THREE TIMES A LADY

Mia's eyes widened in amazement.

Jordan's body was well toned and muscular. His stomach was hard and rippled above the navy swim trunks he wore. And those legs looked like they had the power to walk a thousand miles. The wet material clung to and outlined the long, impressive length of his malehood.

Who knew that beneath those oversize sweat suits and wrinkled clothing was the body of an Adonis? She felt like a voyeur, but could not look away as he stretched each of his muscles with slow, controlled movements. The lights surrounding the pool shimmered on his body as they reflected off the beads of water.

Her heart fluttered in her chest, and her stomach felt tight with nerves she couldn't explain. "Oh no," she moaned as she recognized the feeling she was experiencing. "I want Jordan!"

BOOK YOUR PLACE ON OUR WEBSITE AND MAKE THE ARABESQUE ROMANCE CONNECTION!

We've created a customized website just for our very special Arabesque readers, where you can get the inside scoop on everything that's going on with Arabesque romance novels.

When you come online, you'll have the exciting opportunity to:

- View covers of upcoming books

- Learn about our future publishing schedule (listed by publication month and author)

- Find out when your favorite authors will be visiting a city near you

- Search for and order backlist books

- Check out author bios and background information

- Send e-mail to your favorite authors

- Join us in weekly chats with authors, readers and other guests

- Get writing guidelines

- AND MUCH MORE!

Visit our website at
http://www.arabesquebooks.com

THREE TIMES A LADY

Niobia Bryant

ARABESQUE
BET
BOOKS

BET Publications, LLC
www.bet.com
www.arabesquebooks.com

*This collection of words
I dedicate to my dozens of cousins
first, second, and third.*

*From the
bricks of Newark in New Jerusalem,
From the
heat of LA in Cali-forn-i-a,
From the
borough of the Bronx in the Big Apple,
From the
dirty south floor in Carolina.*

*But especially to the "furious five":
Tarik, Dora, Timothy, Domingo, and Tajah*

Prologue

The beautiful amber-skinned children sat in a circle on the carpeted floor of their colorfully decorated playroom. But they were not in the midst of a game. In fact, they were very serious and determined. The four pairs of cocoa-brown eyes were focused on the oldest of their bunch, obviously their leader.

"Are we all agreed?" he asked, making eye contact with each of his siblings.

They all nodded.

"Good, then it's Mission: Find a Wife for Dad—"

"And a mom for us," the two smallest children interjected, their voices in perfect unison.

"Right." He nodded. "She has to be pretty and smart—"

"And can bake cookies. Daddy a'ways burns his up," the angelic voices piped in again, twisting their faces in disgust as they remembered his most recent attempt at chocolate chip cookies.

"Okay, let's do it." He stretched his hand out into the middle of their circle, palm side down.

One by one, they each placed one hand on top of another, until they were stacked. "Go . . . Banks!" they shouted in unison.

One

"I have compiled the perfect financial portfolio for your firm's needs." Mia Gordon readjusted the headset she wore, as she paced the floor of her executive corner office.

She knew her trademark pacing was wearing down the wool of her handmade Indian rug, but she didn't care. Pacing kept her blood pumping, and, she believed, increased the blood flow to her brain, further increasing her quick-thinking abilities. To be a successful financial analyst for one of the country's largest investment banking firms, she had to be a quick thinker. That was the reason she was vice president of mergers and acquisitions. She was good at what she did. Damn good.

"Well, let's set up a meeting at your convenience to discuss the numbers," she said with more demand than question. Aggressiveness was another needed trait.

Seconds later she punched the air with her fist, her competitiveness kicking into overdrive as the prospective client agreed to an all-important meeting. This was a nine-figure deal, and Mia wanted it. "Thank you, Mr. Petra . . . oh, okay, Roger. I'll see you this Thursday."

Mia ended the phone call, removing the headset and the cordless phone snapped to the waistband of her charcoal gray Jones New York classic trousers. Renewed energy soared through her. She thrived on her career; at thirty-four she was successful, with a high six-figure income and a reputation for integrity in her work. And this weekend she was moving into her first home. What more could she ask for?

For many years she had worked hard to be a "success story." All through school she had excelled in mathematics, and it was a high school guidance counselor who had introduced the investment world to her as a career choice. The field suited her aggressive and competitive nature perfectly, while allowing her strong mathematical abilities to flourish. After researching investment banking, Mia knew this was the ideal career choice for her. She attended Rutgers University, earning an economics degree, and then moved on to Stanford for her MBA.

With the combination of her education, determination, competitive drive, and firm grasp of numbers, Mia had risen through the ranks. Her beginning years at Stromer, Wiler had been worth the cost of all-nighters and no social life, in her opinion. Those long hours as a junior associate, doing computer analyses, preparing financial reports, and putting together documents for senior bankers to pitch their ideas, had put her on the fast track for advancement.

Her career was her main focus for so many years that sometimes Mia wondered if she would ever have time for a serious and meaningful relationship. Currently, she kept her life organized down to the minute, and there was no slot penciled in for a serious commitment. Thus the occasional dates had to suffice. And even those were business related. Many men couldn't handle her success with the accompanying hefty salary. Their plans usually included archaic and outdated beliefs of starting a family with her, which meant stepping into the role of working mother.

She worked diligently for success, particularly as a minority woman in a field that was only ten percent female. Nothing was going to knock her off track now. Besides she hadn't met the man unique enough to encourage her to make room for him in her life on a long-term basis.

Okay, she was hitting thirty-five, and occasionally she thought about having children. But if she didn't have time to find a man with whom to procreate, then she knew she didn't have adequate time to be a mother. Of course, her parents were pressing the issue, but it was her life, her career, her body, thus her choice.

"Mia."

She glanced over at her speaker phone as her assistant addressed her through the two-way intercom. "Go ahead, Tyresa."

"There's a Tyrell Tarrington on the line."

Mia tapped the fourteen-karat Cross pen in her hand against the computer printouts she was reading. A vision of the light-complexioned, boyishly handsome man filled her. They had met last month when she traveled to Houston to examine a facility that one of her clients was prepared to purchase.

She knew the call was not business related, even if they had exchanged cards for strictly professional reasons. Dating was not a part of her plans this week, not with the meeting she had to get ready for by Thursday with Petra Communications.

"Reese, take a message and tell him I'll be in meetings all day." Her voice was crisp and efficient.

"He sounds yummy, boss."

Mia smiled slightly, shaking her head. "He'll have to be yummy when I get a chance to return his call, which won't be until next week sometime. I want this Petra deal, and I'm going to get it. That comes first and foremost."

"Okay, but I hope you don't regret it."

"I doubt that," Mia said with all seriousness, all thoughts of him and a possible date already fading out of her short-term memory.

Mia checked her slim Movado watch, adjusting her body to comfort in her ergonomic bungi office chair, behind the uniquely designed L-shaped glass desk. It was just 11:00 A.M., and she had a busy schedule ahead of her. Already four hours of the workday were behind her, and she had another eight hours to go. It was a good thing she loved her career, or she would've gone crazy years ago!

Mia was financially able to buy a home wherever she wanted, so a lot of her friends, and especially her parents, were abhorred that she refused to move out of Newark, New Jersey. The city was looked upon as one of the worst in the country, plagued by overpopulation, drugs, and poverty.

The city has been around for 325 years. Only Boston and New York could tout a longer history. It hasn't always been known for poverty, drug abuse, and high unemployment rates. The city was an industrial giant in the past and was now on the rise again being called the "Renaissance City" or "New Newark."

True, the city took a jolt during the riot of '67 that raged hotter than the heat that swirled that summer. And yes, sadly the same issues still existed. The city still showed the effects of the damage created by the protectors and the National Guard and state police that hot summer.

Mia was a firm believer in the best to come for her hometown, and she planned to be there to see it. But she grew up in this city, and she loved it because it helped shape her into the woman she was. Growing up in the Bricks had given her inner strength and grit that helped her in her career. She knew the combination of her street smarts and book sense made her a lethal contender in any field.

She vowed to remain in Newark to see the gradual rise of the city, out of the ashes still remaining from the riot of 1967. Positive changes could be seen already, particularly in the downtown area. But then Newark never was as bad as the statistics and the media tried to portray it. Mia loved her hometown, and she wasn't taking her hefty salary and fleeing as most people—like her parents—did, thinking they were too good for the place where they were raised.

She had no desire to move to South Orange or Maplewood, some of the nearby towns that were seen as more suburban and livable than Newark. Her own parents had fled to Maplewood more than a decade ago. But when Mia began house hunting, she specifically looked within her hometown's city limits and she found her treasure in the Weequahic section.

The sprawling homes were reminiscent of the splendor the city once enjoyed and would see again. The community was filled with lawyers, doctors, local politicians, and blue-collar workers who had scraped and saved to own their own homes, just like people in many other communities across America. In fact the mayor of Newark lived just a block over from the four-bedroom brick home Mia bought.

That Saturday morning of her move, she followed the moving company's truck in her silver Mercedes-Benz CLK coupe from her two-bedroom apartment to her new home. Mia was excited, and watched anxiously as the movers began to unload her furnishings and marked cardboard boxes.

Mia used her key to unlock the stained-glass-decorated mahogany front door. It was solid and sturdy, just like the rest of the house. She used one of the smaller boxes that the movers had left on the stone wraparound porch to hold the door open wide. Excitement was not a sufficient word to describe how she felt. When she stepped into the foyer, she slowly removed her shades and looked around at the empty sun-filled structure. She had loved the house from the first moment she laid eyes on it. Her enchantment with it had flourished even more when she toured the inside.

There was a finished basement, with an attached half

bath, which she would use as her home office. On the first floor, a detailed stone fireplace took up one wall of the spacious living room, and there was a dining room with delicate woodwork and large windows. The pantry was almost the size of a small bedroom, able to hold a freezer easily. A fully equipped kitchen showed the modern updating that the prior owners had completed. Lastly, there was a small bedroom off the spacious kitchen, which had most likely served as the cook's quarters.

Upstairs were four bedrooms, and the master suite had its own private sitting room and bath, with a skylight and separate shower stall. The realtor had told her the last owners had also made recent renovations in the bathroom, and Mia loved all of them. Yes, it was quite a home for a single woman with no children. She knew she would probably never use most of the bedrooms in the years to come, but that was still fine by her. She wanted the house, and now she had it.

This beautiful dwelling was hers, another testament to her successful career as a focused businesswoman. Already she felt as though she was home. Mia looked forward to the many treasured hours of peace, quiet, and serenity she would spend in it—alone.

"Good morning, good morning to the Renaissance City. This is Tabitha Wilcox here to lead you through this beautiful Saturday morning. It's 8:00 A.M. so rise and shine with your jazz central station. How's a little Miles in the morning to make you move?"

Jordan stretched his long-limbed frame where he lay on his stomach in his king-size bed as his clock radio turned on. It did its job and awakened him, even if he wasn't ready to leave the comfort of his bed. He groaned from underneath his pillow and slowly opened one eye to peer at the brilliant yellow disk in the sky through the windows. Quickly he shut the eye.

He definitely was not a morning person. He longed for the days when he could lounge in bed all morning until the energy he felt drained of returned. The cool crispness of the sheets was heavenly against his naked chest. The pillows felt like fluffy white clouds surrounding his face with softness.

In his more carefree days only the sweet intimate scent and feel of a woman lying in his arms could awaken him with a smile at this time of the morning. Especially someone like Marisol, his last girlfriend of about three years ago.

How often had the beauty complained of the lack of time he had for her? At one point she began to accuse him of using her just for sex. She had been a total delight between his sheets, but he had been insulted by her opinion of him. The relationship had quickly faded after that.

Last he heard, she had latched on to a retired basketball player who had plenty of time to pamper and spoil her the way she craved. Jordan had to admit that the thought of Marisol stirred his blood. She had been his total fantasy come to life in bed.

But alas a woman that was good emotionally, socially, financially, *and* sexually was what was good for him and his children. Marisol had not been that woman. Would anyone be able to fulfill all the needs he had, which included the welfare of the children he cherished and loved?

So here he was alone with no woman in his life or his bed. He didn't want to but he *had* to get up.

In his latest novel, he was up to the part where he described his characters' personalities, and detailed their connection to the murder victim. This was a very vital part of a good mystery novel. It was why he was one of the best in his genre.

Jordan threw back the thin sheet covering his body, his mind totally focused on the newer ideas already forming for the novel. When it came to his writing ca-

reer, his focus never wavered, thus all thoughts of the
lack of a lady in his life evaporated like steam. Excitedly
he sat up and slid on his tortoiseshell spectacles. He bit
his bottom lip in concentration as he jotted notes on
the pad he kept by the bed. The words flew from his
brain and down onto the paper.

"I can't wait to get started," he said aloud, quickly
standing and stepping out of his pajama bottoms.

Even as he showered and brushed his teeth, his mind
remained centered on his novel. Since he worked from
home Jordan wasn't really concerned over what he
chose to wear. His top priority was comfort. Besides,
what did it matter what he looked like, who would see
him? His faded, well-worn, and wrinkled army-green
sweatpants and red T-shirt were quite a sight as he made
his way downstairs.

His office looked almost as disastrous as his appearance, with the piles of papers on his desk and the disheveled stacks of books crammed into every available
space of the sizable area. This was his office, and he
loved it just the way it was with the rich mahogany and
brown decor. The clutter was his own form of organization. His sanctuary. A place to get lost in his own world
of murder and mayhem, characters, plot lines, and true
storytelling.

Eagerly he sat at his desk. Soon his fingers began to
fly over the keyboard. His thoughts became lost in the
world of his character Slim Willie in his latest install-
ment of the crime-solving series.

*Slim slowly opened the door to the community center. His
tall frame made an eerie shadow against the floor of the
dimly lit gymnasium. He was just about to step inside
when a large* Boom! *halted his steps.*

"Daddy! Daddy! Someone's moving in next door!"
Jordan jumped at the sound of his children's screeching voices, accidentally knocking over the cold cup of

coffee he had fixed for himself yesterday and forgotten to discard. Frantically he righted the cup, dismayed as the brown liquid spread over the top few pages of his manuscript. Thank God it was just the rough draft.

He sighed as he lifted up the now wet and stained pages with his index finger and thumb. Liquid dripped off them down onto his cluttered desk. Flinging them into the already overflowing wastepaper basket, he eyed the three of his five children.

"What did Daddy say about barging into his office while he's working?" He tried to make his voice stern as he looked at them over the rim of his glasses. As always they slid to the end of his long aquiline nose.

"Daddy, you're talking in third person again," his eleven-year-old daughter, Tia, said wryly.

He pushed the glasses back up onto his face with his index finger. "Children, Daddy—"

"Has a deadline," they said in unison, with the twins saying *deadwine* since neither could pronounce the letter *l* properly.

Jordan looked startled, before he continued. "Well, writing is how Daddy—"

"Pays the bills," they chimed in again.

"Stop doing that," he yelled in frustration, and then instantly regretted it as four-year-old identical twins Aliya's and Amina's eyes filled with hurt tears.

He rushed from behind his wooden desk, nearly tripping over the wastepaper basket in his usual clumsy manner. "I'm sorry, girls," he apologized, stooping down to embrace them tightly. "Don't cry."

Tia moved over to pat him on the back, a consoling gesture. "It's okay, Dad. We all know how postal you get when you're near your deadline."

Jordan looked up to wink at her, his spectacles again precariously perched on the end of his nose. This time Tia pushed them up with her slender finger, and he smiled. "Now, what's this about new neighbors?"

"There's a big moving truck parked outside. Rajahn and Kimani went next door already—"

"They did what?" he exclaimed, rising.

The twins each reached for one of his large hands, jumping up and down with excitement. "I hope they have kids we can pway with," Amina said, sighing, and Aliya agreed with eager nodding.

Tia snorted. "As if there ain't enough kids 'round here already."

Jordan looked back at his computer terminal with longing. He had been deeply engrossed in his work. His creative juices were flowing. This was his element.

It would have to wait, even if he didn't want it to. He had nosy children to retrieve and new neighbors to meet.

Mia opened wide the back door in the kitchen, allowing the fresh summer air and sunshine to fill the room as she began to unpack her dishes. Carefully she washed and dried each one to remove the residue left over from the newspaper they'd been wrapped in. She touched the maple-wood cabinets with frosted glass panes with pride as she placed the dishes in them. It was a large kitchen, and she couldn't wait to see it decorated. Mia expected it to be a showpiece like the homes in *Beautiful Homes & Garden*.

"Where's the rest of your family?"

Mia yelled out in fright and dropped the ceramic plate she held in her hand. It crashed to the floor as she whirled around to face the open back door. A slender child of around eight with round spectacles stepped into the kitchen, dressed in cut-off jeans and an orange tank top. The part in her hair was hopelessly uneven and her two ponytails were fuzzy.

Mia prided herself on always remaining composed, but right now her heart was pounding frantically against her chest, and she was shaking. The child's sudden appearance had scared her witless. "Where did you come from?"

"I live next door. My brother Rajahn's outside. He's scared to come in but I ain't," she said with pride.

"It's 'but I'm not,' " Mia said offhandedly, her hand over her heart.

The little girl scrunched up her pretty face. "Huh?"

"Ain't, isn't a proper word, so don't use it."

She smiled, revealing clear braces. "Oh yeah, my daddy tells us that all the time."

"Well, neighbor, what's your name?" Mia asked, as her heart finally slowed to a normal rate.

"Kimani Lashelle Banks."

"That's a beautiful name. I'm Ms. Gordon."

The little girl nodded slowly several times as she peered up at Mia through her glasses. It made Mia feel as if she were being examined under two magnifying glasses. "Where's Mr. Gordon?" the girl said.

"Excuse me?" Mia was surprised by the question. Kids these days!

Kimani sighed, tapping her slender finger against her chin as she circled where Mia stood. Her sneakered feet crunched on the shards on the floor. "You know, your husband?"

"Be careful of the glass, Kishani."

"Kimani," she corrected.

Mia put her hands on the child's slender shoulders to direct her away from the mess. "Right . . . Kimani. And I'm not married."

Kimani's face lit up, as she smiled brightly. She really was adorable, and Mia instinctively returned her smile.

"Oh," Kimani said suddenly, as she remembered her sibling's other request. "Can you cook and bake cookies? You got a boyfriend? Are you smart? Do you like kids? Is that your car outside? Are you rich like my daddy?"

Mia looked down at her with a wide-eyed, shocked

expression. She felt as if she were being interviewed by a mini Queen Latifah. "Why?"

Before she could get an answer, she was startled again as her doorway was suddenly filled with activity. Turning, her eyes widened farther. A disheveled-looking man and four children stood on the small brick porch of her house. Mia eyed each one quickly.

A tall handsome boy in his preteens, obviously the brother of whom Kimani spoke since he was the only male child in the bunch. An angelic girl of about eleven, whose ponytail was as disastrous as Kimani's, winked at Mia mischievously. The cutest and chubbiest twin girls Mia had ever laid eyes on each sucked a plump thumb and clutched the legs of the man's ill-fitting hideous army-green sweatpants. The girls were about four, and their hair yet another example of a sloppy attempt at combing.

The man looked as if he just got out of bed after sleeping in his clothes all night. His glasses were too large for his slender face, and from the way he kept pushing them up on his nose, they needed to be adjusted.

What a crew!

Behind Mia's back, and so that her dad didn't see her as well, Kimani gave Rajahn a thumbs-up sign. "Ms. Gordon, that's my dad, he writes mysteries; and my brother, Rajahn, he's addicted to his Sony Playstation; and my older sister, Tia, she has a smart mouth; and my little sisters Amina and Aliya, they *love* the Teletubbies."

Each person waved as Kimani introduced them, and Mia smiled at them, thinking, *My God, one more and they could play the Brady Bunch.*

"Hi, I'm Jordan Banks. I hope Kimani hasn't been annoying you. She can be a bit talkative."

His voice was surprisingly deep. For some reason Mia had expected a high-pitched nasal tone. She was momentarily taken aback by it. "Uhm, nice to meet you.

I'm Mia Gordon. Kimani has been no trouble at all. She's a very bright . . . and inquisitive girl."

"Welcome to the neighborhood," he said, already seeming distracted as if his mind were elsewhere. "We'll leave you and your family—"

"No, no," Mia interjected. "I live alone."

He nodded. "Well, welcome to the neighborhood. I'll try to make sure the children don't bother you."

"I'm sure they'll not be a problem," she assured him.

"Does that mean I can come visit you, Ms. Gordon?" Kimani asked, as she looked up at her with a toothy brace-filled grin.

"Sure, although I'm pretty boring," Mia warned playfully.

"Okay, kids, let's go." They all said good-bye, sounding like a class.

She watched from her back porch as the brood walked through a break in the hedges that separated their homes. Suddenly Jordan tripped over something and stumbled, falling through the hedges onto his stomach. Embarrassed for him, Mia jumped back so that the group wouldn't know that she had seen him fall flat on his face.

"Daddy, one of these days you're gonna really hurt yourself. You're always so clumsy." She heard one of his daughters chide him, causing her to stifle a laugh as she closed the solid back door.

As Mia swept up the broken dish, she recalled that no one made any mention of his wife or their mother. Surely he wasn't raising five children alone. Although that would explain the disheveled state of the girls' hair. Not many men were adept at creating a neat hairstyle; he looked as though he barely managed to get himself together in the mornings.

God bless him anyway because she couldn't imagine having time for one child to raise, far less five. In this day and age five children was a lot. *Better him than me,* she thought.

The movers had unloaded all the furniture, pictures, and lamps and even set them up to her specifications, leaving only the boxes in each room to unpack. That would take no time at all because she was an admitted neat freak. Each box was labeled and filled with items for only the room designated.

As she moved from room to room on the first level, she caught glimpses of the children through the windows playing on their large brick front porch next door. Frequently they seemed to be looking toward her house, and Mia felt that they might be discussing her. But she just laughed it off. She refused to be paranoid about little sweet, harmless children with angelic faces. They were total innocents.

"Man, can you believe our luck?" Rajahn asked his siblings. He turned to Kimani. "What were y'all talking about in the kitchen, Kimani?"

She closed the Rosa Guy novel *The Friends* that she was reading. "She's not married but I didn't get to see if she could cook or not."

Tia raised a brow. "I don't think it really matters."

Rajahn looked down at where Tia sat on the porch step beneath him. "Why not?" he asked.

She rolled her eyes heavenward. "Hel-lo! Am I the only one who noticed that she and Dad didn't even look twice at each other?"

They all got quiet because they *had* noticed the lack of interest between the adults. The twins, picking up on the somber mood of their elder siblings, left their motorized bikes on the lawn and came to sit on the bottom step of the porch together.

Tia was right. Ms. Gordon and their dad had not shown any interest in each other. Not like the men and women they saw on television. Not even like the way Rajahn felt when he saw Tasha, a girl in his science class last year. Nothing.

But Ms. Gordon had to be the one. Just last weekend they had made the pact to find Miss Right for their dad, and this weekend Ms. Gordon moved into the house next door. It was as if God had sent her. She was the one.

"We'll just have to work hard to make them realize they belong together," Rajahn said with determination. "And we'll do whatever it takes."

Inside the house, Jordan removed his glasses and rubbed his eyes with his fingertips. He leaned back, stretching his long frame, but almost toppled backward completely. He had to yank his upper body forward to keep from falling, his arms straight ahead of him for balance. Smiling briefly, he shook his head. His physical coordination had been challenged since before he could remember, and he didn't suppose he would ever grow out of it.

Deciding to take a break, he walked over to the windows of his mahogany and blue office to look out at the front porch. The summer sun was shining brightly as he watched his five children assembled there. He felt his heart swell with love for them all.

They were the reason he worked hard and spent long hours in front of that computer, letting his ideas flow from his brain to his fingertips as he created—he hoped—another best-selling novel in his Slim Willie detective series. The children deserved the best of everything, and he wanted to give it to them, especially after the hard times they had already experienced in their short lives. They all had a tragic tale of their own to tell. He was just hopeful that his introduction into their lives would lead to a happy ending for them all.

In college, Jordan had become a volunteer mentor to at-risk youths at a community center in his neighborhood, using the wonderful relationship he had with his own father to guide him.

Five years ago he had been introduced to a young

scraggly boy of eight, who had been caught shoplifting from a downtown Newark clothing store. Part of the boy's punishment had been enrollment in the popular and successful Man-to-Man mentoring program at the center. Jordan had instantly felt an affinity to the child. He had a tough-guy attitude but the fear and vulnerability in the boy's eyes were clear. After a few rough moments after their first meeting they had developed a tight bond. Jordan became many of the things Rajahn had needed in his life: friend, father figure, inspiration, and a good example.

Never would he forget the night Rajahn had walked to his apartment in the Hallmark Building and flung himself into Jordan's arms when he opened the door. His thin body had been racked with tears as he clutched his mentor's waist. It took some time to calm him down but he eventually explained how he had found his mother dead in their apartment. Rajahn had told Jordan how he had remained with her lifeless body until the ambulance he called had arrived. Fearing child protective services would find him and send him to a strange foster home, the gutsy boy had sneaked away and come straight to his mentor and friend.

Since that night Jordan had considered himself Rajahn's guardian and moved the boy into his home without a moment's hesitation. Going through the proper channels, he became first his foster parent, and then adopted him a year later. Now he had a son whom he loved and cherished.

Next he adopted Kimani. She had been in the foster-care system since birth, when her teenaged mother had deserted her at the hospital before running away. Jordan had seen Kimani's picture at the youth center where he volunteered and had been enchanted by the little girl with the crooked teeth and the big glasses. Kimani's mother, who had been arrested not long after for abandoning her child, had signed over all legal

claims to her daughter, and Jordan had willingly
adopted her. That was three years ago.

Then came Tia. Until she was nine she had been
raised by her grandmother. But when the elderly
woman passed away from a fatal stroke, there had been
no other family members to raise the little girl. This
time the director of the youth center had brought Tia
to his attention. Jordan had been a little hesitant about
his ability to raise three children, but because of his
writing career, he was a wealthy man, he had a large
home, and lots of love to give. He just couldn't see himself saying no. So Jordan gladly added her to his family;
Tia's outgoing personality and slightly weird sense of
humor had won him over.

Last came the twins. Ever since they were two, Jordan
had them in his care. Their father, his best friend, had
killed himself, distraught over his wife's death from cer-
vical cancer six months before. Jordan had immediately
upheld his godfather duties and took over raising the
little angels when no other family members seemed to
want to claim them. He constantly wondered who could
deny the chocolate cherubs.

So then they were five.

He loved each of them as if they had been his natural
offsprings. Rajahn with his inner strength, Tia with her
endless humor, Kimani with her intelligence, and the
twins with their unconditional love. Thankfully they
were all well-adjusted and happy, and there was nothing
more Jordan could want in life besides that.

Of course he knew the children wanted more of his
time, but at least he was in the house, always available
to them, even if he spent most of his time in his office.
But thank God for Ms. McKnight, the middle-aged
woman he paid to come in three days a week to tend
to the house. The woman was truly a godsend, especially
without a constant female presence in the house.

Sometimes Jordan wondered if the children felt the
lack of a mother figure in their lives. They had never

made any mention of it to him. Besides, it would take a very special woman to choose to be a mother to a ready-made family.

It had been sometime since he had a serious relationship. He had to admit that it got lonely sometimes. And he was like any other male with normal needs and urges. But it was all simply mind over matter. Perhaps he would fall in love one day, perhaps not. It wasn't a major issue for him, his children's welfare and his career were.

Once the novel was completed and sent to his publisher he would have some free time to spend with the children. Maybe he would take them all on a trip to Disney World like last summer. Keeping up with five children in the wonderland had been a handful, but worth it.

But for now his focus had to be on getting more work done before it was time for him to prepare lunch. Ms. McKnight had the weekends off, so the cooking duties were left up to him. Sighing, Jordan turned away from the window, his mind already lost in the world of Slim Willie.

Two

Night life in the city was invigorating and intriguing to Mia. Regardless of the temperature, she loved to drive with the window down, allowing some of the night air to breeze through her vehicle. She loved to open the sunroof and peer up at the stars in the sky when at a stoplight. She loved city life and wouldn't give it up for anything.

Almost reluctantly she turned her car around the corner that would take her home, honking her horn briefly at a neighbor who was on her way to the corner store with her small child. Mia parked in the two-car garage behind the house. The digital clock on her console glowed a neon 8:48 P.M. The street was dark and quiet. As she walked to the back porch of her home, she glanced over to her left to the brightly lit house next door.

The Bankses' home was a large two-story structure and probably had been elegant at one time but now the white paint was peeling and the yard was in need of landscaping. Obviously Mr. Banks was as careless with the upkeep of his home as he was with his own appearance.

Since she moved in two weeks ago she'd seen him twice during the weekends and he had looked as disheveled as he had at their first meeting. Plus he had to be the clumsiest man she'd ever met. She would advise anyone who chose to be in his company to give him his own personal space of about five feet, just in case he stumbled over his unhemmed pants and fell. And why didn't he just get those awful glasses adjusted so that they would fit? Then he wouldn't have to keep pushing them up on his face all the time.

Mia believed that if his head weren't attached to his body he would lose it. She shook her head in bewilderment. The man was truly an enigma. She was amazed that he could compose his thoughts enough to actually write a book.

What she could commend him on were his children. They were all polite, well-behaved, and bright. Tia did push the limits sometimes with her quirky sense of humor, but overall she was adorable. And they loved their father dearly, filling Mia in with honesty on how they came to be adopted by him. In fact, they filled Mia in on quite a few facts about Mr. Jordan Banks. Way more than she wanted to know about his taste in music and food, and some rather odd facts. Right now she could sweep a game show if all the questions were about him.

And the children seemed enamored of her and Mia couldn't fathom why. Surely, to children, her life and her orderly house would be boring. But they visited her nearly every weekend, on and off, quizzing her about herself until she felt dizzy. Although she didn't mind their company, Mia was definitely not used to their endless exuberance and energy, and felt more than a little overwhelmed by the five children. And they always seemed to choose the worst possible time to drop over, like when she was engrossed in work in her home office. Though in all fairness it was hard for her to recall any long periods of time when she wasn't working.

Sighing, she climbed the stairs illuminated by the light poles in the backyard and used her key to enter the house. What went on next door was not her concern, especially since they were not abused or neglected. So what if he had no idea how to do little girls' hair, how many men did? Was it any of her business if he needed to spend more time with his beautiful children? Closed up in an office from seven to seven every day wasn't healthy—

"Whoa," Mia said aloud. "Who am I to judge? After a twelve-hour workday, am I not headed to my office to work some more right now?"

"But *I* don't have children," she answered herself with satisfaction as she descended the stairs into her brightly lit basement office. "It's just me, myself, and I. Just the way I like it."

In an effort to always find ways to keep herself energized to work even harder Mia had decorated the entire sublevel in yellows, oranges, peaches, and brilliant white. Area rugs of the same colors were scattered over the hardwood floor. Brass ornaments adorned the walls and every other available space. Fluorescent track lights illuminated off the clear glass contemporary office desk and matching low-slung tables. Even at midnight the room glowed just as brightly as the morning sun. It was like its own energy force, and Mia drew upon it.

She hadn't even wasted time to dash upstairs and change out of the Dion Scott navy suit she wore. Mia removed the contemporary cropped jacket and settled into the chair in front of her desk.

As soon as she got comfortable, the telephone began to ring. Mia typed in her password with her right hand and picked up the cordless phone on her desk with her left. "Gordon here, uh . . . I mean hello," she said laughing lightly at her slip in using her usual office greeting.

"Yes, uhm, hello. This is Jordan . . . Jordan Banks from next door."

As he stumbled through a greeting, Mia was busy thinking, *What does he want?*

"Hello, Mr. Banks." She switched the phone to between her cheek and her shoulder, as she typed on the keyboard with both hands. "How can I help you?"

"Well, uh . . . I hate to bother you. I know you just got in from work, but . . . well . . . I need to ask—"

Mia visibly jumped as a small child—no, children—began to cry out frantically. She stopped typing and raised a finely arched brow. "Yes, Mr. Banks?"

"Amina and Aliya, please stop crying. Daddy's on the phone," Mia heard him say in a harried voice, but the children only cried louder.

"Mr. Banks!" she yelled into the phone, hoping to regain his attention so that she could hang up and get back to work.

"Uh, yes, Ms. Gordon. I'm sorry about the noise but that's the reason I'm calling."

She couldn't even begin to imagine the connection between herself and the twins crying. "Yes, Mr. Banks?" she asked again, her voice clearly impatient.

"The girls, it's their bedtime and they're hollering their heads off for you."

"For me?" she shrieked in disbelief. *I've only known them two weeks,* she thought. *Why are they hollering for me?*

In the background Mia heard the twins begin yelling her name, sounding like sanctified churchgoers calling for Jesus Christ.

"Look, Ms. Gordon. I wouldn't ask if I weren't near a nervous breakdown and afraid they were going to make themselves sick. Damn, they've been going at it for the past twenty minutes. I usually work on my novel after they're in bed. I . . . I . . . look, please?"

The desperation in his voice was obvious, and Mia pictured him more disheveled than ever, probably fidgeting with his ill-fitting glasses in a hideous shirt and purple sweatpants with red and black Air Jordans that had seen better days. A total stranger was pleading with her to come into his private domain and help soothe *his* children. She was a woman who hadn't held an infant in years and felt the only bit of inadequacy in her life when she was *around* children. The whole situation was insane and bizarre.

Then why was she going?

"I'll be right over, Mr. Banks."

He expelled a sigh of relief. "Thank God."

Mia smiled as she hung up the phone. More out of habit than necessity she exited from the computer program before walking up the stairs and out of the front door.

He really needs to work on his front yard, she thought, deciding to give him the name of her landscaper as she closed the gate behind her and quickly walked up the path. Toys were strewn over the wide front porch and steps, bicycles lay scattered on the uncut grass like confetti. She looked over at her own neatly mown lawn, trimmed hedges, and leaf-free backyard and wondered how the family could function among their chaos. It really wasn't that expensive to hire someone to come in and do the work, just as she did.

Before she could even knock, the front door swung open wide. "Hello, Ms. Gordon."

She smiled down into Kimani's bespectacled face. "Hello, little Miss Kimani."

"Everyone's upstairs. Come on," she said over the echoing loudness of her twin sisters' cries.

The house was neat but well lived in. Mia had expected it to be a disaster area like the front yard. Then she remembered the children telling her about Ms. McKnight, their part-time cleaning lady and cook.

Mia actually liked the mahogany and leather furnishings and decor with accompanying African sculptures and art adorning the beige walls. Pictures of the children were everywhere.

The twins' yells had been excruciatingly loud over the phone; they were deafening inside the house. Mia followed Kimani, who sprinted up the stairs with energy a thirty-four-year-old could only reminisce about. The closer Mia got to the second landing, the louder the twins' cries rang in her ears.

Kimani peeked her head out of a lit doorway to Mia's

left. "Come on, Ms. Gordon," she said impatiently, waving her hand.

The twins' bedroom was large and filled with children's furniture in pretty pastel colors. Everyone looked up at Mia when she entered. Vaguely she noticed that there were no tears in the twins' bright brown eyes. Her eyes landed on Jordan and quickly moved away.

"Hewwo, Ms. Gordon," Aliya and Amina said in cheerful unison, after their yells finally winded down to blessed and blissful silence.

"Thank heavens," Jordan sighed from where he stood between their beds. He lifted his glasses and massaged the bridge of his nose.

Mia had quickly taken in the oversize bulky sweat suit he wore, with a dismissive air, before refocusing on her reason for even being there. Smiling she moved past him to kneel between the beds. "Hello, girls. What's wrong? Aren't you sleepy?"

Both she and Jordan jumped as the bedroom door closed behind them. They turned and saw that the other children had quickly and quietly left the bedroom. Briefly they looked at each other before refocusing on the twins.

"We wanted to see you before we went to sweep," Amina said innocently.

Mia nodded slowly, as if she understood her logic when in fact she did not. "Okay, but why were you yelling at the top of your lungs? That wasn't very fair to everyone else in the house."

The girls looked over at each other where they lay in their respective beds, before looking back at Mia. " 'Cause Daddy wouldn't call you," Amina answered, obviously the more talkative of the two.

Mia heard Jordan mumble something under his breath, but she ignored him. "What did you want to see me for?"

Again they looked at each other. " 'Cause we wike

you," one of them answered in total sweetness and innocence.

Mia smiled, touched by the answer. Who wouldn't be? She rose and leaned over to kiss each of them on their forehead. "And I like you, but it's your bedtime so good night, girls," she said softly.

"Okay, girls, say your prayers," Jordan said from behind her.

Amina held out her hand for Mia, and Aliya reached for their father's large hand, which they both immediately took. "Daddy, take Ms. Gordon's hand," Amina insisted, with wide-eyed innocence.

Jordan looked flushed by the request and was more than a little hesitant. His beautiful next-door neighbor made him nervous. Anxious to get back to work, he stepped closer to her and took Mia's hand in his, engulfing it. He lowered his head, ignoring her shocked expression. Jordan was very aware that she probably disdained his touch. "Go ahead, girls."

"Now thy way me down to sweep. I pray the Word my soul to keep. If I should pass before I wake, I pray the Word my soul do take. God bwess Daddy, Rajahn, Tia, Kimani, Grandpa, and Ms. McKnight—"

"And our new friend, Ms. Gordon," Aliya amended, instantly gaining her twin's earnest nod of approval.

"Amen," they finished in unison.

Mia gratefully pulled her hand out of Jordan's warm grasp. "Good night, ladies."

Jordan leaned down and kissed each of them. "Night."

They left the room after he dimmed the lights, closing the door behind him. "Thanks again, Ms. Gordon."

"Mia."

"Uh, okay . . . Mia. Thanks. The children are all quite taken with you." He strode over to three rooms, presumably to look in on the other children.

"I like them as well." She moved to take the stairs,

very much aware that he followed behind her. *I hope he doesn't trip and send us both rolling down these stairs!*

They reached the bottom landing with no complications and when Mia turned to face Jordan, she saw him look toward a closed door with longing. She knew it was his beloved office, and she was just as anxious to get back to work herself. "Well, good night, Mr. Banks."

"Jordan."

"Right."

"Would you like me to walk you next door?"

"No, that's okay. I'm sure I'll be fine."

He nodded and glanced back at the closed door. "Good night, Ms. Gordon . . . uh, Mia."

She didn't hear the front door close until she had stepped onto her own front porch. Mia could have sworn she heard him yell out, but she didn't get alarmed. *Nine times out of ten,* she thought. *He stubbed his toe. That man is a disaster waiting to happen.*

She quickly walked into the house and was soon downstairs in her office, blissfully engrossed in work.

"Damn it," Jordan swore, as he bent to rub his throbbing toe. His foot seemed to always be drawn to the leg of the small wooden table in his foyer, like metal to magnet. He winced as the toe pulsated with pain.

Limping slightly, he walked to his office and closed the door behind him. It was among the chaos of his cluttered office, the only room in the house deemed for his use only, that he found peace. There *was* a method to his madness. The clutter was his own form of organization, actually. He might not remember where everything was exactly, but he knew that it was somewhere in his office.

Jordan was anxious to get back to work. "Now if only I can find my glasses," he mumbled as he searched among the clutter on his desk. "What did I do with them?"

Dejected, he slumped into his swivel chair. He could hardly see a thing without his specs. He felt a bit of anger at himself. Just like his house and car keys, he couldn't seem to ever keep up with his glasses.

Jordan dropped his head in his hands, trying to retrace his steps around the house. It was then that his glasses slid down off his head, landing with a soft plop on his nose. He laughed at himself lightly. His father used to tease him that he would forget his head if it weren't attached.

He reread the last few pages he had written to pick up his flow of thought again. But even as he tried to focus on his writing and become as absorbed as he usually did, he couldn't. It was almost as if he could still hear the twins' frantic crying echoing around him. The whole scene had been odd. Never had they acted in such a way, and all because they wanted to see Ms. Gordon.

Jordan knew the children were fond of her, because they spoke of her quite often, very often—too often. Just when he was trying to finish up his plot line, one of the children would enter his office and wait one hot second before going on a twenty-minute tribute to the "Oh so pretty, oh so smart, and oh so nice Ms. Gordon."

Frankly he could clearly see she was pretty with her heart-shaped face, full pouty lips, high cheekbones, and dimpled chin. Okay, she was gorgeous and totally unaware of it, which made it all even more endearing. To be a financial analyst with an MBA from Stanford she had to be very intelligent, he knew, but nice? *Two out of three ain't bad.*

Obviously her manner with the children was better than it was with him. She had a way of looking at him with those deep-set eyes that made Jordan doubt himself. Mia Gordon was standoffish and distant. He had the distinct feeling that the woman didn't like him. He had put off calling her tonight for as long as he could, until he thought the twins' yells would burst his eardrums.

Even at close to nine P.M., she was still dressed in her tailored navy skirt and white tuxedo blouse. She looked down at him, but at least *he* knew how to relax and be comfortable.

"Good work but next time don't yell so loud," Rajahn whispered to the twins.

After they had made sure the coast was clear, the children had stopped pretending to be asleep and sneaked out of their bedrooms to tiptoe back to the twins'.

"You said to keep crying and don't stop 'tiw Ms. Gordon came over," Amina complained, her mouth pouting at her brother's disapproval.

"Yeah, but not to give everybody a migraine," Tia drawled.

"Forget about that, what happened after we left?" Kimani squinted as she peered into their faces, having forgotten to grab her glasses from her nightstand.

They both shrugged. "We don't know."

"Oh, bro-ther," Tia groaned.

Kimani looked heavenward for assistance. She thought for a second. "Did they kiss?"

"No," they both giggled, holding their hands to their mouths at the thought of that.

"Did they talk?"

"Nope."

Tia put her hands on her slender hips, turning to glare at Rajahn. "You mean we listened to them hollering, for nothing? Bright idea, Raj. Oh yeah, real bright," she said sarcastically.

"Aw, shut up, Tia."

"Will you two keep it down before Daddy knows we're up," Kimani hissed, turning to squint in their direction.

"They did howd hands when we said our prayers," Aliya said brightly, as if she just remembered.

All three swung their heads to look at the twins. "Why didn't you say so?" Rajahn asked impatiently.

"You didn't ask," Amina said simply.

"It's something," Kimani said, sighing.

Tia rolled her eyes. "Not much."

Rajahn moved toward the door. "We'll just come up with something else is all. Now get to bed and good night."

The next morning Minnie McKnight used her key to enter the house of her surrogate family. The sun entered the space brilliantly as she did. Soon she was in the small kitchen starting breakfast. She hummed an Ella Fitzgerald tune as she set the table in the adjoining dining room.

Ms. McKnight went about her tasks with love. She felt as close to this family as anyone could. They were her little bunch. Who would have known, when one of her church sisters mentioned the caregiving position to her, that she would bond so quickly?

It was hard not to love them. The children were all sweet and affectionate, and endearing with their tragic beginnings. And Jordan, well, he was like her son with his sweet, clumsy nature. It was his kind heart that gave him a special soft spot in her old heart. If only he would find happiness in his own heart. He needed a good woman to love him, and the children needed a mother. No matter how many hints she tried to drop in his lap, he ignored them all.

The children and those novels were his life. But he was a good man, the kind all the women were complaining didn't exist. It would take a very special woman indeed to win Jordan's heart and to see past his flaws to the wonderful man he was.

Minnie smiled when she envisioned him with the

strength needed to raise children but still holding on to the tenderness to kiss and hug them for days.

She'd fight tooth and nail for her little bunch. This was her family, and they deserved nothing but the best that life had to offer. She needed them just as much as they needed her. She got just as much pleasure from doling out hugs as they did receiving them. Minnie would give them the world if she could.

By the time the occupants of the house began to stir, the table was filled with steaming platters of scrambled eggs, buttermilk pancakes, and country-fried ham. One by one the children dragged into the dining room to claim their usual seat at the large round table, still dressed in their pajamas.

"Good morning, children," she said in greeting, as she filled their glasses with orange juice. "And what did we dream of last night?"

The children all smiled, even Rajahn, who she believed would soon feel too old for the ritual. Every morning she worked she would ask them to try and recall their dreams from the previous night.

"I dreamed about being MVP of our b-ball championship coming up," Rajahn said with pride, as he stuck a fork in the stack of pancakes and lifted three from the pile to put on his plate.

"Well, keep dreaming, big brother, because Michael Jordan you're not," Tia drawled.

Ms. McKnight gave her a chastising look. "Tia, must you always have such a sharp tongue? What did *you* dream of?"

Tia took a sip of her juice. "I dreamed I was being chased by rabid monkeys and they clawed my sto—"

"Tia!" Ms. McKnight cut her off sharply. "Please, before you frighten the twins. What an odd little girl you are!"

Tia just laughed and shrugged, turning her attention to her eggs.

"Well, Amina and Aliya. What did both of you dream

of?" she asked, stooping down to wipe syrup from their mouths. "Oh, let me guess—"

"Teletubbies," the rest of the children said dryly in unison.

The twins laughed and clutched their stomachs as Minnie kissed their soft downy cheeks. Just then they all heard the sound of slippered feet dragging across the wood floor.

When Jordan entered the dining room, six pairs of eyes were on him. "Morning," he muttered, grouchy as ever. "Breakfast smells good, Ms. M."

"Thank you, Jordan." She took a seat at the table, fixing her own plate. "Kimani was just about to tell us what she dreamed about last night. Kimani?"

"I dreamed of my birthday Friday," she said, sighing in happiness.

Jordan heaped his plate full. "Have you made up your mind what you want for dinner Friday? Your birthday, your pick."

"I want to invite Ms. Gordon."

The forkful of eggs and pancakes he was about to shovel into his mouth froze midway. "Ms. Gordon?"

"Isn't that the young lady who bought the house next door?" Ms. McKnight asked. "I haven't had the chance to meet her yet. She's never home by the time I leave."

Kimani, Tia, and Rajahn looked at Minnie, nodded, and then swung their heads back to their father. They were obviously awaiting an answer. "Please, Daddy. She's really nice and I like her. And it's *my* birthday dinner," Kimani whined.

He swallowed over the lump in his throat. "Of course . . . yes, you may invite her."

Ms. McKnight pondered his pained expression, before she turned her attention back to Kimani. "What would you like me to cook, sweetie?"

"Lasagna and a chocolate cake."

She nodded. "And I'll make the lasagna extra cheesy with sausage, just the way you like it."

Jordan groaned as he imagined the heartburn he would have to suffer through Friday night after dinner. Thing was, he didn't know if it would be from the spicy meal or the straitlaced guest from next door.

Three

"Congratulations on snagging that big Petra Communications deal."

"Yeah, thanks," Mia said vaguely, her thoughts more centered on the rack of girls' dresses through which she was browsing. She snatched up a pretty floral dress with a matching straw hat. "How about this?"

Her executive assistant, Tyresa, shook her head in disapproval. "Too dressy."

She held up another one. "This?"

"Too boyish."

Mia threw a nasty look at her. "Look, Reese. I'm stressed. I have less than ten minutes to find Kimani a gift, get it wrapped, and make it back to my office in time for my three o'clock meeting. I brought you with me to help. So . . . help!"

Tyresa sighed. "Why did you wait until the last minute? That's certainly not like you, Miss Organization."

Mia turned away with a sheepish look. "I forgot," she mumbled.

"Huh?"

"I forgot, okay . . . sue me," she said louder, drawing odd looks from fellow shoppers in the department store of the mall. "Thank God I wrote it in my daily planner Tuesday when she invited me. I promised her I would come to her birthday dinner."

Tyresa held up a neon green-and-pink striped jumper. They both frowned in distaste before Tyresa quickly hung it back on the rack. "I thought you said your neighbor was a weirdo."

"I did not say he was a weirdo. I said he was odd." Mia checked her watch again. "Let's find a toy store. This isn't working out like I hoped."

"Is he cute?" Tyresa asked as she tried to catch up with Mia who was striding quickly out of Lord & Taylor toward Kaybees.

Mia's steps faltered. "Is *who* cute?"

"Jordan Banks. My husband loves his mystery novels. So is he cute?"

"He . . . he . . ." she struggled to find the words to describe him. "He's not ugly, but his glasses are entirely too big for his face, and he always looks like he pulled his clothes out of a hamper. He's . . . he's sort of nerdy."

"Nerdy?"

"Yes. He's a clumsy nerd. Very Steve Urkel-like," Mia said as she picked up a child's portable computer. "But his kids are adorable, and for some odd reason they like me, and I like them too. For Kimani, I will sit through dinner with him and pray he doesn't trip and spill food in my lap."

"He's single, right?" Tyresa hinted.

Mia grabbed a computer box and headed straight for the cashier. "Don't go there, Reese, please."

"Why not?"

"The man has five children." Mia gave her a look as though she was crazy for even thinking along those lines. "And did I mention he's nerd *and* he has *five* children? Five, Tyresa. One more and they're the Bradys, not the Bankses."

"Okay, I'm sorry. I just—"

"Look, any chance of Jordan Banks and me hooking up are the same as a snowball's chance of staying frozen while rolling around in hell."

* * *

Her office was her sanctuary, and not many things penetrated her harmony. Only one thing, or rather one person, could cause the tension she felt fill her body. Mia leaned back in her chair and counted to ten, steeling herself to take the call her secretary just announced on line one. But was there ever enough time to really prepare? With one last silent prayer Mia picked up the line.

"Hello, Mother," she said with obvious forced gaiety. "How are you doing?"

"I'm doing as well as an old woman can without grandchildren to look forward to seeing."

Mia closed her eyes, riding out a wave of intense irritation. *Does she ever let up?* "What can I help you with, Ma?"

"I had a doctor's appointment today with my cardiologist, Dr. Blanchard. Did I ever tell you about him?"

Every chance you get. "Yes, Ma, you did. Is everything okay?" She swiveled in the chair to her left to look out at her scenic view of the sun beginning to set. The soft pastels of the lavenders and varying tones of blues swirled together in the sky with a hint of burnt orange streaking across.

"Yes, but I didn't call to discuss my checkup."

Uh-oh, here it comes. Mia steeled herself.

"I told Dr. Blanchard all about you this time, and I even showed him a picture. I gave him your phone number," she said with satisfaction.

Is this woman crazy? "You did what!" Mia shrieked.

"You're not able to find a man on your own," her mother snapped, her tone condescending. "I told him to call you tonight for dinner and maybe a movie."

Mia marveled at how her mother sounded as if that settled the entire matter. "Well, I won't be home tonight so he'll have a very stimulating conversation with my answering machine."

"And where are you going?"

"One of the little girls next door is having a birthday

dinner, and I was honored to accept her invitation. I'm looking forward to it actually."

Her mother gasped in shock, and Mia could just see her swooning with her usual overdramatic manner. "You're going to miss out on a dinner date with a prestigious and wealthy doctor to eat dinner with a bunch of kids at your next-door neighbor's house . . . in Newark!"

"Yes, Mama. And did you forget that I grew up in Newark, just like you?" *Oh, she'll hate that one.* "As a matter of fact my meeting ran over, and if I don't leave now I'll be late. Tell Dad I love him, and I'll call this weekend. Bye."

Mia shook her head at her mother's assumptions as she filled her leather attaché with files and pulled the colorful shopping bag holding Kimani's wrapped gift from under her desk. This was one of the first times in months that she was leaving her office before 7:00 P.M.

Rajahn knocked on his father's office door before he walked in slowly. "Dad?"

Jordan was so focused on his writing that it took several attempts from his son before he heard him.

"Dad!"

Jordan finally looked away from his terminal. "Yes, Rajahn."

"Ms. McKnight said to tell you that dinner's almost ready."

He nodded, already turning back to his terminal to reread what he had just typed. "I'll be right out."

"Uh, Dad? Aren't you going to shower and change."

Jordan looked up again in surprise. "What's wrong with what I have on?"

"A green T-shirt and burgundy sweatpants, Dad?"

He stood and looked down at himself. "Bad, huh?"

Rajahn grimaced. "Worse. Don't you wanna style like me?" Rajahn asked, dressed in GAP khaki shorts, with a tan and brown GAP plaid shirt worn open with a white tank top underneath.

They heard the doorbell ring. "That's probably Ms. Gordon. Maybe you should go up now, Dad."

He eyed his son suspiciously, wondering, *Since when does he care about how I dress?* "Let me just save this."

Rajahn turned to leave, his thin body swamped in the purposely oversize clothing. "Oh, and, Dad, I knew you would be rushing so I laid out something for you to put on."

Jordan stared at the door a long time after it closed.

"It's nice to finally meet you, Ms. Gordon," Ms. McKnight said, as she led Mia into the living room. "The kids talk about you so much."

Mia smiled. "They're great kids."

"So you don't have any children of your own?" she asked as they took seats on the plush cocoa leather sofa.

Mia stiffened at the question, immediately defensive. Was Ms. McKnight like the many other people who thought it odd for a thirty-four-year-old woman not to have children? "No, I don't."

"The way they pester you, that's a good thing," Minnie said, laughing heartily, her slender shoulders shaking.

"Where *are* the children?" Mia asked, looking around as she relaxed again.

"The girls all started day camp at the local community center. The van should be dropping them off any minute now. Rajahn's probably playing those video games of his in the playroom downstairs."

"Hi, Ms. Gordon."

Mia and Ms. McKnight turned as Rajahn walked into the living room. "Speak of the devil," Ms. McKnight said, smiling up at him warmly. "Come on and sit. Keep Ms. Gordon—"

"Call me Mia."

She nodded, instantly taking a liking to the pretty woman with the dimpled chin that made her even more intriguing. "Okay, keep *Mia* company while I check on dinner. Did you tell your daddy?"

"Yes, ma'am."

"Good."

She stood and bustled out of the room, and Rajahn came to sit on the sofa beside Mia. "So you don't go to day camp with your sisters?"

His expression said, *What? Are you kidding?*, but he only replied, "Naw. I have a summer basketball league. Besides I'm too old for day camp."

Mia smiled. "Of course you are. I'm sorry."

"Do you like basketball?"

He's really going to be a heartbreaker, Mia thought, as she looked at him. "Yes, I watch when I get a chance. I'm a loyal Nets fan even if there's never a post season for them. But unfortunately I'm usually so busy with working that I miss a lot of their games."

"Yeah, my dad works a lot too." Rajahn's face saddened. "We don't get a chance to do things like we used to, but he's a real good father though."

"You love your dad a lot, I can tell."

"He always tells us that adopting us was better in some ways than having his own kids because he got to pick exactly the children he wanted." With bashfulness, the thirteen-year-old young man ducked his head.

She reached over and smoothed his short hair. "And he did a real good job at choosing you all."

"Thanks."

"Excuse me."

They both turned to find Jordan walking into the living room. Rajahn groaned and lowered his head in his hands because his father had not put on the suit Rajahn had laid out. Mia thought his appearance was a *big* improvement. The lightweight linen shirt and baggy blue jeans at least fit him and were, for him, amazingly wrinkle free.

"Hello, Ms. Gord—Mia."

"Hi, Jordan."

Rajahn stood, almost as tall as his father. "I think I hear Ms. M calling me." He dashed out of the room.

Mia made a face. "Funny, I didn't hear her."

"Neither did I," Jordan said as he stepped farther into the room.

Mia watched as he took a seat adjacent to her in a plush maroon leather armchair. They sat in silence, smiling briefly at each other when their eyes would meet as they looked around the living room.

"So you're a writer," Mia said, hoping to break the uncomfortable silence. Having small talk with Jordan was not a part of her plans for the evening, but to not do so would be rude.

"Yeah, yeah, I am." He pushed his glasses up with his index finger. "I write mystery novels."

"My assistant's husband, Royce, is a huge fan of yours." Mia smiled, transforming her face. "She's been nagging me to have you sign his copy of *Murder by Moonlight*."

Jordan looked uncomfortable under the praise. "That was my first novel. I wouldn't mind signing it."

"Really? Thanks. I'll bring it over soon. She wants to surprise him."

Jordan nodded. "Of course. Fans like him keep me working, and with five children who love nice things I need as much work as possible," he joked, obviously already wealthy.

They both laughed at that. Mia was again surprised by his deep voice. It was . . . hypnotic, putting her at ease. "I wish I had more time to read like I did when I was in college, but I'm always so busy working."

He nodded in agreement. "I understand, believe me. I spend so much time thinking about my story line, researching it, writing both the rough draft and then the second draft, that I never read anything but my own work. Whatever time I'm not working I try to spend with my kids."

"That's why I haven't started a family yet. I worry that I won't be able to give children the time they need." Mia was surprised at what she just revealed to him. *Why did I just say that?*

"With five of my own, believe me it's not easy. It's a job beyond the regular nine to five, five days a week."

"I could never imagine being able to cope with five children, especially with my job. I usually put in twelve hours a day at the office and still wind up bringing work home."

"Wow, and I thought I worked long hours. How do you do it?" He looked at her with amazement.

"I love what I do, so it doesn't even seem like work."

"Maybe I should consider investing, especially for the children." Jordan leaned forward in his chair, looking at her intently.

"Investing is a positive thing for everyone. I can refer you to one of my associates if you're interested."

Jordan nodded. "You wouldn't be able to handle it for me?"

"Most of my clients are corporations dealing with mergers and acquisitions mainly." Mia began to fill him in on several different investment ideas that he could consider. Her eyes brightened considerably as she leaned forward and spoke to him. She accentuated her words with sharp hand movements and keen eye contact.

Jordan could see why she excelled in her field. Her excitement about the endless possibilities in investing was infectious. He actually felt fascinated by the bright glitter in her eyes. She loved what she did just as much as he drew energy and life from writing.

The movement of her pouty full lips fascinated him, and he stared at them in fascination as she spoke. As she leaned forward the faint scent of her perfume, something all too sweet and intriguing, drifted to him.

And the edge of her lavender lacy bra showed as her silk shirt hung slightly away from her cinnamon flesh.

"One of the associates at the firm should be able to create an optimal investment portfolio for you," she finished, her voice firm and businesslike.

"If you could recommend someone, I'll call to set up an appointment."

"No, better yet, I'll have Victor Pennington contact you first thing Monday morning if you like."

He nodded his approval, and they fell silent again. It was awkward and left way too much time for Jordan to keep from envisioning the delectable sight of her lingerie. "You said you used to read a lot in college? I'm curious, what types of novels?" he asked suddenly, an effort to get his thoughts on more neutral ground.

"Uhm," Mia hedged in embarrassment. She mumbled the answer deeply under her breath.

"Sorry, I couldn't hear you."

She cleared her throat. "I said romance novels."

Jordan obviously thought that was the funniest thing he'd heard in a while as he burst out laughing, tears actually forming in his eyes behind his glasses. Mia wanted to know what was so amusing, and the stern look she gave him spoke volumes.

He bit his bottom lip to stifle any more laughter. "I'm sorry, it's just—"

"Just what?" she snapped, her eyes momentarily flicking down to his even white teeth.

"You seem very practical and straitlaced—"

"Straitlaced?" Mia threw him a cold look. "Whatever. Look, I said it was while I was in college, okay?"

"Of course."

"Okay, Mr. Best-selling Mystery Novelist, when you're not penning whodunits, what do *you* read?"

"Self-help books," he said with pride, as he pushed his glasses back up on his nose.

Mia raised an arched brow, and gave him a withering look. "How appropriate."

He looked stunned by her sarcastic remark, but didn't have a chance to question her as the girls barreled into the room at top speed.

"Hi, Daddy. Hi, Ms. Gordon." They all greeted the adults.

Mia watched as each girl hugged Jordan around his neck, before they moved to gather next to her on the sofa. She smiled down into their pretty bronzed faces.

"Hello, girls, and happy birthday, Kimani."

Kimani smiled broadly, as she swung her legs off the edge of the chair. "I'm nine today. I'm a big girl," she said with pride.

"Well, of course you are," Mia agreed.

"I had a party at camp but we didn't eat a lot because I remembered my special dinner."

"I'm starving," Tia complained. "My stomach's straight growling."

The twins moved to climb into their father's lap. "So am I, Daddy," Amina whined.

"Ms. McKnight will let us know as soon as dinner is ready." He bounced a twin on each knee to their giggling delight. "How about telling me what happened at camp today, Tia?"

"Same-o, same-o, Daddy. We play, have a snack, play some more, eat lunch, play some more, take a nap, wake up and eat another snack, and then . . . that's right, you guessed it, we play some more," Tia droned. "Only thing that changes is an occasional field trip to go swimming or roller-skating. Same as last year and the year before that and the year—"

"We get the idea, Tia," Jordan interrupted firmly.

"And they'll be doing the same ole thing next—"

"Tia," he barked shortly.

"Sorry, Dad," she immediately apologized, flashing him a bright smile that instantly won him over.

Mia was again amazed by his rapport with the children. They were obviously a family that loved one another unconditionally. He had brought these children

who had memories of less-than-perfect past lives together and somehow successfully blended them into
one cohesive unit. It was as if they had been growing
up together their whole lives. For that, Mia had to admit
that Jordan was special.

"Daddy, where's my present?" Kimani asked, as she
comfortably leaned on the lap of Mia's pinstriped, tailored suit pants.

Jordan looked around in surprise. "Who said I got
you anything?"

"Don't play, Daddy," Kimani whined.

Mia had been appalled, thinking the man had been
absentminded enough to forget to buy his daughter a
birthday present but as he smiled at Kimani she realized
he was only teasing.

"And I do believe there's a gift for you . . . right here!"
Tia held up the bright shopping bag by Mia's feet.

Mia removed it from her grasp gently and set it back
on the floor by her feet. "Curiosity killed the cat, little
Miss Tia."

"Yeah, and satisfaction brought him back," Tia said
smugly.

Jordan gave her "the look." "As you probably know
by now, Tia Iman Banks is our resident smart mouth."

Mia smiled when Tia stood and took a mock bow.

One of the twins twisted in his lap and pulled his
glasses off his face with a delightful giggle. She put them
awkwardly on her face, chanting, "I got Dad-dy gwasses.
I got Dad-dy gwasses!"

Jordan moaned in exasperation. "Amina, give Daddy
back his glasses."

He maneuvered them from her grasp and slipped
them back onto his face. Amina hugged him around
his neck, nearly knocking her twin off his other knee.
"I think you wook best without those gwasses, Daddy."

Yes, my God, he does, Mia thought to herself as her eyes
widened in shock. She was completely floored by how
not having on those oversize, ill-adjusted spectacles

drastically changed his looks. Hidden by the mask of those large awkward glasses was a smooth handsome face. It was rugged with its strong lines and bronzed caramel complexion. Very Denzel Washington-like.

The man was gorgeous!

It was like seeing Clark Kent remove his glasses and becoming Superman, or Steve Urkel becoming Stephon Urkél. All by the simple act of removing glasses. Okay, so he wasn't Superman. He was still clumsy and absentminded, but Mia now realized he was very handsome indeed. Her heart skipped in her chest, and she was shocked by her reaction. She couldn't take her eyes off him. She had just seen the man in a whole new light.

The sound of Rajahn's feet pounding on the floor proceeded his coming to a screeching halt in the doorway. "Ms. M says dinner's ready."

"Thank you, Jesus! I'm starving," Tia said, before walking out of the living room behind her fast-retreating brother.

Kimani stood, quickly grabbing the twins' hands and pulling them behind her. That left Mia alone with Jordan again. He stood and waved his hand before him. "Ladies first, Mia."

Suddenly the sound of her name on his lips was . . . enticing! She stood, picking up the bag holding Kimani's gift. "Thanks," she said softly.

Mia left the living room but immediately swung around when she heard him yell out. He stumbled but quickly corrected his tall frame. She watched as he stooped down to pick up something in his path.

"Uh, one of the girls' toys," he mumbled, obviously embarrassed that he had almost fallen flat on his face in front of her.

Well, right in back of her, technically. The man was a walking disaster. Mia just forced a smile and left the room. It didn't matter how he looked, he still was just an absentminded klutz. *Hello, Mia, welcome back to reality!*

* * *

After the delicious dinner of lasagna and Caesar salad, Ms. McKnight entered the dining room carrying a seven-layer chocolate cake topped with chopped walnuts and nine lit candles.

They all joined in singing "Happy Birthday" as Ms. McKnight set the cake down in a cleared spot in front of Kimani. The candles reflected off her glasses in the dimly lit room as she eyed the cake eagerly.

"Blow out the candles after you make a wish, Kimani," Jordan instructed from where he sat at the head of the table. His own glasses reflected the lit candles as well.

"Uh, Dad, that's not very sanitary," she said, before using her paper plate to fan the flames out instead.

Mia hid her smile behind her hand. "Happy birthday, Kimani," she said, leaning down to kiss her smooth cheek.

Ms. McKnight sliced the cake and handed everyone a nice-sized piece. She smiled sweetly at Mia as she handed her the cake. She immediately liked the rapport she saw between the woman and the children. In just a few minutes she had seen Mia be more affectionate and aware of the children than Marisol had been in months. Just too bad the bright and extremely beautiful woman did not show the same feelings for their father. They would make quite a handsome couple. *Time changes many things,* she thought as she sat down.

"You grew up in Newark, Mia?" Jordan asked.

She sat to his immediate right at the table and looked over at him briefly. "Oh, yes. I'm a Brick City baby and proud of it. You?"

"Yup, although my father is originally from Virginia. He moved back after my Mom passed. There is nothing like growing up in the Bricks."

Mia nodded in agreement. The Bricks was the unofficial nickname of the large city mainly because of the large amount of brick-constructed projects that had been in the area. A part of the revitalization effort in the city was the relocation of the project residents to smaller buildings and town houses so that the older buildings could be destroyed.

"It was really hard for me in college. I felt like I was always having to defend where I came from. I spent so much time of my college years angry."

Jordan nodded in understanding. "It wasn't as bad for me. I attended Essex County College before moving on to Rutgers downtown."

The adults began a discussion on the mayor's effort to renovate the city, and the children enjoyed their cake. They were just happy that Ms. Gordon and their father were talking. Their smiles turned to frowns when Mia suggested that Jordan show the children more of the culture to be found in the city. Touring the historical buildings and going to the museums and other events like the annual jazz festival were not their idea of fun. Their interest did pick up again when the adults began to discuss the Universoul Circus.

"A circus with nothing but Black people, Ms. Gordon?" Rajahn asked.

"Uh-huh, I have pictures from when I went with the church, but you have to see it in person."

"Can I see the pictures, Ms. Gordon?" he asked with excitement.

"Yeah, me, too, Ms. Gordon?" Tia asked, before taking a big gulp of her milk.

"I'd like to se them, too, Ms. Gordon?" Kimani piped in, sucking icing from one of the candles, which Mrs. McKnight immediately took from her with a scolding frown.

"We wanna see them, too," the twins added, their faces nearly covered with chocolate icing.

Mia looked into each of their expectant faces, completely put on the spot. What else could she say but, "Okay"?

Jordan saw the look in her eyes and knew the woman felt like a deer caught in headlights. They were his children, and he felt overwhelmed at times when they were all together and clamoring for his attention. He bit back a smile before coming to her rescue. "I would like to see those photos as well. If you don't mind, maybe you could bring them over here for all of us to see one day."

"Uh, yes, that would be fine. Perhaps sometime this weekend?"

"Can you do it after my basketball game tomorrow?" Rajahn asked eagerly. "In fact, would you like to come to the game? You said you like b-ball, remember? Then you can check out my skills on the court."

Mia smiled as he imitated shooting a basketball, but that didn't mean she was going to allow herself to be backed into another corner by five sets of adorable brown eyes. Her life was becoming too enmeshed with this rambunctious bunch. Saturdays were her down time, and that's only if she wasn't *still* working. No, she was not giving up her solitude to spend the afternoon with five children at a basketball game. These children were wrapping her around their fingers, roping her into things totally out of the norm for her. It didn't matter that they were adorable, or that they looked suddenly solemn as she hadn't yet answered, or that Tia held her hands together and mouthed *please,* or that Kimani threw her that adorable brace-filled smile, or that the twins were nodding yes eagerly. She didn't want to go, and she just had to tell them no. Right?

"Okay, I'd love to go," she answered instead.

They all jumped up and down excitedly in their seats, and Mia felt like a big sucker.

"Did you enjoy your birthday?" Jordan asked Kimani as he tucked her summer spread around her.

"Yes, and thank you for the gold earrings and necklace set. It's just what I wanted. I'm glad you didn't for-get."

"Your notes left all over my office helped a lot," he said dryly, before tweaking her nose playfully and affec-tionately. "Did you like all your other gifts?"

"I loved the collection of books Grandpa sent me." She ticked off a finger as she listed each gift. "And Mrs. McKnight gave me three outfits to start school with in September, although they're dresses. Ms. Gordon's computer is off the hook—"

"It's what?" Jordan interrupted in confusion, push-ing glasses up on his nose.

"That means it's *real* nice, Daddy."

"Oh, okay."

"Tia promised not to tease me for the whole week-end, Rajahn drew a picture of me, and the twins gave me the beaded bracelets they made at camp." She fin-ished with a smile.

"I guess you have a lot of thank-you cards to give. Do you want to use the computer to make some?"

Kimani's eyes widened in shock. That was a *big*-time offer, because he didn't let anyone use the computer while he was working on a book. *Daddy must be in a* real *good mood.* "Really?"

"Yes, but it's time for bed now." He leaned down to kiss her cheek and leaned over to turn off the teddy bear lamp on the white bedside table.

"Daddy?" she called out when he moved toward the door.

He turned, cloaked by the darkness. "Yes, Ki."

"Don't you ever want to get married?" she asked.

He sighed and walked back across the room. Of course he stumbled over something, possibly his own feet, and yelled out. With the lights on he was clumsy enough, but in total darkness . . .

"Daddy, are you okay?" she asked, as she reached over to turn on the lamp.

"Yeah, I'm fine." He came to sit on the edge of the

bed, his foot throbbing from walking into the bedpost. "Are you worrying about me getting married one day? You know I'll always love all my children regardless."

"Please, Dad," Kimani drawled. "I'm worried about you *not* getting married one day."

He laughed. "Listen, when and if I find the right woman, I'll get married. Don't worry about your old man."

"But you *would* marry the right woman, right?"

"Of course."

Kimani smiled after he left the room. *Well, have we got the right one for you, Daddy.*

Mia listened to the message on her answering machine again.

"Hello, Ms. Gordon. This is Terrence Blanchard. Dr. Terrence Blanchard. Your mother passed on your number to me, and I thought we might enjoy a date sometime but I can see you're not home. Call me when you get a chance at 555-2000. I look forward to meeting you, you're a very beautiful woman. So call me. . . . Bye."

Mia had to admit, his voice was nice and deep and cultured. She was intrigued. Bet he didn't wear wrinkled sweatpants and oversize tees, or funny glasses. And rest assured he didn't trip all over himself like a klutz! Maybe she *would* call him.

Four

Mia awoke early Saturday morning in good spirits. She stretched her long, slender limbs in her queen-size bed beneath the white Egyptian cotton sheets. Glancing over at her alarm clock on the bedside table, she saw that it was just a little after seven, and the sun was already shining brightly.

Last night at the Bankses' had not been as bad as a root canal as she thought it would be. Of course, after being used to growing up an only child and then living alone as an adult, she hadn't heard that much talking and laughing during a meal since her college days. And after being unnerved by it at first, she had actually begun to feel it was kind of nice.

But she still loved her solitude. It was moments like these, lying alone in a quiet house and just being able to relax, that Mia cherished the most. She was a huge fan of meditation, and she could not imagine ever being able to effectively focus on her thoughts and to reflect if she were in the household next door. Both were huge parts of achieving an optimal meditative state.

As she lay languid and calm in her bed, her hand lightly twirling a ringlet of her ebony hair around a slender finger, she thought of Jordan. Not the clumsy, unorganized man with the ill-fitting glasses, but the surprisingly handsome man beneath the mask.

"Damn," Mia said in a soft whisper, as she clearly envisioned his masculine beauty. The smooth mocha com-

plexion, his thick full brows above clear mocha eyes.
Lush and long lashes framed those brandy-tinted eyes,
and that effect considerably softened his high cheekbones, long aquiline nose, and square chin. And he had
the most luscious lips she had ever seen. Suckable lips.

All through dinner last night she had kept sneaking
glances at him, still amazed by the temporary transfor-
mation. Why would he willingly detract from his own
looks?

Maybe she was too hard on him. The man worked
out of home, was raising five active children alone. What
reason would he have to be dressed to the nines like
all the men she worked alongside every day? It would
be odd for him to be in tailored suits all day.

But that didn't excuse his clumsiness. The man
seemed to have two left feet and a perpetual black cloud
of bad luck looming over him.

Sighing she eyed the book lying on her nightstand.
It was Tyresa's husband, Royce's copy of Jordan's first
book, *Murder by Moonlight*. Picking it up, she opened it
and read the first page.

After skimming through the first paragraph, more
out of curiosity than anything else, Mia found herself
getting comfortable to read the story that had so instantly captured her interest.

"Tia, you grab the milk. Kimani, you get the cereal.
I have the bowls and spoons," Rajahn yelled over his
shoulder as he left the kitchen, headed to the door in
the foyer that lead down into their playroom.

He heard his four sisters following him as he turned
the huge sixty-inch television on to one of the Saturday
morning cartoon shows. "Hurry up, y'all. I wanna get
my grub on!"

The twins came down first, still dressed in their pajamas and clutching their precious stuffed toys. Carefully, as their dad had taught them, they held on to the
railing as they went down the stairs. Immediately they

moved to sit on either side of their big brother, whom they adored.

Soon Kimani and Tia also were settled on the carpet in front of the TV as Rajahn poured generous amounts of Fruity Pebbles and milk into a bowl for each of them. This was their usual Saturday morning routine, as they ate and laughed at the antics of colorful cartoon characters.

Rajahn would've much preferred to watch the show about wild animals and their eating habits, but he knew his sisters wouldn't enjoy the program the way he did. It wasn't easy being outnumbered four to one! If only their dad would let them have their own TVs. It wasn't as if he couldn't afford to buy them!

But then Raj was old enough to understand that this was their father's way of supervising how much television they watched and what they watched. He discovered the parental channel block on the cable box when he and his friend Willie tried to watch a risqué program on HBO the night of a sleep-over. Willie and he were thoroughly disgusted and disappointed when they couldn't tune in the channel!

Sighing, Rajahn reached for the box of cereal to pour another bowl to feed his constantly growing appetite. The children all heard the stairs creak under their father's weight. Moments later the door opened at the top of the stairs.

They all turned to look up. "Good morning, Daddy," they greeted in unison.

"Morning," Jordan grumbled, also clad in his night-clothes—a T-shirt with his college alma mater and striped pajama bottoms. "Don't waste any cereal on that carpet, I just had it cleaned."

"We won't, Dad," Rajahn assured him.

Tia raised her spoon to her mouth, her way of drinking the sweet milk left behind after she had eaten all of the cereal. Slyly, she cut her eyes up at him, "Why don't you have on your glasses, Daddy?"

He walked down the stairs and sat on one of the bean-bag chairs lining the wall with a grimace. *I'm getting old!* "When I woke up this morning I found them in my bed broken in half. I must've slept with them on, although I'm sure I placed them on the nightstand before I went to bed." He sighed. "I guess I'll have to go and get another pair some time this week. For now I'll have to use those stupid contacts. Rajahn, be sure to remind me to call Elegant Eyes downtown and make an appointment."

"A'ight, Dad," he said, his mouth filled with cereal and milk.

"No!" Tia yelled out suddenly, her pretty face frantic. Everyone eyed her oddly. She flashed her smile to throw them off. "Daddy, why don't you just wear contacts from now on?"

At the nudge she gave Kimani, her sister joined in with her. "Yeah, Dad, you should try them out. Then you won't have to worry about keeping up with your glasses like I do."

"Or breaking them," Rajahn joined in at Tia's hard, meaningful stare.

"You wook good without your gwasses," Aliya agreed, restating her comment from the previous evening.

Jordan moved to stand up, with effort, from the bean-bag chair. The chairs were well suited for children, but not an inactive thirty-five-year-old man! "Well, I'll have to keep using the contacts until I get another pair of glasses."

"They aren't so bad, are they, Dad?" Tia asked hopefully.

He blinked rapidly. "They just take a little getting used to. Look, I have to go to Staples to get some office supplies, so everyone be dressed by nine o'clock."

"Aw, man, I don't wanna go," Tia whined.

"Me neither," Kimani added, her mouth as pouted as her sister's.

Jordan sighed as he headed for the stairs. "Ladies,

let's not give Daddy a hard time," his voice floated down before they heard the door close behind him.

"I broke Daddy's glasses," Tia said with pride as she stacked her empty bowl inside of her sisters'.

"What!" both Rajahn and Kimani exclaimed.

The twins covered their mouths with their hands, saying. "Oooooh. You're gonna be in trou-bwe." They drew out the first syllable of *trouble* in a sing-song fashion.

"Why would you do a stupid thing like that?" Rajahn moaned, looking at her as if she had two heads.

"For your information, yesterday when Aliya took Daddy's glasses off, I was lookin' dead in Ms. Gordon's face." She looked smug.

But her siblings all looked over at her as if she were crazy, not understanding the satisfaction she obviously felt. "So?" Kimani snapped.

Tia loudly released air through her heart-shaped mouth in exasperation. "So . . . I saw how she looked at him differently without those big ole glasses on. It's like she thought he was cute . . . without the specs."

At their looks of disbelief, she insisted, "I saw it, and then she kinda stared at Daddy with a goofy look."

"Daddy does look cuter without those glasses," Kimani conceded, now believing her adamant sister. "Even the twins think so."

Rajahn nodded with a smile. "So we need to keep him out of those glasses. They are funny-looking, but he loves them."

"Maybe he'll pick some that suit his face better," Kimani added.

"I say scrap the glasses altogether." Tia frowned. "And while we're at it, wouldn't it help if Daddy wasn't always around the house in those funky sweatpants and T-shirts he loves?"

"He does need some style," Rajahn agreed.

Tia stood and stretched her slender frame. "Right

now, I'm going to ask Ms. Gordon if I can stay with her 'til y'all get back."

"Us too, Tia," Kimani said, referring to herself and the twins in totally broken language, uncharacteristic of her. "I mean, the twins and I would like to stay with her as well."

Tia rolled her eyes heavenward and waved her hand. "Whatever."

"I'm going with Dad. It'll give us a chance for a man-to-man conversation," Rajahn said seriously.

"And who's the other man he's supposed to talk to?" Tia scoffed.

Rajahn shot her a nasty look. "Shut up, Tia."

"Come on, let's go call Ms. Gordon," Kimani insisted, acting as a buffer between her two older siblings.

The girls, led by the twins, all headed up the stairs carrying the remnants of their breakfast with them. Rajahn turned to his wild animal program with a satisfied smile. "Oh, and y'all work on Ms. Gordon," he yelled up to them. "If we work this right she'll be a Banks before Thanksgiving."

"And you're sure it's okay for the girls to stay here with you?" Jordan asked, as he stood on Mia's porch looking down at her.

Mia nodded with a smile, not showing the slight apprehension she felt at "baby-sitting," even if the girls were no longer babies.

He smiled in return, his teeth brilliant against his bronze skin and supple lips. Mia felt her heart speed up. *Whoa, Mia, what's going on with you girl?*

Okay, she was willing to be honest because she knew *exactly* what was wrong with her. When she opened her door this morning, she certainly hadn't expected to see Jordan standing there looking devilishly handsome without his glasses. Once again her reaction to him was instantaneous. The man was gorgeous. Why did he hide

it? She was stunned by just how raw and sensual his
looks were. He was one of the finest men she had laid
eyes upon in a long time.

Mia cleared her throat, amazed at her thoughts of
how those long narrow fingers would feel caressing her
neck—and beyond. "It's no problem at all, Jordan,"
she assured him with honesty.

"I won't be long. Girls, be on your best behavior."
He gave a stern look to Tia in particular, who stood
behind Mia in the foyer with her sisters.

"Where's Rajahn?" she asked as she looked past his
broad shoulder outside.

Jordan stepped aside so that she could see his son
sitting in the passenger seat of the silver Land Cruiser.
"He decided he wanted to ride with me. Also, he asked
me to remind you of his game today at one o'clock."

Mia smiled at Rajahn and waved at him. "Please tell
him that I haven't forgotten that or the pictures from
the circus," she said, surprising herself with the re-
minder she had felt cajoled to make yesterday at dinner.

He laughed, the crinkles at his eyes deepening. The
sound was rich and deep. "I told Raj that it might be
best to postpone that for another day with you keeping
an eye on the girls for me."

"Okay, but it wouldn't have been a problem at all."

The children looked on with pleasure as they
watched their dad and Ms. Gordon talking. Tia nearly
burst with pride. Her father looked so handsome without his glasses, almost as cute as the rapper Mase, who
was her all-time favorite performer. On top of that he
didn't trip over his own feet or anything. *Daddy's on a
roll!*

"Okay, girls, I'll see you in a little bit."

"Bye, Daddy," they answered in unison.

Mia closed the front door and eyed her guests a little
warily, unsure of what to do to keep them occupied and
out of trouble. Suddenly, an idea formed. They were
adorable and loving children, but their fuzzy, well-worn

hairstyles left a lot to be desired. *I'll kill two birds with one stone.*

Smiling she clasped her hands together in front of her chest. "I know exactly what we ladies will do to keep ourselves occupied until the men return."

Jordan's mind was half on his driving and half focused on the memory of Mia's flowery scent, her beautiful face with that oddly dimpled chin, and the sight of her shapely legs in shorts. She was brains and beauty, a lethal combination for any man.

"Dad, don't you ever think about getting married? I mean, you're not getting any younger."

Jordan started in surprise before glancing over at his son. Déjà vu? Yes, except that it was Kimani who had asked him the same exact question, just last night. Coincidence? Maybe. "Don't tell me," he drawled, as he steered the sizable SUV easily. "You're worried I'll never get married, right?"

Rajahn's face brightened with pleasure. "Yeah," he said excitedly. "How'd you know?"

"Lucky guess?" he answered weakly.

"Wow, Dad, you and I are here." He used his index and middle fingers to make a V, moving it from near his eyes toward his father's, indicating they were on the same thought level.

Jordan smiled. "I wish we could be here about keeping your room clean," Jordan joked, imitating the gesture his son made.

"Yeah, Dad."

They rode in companionable silence for a few moments before Rajahn started to glance over at his father frequently. Jordan finally noticed and asked, "What?"

"I gave you time to think over the question, so now what's the answer?"

He looked over at his son. Rajahn was really becoming a man. In five short years Jordan had watched him grow from a smart-mouth boy to a well-mannered polite young man. In many ways this man-child was his biggest pride and joy.

"Hey, you know what, Raj?" he asked suddenly. "I love you, little man."

He balled his hand into a fist and reached over toward his son, who immediately did the same with his own hand before lightly tapping it on top of his father's, giving him a "pound."

But he still moaned, "Dad."

"Hey, you're never too old for me to show you love. This way when you're old enough for a lady friend you won't be afraid to show her the affection she deserves." Frequently he liked to have these one-on-one talks with his son on the proper treatment and respect for women. He hoped the lessons he tried to teach would remain with him forever.

"Dad, you need to take your own advice." Rajahn leaned forward to turn down the radio's volume.

"What's that?"

"If I had a shorty like Ms. Gordon as my next-door neighbor I would try to push up on her."

"Drop the slang, Raj, so that I know what you're saying."

He sighed. "Okay. Ms. Gordon is a real pretty lady. She's nice and smart and cool and *single*. If I were you I would ask her out on a date."

Ask Mia Gordon out on a date!

He thought of his neighbor, and surprisingly a clear image of her standing in the midst of cluttered ceramics in her kitchen filled his mind. It was replaced with a picture of her the night she came to check on the twins, finally to be overcome by the sight and smell of her this morning. She was pretty with her jet-black riotous curly hair framing soft feminine features, and the most gloriously full lips that just begged to be—

Oh yeah, he noticed that she was quite pretty in a straitlaced kind of way. Okay, okay, just damned pretty, period. When he saw her that first day in her kitchen conversing with Kimani he had immediately noticed her physical appeal, but Mia Gordon and he were as different as night and day, oil and vinegar, happiness and depression.

She was a career-focused, single woman with no children, and he was a father of five who worked out of his home. Can we say "Not a match made in heaven"?

"Believe me, son, Ms. Gordon is a very attractive woman but I have no intention of asking her out on a date."

Jordan didn't see the crestfallen look on his son's face as they exited Route 22 to get onto the entrance ramp of the Garden State Parkway headed toward home.

"Now," Mia sighed with satisfaction as she finished the last tiny plait of Kimani's shoulder-length hair. "You're all done, and my fingers are saying 'Hallelujah!' "

She had washed and conditioned each of the girls' hair and then blow-dried it before greasing their scalps with an herbal pomade. Taking a seat on the couch, she settled some old throw pillows on the floor. One by one she had sat the girls on the pillow between her legs and plaited their hair into tight and tiny corn braids that should last through the rest of the summer.

It reminded her of the precious moments she used to share with both her mother and grandmother, who had passed on. Her fingers felt cramped but it gave her a warm feeling that was new to her, a feeling of contentment. The girls' pleasure at the results made her feel good.

"You know what, I have some wooden beads from when I had my hair braided during a trip to Africa," she said with excitement as she remembered them. "Kimani, run upstairs and look for a small box in the top drawer of my dresser."

Quickly the little girl returned with the beads and Mia sat each of them on the pillows on the floor again, using small black rubber bands to secure the beads to the ends of each braid. Tia was the last to have hers applied as her sisters twisted their heads to make their own beads click.

Tia allowed her face to fall softly against Mia's inner thigh. It had been so long since she had her hair braided. Just like her sisters, she felt this as a bond mothers and daughters shared. She just knew this woman was meant to be their mother.

Mia smoothed her hands over Tia's head. "We're all done, Miss Tia."

She wasn't even aware of her mothering tone, but the girls all heard it and felt warmed by it. Didn't their father understand little girls needed mothers to braid their hair, kiss their boo-boos, hug them only the way a mother could, and teach them about boys? They had a father who was very loving, and now they wanted a mother to complete the set the way it should be. Parents. A daddy *and* a mommy.

Tia stood and walked over to the large mahogany-framed mirror on the opposite wall of the living room. Because of her unusually tall height, she was able to see her head in the reflection. Each braid was evenly parted and neatly braided. Her scalp shone from the herbal pomade Mia had smoothed on. A smile broke out on her pretty slender face.

"So do you like it?" Mia asked, coming to stand behind her in the mirror. "You all look like beautiful little Nubian princesses."

"I like it a lot, Ms. Gordon," Tia said shyly, breaking the warm gaze they shared in the mirror. Seeing her hair like that reminded her of when her grandmother had still been alive to care for her. "Thank you."

"You're very welcome." Turning, she smiled at Kimani and the twins where they all sat on the mahogany tuxedo sofa. "I just hope your father doesn't mind. Maybe I should have asked him first."

"Believe me, Ms. G," Tia said from behind her with her usual spunk back in place. "Dad will be happy. He always gets so postal when he has to do our hair. Ms. M always gives us those big ole down-south dookie braids looking like Celie from *The Color Purple.*"

Mia laughed and moved to reclaim her seat on the sofa. One of the twins immediately moved to sit on her lap. "Uhm, speaking of your dad, why isn't he wearing his glasses?" she asked, as a vision of him standing so vibrant, strong, and handsome on her porch this morning filled her thoughts.

"Tia broke them," Amina answered innocently as she fingered one of the beads on her hair.

Both Tia and Kimani threw her a furious stare, which with the bliss of a small child, Amina ignored.

Kimani laughed nervously, pushing her own glasses up on her face. "What she *means* is, Tia broke them by accident."

"We all think he's cuter without his glasses," Tia inserted, her eyes carefully on Mia. "What do you think, Ms. Gordon?"

Mia was startled by the question, and it showed on her pretty face. She shifted in her seat under the intense gazes of four pairs of eyes. Okay, when she heard the doorbell ring this morning she had of course been expecting the girls because she agreed to let them come over to the house when they called her, but she had not been expecting to come face-to-face with Jordan Banks à la no glasses.

Yes, he was cute. Beyond cute. He was gorgeous in a classically handsome way. As she stood just a few inches away from him she had been well aware of the fact. But she was not going to tell that bit of information to these little girls.

Mia was saved from answering as her cordless phone

began to ring loudly. She leaned behind Kimani to reach for it but felt nothing but air. Tia had snatched it up before she could get it herself, and with one of the twins in her lap, she hadn't wanted to move too suddenly.

"Hello, Mia Gordon's residence."

"Tia, give me my phone," she demanded sternly, her hand outstretched. Moving to get the child out of her lap, Mia stood and held out her hand again when the little girl seemed to ignore her.

"Who's this? Dr. who?" Tia asked, looking up at Mia as she held her hand over the mouthpiece of the phone. "Are you sick, Ms. G?"

Mia took the phone from her with an agitated sigh. *That's why I don't have children. They're just too grown!* "Hello, this is Mia," she said with forced patience.

Tia moved to sit on the sofa in the spot Mia vacated, shrugging at Kimani's questioning look. They both turned to look at Mia.

"Oh, yes, hello, Dr. Blanchard . . . Okay, Terrence." She laughed huskily and turned her back to the children when she noticed them staring at her.

They still listened carefully to her side of the call.

"Yes, I did get your message last night but before you say anything else, let me please apologize for my mother," she said, seriously.

"If it gives me the chance to know a beautiful and smart woman such as yourself, then I want to thank her." His voice was smooth and rich.

Mia smiled at the compliment. "I'm just sorry you have an advantage over me in that aspect."

"Well, let's rectify that tonight."

Mia nodded, clutching the phone to her face. "That would be nice."

The girls looked on grimly as Mia made plans to meet him at a restaurant, The Jazz Spot, for dinner at seven. Tia, knowing it was a man on the phone, understood that making an appointment to meet with a doctor wasn't usually at night . . . wasn't at a restaurant . . . and wasn't something to make Ms. Gordon smile like *that!*

"Okay, I'll see you later then? Bye." Mia disconnected and turned to see the crestfallen faces of Kimani and Tia. The twins played with each other on the floor with the toys they had brought over with them. "Why the gloomy faces, girls?"

Their spirits plummeted. What chance did they have of hooking up their father and Ms. Gordon if she got a new boyfriend? This was a definite hitch in their plans. But how could they explain that to her?

Instead they mumbled, "Nothing."

Mia was confused by the sudden change in their attitude and had no clue what had brought it on. But she was still pleased by her upcoming date this evening. Of course she would have loved to know what the good doctor looked like. Going on her mother's judgment alone was scary to say the least.

Maybe he would be tall, between six feet and six foot three, with clear eyes with brown liquid depths that shimmered like brandy. And maybe he would have smooth masculine lips with even white teeth that glistened when he smiled, and a strong defined chin—

Whoa, Mia!

The doorbell chimed just as she realized that she was describing Jordan Banks. She walked quickly to open the front door, the girls immediately lining up behind her. She came face-to-face with him, all six feet two inches of him, complete with brandied eyes and smooth brown lips.

"Hi, Jordan," she said, flustered by her thoughts of him.

The girls filled the doorway, surrounding her as they heard their father's name. He smiled in surprise. "Look at all my beautiful little ladies," he exclaimed.

"You wike it, Daddy? Ms. Gordon braided our hair," Amina said, the first to step out onto the porch. She swung her head to shake the beads.

"I don't just like it, I love it." He leaned down to finger one of her braids before looking up at Mia suddenly.

Their eyes met over Amina's head, and Mia felt herself drowning in those liquid pools. "Thank you, Mia. I don't know what to say."

He was extremely touched that she had put so much time and effort into his daughters' hair. It was one of the most kind and unselfish things anyone had done for him. Honestly he had thought the girls would spend the time with Mia entertaining themselves while she worked. Obviously he had been wrong. So very wrong.

"I hope you don't mind. Perhaps I should have asked your permission first?" She placed her hand on Kimani's thin shoulder, finally breaking the look between them. It left her breathless and . . . confused.

"No . . . no . . . I don't mind one bit. I don't know how to thank you." He looked down at his sneakered feet sheepishly. "As you could tell I'm not very good with doing their hair."

They both laughed softly at that.

Rajahn walked up onto the porch. "Ms. Gordon, are you still coming to my game this afternoon?" he asked, his voice hopeful.

Oh, Lord, I forgot all about it! How could she still go when she had a date to prepare for by seven? That meant finding something to wear, doing her hair and makeup. There was no way she was showing up to a blind date with only last-minute preparations because she had spent her entire afternoon at her neighbor's child's basketball game.

Tia and Kimani looked at each other, both knowing that she was thinking of her date at The Jazz Spot. Would she still go to the game with them? Only Ms. Gordon knew the answer, so they both turned to her.

"Of course I'm still going, Raj. I wouldn't miss it for anything," she answered.

Jordan blinked rapidly and Mia knew it was because

of the contacts he wasn't used to wearing. "Do you know how to get to Weequahic Park?"

Rajahn looked confused. "Why take two cars? We can all ride together. You have plenty of room in the SUV, Dad."

Jordan and Mia looked at each other before looking away quickly. "It's up to Ms. Gordon. Of course you're welcome to ride along with us. It is the most practical thing to do."

Mia nodded, not allowing herself to look at him again. "What time should I be ready?"

He glanced down at his watch. "In an hour would be good."

"Okay."

She watched, framed by the doorway, as he led his five children to their house. Why did she feel a wave of nerves shimmy across her skin? Was it her date with Dr. Blanchard, or her odd and disconcerting sudden awareness of Jordan Banks à la nerd extraordinaire?

Five

"Jordan? What happened to your face?"

They were all piled in his Land Cruiser, with Mia riding in the front with him. She had wondered about the bandage on his forehead as soon as she stepped out of the house to join them. The question had overwhelmed her until she just finally had to ask him, although she was pretty sure that he would tell her it was self-inflicted.

He looked away from her, his brown eyes warm with embarrassment. It was bad enough he had to wear the bandage, being that it was hardly conspicuous in size or color against his mocha complexion, but did she have to mention it as well? He motioned with his index finger to push up his glasses, before he remembered that he had on contacts. Still he felt the sensation that the glasses were on his face, sliding down his nose as they usually did. Turning the vehicle into the park's entrance, he soon pulled into an empty parking space.

Was he stalling to answer the question? Of course he was! The truth was totally embarrassing.

"Daddy hit himsewf on the head with one of the kitchen cabinets," Amina answered, holding her hands over her mouth as she giggled.

Aliya joined her twin in the humorous delight. Kimani tried to shush them. Tia mumbled something about brats under her breath and Rajahn just shook his head, before lowering it to his hand. Jordan sighed.

"Oh, my God! Are you okay? Did you black out? Do you need stitches? Is it still bleeding?" Mia answered her questions like rapid gunfire, one after the other, leaving Jordan feeling slightly dizzy. She had turned in the leather seat to look at him, her pretty face filled with concern.

This man is going to kill himself! she thought with amazement.

Jordan shook his head. "I'm fine. It was just a small break in the skin." *My children just made me embarrassed as hell, but what's a little humiliation among family?*

Mia reached over to gingerly touch the bandage, and he winced visibly. "Let me look take a look at it," she said softly, smiling when he turned in his seat to face her.

They were just inches apart as she raised her hand to gently pull back the bandage, working the adhesive from his skin. Her eyes widened at the angry reddish break in the skin. "Are you sure you don't need to go to an ER?" she asked softly.

Jordan swallowed over a sudden lump in his throat as he felt the sweet softness of her breath caress his face. Her perfume was an odd mix that was subtle but alluring. It reminded him of a soft, sweet cool breeze that surprisingly had the power to blow him completely off his feet.

Her eyes dipped down from the injury to look into his eyes. Their gazes locked for a few brief moments before Mia cleared her throat and looked away first, her hands suddenly shaking.

"It'll probably heal better if you let it get some air," she advised before removing the bandage at his slow nod.

"Thanks, Mia."

She balled the soiled bandage into a napkin before tossing it into a small trash bag he kept in the front.

"I've had way worse accidents than this and sur-

vived," he assured her, a testament to his clumsiness.
"Believe me."

"One of these days you're gonna kill yourself," she
muttered before climbing out of the SUV.

The children climbed out behind her, and Mia un-
buckled both of the twins before lifting them down to
the ground. Together they all made their way over to
the bleachers surrounding the blacktop basketball
court. People were scattered about, some sitting on the
bleachers, others loitering on the grass enjoying the
warmth and brilliance of the sun. It was a beautiful summer day in the city, and the inhabitants of the park were
certainly enjoying it.

They all sat together on one bleacher, with the children sitting between Jordan and Mia, as Rajahn ran to
meet his teammates, all dressed in their oversize basketball shorts and jerseys. Jordan conversed freely with
many of the other parents there, and immediately introduced Mia to everyone as his new next-door neighbor. They both ignored the looks of disbelief everyone
gave them because they obviously thought the two were
involved.

Couldn't two adults, who were both single, be at an
event together and not be *together?* Obviously no one
else thought so.

They were unaware of the attractive family they
made. Jordan's chiseled good looks were the perfect
compliment to Mia's beauty. The children, although no
blood relation to Mia, nor Jordan for that matter,
seemed like testaments to the attractive couple's union.
Both conversed with the children, answering all their
questions, and they worked together to stop any unruly
behavior.

As the game began Mia was busy thinking about the
moment when her eyes had met Jordan's. Never had
she shared such a simple and intense gesture with someone. It had been like being kissed by the sun's rays and
comforted by a blazing fire in the dead of winter. Look-

ing into his eyes had revealed a lot about herself and her newfound attraction to this man she had once disdained. Allowing herself to flourish in this sudden awareness of him was a definite no-no. The man had five children, for God's sake. She would have to have a death wish to take that on!

Jordan glanced over at Mia out the corner of his eye. Having her fret over his last in a long line of self-inflicted injuries had been disconcerting. For so many years he had to be the one to kiss boo-boos and give assuring words to his injured children. It was a new sensation to have someone tend to him, particularly a woman—a vibrant and attractive woman whose hands were as soft as cotton, whose scent was as intoxicating as an aphrodisiac, and whose eyes had the power to hypnotize. Gone were the condescending and degrading looks in her eyes whenever she saw him. Somewhere along the line they had been replaced by softness and concern, like today.

Why hadn't he realized before that she had the most incredible almond-shaped cinnamon-brown eyes? And her perfume was enticingly noticeable without being overpowering. And who knew she had such nice legs! He was used to seeing her in her professional attire that was attractive but hardly accentuated her shapely figure like what she wore today. Oh, no, in her colorful orange stretch tank top and form-fitting Capri jeans, he definitely felt like he was seeing an all new Mia Gordon. Jordan liked this one better. It reminded him more of the laid-back style he favored.

It seemed that beneath the sharp professional image, Ms. Gordon had one helluva body, which immediately conjured thoughts of sweating, gyrating nude bodies lost in mindless physical bliss.

As the game progressed Mia was as enthusiastic as the girls in cheering Rajahn on. That turned him on even more. He loved it that she was making a spectacle of herself and not caring one bit. His earlier assumptions about her would never have imagined this woman in such a carefree manner. He had to force himself not to stare at her in fascination and pure lust.

When Raj shot a clean three-pointer, she jumped up off the bleacher and started chanting, "Go, Raj. Go, Raj."

The girls joined in with her, becoming his unofficial cheerleading squad, which Rajahn loved. He used his hands to "raise the roof" as he smiled up at them.

"Your wife must have been a cheerleader in school."

Jordan turned to find an attractive woman in her early thirties on the bleacher seat above him. "Oh, she's not my wife, she's my—"

She leaned closer to him. "Your girlfriend?"

He leaned away slightly. "No, she's my next-door neighbor."

"Aah," she sighed with satisfaction, before moving down to sit next to him. "Amanda Langston. And you're . . . ?"

He took the slender hand she offered, flustered by her forthright personality. "Jordan Banks."

She grasped his hand a moment longer than he thought necessary. "Now that's a familiar name, why is that?"

"I'm a writer," he answered, pulling his hand from her grasp.

"Wow, I'm a freelance reporter for the local newspaper, the *Star Gazette.*"

"Are you covering the game?" Jordan asked. "My son's playing."

She looked toward the handsome young man he pointed out, not noticing any real resemblance between the two. "Actually I was just enjoying a walk around the park when I spotted you and decided to walk over to check you out."

Rajahn scored another three-pointer at the buzzer that signaled halftime. Mia turned to Jordan as she and the girls continued to cheer loudly. But her cheers froze

in her throat when she saw him in deep conversation
with a very attractive woman. Quickly Mia scanned the
woman's angelic pretty features with her jets-black
cropped hair and perfectly applied makeup. She looked
like an ethnic porcelain doll. Very Halle Berry-like.

The girls looked up at Mia and after seeing her odd
expression, they followed her gaze. Tia instantly
squeezed past the twins to tug on her father's T-shirt.
"Daddy? Daddy, who is she?"

Jordan smiled up at Tia and then looked over at the
four pairs of eyes on him. They all were curious. "This
is Amanda Langston. Amanda, this is Mia Gordon, my
next-door neighbor, and these are my four beautiful
little girls, Kimani, the twins Aliya and Amina, and the
inquisitive one is Tia."

Mia reached around the girls to shake the woman's
hand. "Nice to meet you."

"You as well," Amanda said, before smiling warmly
at each of the children, who only waved shortly in return. "I was just trying to talk Jordan into granting me
an interview."

The girls all moved closer to Mia, and Amanda instantly felt their rejection.

"You're a reporter?" Mia asked, her eyes squinting
against the sun.

"I'm a freelance writer for the local paper." She
reached over to lightly touch Jordan's hand. "I think
our readers would enjoy a story about a successful
hometown writer. So will you do it?"

Mia looked down at the woman's hand lightly resting
on Jordan's. She didn't look away from it until Jordan
coughed nervously and moved his hand. Mia didn't
know why, but Jordan looked directly at her after that.

"Come on, girls. Let's leave your dad and Ms. Langston alone," Mia said suddenly, grabbing the twins'
hands. "I feel like some ice cream."

Jordan started to protest. Amanda was far too forward, and she made him nervous. Frankly he didn't

want to be alone with her, but as quick as can be Mia and his daughters climbed down off the bleachers and headed for the vendors on the other side of the court.

"So, Mr. Jordan Banks," Amanda purred, leaning in close to him. "Shall we set up a dinner date for the interview?"

He shifted uncomfortably in his seat. The woman held none of Mia's reserved composure. In the past he would have had to admit that the fact that she was gorgeous would've blinded him to whatever she lacked in other areas, but meeting an incredibly complex woman like Mia who offered much more than just beauty made him realize that he should search for more in his bed-mates and girlfriends than just their looks. Turning, he looked for and found Mia and his children all sitting on a park bench with ice cream. He started in surprise when he realized that Mia was already looking across the court at him!

"You're much prettier than she is, Ms. Gordon."

Mia looked down into Kimani's bespectacled face. "Huh?"

Kimani grabbed Mia's hand. "I said you're much prettier than her."

"Oh, Kimani, don't be silly. Ms. Langston is a very attractive woman, and I'm sure your father thinks so as well."

"But we don't like her, do we?" Tia asked her siblings, her tongue coated pink with strawberry ice cream.

"No," they all said in unison, causing Mia's eyes to widen in surprise.

"Now, girls, that's not fair. You don't even know her, and she seemed very nice." Mia looked back over toward Jordan and Amanda. "Your father seems to enjoy her company."

Whoa! Pump the brakes, Mia. Is that jealousy in your voice?

Rajahn ran up to them, his thin tall body still damp

with sweat. "Who's that with Daddy?" he asked, before sneaking a bite of one of the twin's ice cream sandwiches.

"Some hoochie," Tia said, sneering.

"Tia!" Mia gasped, shocked. "That's an awful thing to say. I'm sorry that you feel the need to address another female in such a manner. We get enough of that name-calling from men, right?"

Tia, feeling properly chastised, nodded. "But I still don't like her," she muttered.

Mia sighed, feeling totally incapable of making this little girl understand the importance of women respecting one another, through words and actions. "Rajahn, the lady's name is Amanda Langston. She's a reporter from the local newspaper."

"Maybe she just wants to interview Dad?" Kimani said, not sounding sure herself."

They all, including Mia, looked back over across the court at the couple as Amanda leaned over and whispered something in Jordan's ear, her hand lightly touching his thigh. Whatever the woman said made him smile.

"Looks like she's trying to push up on Daddy to me," Rajahn said, sneaking a peek at Mia's face to gauge her reaction.

Looks like that to me too, Mia thought.

Rajahn smiled, seeing the odd look on Mia's face as she continued to watch his father and the lady across the court. He wished he could talk more but he saw his team gathering to resume playing. "The next half is about to start. I'll see y'all after the game, 'kay?"

"Bye, Rajahn," the twins sang, waving to their brother's retreating figure. Their hands and faces were ruined by the fast-melting ice cream.

"Man, y'all sure made a big mess," Tia complained, looking down at the twins.

At hearing her complaints, Mia turned from staring at Jordan and his new friend to look down at the little girls. She immediately grimaced at the sight. Had she not been so preoccupied with minding other people's business, then she would have properly supervised the twins. Now they resembled two miniature disaster areas. *Great baby-sitter I make,* she thought.

"Tia, you and Kimani go over to the ice cream vendor and get some napkins for me, please."

They both ran the short distance together, returning moments later with a stack of napkins. "Here you go, Ms. Gordon," Tia said, handing them over to her.

"I wuv ice cream," Aliya said, giggling, which caused Mia's spirits to lift a little.

Mia smiled at her. "Yes, but most of it is on your clothes, and not in your stomach where it belongs. I really should have paid more attention to you little dumplings."

Tia used napkins to clean up Amina, sighing, "Don't worry, Ms. Gordon. Every time these two get ice cream, they always make a mess."

Mia handed the soiled napkins to Kimani to discard in a nearby trash can. "Even with your dad?"

Tia stopped dabbing the napkin on Amina's pink floral T-shirt to look over at her. "Especially with Daddy."

She laughed at Tia's cornball expression before standing. "Let's go get our seats, ladies. We have an MVP to cheer on!"

"We could meet at my apartment. I'll cook dinner."

Jordan barely heard her as he looked across the court at Mia gently cleaning the hands of one of the twins. *She sure looks good squatting down like that.*

As he watched her he felt his breath catch suddenly. He felt spellbound. Mia's face had suddenly broken into a bright wide smile that truly transformed her. As she flung her head back in carefree laughter, with the wind blowing the long strands of her hair from her face, she looked so relaxed and beautiful. Radiant. Approach-able. Different.

He felt an intense desire to see her laugh and smile like that for him. Surely the brilliance could lighten the darkest storm-filled skies.

"Jordan?" Amanda lightly patted his leg. "Jordan? Yoo-hoo!"

He slowly turned to face her. "Yeah?"

"I said we could do the interview at my apartment and I'll cook dinner." The offer for much more was in her eyes.

Jordan shook his head. "I'm finishing up my latest novel, and it would be best if we conducted the inter-view in my home."

"Oh, that's fine with me," Amanda said, immediately envisioning a quiet evening with him. Of course he would have to do something with his brood, but that was his concern . . . not hers. "Should I bring any-thing?"

Jordan looked confused. "Just your tape recorder, and a pen and pad, I guess."

Mia and his children climbed up on the stands to reclaim their seats, just as the second half of the bas-ketball game got under way. Tia moved to squeeze in between her father and Amanda, forcing them to sepa-rate to make room for her. She took the seat with a sigh of satisfaction.

"Daddy," Amina whispered to him, "we had ice cream."

With a bemused smile, he eyed her stained T-shirt and shorts. "I can tell," he said dryly, before tweaking the tip of her sticky nose.

Rajahn had a good second half but Mia was much more reserved in her cheers for him. With his at-the-buzzer three-pointer, his team won the league's cham-pionship game. Jordan stood, and Tia immediately jumped to her feet beside him. "Ms. Langston, I'll see you tomorrow afternoon then."

Tia eyed the woman with open hostility, but turned to her father with a perfectly angelic face. "Why, Daddy?"

He hugged Tia to his side. "Ms. Langston is doing an interview for the local paper. I'm sure glad that Mia braided your hair since we're taking a picture as well."

"Really, Daddy?" she said, sighing, turning to face the woman again. "I guess that's why we all love Ms. Gordon so much."

Amanda clearly picked up the signals the child was sending, and was a little put back by her. "Uh, well, I'll see you tomorrow," she said, flustered, before leaving the stands.

"We'll *all* see you tomorrow," Tia called after her with false sweetness.

The group stepped down off the bleachers just as Rajahn ran up to them. Jordan smiled with pride at him, just as he did when any of his children excelled. "Good game, son," he said, as he hugged him to his side.

"Yes, congratulations, Rajahn," Mia joined in with a smile.

"See, Ms. G, I told you I got game."

"You sure do," she said softly with a wink.

"I think this calls for a celebration dinner, anywhere you choose, Raj," Jordan said, as he bent over to pick up one of the twins.

Rajahn swung the other one into his arms as he thought it over. "I guess, for the little rug rats," he said affectionately, as he tickled Aliya, "I choose Chuck E. Cheese."

His sisters all cheered in pleasure at his choice, just as he knew they would. Mia thought he was a sweet older brother.

"You will join us, Mia," Jordan asked, turning to face her.

He looked directly into her eyes, and Mia seriously thought about having her head checked because she felt her heart flip. Coughing, she looked down at her Movado watch. It was only a little after four but she had a date for which to prepare. She wanted to look and be at her best. "I'm sorry but I have a date tonight. So if you could just drop me home, I'd appreciate it."

Jordan looked at Mia, long and hard. "A date?" he asked.

"Yes, you know, two people going out and having dinner, or seeing a movie. You really need to get out more, Jordan," she joked, purposely ignoring the crestfallen looks on all the children's faces.

"Of course," he said, feeling surprisingly disappointed that she wouldn't be joining them. Another unknown emotion caused his stomach to burn.

As they walked to the SUV, Mia had the distinct feeling of being a spoilsport. Everyone climbed into the vehicle, with Rajahn being sure to strap in the twins. The older children buckled their own seat belts.

"So, uh, who's your date?" Jordan asked suddenly, when he pulled the SUV to a stop at a red light.

Mia glanced over at him before answering. "He's a doctor. You wouldn't know him. In fact, I don't really know him. It's a blind date, believe it or not."

"I bet he's ugly and bald, just like our doctor is," Tia piped in from the seat behind them.

"Tia!" Jordan and Mia both said in reprimand.

"Sorry," she said, sounding as though she only half meant it.

They rode the rest of the distance in silence. As the SUV pulled to a stop in front of her house, Mia turned in her seat to look at the children. "Make sure you have enough fun for me at Chuck E. Cheese."

"I don't even feel like going anymore," Rajahn muttered, looking out the window at their dark rambling house.

"Me neither," Kimani said.

"Can't we just go inside, Daddy?" Tia asked, after

she shot the twins a hostile glance to keep them from
pleading to go to Chuck E. Cheese.

It was Jordan's turn to twist in his seat to look at his
children as if they were aliens. "Let me get this straight.
Everyone complains that I lock myself up in the office
too much, and I agree to take everyone to Chuck E's
for an evening of gooey pizza, puppets, and arcades,
and no one wants to go?"

"No, sir," the older children all answered in unison.

Jordan was flabbergasted, and Mia was filled with
guilt. The children had been all revved up to go, until
she had declined the offer to join them.

"Can we just go inside?" Tia asked again, already
having unlatched her seat belt.

"Yeah, go ahead. Raj, you have your key? I want to
pull the car into the garage."

"Yes, sir," he answered, before climbing out of the
vehicle behind his siblings.

"I feel awful, like I just rained on a parade," Mia
moaned, as she looked out of the window at the group
entering the house.

"Don't be ridiculous.. If the kids want to sulk and
miss out on fun because you have other plans, then
that's their decision." Jordan smiled at her. "A child
will twist you around his pinky if you let him."

"I know you're right, but that doesn't stop me from
feeling bad." Mia reached for the door handle. "Bye,
Jordan."

She opened the door and placed a slender leg out
to step down.

"Mia?"

She turned in the seat to look over her shoulder at
him with a questioning look.

"Have a good time on your date," he said softly.

Mia smiled. "Thanks, I will. Do me a favor?"

"What's that?" a

"Order them a pizza."

He laughed. "I'll do that."

Jordan watched and waited until she entered the house. She was off to go prepare for her date. Why did the thought of that irk his nerves so badly?

"What a lousy day this turned out to be!" Rajahn moaned, as he slumped onto a red beanbag chair in front of the big-screen television in the playroom.

"Tell me about it," Tia agreed. "First, Ms. Gordon has a date tonight and then that hooch—uh, the newspaper lady is coming here tomorrow to paw all over Dad."

Kimani grabbed the other controller to the Sony Playstation, pushing the start button to allow her to enter the martial arts game her brother was currently playing. "It might be too late to do anything about Ms. Gordon, but we can get rid of Ms. Langston easily tomorrow."

Her older siblings turned to look at her, and she explained her plan.

Six

Mia checked her appearance in the full-length mirror of the ladies' room. She really did look good in the maroon silk-lined tube dress she wore with strappy matching stilettos. Her hair was pressed and curled into a flip and she had carefully applied neutral eye shadow to her almond-shaped mocha eyes.

Okay, she looked good and when she entered the restaurant and was led to Dr. Blanchard's table, it was to discover that he looked *damn* good as well: tall and athletically muscular, with aristocratic features and a light complexion. The navy suit he wore was hand-tailored and fit his frame well, and his Italian leather loafers were so nicely polished. His posture, his diction, and his appearance spoke of wealth and a superior class. He was everything she usually found herself attracted to: a professional man with no children, who enjoyed the finer things in life. Someone she could date, when she did date, and enjoy the present with him without having to contemplate a future.

He was the epitome of the anti-Jordan.

So they both looked great, and the restaurant was excellent, the conversation stimulating, and the mood right for starting off a new romance. Then why was she thinking of an absentminded writer, who was clumsy, and had five rambunctious children? Why did she feel as though she'd rather be at Chuck E. Cheese with them, than at a four-star restaurant with a handsome, eligible doctor who seemed very interested in her?

Mia was seriously considering going to a therapist because obviously she had serious head problems. Sighing, she picked up her round beaded purse and left the ladies' room. She was resolved to enjoy her date and not ponder a walking disaster with a large ready-made family.

Jordan balled up the piece of paper he had just printed out. The words he had typed were as jumbled as his thoughts. He couldn't seem to focus and concentrate as he usually did when he was working. Aiming, he fired the ball into the already filled wastepaper basket. He sighed heavily as it missed completely.

How could he concentrate when thoughts of almond-shaped mocha eyes and long shapely cinnamon-brown legs plagued his thoughts? And the vision of her face bright and beautiful with laughter filled his vision a hundred times or more. Constantly he thought of Mia on her date. He had seen her leave for it an hour ago, and she had looked exquisite, so unlike her tailored business appearance yet again.

When had she claimed a place in his consciousness and awareness? When had everything changed for him? He was attracted and intrigued. Of course he knew it was not a course or path to follow.

Something in her mocha depths had drawn him in, and now she dominated his thoughts. He felt himself sinking.

Mia pulled her car slowly up into the driveway and then into her backyard blessed with light from the full moon. Tonight had been a very confusing night for her. Frankly she longed for the whole day to be over. Tomorrow she would awaken, and everything would be back to normal. She would disdain Jordan, ponder all his faults, and avoid him at all costs, as usual.

Okay, yes, she had come to discover that he was physically attractive. And his rapport with his children was a testament to his loving personality. But he was not the man for her.

Then why has he been on my mind? And why am I jealous of the gorgeous reporter?

Mia groaned as she entered the dark house through the back door leading into her kitchen. Clicking the lights on, she dropped her keys and purse onto the counter. She fixed herself a glass of orange juice and Crown Royal, carrying it with her out of the kitchen to the front hall.

Her plan was to change into something comfortable and head right to her office. Carefully she climbed the stairs and entered her bedroom in the darkness.

Mia groped the wall for the light switch near the doorway, soon illuminating the entire room. It was stuffy and warm, and she immediately crossed the hardwood floors to open the windows against the back wall. Raising the venetian blind, she locked it into place with the cord. Without the blind blocking her view, Mia was able to look down at her backyard and into a portion of Jordan's.

Someone was enjoying a late-night swim in the built-in pool. She leaned in closer to peer out. She already knew it had to be Jordan. He swam as if trying to outrun something, his arms slicing through the water easily, his legs furiously helping to propel the rest of his body forward.

Transfixed, Mia remained bent over to get a closer look.

Who knew the klutz could be so athletic? she thought.

But it was when he swam over to the built-in steps of the pool and began to climb up out of the clear depths of the water that she was truly amazed.

"Oh, my," she said, sighing, her mouth ajar as her eyes widened in amazement.

Jordan's body was well-toned and muscular. Definition of every sinewy detail was slicked with water. His stomach was hard and rippled above the navy swim trunks he wore. And those legs looked to have the power to walk a thousand miles. His arms seemed strong enough to lift the entire world above his head. The wet material clung to and outlined the long, impressive length of his malehood.

"I'll be damned," she whispered.

Who knew that beneath those oversize sweat suits and wrinkled clothing was the body of an Adonis? She felt like a voyeur, but could not look away as he stretched each of his muscles with slow, controlled movements. The lights surrounding the pool shimmered on his body as they reflected off the beads of water.

Mia felt disappointed as he threw his bath towel around his neck and entered the house. He was gone from her sight, and she felt the loss intensely. Finally and slowly, she straightened, stepping back from the window. Her heart fluttered in her chest, and her stomach felt tight with nerves she couldn't explain.

"Oh, no," she moaned, free-falling back onto her bed, as she recognized the feeling she was experiencing. "I want Jordan!"

Twenty laps in a pool he was seriously considering having heated, and still the thoughts he tried to erase from his memory remained. Sighing he used the towel to dry his upper body and then his feet before walking into the house through the kitchen.

Jordan wasn't in the mood to write, an oddity for him. His thoughts wouldn't gather anyway. He felt as if his mind were like confetti blowing in the wind. Somehow he knew if he were able to snatch those fragments together it would be a mosaic of the beautiful Mia Gordon. He checked on each of his children, who were all sleeping comfortably, before entering his bedroom in the middle of the hall.

Besides his office, this room was also his sanctuary, and it was decidedly more fastidious than his little disaster area downstairs. The room was done in shades of ivory, brown, and burgundy—his favorite colors—and various lighting fixtures filled every nook, cranny, desk, and dresser in the suite. He loved it here. This is where he would sit and read for hours when he found the time.

After turning on the ceiling light, Jordan instantly pulled off the wet trunks, walking naked to his adjoining bathroom to hang them over the shower to dry. Turning the water on steaming hot, he stepped under the pulsating spray, lathering himself to remove the chlorine from his skin. If only he could wipe all thoughts of his next-door neighbor from his mind just as easily. *What the hell is wrong with me?*

Yes, she was an attractive lady, but he didn't want an involvement with her. And would she want one with him? He doubted that very highly.

For so long his entire focus had been raising his children and writing the mystery novels that he loved so much. It didn't occur to him that some aspect of his life was missing. Lord, he hadn't been on a date in years. But as he moved through life with concerns for just his children and his work, he hadn't even realized the lack of a lady in his life. He was a normal man with normal urges, but his family and his writing career had always come first.

Not until a certain lovely lady, who was a hopeless workaholic, had moved in next door.

Was it because the kids loved her and constantly drew her into their lives? A role she had no experience with but filled nonetheless to please his children?

Or was it because of the softness of her hand upon his forehead earlier when she touched him?

Or was it the sweet simple scent of her perfume?

Or the way her smile was just a slight lifting of her mouth, barely discernible but enough to transform a cute face into a beautiful one?

Or that dimple in her chin that made him want to lick in its depths?

But to sit and ponder Mia was stupid. It was obvious that she was not interested in him. Even though she liked his children, he truly believed that she could do very well without laying eyes on him!

After one afternoon in her company, he was caught in a spell where he would love to see the reserved and composed woman in his bed, under him, writhing in pleasure, her eyes glazed as he stroked deeply inside of—

Down, boy!

So intent on his daydreaming he was, that he didn't realize that the water had become cold. But that was a blessing in disguise as it doused the flames of desire that had risen in him and caused the stiff hardness of his malehood to recede.

"Why, Lord?" he asked, actually looking upward at the ceiling. "Why after all this time did I have to want a woman who doesn't want me?"

Jordan wrapped a robe around his damp body as he stepped out of the bathroom and into his bedroom. He strolled over to the eight-drawer bureau, immediately reaching into the top drawer for a pair of the well-worn sweatpants that he favored.

He started when he felt nothing but air. Startled, he looked down into the drawer. It was empty! Frantic he checked drawer after drawer after drawer. Each time he came up with the same thing . . . nothing!

A rather dramatic shriek crept from the back of his throat as he raced to the closet on the opposite side of the room, nearly slipping on the hardwood floors.

"Calm down, just calm . . . down," he kept telling himself, as he jerked the closet doors open. "This is all a horrible nightmare."

The closet was empty as well, and his roar of disbelief echoed inside it. Gone were his pairs of precious well-worn sneakers and athletic sandals. Jeans faded by numerous washings, just the way he liked them . . . gone! The casual clothing he had cherished since college . . . gone! Nothing was left but a suit and a new pair of shoes he bought last year to attend a funeral.

He smelled a rat! No, no, he smelled five little rats. Did they think he'd be crazy enough to believe that someone broke in and stole just his clothing? Grumbling he pulled on a housecoat the children had bought for him three years ago that he had never worn. He was making his way to Rajahn's room when the doorbell rang.

With a groan he turned and headed toward the stairs. The bell rang a second time and in his haste to get downstairs one of his damp feet slipped against the waxed hardwood floor. Jordan yelled out as he tumbled like a 187-pound ball down the flight of stairs. Head over feet, then feet over head, until he fell to the bottom with a large thump. Luckily, he was still all in one unbroken piece.

"Sweet Jesus," he moaned, lying on his back. One of his feet still rested on the bottom step, his eyes closed as he breathed deeply.

"Dad, are you okay?"

Jordan opened one eye to see his son at the top of the stairs looking down at him with concern. He moved his hand to correct the haphazard state of his robe before answering, "Yeah, yeah. I'm okay."

"Jordan? Jordan! Are you okay?"

He looked over his head at the door. The dark outline of someone pressed to the small diamond-shaped frosted pane at the top of the door was clearly shadowed. *What have I done to deserve this?*

As he struggled to get up, Rajahn flew down the stairs like lightning and jumped over his body to open the front door. He then turned to offer his father a hand. "You okay, Dad? What happened?"

Mia immediately stepped into the house, concern clearly written on her face. "I heard you fall. Are you okay, Jordan?"

He had a little more pride now that he was once again standing on his feet with his son's assistance. "I'm fine . . . I'm fine."

Rajahn headed back up the stairs. "I'm going back to bed. You're in good hands with Ms. G, right?"

Remembering why he was without proper attire, Jordan called up, "Rajahn, do you now what happened to my—"

The solid closing of his son's bedroom door cut him off.

Mia lowered her eyes, but found herself sneaking another peek at the smooth hair covering Jordan's chest, which showed through the gap in his robe. She forced herself to look away again. When she glanced back this time her eyes widened at the muscular thigh that was revealed through the flap of the robe. *My word!*

Jordan sighed, facing Mia. Quickly he scanned the powder-blue satin shirt and tailored skirt she wore. *She's still sexy in that stuffy business uniform. Hell, sexier even.* "Can I help you with something, Mia?"

"I found one of the twin's toys in my living room, and I thought they might need it to sleep with." She held out a plush Teletubbies doll.

"So that's where it went," he said, accepting it. Briefly their hands touched and both flinched. Jordan cleared his throat. "Uhm . . . Aliya was looking for this before she went to bed tonight. I thought she had left it in the park today."

"I figured she would want it," she said with a smile, looking everywhere but at him.

Jordan looked at her, very much aware of how she

seemed to avoid his eyes. When she glanced at him out of the corner of her eyes and flushed, he had the distinct feeling that she was uncomfortable about his state of dress, or rather undress. This thought made him want to smile, but he didn't.

"So, Mia, how was your, ah, uhm, your, ah, your date?" he asked, about to raise his hand to his face in a nervous gesture that was now becoming bothersome without actual glasses to adjust.

She looked over at him and found him watching her with a serious expression. Immediately she diverted her gaze to a spot above his head. "It was nice."

Actually this was the first she had thought of Dr. Blanchard since she left the restaurant after their date ended. This man standing here, obviously very naked beneath the short robe had occupied her thoughts. And she couldn't for the life of her understand why.

"Did you order the pizza?" she asked.

He nodded, crossing his arms across his chest, causing the robe's hem to rise higher on his muscular thighs. "I sure did, and they loved it, although they all said they missed you."

"I missed them, too," she said with honesty.

His stomach grumbled loudly. "I think the mention of the pizza got me going," he said with a laugh. "There's some left over. . . . Join me for a slice?"

At dinner she had hardly eaten any of the grilled salmon she ordered. She could really go for a greasy slice of pizza. *I just wish he'd get dressed so that I'd stop feeling like a pervert!* "Sure," she answered with a smile. "Uhm, Jordan?"

He turned. "Yeah?"

"Wouldn't you like to, uhm, you know, go get dressed?"

Jordan tightened his robe around him. "I would if I had something to dress in."

"Huh?" Mia asked, trying to keep her eyes from slipping down to look at how the thin cotton of the robe lay snugly against his maleness, leaving her with quite an impression.

"All of my clothes are missing," he explained, blinking his eyes rapidly. "And I smell five little rats who must've done some spring cleaning with my wardrobe."

Mia thought of the casual well-worn clothes he favored. *If they did toss them out, then they did him a favor! Good riddance to rubbish.*

"Does my being in my robe bother you, Mia?" he asked, his voice low, husky, and slightly mocking.

Mia looked up at him, startled by the question. What should she say? Yes, it bothered her. Seeing him just one thin layer away from total nakedness, especially after spying on him by the pool, made her want to walk over to him and slowly remove the robe. She envisioned him still moist and her licking every drop of water from his well-toned muscular body.

Shaking her head, she lied, "No, it doesn't bother me at all."

"Good." Jordan led the way into the kitchen with Mia close behind.

She focused her gaze on the back of his head, not following the temptation to look down at his hard buttocks pressed against the cotton of the robe. Okay, she looked once, but that's all!

He reached into the refrigerator for the pizza box and turned to the oven. "I'd rather heat it in the oven if you don't mind the wait. The microwave makes the crust soggy."

"Sure, but you know what," she said, moving to take the box from him and set it on the counter. "Somehow 'Jordan' and 'hot stove' in the same sentence don't sit well with me. You sit, and I'll do it."

Jordan laughed. "I'm not a total klutz."

Turning from where she was cutting two slices of pizza, Mia looked pointedly at the bruise on his forehead. "Whatever, Jordan. Sit!"

"Funny, Ms. Black Corporate America in the kitchen. Never would've imagined it."

"Yeah? Well, me neither. I can't cook, this is as far as my culinary skills go," she admitted unashamedly.

Jordan laughed. "I'm going to sit back and enjoy this," he said, as he took a seat at the small round table in the center of the spacious kitchen. "The plates are in the cupboard to your left, and the glasses to your right. The cookware is underneath the counter, and the forks are in the drawer by the fridge, which holds your choice of drinks."

With that he said nothing else. Jordan just watched her as she moved around the kitchen placing the two slices on a baking sheet and sliding it into the preheated oven. Next she pulled down plates, glasses, and silverware before setting them on the counter.

Watching her move about his kitchen felt comfortable to him. And he noticed little things about her as he watched her closely, drawn like a moth to a flame.

She moved with grace, almost walking just on the tip of her toes in the heels she wore. And those shoes, he noticed, broke away from her conservative image. They were stylish and high heeled, perfectly offsetting her delicate ankles and the long, shapely legs he now knew hid underneath those damn skirts of hers. Mia was a slender woman but had those dangerous curves as her hips blossomed into an hourglass shape. Not even her straitlaced clothing could deny that fact.

Frequently she tucked her long curly hair behind her left ear with her forefinger. And she liked to bite on her full bottom lip, wearing off the lipstick she wore and exposing soft, fleshy lips.

"Jordan, do you want fruit juice or soda?" she asked, not aware of the arousing sight she made bent over looking into his fully stocked refrigerator. Her skirt rose just a fraction in the back, exposing just enough of her well-toned thighs to drive him wild.

She wiggled her hips in an innocent little dance, and

he was hypnotized by the movement. He felt like grinning and howling to the moon like a wolf.

"Jordan?" she called to him, turning to look over her shoulder.

Coughing, he looked away, crossing his legs to hide a rather embarrassing erection. "Uh, fruit juice is fine," he finally answered in a strained voice.

Mia eyed him with an odd expression before turning to pull the large plastic bottle of fruit juice from the refrigerator. As she faced him again she realized then that Jordan was staring at her, and she suddenly became nervous under his gaze. "Here," she said suddenly, setting the bottle next to him on the table. "Pour."

Meanwhile she pulled the baking sheet from the oven with a mitt and transferred the crispy slices to plates. "Here we go," she said, setting a plate in front of him before taking a seat. "Careful, Jordan, it's hot."

Mia picked up a knife and fork and began to slice off a bite-size piece. She was just about to place the fork into her open mouth when she saw Jordan looking at her with a shocked expression. Freezing, she cut her eyes over at him. "What?"

"Is that how you eat pizza?" he asked. *Damn, she's uptight!*

"Yes," she said defensively, before putting the fork and the gooey pizza into her mouth. "It's much neater this way."

Jordan laughed. "*This* is how you eat pizza, Ms. Gordon."

He picked up the thin-crust slice and folded it in half from the crust to the point, before raising it to his mouth to take a large bite. "See," he said, with a mouthful of food, grease trickling down his arm. "You *never* eat pizza with utensils. Now you try it."

Mia looked at him. "No, you eat your way, and I'll eat mine my way. Thank you very much."

"Come on, Mia, loosen up. Try it," he pleaded, before giving her a soulful face.

She laughed and then said, "No," with the utmost seriousness.

"Please," he dragged out playfully, lifting his still-folded slice to her mouth. "Pretty please with sugar on top."

He forced a smile from her before she leaned forward to take a small bite. *Okay, it is better this way but I'm not admitting that to him!*

"Better, right?" he asked with surety.

"I don't see any difference, really," she lied.

"Whatever."

He laughed in victory when she picked up her slice and folded it before taking a bite, avoiding his smug look. "I knew it."

"Aw, shut up, Jordan," she grumbled, using a napkin to wipe the grease from her fingers.

They ate in silence, each sneaking covert looks at the other, neither aware that their thoughts ran along the same lines. They were very aware of each other, something that continued to surprise them both.

Mia would never have guessed she would be sitting in Jordan's kitchen eating pizza while he wore nothing but a robe, and it wasn't half bad.

"Who knew it could be so quiet around here?" she said, before taking another bite.

Jordan laughed. "Only after nine o'clock when everyone's asleep. Sometimes the silence is a pleasure while other times it's disconcerting."

"What made you decide to adopt?" she asked suddenly, taking a sip of juice.

"I became a mentor while in college. I wanted to impress on young black boys who didn't have the proper male influence, all the things my dad had taught me. These things helped to mold me into a positive figure who is flourishing. I really believe that mentoring and programs similar to that model are a part of what Newark needs for its revitalization. We have to let our young black boys grow up knowing that there are choices to be made in life. The right ways and the wrong ways."

He spoke with passion and brilliance in his eyes, and Mia was drawn in by them. It was uplifting to come across someone who felt just as passionately about this city as she did, if not more. She listened as he continued.

"Mentoring then became adopting because of the relationship I had developed with Rajahn before his mother passed away."

Mia cocked her head to the side as she looked at him with a half smile. "That still doesn't really answer my question. Why do you believe in adoption, Jordan?"

He thought his answer over before speaking. "There are vast numbers of children, particularly minority children, here on earth already in need of a loving and supportive home. I have the resources, the time at home, and I love children. It seemed to make sense for me. It met my needs to have children and their need to be loved."

"You really are a special guy for taking on the challenge, Jordan," she said with honesty. "Of course they're all wonderful children."

"What about you? You never really thought about having a family of your own?"

"Since college I've had a very demanding career that never left time for me to miss out on having a family. And I never really thought of myself as motherly. I look at you with your children, and I honestly don't believe I, as a woman, could be as good with them as you are."

"You know what I think?"

Mia took another bite of her pizza. "What?"

"I think you truly underestimate yourself," he said, his voice low and husky as he looked into her eyes. "In fact, I have a feeling you're a 'three times a lady' lady. I can see you as a success in your career, a wonderful and loving mother, who still is able to keep her man happy."

Mia flushed with warmth, deeply touched by his words. "Thank you, Jordan," she said, her voice hushed and heartfelt. "That is the sweetest thing anyone has said to me—ever."

She jumped in her seat when he reached out to lightly rub his thumb on a spot near her full bottom lip. The spot he touched tingled. "Pizza grease," he explained softly, looking at her.

"Thank you." She forced herself to break their intense gaze. "Three times a lady, huh?"

He nodded and smiled. "Definitely."

Clearing her throat, Mia stood, picking up their plates to carry to the sink. Her heart hammered in her chest as she stood over the sink breathing deeply and slowly. She was trying to calm the nerves he shattered with his words, his look, his touch. *Ooh, the brother can be fierce when he wants to, huh! Fight it, Mia, you have to fight it!*

"Mia?"

She shrieked and dropped the plate she had in her hands when she turned to find him so close to her. He held their used glasses. "Yes?"

"I was going to say to not to wash the dishes, I'll put them in the dishwasher before I go to bed."

Mia stepped back, trying to put some distance between herself and his nearly nude frame, feeling the unrelenting hardness of the countertop against the small of her back. Her eyes dipped to look at the smooth flat hair on his chest that peeked through the robe. Jordan's clean soapy, masculine scent surrounded her. His nearness was overwhelming. Quickly she looked away.

"Don't cut yourself," he warned, after she turned back to the sink to pick up the broken shards of the plate.

"I'm really sorry about this. I guess it's my turn to be clumsy tonight."

"Yeah, and I thought that was my job," he joked.

That made her smile.

Mia turned to face him and then quickly squeezed past. Even though he didn't touch her, the air surrounding them was filled with charged electricity. Mia felt as if the air he created around them pressed just as hard and firm as boulders around her body until she was breathless with want of him. "Uhm, thanks for the pizza, Jordan," she said, heading with determined strides for the front door.

He followed behind her, his eyes dipping to watch the movement of her hourglass hips and tantalizing buttocks against the tailored skirt. The woman was lethal. "Thanks for keeping me company."

"Good luck on your interview tomorrow," she said, stepping out onto the porch. "Bye, Jordan."

"Mia."

She turned in response to him softly saying her name. He had stepped onto the porch behind her, the light from the foyer shadowing his form. Mia swallowed over a sudden lump in her throat as she thought she saw the clear outline of his maleness hang between his strong muscled thighs. *My Lord!*

Jordan looked down at her under the small illumination offered by the porch light. "I . . . uhm . . . oh, forget it," he snapped, before lowering his head to lightly touch his lips with hers.

It was soft and sweet and all too brief.

"Good night, Mia," he mumbled, before turning with more agility than she ever could have imagined he had outside the pool to enter the house.

Mia touched her lips with a slightly trembling hand as his front door closed. *Jordan kissed me!* she thought frantically. *And it was good!*

Before she could change her mind, Mia knocked lightly on the door. Jordan immediately jerked it open, and she reached up to capture his handsome face in her hands. Slowly she raised her head to kiss him with all the passion he released in her like a tidal wave. They floated in the tides of desire together, entwined.

Jordan moaned before lifting her soft pliant body up to his own steel frame, his arms tightly wrapped around her waist. Their tongues discovered each other in rapturous delight with heat and blinding want. They kissed with fierceness and hurried movements as they discovered a one-of-a-kind passion. An unexpected passion.

Mia felt Jordan's lengthy erection against her stomach, his robe offering no cover to his obvious desire. As he licked the contours of her mouth, she shivered, relenting to the delights he bestowed upon her. This was beyond anything she had ever experienced. Better than a hot fudge sundae on a blistering summer day. Better than sitting in front of a fireplace during a winter storm. Better than water to a person dying of thirst in the desert. Better than any- and everything.

Jordan reveled in the feel of Mia's soft plump breasts crushed against his chest. Their mingled moans of pleasure and grunts of want thrilled and excited him. He was sure her mouth tasted sweeter than the rarest of nectar. He never wanted it to end.

But Mia broke the kiss, jerking her head back from his. "No, Jordan, no more," she gasped, panting and breathless.

Reluctantly he released her, his erection tenting the cotton of his robe and exposing the sight of the curly hairs climbing up his thighs. He was slightly embarrassed that he was so moved by their kiss that he lost all capability of speech.

Mia stepped back, visibly shaken. "I'm sorry, Jordan, that was a mistake."

She turned and fled to her house before he could speak, moving through the break in the hedges separating their homes to disappear from his sight but not his thoughts.

Seven

"Let me get this straight," Jordan said, looking at his children, whom he had called upstairs from their playroom. "You tossed out my clothes because . . ."

They all looked at one another uncomfortably where they sat lined up on the leather couch in the living room.

"Dad," Rajahn said finally. "You need new clothes."

Silently Jordan counted to ten. When he spoke, it was slow and deliberate, a struggle for control. "So . . . you . . . all . . . took it . . . upon yourselves . . . to do some . . . spring cleaning . . . in my closets and dressers."

Solemnly they all nodded, realizing how angry their father was at their actions. They knew they had to be honest. What else could they say? That someone broke into the house and only stole his old clothes?

"While you were destroying my personal items, in my bedroom, did anyone remember the interview I have this afternoon with the local newspaper?"

"Sorry, Dad," Rajahn mumbled, looking down at his lap.

Jordan continued to pace in front of them, dressed in the only clothing they didn't get rid of, his wool tailored suit. Can we say not appropriate attire in the hot, hazy, and humid summer weather? He felt as if he were shaking hands with the devil in the bowels of hell. And the suit itched like nothing that could ever be imagined.

He was just grateful that his children hadn't destroyed his underclothing. Now *that* would've been unbearable without his boxers acting as somewhat of a barrier. Right then he decided to have central air installed throughout the house.

"What if I got rid of your video games and comic books, Rajahn?" he asked, stopping in front of his son.

"And, Tia, what if I threw out all your Phase posters?" he asked, moving over to stand in front of her.

"That's Mase, Dad," she said quietly, dropping her head under his chastising stare.

"Whatever," he said tightly, before moving on to Kimani. "What if I threw out all your books?"

"You're right, Dad. I'm sorry," she said, her voice soft as she dropped her head as well.

Sighing he moved to squat down in front of the twins, causing the scratchy wool to press even closer to his thighs. "Were you two in on this as well?" he asked softly.

Tears glistened in both of their eyes and their bottom lips quivered as they both nodded slowly. "We carried out the sneakers," Amina admitted.

Jordan expelled a deep breath before standing. He sat in the chair adjacent to the couch. "My own kids sabotaged me."

He looked down at his watch. It was 9:30 A.M. The mall opened in half an hour. He had to get out of the suit before he broke out in a rash. "To teach you respect for other people's property you're all on punishment for two weeks. No television, no video games. Today you all will give your bedrooms a good cleaning, since you seem to enjoy it so well. Oh, the playroom, too."

They all groaned in dismay.

"That's all I can think of for now but as soon as I can add to your list, you'll all know about it." He stood, scratching at an insufferable itchy spot on his thigh. "Go upstairs and get dressed. I'll have to go to the mall and buy new clothes."

"We're sorry, Dad." Rajahn spoke for his siblings and himself.

"No, I'm sorry. You have no idea how uncomfortable this suit is outside of one of the rooms with an air conditioner."

I kissed Jordan last night, and it was good!

Mia looked into her own reflection the next morning as she stood at the bathroom sink. Had last night been a dream? Had she really knocked on Jordan's door and initiated a passionate kiss that left her with erotic dreams of him all night?

Okay, yes, she had, but only after he kissed her first!

Jordan Banks was *not* the man for her. The man had *five* children. That was a big—no, a *gigantic* deal for Mia, as a single woman with a thriving career, her own home, and no commitments besides mortgage and a car payment, and a few high-limit credit cards.

Who cares if in his arms she had discovered the most profound passion in her life?

Even as she brushed her teeth she scoldingly eyed herself in the round mirror above the sink. *You, my dear, have written a check your ass cannot cash!*

Just as she leaned down to rinse her mouth, the phone on her bedside table began to ring. She jerked her head back up and eyed the phone from where she stood warily.

Oh, God. What if it's Jordan? What if he wants to get into a relationship? What do I say to him? How do I reject him without causing bad blood?

Persistently the phone continued its ringing until finally Mia quickly rinsed her mouth and wiped it with a damp towel before moving across the floor to answer. "Hello," she said hesitantly.

"Mia? Hi, this is Terrence."

Her tensed body immediately relaxed with relief, yet

she still felt the sting of disappointment. "Hello, Terrence. What's up?"

"I had a wonderful time last night. I didn't want it to end. How about you?"

"Me, too."

"I thought we might spend the day together. How about it?"

Mia formed her mouth to deny his offer because she had a lot of work she wanted to get to today. But then she thought of Jordan continuing to plague her thoughts. Not even work could keep that kiss out of her mind; maybe Terrence could. "Yes, I would love to," she answered with false brightness. *A day in the company of a handsome doctor will keep that walking disaster from next door out of my thoughts.*

I hope!

"Dad, do we really have to clean our rooms?" Tia asked from her seat in the Land Cruiser. "In the end everything turned out fine. The lady at the store helped you pick out all new gear. And might I add, you look supa-dupa fly in the outfit you're currently sportin'?"

Jordan eyed her in the rearview mirror with a raised brow. "Don't forget you all have to clean the playroom as well."

He was about to pull into his driveway when he noticed Mia stepping out onto her front porch looking beautiful in a turquoise strapless sundress that completely blew his mind, but not more than the fact that she moved to stand beside a tall distinguished-looking man. Jordan immediately parked on the street in front of his house instead of the driveway, behind a blue foreign sports car.

Through the windshield Mia looked over at him. Their eyes met, and she immediately looked away with a brief wave before turning to her date with a smile.

The children's heads all whipped around to look at

their father as he began to grumble under his breath. They honestly believed he was losing his mind. "Dad?" Rajahn said hesitantly.

Jordan looked at his son, and then noticed all the stares. "Let's move it. You've got rooms to clean."

Dejectedly they began to pile out of the SUV, all exiting on the side near the sidewalk just as he had taught them. Jordan watched Mia and her date descend her steps. She stopped to talk to the children who were all gathered around staring openly.

"Last night she kisses me and this morning it's like I don't even exist," he muttered, as he climbed out of the SUV. "Just what kind of game is she playing?"

This wasn't a part of their plan. He wasn't a part of the plan. The children all eyed him, the look in their eyes clearly proprietary. As Mia introduced each of them to the man, the look did not change one bit. They disliked him. Clearly. Not because he was a bad person, because they didn't know him. He was dating the woman they all wanted their father to marry. That's why they detested the very sight of Dr. Terrence Blanchard.

They had to scare him off. What if Mia married him instead? They could not let that happen.

"Wow, is this your car?" Rajahn said in awe, moving over to the curb to peer inside, his hands pressed to the glass.

His siblings all followed, being sure to stay on the sidewalk, as they literally pawed the car. The smudges they were leaving on the shining automobile were clearly evident. The doctor's cry of outrage mingled with the children's exaggerated awes.

Mia watched as Terrence's handsome face became pain-stricken as the children mauled his treasure. She moved over quickly to pull each of them from their target. "Children, don't."

They all moved away to stand in front of him. "We're

always over at Ms. Gordon's house—all of us," Tia said with emphasis. "It's like our second home."

Mia whipped around to eye Tia suspiciously, just as Jordan walked up to them. He stopped right next to her, and Mia became a fit of nerves. Again she felt that wall surrounding her. The electricity seemed to be in the air between them. Just the memory of the kiss and being so near to him aroused her. Mia crossed her arms over her chest as her nipples hardened into tight buds that ached for his attention. "Hello, Jordan," she mumbled, moving over to stand next to Terrence.

The doctor was staring down with an odd and wary expression at the children gathered around him. He felt like a male version of Dorothy in *The Wiz* when she was in Munchkinland.

Mia thought he looked like a deer caught in headlights. "Terrence, this is my neighbor—"

Her words faltered as a car door slammed. Everyone turned to watch as Amanda crossed the street toward where they stood. Her cherry-red Miata glistened in the sun. The woman looked as if she were headed for the beach instead of a professional interview in the form-fitting knit halter she wore with snug cut-off jeans, both spotless white.

"Oh, brother," the children groaned.

Jordan had completely forgotten the interview as he glanced down at his watch. Amanda stepped onto the sidewalk with a bright smile on her pretty face, immediately moving to stand close to him. "Hello, everyone."

The children waved halfheartedly, Terrence nodded his head, Jordan stepped away from her to give them some distance, and Mia's eyes dipped to watch Amanda's hand lay possessively on his arm, causing her stomach to clench in jealousy. *Vamp!*

"As I was saying, Terrence, this is Jordan Banks. Jordan, this is Dr. Terrence Blanchard." She slid her arm around her date's as he leaned forward to shake hands with Jordan.

"This is Amanda Langston. She's here to in—oof!" Jordan moaned as the woman lightly elbowed him in his side.

Terrence glanced down at his gold Movado museum watch with a bored air. "Mia, we best be going or we'll be late."

"Okay. Good-bye, kids. Jordan, Ms. Langston."

"Come on, kids, your rooms are waiting."

They all began to walk through the gate into the unkempt front yard. Amanda wrapped her arm around Jordan's more snugly, pressing her full breasts against him as they followed the children up the walkway.

I wonder when their baby-sitter is going to arrive? she thought.

Mia turned on Terrence's arm to walk to his car. Her thoughts filled with Jordan. What did he and the vamp have planned for their afternoon? *Surely not too much with the children around?* she thought with satisfaction.

She looked over her shoulder. Jordan glanced back over his as well. Their eyes met and held, even as their bodies continued to move forward, away from each other. Both wished that they were the couple off to share a romantic day together.

With one final melancholy wave, Mia broke the look and slid onto the plush black leather seat of Terrence's Porsche. She turned in time to see Amanda jerk Jordan inside the house and close the door firmly behind them.

God, why do I even care?

A knock sounded on his closed office door, and Jordan looked up in irritation. His children were really pushing the boundaries of sanity. Ever since he and Amanda had entered his office to conduct the interview, just under five minutes ago, every last one of his children had interrupted them in succession. Each claimed a dire need to ask him a question concerning the cleaning of their bedrooms.

The look on Amanda's face was clearly annoyance. There was no baby-sitter. Thus her visions of them conducting the interview over a light lunch in the seclusion of his sizable home faded into thin air with a poof—fast. Never had she imagined being ushered into an old cluttered office with his pesky children knocking on the door every few seconds. This place was a circus, and Jordan was the ringleader. If it weren't for the way the sight of his body and toothy smile made her underwear moist she would've hightailed it out of there four minutes ago.

"Excuse me, Amanda," he said, rising to walk over and snatch the office door open.

Tia and Kimani stood before him holding a platter of sandwiches and a pitcher of fruit punch with two glasses. They smiled sweetly up at their father. "We thought you might be hungry," Kimani said.

They both pushed past him to enter the office. "Lunch is served," they sang in unison.

Well, look at my little angels, Jordan thought with pride. *Now that was sweet.*

The loud banging and splash from inside the office interrupted his thoughts. He had just turned on his heels to walk back into his office when Amanda pushed past him roughly. Her white outfit was splashed with red color as it dripped down her long shapely legs to puddle around her sandaled feet.

She eyed him in fury. "Forget the interview. Just forget everything. You need to whip those little brats," she screamed, before stomping her foot in frustration, which caused more of the red liquid to splash against her legs.

With one last murderous glance she stormed out, slamming the door so hard that the sound seemed to echo and reverberate throughout the house. Moments later the sound of tires squealing against pavement could be clearly heard from outside. And she was gone.

Inside the office Tia and Kimani gave each other a pound with big smiles on their pretty, innocent faces.

"Tia, Kimani!" their father roared, coming to stand in the doorway.

They quickly erased the smiles.

Mia stretched lazily, stifling a yawn with the back of her hand. The sun was brilliant in the powder-blue skies above the clear azure of the water, which was calm. It was a perfect day for boating.

Terrence had chartered a yacht, fully serviced by a crew, chef, and steward. Mia had been more than impressed by the elegance of the green, navy, and white decor with brass accents as Terrence had held his hand out to assist her onto the deck. After being settled on the deck in plush lounges with flutes of expensive Moët, chilled to perfection, the captain had put the yacht out to sea.

"Terrence, this is wonderful," Mia said, taking another sip of champagne and enjoying the cool neat feel of the amber liquid as it floated down her throat. "Thank you, I needed this."

He smiled, reaching over to clasp her hand in his. "No. Thank you."

"What for?"

"Giving me the chance to know such a beautiful and intelligent woman," he said huskily.

As Mia looked at him she suddenly envisioned him with glasses on. His impeccable yellow Polo shirt and khaki shorts transformed into a tattered and well-worn T-shirt with equally ragged sweatpants in a horrid shade of green.

"Leave me alone, Jordan," she mumbled.

"Did you say something, Mia?" he asked, his eyes attentive.

She shook her head. "No, nothing at all."

What's wrong with me?

Here she was on a luxury yacht cruising around New York with a handsome and wealthy eligible bachelor, sipping expensive vintage champagne, about to feast on a fabulous surprise brunch prepared by a Parisian chef. They were surrounded by such peace and tranquillity, something she cherished and hadn't had much of lately.

Then why wasn't she enjoying herself?

In an effort to do just that she focused on the lulling rocking of the yacht against the waves. Slowly it wore off the edge she felt. Mia felt determined to enjoy herself.

"Terrence, this is all wonderful. Thank you. You just don't know how much I needed this." She shifted to a comfortable position on the lounge chair, her eyes protected from the sun's rays behind her Ray-Ban shades.

"Work stressing you?" he asked, turning to look at her.

"No, no. I love my career," she insisted. "It's just nice to relax and be surrounded by quiet. It is a phenomenal thing that is greatly unappreciated, believe me."

"That's odd, you're single, living alone, you should have plenty of this quiet that you love."

"With neighbors like mine, I don't think so!" she joked with a laugh that floated and bounced along the waves to echo in the distance like wind chimes. "I've become a magnet for children lately."

"I thought having so many children went out with Afro blow-out kits in the sixties," he drawled, his tone condescending. "How many were in the little brood, eight?"

Mia bristled. "No, just five—"

"Just?" he balked. "Can we say birth control?"

"Terrence," she said sharply.

He turned to look at her, his expression bewildered. "What?"

She expelled a breath. "Jordan adopted each of those children, and he should be commended for that, not condemned. More men should step up to the challenge when it comes to being a father, especially a good one like Jordan."

Mia's tone was scolding and filled with more passion than she realized as she defended him. Her intention had not been to ridicule Jordan. She hated to think of any of those beautiful children to be thought of as a hindrance.

Terrence swung around to sit up on the edge of his lounge chair to face the beautiful woman. He leaned over, taking her soft, manicured hand in his. "Let's not ruin this. Let's toast to a day of rest and relaxation."

She lifted her flute, lightly tapping it with his with a delicate but somewhat resounding *ding*. "Here's to R and R."

Jordan glanced at the wall clock in his office, his fingers pausing in their flight across the keys. It was 9:30 P.M. The kids were all in bed in their now-spotless rooms still sulking over their punishments. He had been closed up in his office since after their dinner of fried chicken and mashed potatoes from Popeye's.

Everyone was accounted for, except Mia.

He hadn't heard any car doors slam, signaling her return. Would she return? Perhaps Dr. Suave had made other plans—overnight plans.

No! He refused to think of Mia warm and compliant in another man's arms the way she had been in his embrace just last night. Funny, it was just hours ago but it seemed an eternity since he had felt the softness of her lips and the sweet juice they had offered.

Last night on the porch, when he saw her beautiful face framed by the light, her mouth, slightly ajar, time seemed to slow down. Jordan had found himself filled with an intense desire to kiss her, and so he had.

Never would he forget the smooth, lush feel of her lips pressed tightly and then lightly against his own. After he had retreated behind his door, amazed by his own actions, the wood separating them physically but not emotionally, his heart had pounded wildly in his chest.

Then he had heard her knock and felt the reverberations against his back. Immediately he had thought she wanted to reprimand him for his forwardness, but when he opened the door, it was to be surrounded by her sweet scent, teased by the first gentle urging of her tongue into his mouth, aroused by the feel of her lush breasts pressed against his chest, and tortured by the clothes that kept them from the most primal contact between man and woman.

Even now, nearly twenty-four hours later, the thought of that kiss caused his loins to tighten in awareness. The heat, the excitement, the pleasure, the passion. It was nothing like he had ever experienced before.

Mia said "it was a mistake" but he knew from her passionate response and catlike purrs from deep in her throat that she had enjoyed it as well. Those moans had not been faked, the way her hands gripped his head tightly had not been imagined, the glassy look in her eyes had been real, and the tightness of her nipples, swelling in desire and straining against her shirt, had been achingly genuine.

Besides, *she* initiated the second kiss and then turned around and said it was a mistake! Typical female, something he thought she was beyond. Now she was out on a date with Dr. Suave, doing only God knew what!

Jordan pushed away from his desk. He gave up on trying to work. Never had anything distracted him so much from writing. Mia. Only Mia.

Sighing he stood, tripping over his paper shredder and sending thin shreds of confetti-like paper into the air. Ignoring the mess, he walked over to the window facing the front of the house. Immediately he jumped back, hiding behind the curtain to peer outside.

Dr. Suave's car had just pulled up to park outside

Mia's house. Jordan knew that he was wrong for spying, but he just couldn't help himself. He just had to know if she was going to kiss the doctor the way she had kissed him last night.

"Okay. He's getting out of the car, stiff as a robot, I might add," he said aloud to himself, as if offering commentary on a sporting event. "He's opening the door for Mia. She's accepting his hand to get out."

Jordan snorted in derision. "How romantic," he said sarcastically, angry at how Mia smiled up at the man, her beautiful face framed by the yellow glow of the streetlight.

"Okay, now Dr. Suave and Mia walk up onto her porch," he said, peering closer in an effort to keep his sights on them.

He couldn't see a thing!

Rushing, Jordan flew out of the office and ran to the other end of the house to the kitchen. Only with his luck would such an awful chain of events be initiated: As he reached the kitchen he stubbed his toe on the metal saddle of the archway, stumbled forward onto a chair, which then propelled him even farther and caused him to hit his midsection on the corner of the counter. Jordan howled sharply in pain, clutching the injured area, falling backward onto the floor. Reaching up, he grabbed the doorknob for support in rising. His hand slipped, turning the knob, causing the heavy door to swing open where it slammed into the side of his face.

Another howl of shock and pain.

Trying to gain control of a hapless situation, Jordan lay still on the cool tiled floor breathing deeply. Slowly he sat up before eventually standing to his feet, only to step down onto an errant fork, which sunk its prongs deep into his bare foot.

"Damn it," he swore, clutching his foot as he winced in pain.

Would it not be his way to lose his balance and topple

over backward onto the back porch out of the open door, rolling down the three steps with expletives to land on the ground with a thud outside?

His entire body ached, and he closed his eyes against sharp darts of pain. *What awful luck was that?*

"Oh, my God, Jordan, are you okay?"

He groaned, refusing to open his eyes and come face-to-face with his shame. It was Mia. Jordan wished he could turn to dust and then be blown away by the night winds.

Eight

Mia dropped down by where Jordan lay, immediately fearing that he was unconscious when he did not respond. "Jordan?"

He slowly opened one eye, and in relief she released the breath she was holding. "I'm okay."

"Is anything broken? Maybe I should stop Terrence, if he hasn't already pulled off. He can look you over." She made a move to rise but Jordan's hand shot out quickly to wrap around her slender wrist.

"No, I'm fine. Let Dr. Suave go, please," he said, wincing as he sat up and then got to his feet with her assistance.

"Dr. Suave?" she asked, her expression at first confused and then reprimanding. "His name is Blanchard. Dr. Terrence Blanchard, Jordan."

"Whatever."

He climbed the stairs onto his back porch and entered the kitchen. Mia followed closely behind, the scent of her citrus sweet perfume reaching and intriguing him. When he eyed the fork lying on the floor he picked it up and tossed it into the sink.

"Do you have a problem with Terrence?" Mia asked as she followed his fast-retreating figure out of the kitchen and down the hall to his office, her heels clicking against the hardwood floors. "You don't even know him."

Jordan limped slightly as he flung the door to his

office open wide. "Look, you're right I know nothing about Dr. Suave—"

"Jor—dan." She sighed at his refusal to address Terrence properly.

He turned and faced her, causing Mia to jerk to a stop to keep from colliding with his tall muscular frame. "Sorry, I know nothing about Dr. Blanchard, but I have many problems with him."

Mia crossed her arms over her ample chest. "Like?"

Jordan took the seat behind his desk. "I don't feel like getting into it with you."

Mia sucked her teeth. "Good night, Jordan. You have time for games, and I only have time for work. In fact, my office is calling me right now."

"You need more than your figures, stats, and computer to satisfy you."

She had turned to leave and reached for the door just as he spoke "What did you say?" Mia asked, swinging around to look at him.

He stood and slowly came back to walk around the desk to stand in front of her. He felt the intensity between them, and it only increased in magnitude the closer he got to her. Jordan looked directly into her beautiful almond-shaped eyes. "I said, you need more than your figures, stats, and computer to satisfy you."

"Oh, really? And how are you so aware of what it takes to satisfy me?"

Jordan smiled, almost wolfishly, pulling her body close to his. "Because I have what it takes," he said softly, before lowering his head slowly toward hers.

The first touch of their lips was electrifying, even if very brief. They both gasped at the pure sweet feel of the kiss, their hearts pounding wildly. It was but a glimpse of more that they could share.

Jordan lifted his hand from where it massaged the small of her back to lightly trace her full bottom lip with his thumb. "You are so very beautiful," he whispered, his breath fanning against her skin lightly. "You don't even know it."

Mia's cheeks warmed, and she dropped her gaze from his. She could hardly believe that it was clumsy, uncoordinated Jordan that awakened desires in her that she had long since ignored in her single-minded pursuit of her career. He told her she was beautiful, and she felt it. He said he had what it took to satisfy her growling hungry needs, and she believed him.

Using both of his hands to lift her face, Jordan lowered his head to gently kiss her closed eyelids, her high cheekbones, her delicate rounded chin with a dimple deep enough to send his tongue for a dip, and finally, deliciously, her lips. "So sweet," he said, moaning, as he licked the contours of the quivering flesh. "So soft."

She raised her arms and wrapped them around his neck, pressing her body against his just as he deepened the kiss. As their lips tangoed, Mia marveled at the feel of her breasts pressed against the hard contours of his muscled chest. She felt light-headed at the feel of his hard, lengthy erection. "Yes, Jordan, baby, yes," she moaned against his mouth, feeling wanton as she gave in to something she couldn't fight.

He sucked gently on her tongue, enjoying the feel and delectable taste of it. His loins ached with sharp desire for this incredible woman who returned his kisses with just as much passion as he gave her. Gone were her straitlaced demeanor and strict inhibitions. God, he wanted her!

Growling, Jordan swung Mia up into his strong arms. Silently she said a prayer that he didn't destroy the moment by tripping and sending them both crashing to the floor. Thankfully he moved over to the leather sofa in the corner by the cold fireplace. He sat, their tongues still entwined as he positioned her pliable body to straddle his lean hips. That caused her sundress to rise up around her hips. The intoxicating smell of her want wafted to him and red-hot desire raced through his veins like fire! Jordan inhaled the aphrodisiac even deeper.

He wanted to touch every bit of her soft curvaceous body. He needed her to touch him the same way, make him feel whole. "Sweet, beautiful Mia," he said, breaking the kiss as they breathed raggedly, gasping for air and control.

Jordan took her hand and placed it over her own heart. "Does the good doctor make your heart race like this?"

He rubbed his index finger gently over her eyelid. "Does he make your beautiful eyes glaze in desire?"

He lightly teased her swollen nipples through the thin Lycra of the strapless dress she wore. "Does he make these hard like me?"

He moved his hand down to stroke the pulsating bud between her legs, just barely sheltered by the damp seat of silk bikinis. "Can he make you wet like this?"

Each time she whispered "no," shaking her head and whimpering like a child as he touched all the intimate parts of her body. No man had awakened these hot pulsating feelings in her before. Just Jordan. Only Jordan.

Their differences didn't matter as passion swirled around them. Nothing mattered in the world but the way they made each other feel. Not his forgetful ways, his clumsy manner, or large family. Not her addiction to her work, nor her straitlaced manner, nor the way she used to look down her nose at him. Nothing mattered at all. Nothing but this moment.

He stared boldly into her eyes, getting lost in the cocoa depths as he slowly worked the top portion of her dress down around her waist. The sight of her two pert breasts and hard chocolate nipples aroused him as nothing else ever had. "Mia," he moaned, before lowering his head to capture one nipple hotly in his mouth.

Mia arched her back, offering him more to taste and feast upon. She felt herself drown even more as he circled one very sensitive nipple with the tip of his skilled tongue. She moved her hands to his head, pressing it even closer to her breasts. "Yes, Jordan. Don't stop, baby. You better not stop," she begged feverishly.

As the soft cinnamon flesh of her breasts surrounded his mouth he closed his eyes in pleasure. He drew in the nipple deeper to suckle as if he were drawing life from it. His hand teased the other exposed nipple, making sure it didn't feel too left out, until he moved over to taste it as well.

Jordan's lengthy erection strained against the cotton material of his new gray sweatpants, wishing it could be buried inside of her softness and not just pressed ever so intimately against her mound. When Mia rolled her shapely hips, pressing the mound even closer against his hardness, he moaned deep from his soul in pleasure.

"Oh, you like that?" she asked, her voice husky and teasing as she looked down at where he feasted on both of her mounds.

He leaned his head back to look up into her glazed eyes. "Just as much as you like this," he said tauntingly, moving his hands up to grasp both of her breasts. He lowered his head to suck deeply at each nipple, moving back and forth between them.

"Yes, my God, I do," she gasped, letting her head fall back in blind bliss.

Mia had just reached to pull Jordan's T-shirt over his head, when the phone began to ring, breaking into the haven of passion they had created. Both struggled to ignore the intrusion but it continued. She moved to suck deeply at the sweet sweat pocket of his neck, enjoying the salt created from their passion. "You better get it, Jordan."

"Hell no," he said with emphasis. He moved his hands to grasp deeply at her soft buttocks. "This is too good to stop."

Mia smiled, pulling his head back to her breasts. "You're right. I don't think it gets any better than this."

His answering machine clicked on. "This is the Banks residence. After the beep leave a message."

Beep.

"Jordan, hey, this is Amanda. I know our *meeting* didn't go too well this afternoon, but I thought it over and I'd like to try again. Call me at 555-3246. Bye, love."

Mia had immediately stiffened at the sultry and husky tone of the other woman's voice. She jumped off Jordan's lap, her breasts swinging as she did. She jerked her dress back up around her breasts with anger, still unable to hide the hardened nipples that strained against the material.

"What's wrong, Mia?" Jordan asked, rising to his feet as her glorious legs and backside were hidden beneath the material as she pulled her dress down from around her waist.

"Nothing's wrong."

Mia moved quickly toward the office door, and Jordan reached out just as quickly to grab her wrist lightly. "Don't go, Mia."

"Look, I'm not in the habit of being a replacement or a stand-in for another woman," Mia snapped, her eyes blazing with anger as she stared him down. "I'm sorry you didn't get to knock boots with Ms. Langston here in your office—"

Jordan began to chuckle, and Mia's words froze on her lips. He looked at her like an indulging father.

She attempted to snatch her hand away but he tightened his hold. "What's so damn funny, Jordan?"

"Contrary to your belief, I was not attempting to seduce Amanda this afternoon, although I believe she wishes otherwise."

Mia looked unconvinced. "So what is it that she wants to try again?"

Jordan had to stifle a laugh. "The interview," he said simply. "After interrupting every few seconds just five minutes after we entered the office, Tia and Kimani made lunch and then accidentally spilled red punch on Amanda. Needless to say she became angry and left."

Mia felt her tension ease. *The vamp needed to be dressed in red anyway like the sneaky devil she is.* "So are you going to call her?"

Jordan was loving it. Mia was jealous! He swore if she kept on with it she would turn completely green. Mia was jealous of Amanda! As if the other woman could ever compete with her. Amanda was nothing compared to this beauty who stood before him with pouting lips and eyes that flashed like lightning.

He looked at her, very tongue in cheek, rubbing his thumb in tantalizing circles against her inner wrist. "That depends on whether you plan on seeing Dr. Suave again—"

"That's none of your business," she scoffed, enjoying the tingling awareness of his hand against her skin.

Jordan smiled. "Oh, and my . . . affairs with Amanda are yours?"

"I could care less about your relationship with her," Mia snapped.

"Yeah, right."

"What is that supposed to mean?"

Jordan took each of her hands in his. "It means that you get just as jealous at the thought of me with Amanda, as I do thinking of you and Doc."

"I'm not jeal—"

"Admit it," he interjected, slowly lowering his head.

"I'm not jeal—"

"Admit it, Mia," he interjected again, just before touching his mouth to hers.

She closed her eyes against a sweet drowning wave of pleasure. "I'm not jealous, Jordan," she insisted softly, lying.

"Well, I was jealous," he said, just as softly, before touching down on paradise again with his lips. "I hated to think of him kissing you like this. Especially after what we shared last night."

Mia's eyes shot open, and she leaned back to look at him. "You're jealous?"

"I was jealous."

"Was?"

Jordan hugged her close to him. "You're not going to see him anymore," he answered with confidence.

Mia stiffened. "You're telling me not to see him again? I'm sorry but I thought my father's name was Warren, not Jordan."

This time he leaned back to look down at her. He saw the battle brewing in her eyes. "You're right," he acquiesced, not wanting to ruin the bliss of her being in his arms right now. "Forgive me?"

The tension in her eased. Mia was a loner and not used to being told what to do. If that were so she would get along fabulously with her overbearing mother. As long as he realized that, then she didn't have to tell him so. "Yes, I forgive you, Jordan."

He massaged the soft mounds of her buttocks, causing Mia to moan deeply in pleasure. "Did he kiss you?"

She was busy nuzzling her face in the hollow of his neck, enjoying the feel of his own strong buttocks. "Huh?"

"Did he kiss you?"

Mia shook her head, thoroughly distracted by the wonders he was creating.

"Swear?"

She nodded, her eyes closed with a soft smile on her lips.

Jordan kissed the corners of her mouth before deepening the kiss with his eager tongue. There was so much of her body he wanted to explore, but kissing would have to do for now. He sucked her tongue deeply as if leaving a brand.

Mia followed his lead and did the same to him. They both moaned and shivered. She felt as if her womanly flesh were floating in a pool between her legs. Jordan was sure he could destroy a building with the stiff hardness of his member.

"I could kiss you like this all night."

"Me too," she said. "But I have some work to get to tonight for an early meeting in the morning."

Jordan felt, and looked, disappointed. "Do you have to go now?"

Mia nodded, using her thumb to remove the smudges of her lip gloss from his mouth. "Don't you have a novel to complete?" she reminded him.

He looked over at his computer. This was a first. Never had he had to be reminded about writing. This incredible woman with the haunting eyes and a pool-deep dimple made him think of her and nothing else.

She kissed him briefly. "Good night, Jordan."

"Let's go out to dinner tomorrow night. Just you and me," he said suddenly, as if the idea just occurred to him.

Mia lowered her head. This all was moving so fast, so quickly. She felt as if she were at the top of a cold icy mountain with skis on, sliding down at an unstoppable speed with the view of trees and other icy peaks whizzing past her toward the heat and red blur of some emotion she wasn't ready to claim. But it was just dinner, right?

"Okay," she said slowly. "But what about the children?"

"I'll ask Ms. McKnight to baby-sit."

Jordan leaned down and kissed her again. Mia became lost in the passion. Her nipples hardened until they ached, her heart raced, and her womanhood swelled again. God, she wanted him—badly. She knew she had better leave now before they sank to the floor and took their passion to the ultimate level in the middle of his office. Rug burns and all. "No, no more, Jordan, please," she begged, not sounding at all as though she meant it.

He massaged her breasts, teasing the nipples with his

thumbs, and Mia whimpered, her knees buckling beneath her. He laughed huskily, as he supported her with a strong arm around her waist. "You have no idea how beautiful you are when you're hot with desire."

She smiled, swatting his hand away. "Thank you, I think."

"Mia?"

"Yes."

"Are you going to see Doc again?"

Mia looked at him directly and seriously. *At least he asked this time? What's the use? Terrence leaves me cold while Jordan holds the power to warm me with his unique brand of passion.* "No."

"Good," he said, his pleasure evident. "I'll see you tomorrow at eight?"

"You most certainly will."

They kissed one last time before he walked Mia to the front door. His eyes stayed on her until she entered her house with one final wave. He headed straight upstairs for a very cold and not very satisfying shower.

"You look tight, Dad," Rajahn said, looking at his father's reflection in the mirror.

"Tight?"

"That means nice, Dad."

Jordan playfully air-punched at his steadily growing son, who would soon be taller than he. "Why not just say that?"

Rajahn shrugged. "I don't know."

Jordan felt satisfied with his appearance in the full-length mirror. The lightweight khaki suit he wore complimented his complexion. His hair was newly faded and his new cologne, Joop!, had him smelling "tight."

Jordan was more than ready for his first date with Mia. He hoped it was only the first of many to come. Physically they connected. Now it was time to see if they got along socially—without the children—so that they could get into an emotional involvement that might lead anywhere and everywhere.

"You know what, Pops? I should've bet you."

"Bet me? When, and what?"

"You remember. I asked you why you didn't ask Ms. Gordon on a date, and you said, and I quote, 'I have no intention of asking her out.' Remember?"

"Hah, hah, hah," Jordan said, forced to swallow his earlier words.

"I'm really glad you and Ms. G are finally getting it together," Rajahn said seriously.

"Finally?"

"I guess I can tell you now. The other kids and I have kinda been doing little things to get you two together."

Jordan turned to look at one of his five pride and joys. "Like?"

"Like, uhm, inviting her places, or making sure she came over to the house—"

"Like getting rid of Amanda Langston?" he asked with sudden enlightenment. "And throwing out my clothes?"

"Uh, yeah. I mean, yes, sir."

"I have just learned to never underestimate children," he muttered. "Look, no more matchmaking, okay?"

"Yes, sir," Rajahn said, realizing now that it might not have been so wise to tell his father about Mission: Find a Wife for Dad.

Rajahn fretted for nothing because Jordan was in too good a mood to fuss about anything tonight. Besides, the fact that the kids played matchmaker had brought him closer to his beautiful neighbor. If not for them they would have probably just waved at each other from their separate yards and not discovered the one-of-a-kind passion they shared. He would have continued to see her as an uptight workaholic who didn't know how to relax. While she would still be looking down that beautiful nose at him as if he were a fly sitting atop a pile of dung. Besides, to him their harmless schemes just meant that they approved of her, which just increased his opinion of her even more. So how could he be mad at his children?

Jordan walked out of his bedroom after briefly hugging his son to his side. When he got to the bottom of the stairs his girls were just coming out of the kitchen. All their chattering stopped as they caught sight of their father.

"Uhm, uhm, uhm. Check you out!" Tia exclaimed, coming over to reach up and smooth his tie. "You look tight, Pops."

Jordan struck a GQ pose, causing them to burst into a fit of giggles. "So, I'm most of that?" he asked.

Kimani sighed. "It's 'all that,' and, yes, you are."

"Right."

"Uh, Dad, try not to do anything goofy," Tia said.

"Please don't trip—" Kimani interjected.

"Or spill anything on yourself or Ms. Gordon," Tia finished.

Jordan looked down at them with a bemused expression. "Anything else?"

"Don't forget the flowers," Amina advised.

"I won't," he assured her with a wink.

It was a quarter to eight. He was sharply dressed, smelling good, had what the children told him were Mia's favorite flowers in the fridge, Ms. McKnight was on her way, and he was filled with anticipation of the night of beginnings to come.

All he needed now was his lovely date.

Mia removed her dress-length pale pink suit jacket as she entered her spacious office at Stromer, Wiler. She rolled up the sleeves of the crisp white hand-sewn cotton business shirt from India. With plenty of energy at the prospect of landing another bigwig client, she jumped into the mental pile of her beloved numbers and figures. She hadn't even spent the bonus she received for snagging the Petra Communications deal yet, and here was another conquest to push her even further up the corporate investment ladder.

Just after lunch she had got word that Pencom, a large computer software company that she had been trying to snag, had finally accepted her proposal for its acquisition of Tech Inc., a smaller and less competitive software company with innovative ideas and new products. Because of a meeting with all the department heads at Stromer, Wiler, that had lasted late into the afternoon, she had to work into the night, researching and fine-tuning the deal to get ready for the appointment she had in the morning with all the key players in New York.

Mia thrived on this, enjoying the feeling of her heart pumping and racing as she took her seat in the bungi chair of her office at work. She felt she worked best under pressure. This was her element, and she thrived in it.

As she turned her computer terminal on, typing in her password, Mia's attention was totally focused on her work and nothing else.

Jordan glanced down at his watch, trying hard not to let his emotions overrule him. Over the past hour he had wavered between anger and fear. Neither offered him any solace as he paced the entire length of his front porch.

It was 9:30 P.M. Mia was late and they had already missed their dinner reservations at the Fifty-seven Fifty-seven Bar and Restaurant in New York. If it weren't for the fact that she lived next door to him, he would think he was being stood up. But she hadn't come home at all yet.

What if she had been in an accident? Or what if that expensive sports car of hers had left her stranded on the side of the road during her commute? Or—

No! As fear claimed him again, almost clawing at his throat like a rabid dog, Jordan forced from his thoughts the idea of any danger befalling Mia. Especially if she was just sitting around somewhere avoiding him and their first date. He thought of her out to dinner with Dr. Suave, not caring that he waited like a fool with a bouquet of lavender and white roses, her favorite according to his children.

Jordan left his porch, the streetlights casting an eerie yellowish glow to the night, and walked over to Mia's porch. He took a seat on the top step.

Where is she?

Mia smiled with satisfaction as she printed out the data she collected and then saved the information on both her hard drive and a disk. One copy she placed in a manila folder and slipped into her Coach briefcase, the other she locked in the top drawer of her glass desk.

As she left the office Mia glanced down at her Movado watch. It was just after 10 P.M., and she was too wired to be sleepy. She felt like dancing or going jogging, anything that kept the blood pumping through her body.

But Mia was realistic. She knew she would just go home, put on some legendary jazz greats, and sip on a glass of expensive merlot while she soaked in an herbal aromatherapy bubble bath. It was a ritual, and with her successful track record, there was no need to change now.

This is how I pay the bills!

Now that was Jordan's favorite say—

Oh my God! Mia came to a stop in her path to the elevator, totally surrounded by the quiet of the empty offices. *Jordan! I forgot about my date with Jordan tonight.*

She was mortified. How could she have forgotten the date so easily? Last night she had been up thinking of him and the passion they had shared, and tonight she had forgotten him. How? Was she that bad a workaholic that closing a deal outweighed a date with a man who finally made her feel alive?

Mia pushed the button for the elevator, shaking her head. What planet had she floated to today? Maybe she had pushed all thoughts of the father of five from her mind subconsciously because of the conscious fears she had last night about starting a relationship with him.

"Oh, Jordan," she said, as she stepped onto the elevator. "Maybe he forgot as well. He's so absentminded at times."

Her mood brightened as the farfetched thought occurred to her. It was a long stretch. Okay, it was an impossibly long stretch, but it never hurt to hope.

Right?

Okay, that bitter taste in my mouth is the result of the flames of hope being doused.

Mia pulled her car into a spot directly in front of her house, but her eyes were on the solitary figure sitting on the porch. Taking a deep breath, she grabbed her briefcase and climbed out of the vehicle.

What should I say?

Jordan looked up as Mia stepped onto her porch, a vision in pale pink. She looked beautiful. The flowers he had bought for her hung between his knees, the petals swaying against the step like a broom. Pointedly he looked down at his watch, using the light offered by the street lamp to read the telltale dials. It was a quarter to eleven.

"Jordan, I'm—" she began.

"Late," he interjected, his voice as hard and cold as diamonds.

Mia sighed. "Yes, Jordan, I'm late, and I'm sorry."

He laughed harshly with more bitterness than a snowstorm in the dead of winter in Alaska. "You know, Mia, if you didn't want to go out with me, there's a very universal word you could have used—no. Simple word, just two little letters, only takes a second to say it . . . n-o."

"Jordan—"

He stood and handed her the bouquet. "Here, take them," he barked when she hesitated.

Mia was touched. They were beautiful, long-stemmed fragrant roses in her favorite colors. The petals seemed to glow in the darkness, and their calming perfume wafted up to her. "Thank you so much, Jordan. Please let me explain."

When he remained quiet, staring down the street, his profile looking as if it were carved in granite, his powerful hands in his pockets, she continued. "I had a project to fine-tune at the last minute for a meeting in the morning with a new client. I—"

"Oh, I see," he said, nodding his handsome head slowly. "While I've been sitting out here for three hours, not knowing whether to be worried or angry, you were at your beloved office working."

Jordan laughed lightly, removing one hand from his pocket to rub his mouth. He started to reach up to push up his glasses but then remembered he was a part of the contact crowd now. "I see that any of the time I spent worrying that you were hurt or stranded was as big a waste of time as me asking you out in the first place."

Finally, he looked over at her, and Mia was spellbound by just how handsome he was. "Jordan, this is a very important deal."

"You know, Mia, I knew you got a thrill out of working, but I had no idea how absorbed in your career you are."

Mia stiffened. "No more so than you are in your writing," she snapped.

"I didn't stand you up."

"Jordan, we can go out tomorrow night," she said

softly, laying her hand on his arm. "Oh, no I can't, I have a charity auction to attend that my job is giving—"

He jerked from her grasp. "Sorry, I don't give or take mercy dates."

"A mercy date!" she exclaimed, her voice incredulous.

"Look, Mia, you don't have to worry about my children or myself intruding on your precious time being locked up in that damn office of yours. Perhaps you should call Dr. Suave and let him fight for it. But then again when it came time for your date with him I saw there were no important deals."

Mia watched in shock as Jordan walked down the steps. He entered his yard and his house without ever looking back.

Nine

"Good morning, babies. Why the gloomy faces, children?" Ms. McKnight eyed each of the children as they took their seats at the dining room table. No one answered. She started serving the grits, scrambled eggs, and bacon she had prepared for their breakfast.

"So," she said brightly, hoping to steer their little minds to more cheerful thoughts. Instinctively she knew that if she gave them time, one of them would fill her in on their obvious collective trouble without her having to nudge them. "What did everyone dream of last night?"

Again, silence met her. Amazing how in the right context silence spoke volumes.

After taking her seat, she turned to the child to her immediate left. "Kimani?"

She used her fork to poke at the fluffy eggs on her plate. Briefly she looked up at their caregiver. "I . . . I dreamed Daddy and Ms. Gordon weren't mad at each other anymore," she grumbled.

Ms. McKnight's fork halted in its path to her mouth. *Well, I didn't know one of 'em would tell it that soon.* Composing her thoughts quickly, she said, "Who says they're mad at each other?"

Rajahn spoke up for his sister. "We all stayed up waiting for Ms. Gordon to come home for their date last night. When she did we saw her and Dad argue before he walked away and slammed the door coming into the house."

She *tsk-tsked* in disapproval. "And here I was thinking you were all asleep. I thought I heard those floor boards creaking upstairs."

"We're sorry, Ms. M," Tia added, turning to her with troubled eyes so unlike the usual mischief that ruled in the amber depths. "We just wanted to see them leave for their date. Why couldn't she just show up on time? Dang!"

Ms. McKnight said nothing at first. She also was aware that the big "date" did not go exactly as Jordan had planned. "They'll get over it, believe me. Grown-ups always find a reason to be mad at each other because we like to make up. Everything will work out in the end."

The doorbell rang, and they all jumped at the unexpectedness of it. "I'll get it," Ms. McKnight said, rising. "Your daddy's been locked inside that office of his since before I arrived this morning."

As soon as she left the room, Rajahn looked at each of his siblings. "We have to get them together so that they can make up. We've done too much to let them screw it all up now. Right?"

"Right," the rest agreed eagerly.

Quietly, almost whispering, the older children began exchanging ideas. Their food and the gloom they awakened with this morning were momentarily forgotten. They didn't even notice Mrs. McKnight and another person enter the dining room.

"Isn't anyone going to tell their grandpa good morning?" he asked, his voice deep and gruff.

All the children's heads swung to look back at the entrance. Tall, robust, and lovable. With him they knew came more hugs; jokes; the scent of Old Spice; and the hard, sweet butterscotch candy that he kept in his pockets. "Grandpa," they all yelled in excited unison, before dashing from their seats to barrel toward him.

Clinton dropped down to one knee to gather his four granddaughters into his arms. They all closed their eyes and smiled. After hugging them, he reached out to shake his grandson's hand. He wisely knew that the boy felt he was too old for a hug.

"I got presents for everyone," he said with all the fun and excitement of Santa Claus, even if it was the deep of summer. He looked at Ms. McKnight with a roguish wink of his eye. "Are those grits I smell, woman?"

She stiffened. "Yes, it is, *man,*" she snapped.

To her Clinton Banks was an old fool and a flirt, the complete opposite of his reclusive son. Minnie couldn't stand the sight of the gray-haired devil. Okay, yes, she *could* stand the sight of him. He was still an impressively handsome man until he opened his big chauvinistic mouth. The man's thinking was totally archaic and asinine, with plenty of emphasis on the *ass.*

The children all moved to reclaim their seats, and their grandfather stood slowly. "I don't see Jordan so I know where he is. While I go drag my son out of that office, how 'bout getting to fixin' me a big old plate, Minnie."

It was a demand and not a request. On top of that he slapped her buttocks on his way out of the room. "Time's a wastin', woman," he called back over his broad shoulder.

Her mouth dropped open in shock and indignation. "Old fool," she muttered, her voice showing she wasn't quite as angry as she put on.

The morning sun beamed brightly over the city. The sounds of life and laughter in the summer were booming outside already, but Jordan didn't know that. His windows and curtains were closed purposely.

His fingers flew relentlessly across the keyboard in a conscious effort to keep busy so that he wouldn't think of Mia. If that meant getting up at four every morning, like today, then so be it. Because of it he was midway through his second revision and now ahead of the schedule he had set for himself. He cursed himself as he realized that he had failed again. He was thinking of Mia anyway.

His fingers paused above a key. It was no use, she dominated his thoughts and his life. With a deep breath, Jordan leaned back in his chair and placed his hands behind his head to stretch. Last night he had been relieved that she had finally arrived home safely. But the anger he felt at how easily she had forgotten about him ran very deep. He would think of that during odd moments and actually growl in frustration because of it.

He would think of the way she used to look down her nose at him, making him feel inadequate. "So she thinks she's too good for me," he muttered, allowing himself to wallow in his anger for a moment. "She's lucky I didn't think I was too good for her uptight behind."

Foolishly he had thought last night was the beginning of "them," but instead it was the end. Obviously men like Dr. Terrence Blanchard, with their credentials and snobbish mannerisms, were more to her liking. He should have stuck to his original opinions on his neighbor and not let her smile bewitch him. Unwillingly his mind flashed back to that day in the park, their first kiss, the night in his office on the couch . . .

"No, Jordan," he said aloud forcefully to himself, slamming his hands down on the cluttered desk. "Don't think about her."

"Son, I don't know who she is, but she sure has you crazy up in here talking to yourself."

"Dad?" he asked, surprised as he looked up into the face of an older version of himself.

The only difference in looks between them was his father's twenty extra pounds, graying hair, and crow's-feet. Jordan knew that twenty years from now, physically he would be this man.

Standing he reached out to hug his father across the desk, accidentally knocking over the heavy brass desk lamp on the corner of his cluttered desk.

Clinton laughed, before stooping to pick up the lamp. "Still clumsy as ever, son."

"Unfortunately." Jordan smiled, this time safely leaning to clasp his beloved father, mentor, and friend into his arms. "You just got in from Virginia? Did you tell me and I forgot again to pick you up from the airport? I'm sorry, Dad."

Clinton waved his hand dismissively, very aware and used to his son's absentminded nature. "I caught a taxi. I'm here in one piece, so there's nothing to fret over. What's done is done, although sometimes I worry you'd lose your head if it weren't attached to your body."

"I'm just glad you could visit me and the kids," Jordan said with honesty.

"I will tell you what I just became worried about," he said, sitting down on the other corner of the unkempt desk.

"What's that?"

"I want to know why my only child, my son, who has a good head on his shoulders, because I made sure he did, is sitting in his office talking to himself. Tell me about her."

Jordan slumped down into his chair, raising his hand to slowly wipe his mouth—a new nervous gesture without his glasses to push up onto his face. After a long drawn-out sigh, he started to tell his father about his distraction—Mia.

The brief knock at her office door caused Mia to look up from the computer monitor as Tyresa entered, carrying a stack of folders in one hand and a cup of steaming liquid in the other.

"Now I recognize the files I asked for, but what's

that?" Mia eyed the black cup warily as her assistant set it on a clear spot on her desktop.

"Cinnamon tea," Tyresa said with overdramatized relish, taking a seat at one of the chairs facing Mia's L-shaped desk. "Drink up, buddy, because you need it after that meeting this morning."

Mia dropped her head into her manicured hands, dismayed. "I have never been so out of it during a meeting before. Thank God you were sitting next to me to kick me under the table!"

Tyresa smiled. "What had you in such a daze anyway?"

Mia's own smile faded, and she looked out the side window of her corner office. Usually the scenic view of the harbor stretching for miles out calmed her. Many mornings she meditated while looking out on the waters. Sometimes she achieved such an optimal state of peace and tranquillity that she felt as if she were actually floating on the gentle waves she was gazing upon. Today, the view held no meaning, no distinction, no help. If anything she felt as if she were drowning.

She clearly remembered where her mind had kept slipping to this morning. Jordan. He had conquered her dreams last night and destroyed her reasoning this morning. Several times she would be so deep in thought about him that she lost all concept of her surroundings and the people around her. Sort of like an abyss. A Jordan-filled abyss.

And Mia had thought of so many things, but they all had returned to Jordan. When she had laid eyes on him for the first time at her back door with his children and awful spectacles; when he tripped between the hedges separating their houses; the way just the sight of him used to irritate her; the night he called for her to come over because the twins wouldn't stop crying; the first time she looked into that handsome face and those beautiful eyes without the distraction of those glasses; when she looked deeply into those mocha eyes as she touched his forehead in the Land Cruiser; her jealousy at seeing him with Amanda Langston in the park; and the expression of regret on his handsome face when he told her to have a good time on her first date with Terrence. And, oh Lord, that night she saw how glorious the body was that he hid behind old faded baggy sweats and T-shirts. The very same night that damn robe had threatened to open and expose his glory. Or how he taught her how to eat pizza and lightly touched her lips with his thumb.

But that was topped by his kissing her, then she in turn kissing him with passion that exploded between them with more fireworks than the Fourth of July. It had only hinted at the fevered moments they would share on his couch in his office the next night. She blushed and had to fan herself at the thought of the heat they had created.

Lastly, and most consistently, she thought of the anger on his handsome face last night because she had forgotten their first date. Mia still felt as if his comments and most of his anger were uncalled for. But, Lord, he had looked so handsome, and it touched her that he had waited outside for her to get home safely. He was a real gentleman—with a temper.

Jordan.

If only he didn't have so many chil—

No! Mia's brain shrieked. How could she even think of Jordan without his children? Was she that selfish? She had to be, because the fact that he had five children was the major factor holding her back from wanting to be serious about him. She just couldn't fathom herself, a single career woman with no children, suddenly stepping up to the challenge of being a mother to a ready-made family of five.

Sighing, Mia continued to look off into the distance. She wished her tranquil waters offered some solace today. Maybe what had happened last night was for the best. Any idea of something developing between Jordan and her had been nipped in the bud. He just wasn't the man for her. She was seriously considering calling Terrence to pick up the lukewarm relationship they had begun.

"Mia. Mia? Mia!"

She was drawn from her reverie by her assistant's persistent calling. "What, Tyresa?" she asked, turning her gaze from the unsatisfying view to look at her with troubled eyes.

"You're doing it again, you know, drifting. Now what's on your mind, friend?"

"The fact that there's a snowball rolling around frozen in hell," she said softly, with a haunting smile that didn't reach her eyes.

"Seems to me that our young lady just needs something to take her mind off work, if you know what I mean," Clinton said roguishly with a wink.

Jordan looked over at his father in amazement. "Unfortunately I know exactly what you mean," he said wryly.

His father's mind stayed in the gutter—and in the dark ages when it came to women. Frequently he wondered how the old man and his mother had been so deeply in love when she had been such a strong-willed woman. But then his mother had had his father wrapped around her finger. Jordan allowed himself to feel a moment of grief as he thought of her in heaven and not here on earth where he still missed and needed her.

"All the money you got, you could marry her and then demand she don't work," Clinton said with satisfaction, intruding on Jordan's thoughts.

Jordan snorted. "I don't see any man demanding Mia to do anything."

"Oh, she's one of them feminists," his father said with distaste.

"She's a beautiful, intelligent woman who would rather work all night than go out to a romantic dinner with me," Jordan said, resigned and still angered by the truth. "It doesn't matter anyway. We broke it off last night before it even began."

Clinton saw that his son needed advice and decided to keep his usual blunt comments, given more for shock value than actual belief, to himself. "There's something about this woman that has affected you deeply, son. Maybe instead of being angry, you should talk to her. From what you told me she has one of those high-demanding careers, and that means compromise for any man in a relationship with her."

Jordan's eyes widened as he looked at his father in fast-growing amazement.

Clinton continued. "This young lady sounds like someone used to setting her own rules because she lives alone and makes her own money by working a lot. You work a lot, too, Jordan, but your schedule can be more flexible than hers. She'll need room for adjusting to a relationship. It's like living alone and making compromises for a new roommate. Everything takes time. You understand, son?"

Jordan didn't answer. He just continued to look at his caveman-mentality father step into the twenty-first century with his thinking. Who knew?

"If that doesn't work then give her a good tumble."

Jordan dropped his head to his chest as the father he was used to stepped forward again.

Mia reached into her briefcase, extracting Tyresa's husband, Royce's copy of Jordan's first book, *Murder by Moonlight*. She hadn't gotten him to sign it, and she doubted she would have the chance now. "I stayed up all night reading this," she said as she pushed it across the glass top to Tyresa. "It was good. No, it's excellent. He writes with such clarity and vision. It's lyrical and descriptive. I'm amazed that it came from Jordan actually."

Tyresa eyed her boss with shrewd eyes as she thumbed through the well-worn hardcover book. Mia had just filled her in on her tumultuous and passionate beginnings with Jordan Banks. The mixed emotions her friend felt were evident. As she continued to flip through the book she wished her husband didn't have the awful habit of removing the book jacket when he read. She would have loved to see the photo of the author. She did see that it wasn't autographed, but after what Mia had told her and what she saw in her friend's face, she didn't even question her about it. "So, what about Dr. Suave?"

Mia gave her a stern look at using Jordan's patronizing name for Terrence, but then they both broke into childish giggles. She sighed. "Terrence is handsome, dignified, educated, wealthy, and childless," she finished with emphasis.

Tyresa's mouth formed an *O* she finally realized the biggest barrier for Mia becoming seriously involved with "a good man." "I thought you loved Jordan's kids?"

That same guilt claimed her. "I do—"

"But?"

"But . . . I'm not ready to be a mother to five children. I'm not ready to be a mother, period."

"Oh, so Jordan asked you to marry him?"

"No."

"Then stop jumping the gun," Tyresa told her, leaning forward in her chair to look directly at her friend, boss, and mentor. "In this business it's good to think steps ahead, but in a relationship it may not always be for the best. A date is a date and nothing more, Mia. Sometimes you just gotta enjoy the flow and not fight it."

"I don't know, Reese. I just don't know."

* * *

Mia pulled into the garage behind the house, sighing heavily. She got out of the luxury automobile and looked over at the house next door. The house was brightly lit against the night's velvety black backdrop. She envisioned Jordan in his office, busily typing away at his computer, dressed in his uniform of sweats and a T-shirt.

I sure could go for one of his kisses right now, she thought, as she climbed the stairs to enter her house through the kitchen.

"Ms. G."

Mia whirled around inside the kitchen to look out the still-open back door. Rajahn was standing at the foot of the stairs, slightly cloaked by the darkness. "Hello, Rajahn. Is something wrong?"

"My dad fell in the basement. We need your help," he said in an urgent, rushed tone.

Mia's heart began to pound in her chest. "Jordan fell," she croaked, before dropping whatever she held to race down the steps and through the hedges.

Rajahn followed close behind her.

She entered the house and headed straight through the foyer to the door leading to the kids' playroom in the basement. As soon as she stepped through the archway Mia eyed Jordan standing at the foot of the stairs. Air whooshed against the back of her legs as the door slammed closed behind her. "What the hell?" she shrieked.

The click of the lock being turned sounded loudly. Mia turned and tried to open the door. It wouldn't budge. Jordan raced up the stairs to try the knob as well. Mia's heart hammered as she smelled the scent of man and soap. She felt his heat just an inch or two away from her. She tasted the desire she had for him.

Jordan turned his head over his shoulder to look at her. "We've been tricked."

* * *

Rajahn heard them rattling the knob and trying to force the door open. For a moment indecision was his friend. *Are we doing the right thing?*

His cohorts walked up to him. Tia, Kimani, the twins, and Grandpa. The same doubt clouding his face was mirrored in theirs. This just had to work.

Mia's hand hurt from banging against the solid wood of the door. Her throat was scratchy from trying to threaten, bargain, and plead with their captors.

"I can't believe this," she moaned, turning to look down the stairs at Jordan. "I have a charity auction to attend in"—she glanced at her watch—"one hour."

His snort reached her ears and she raised one finely arched brow. Jordan was mumbling something under his breath. She caught snatches of "workaholic" and "addicted to her job," and she stiffened.

Mia crossed her arms over her chest. "Do something, Jordan!"

"We're outnumbered five, probably six, to two." He came to stand at the bottom of the steps to look up at her. "Looks like the mission is in full force again."

Mia was confused, and her beautiful face showed it. "Huh?"

"Come down."

Her heels clicked against the solid wooden steps as she descended. The faint scent of roses that had only teased her senses lightly before, became stronger with each step that brought her closer to the bottom. *What's going on?*

Mia gasped in surprise. Colorful helium balloons and fragrant flowers were everywhere. Candles of every shape and size were positioned and ready to be lit. A stack of CDs sat by the portable radio on the floor.

She looked back at Jordan in confusion. He just shrugged. She stepped toward the radio, stooping to pick up the stack. Marvin Gaye, Luther Vandross, Sade,

Eric Benet, Kenny Lattimore, Whitney Houston, and many more. Varying artists with one major theme; romance. She replaced the stack.

In the corner, pillows and comforters were piled high. A bottle of champagne chilled in a bucket of ice with two crystal flutes sitting next to it. A picnic basket, presumably filled with food, sat beside that. It was a love nest!

They both jumped as the CD player clicked on. Marvin Gaye's melodic voice singing "Sexual Healing" filled the basement.

The combination of Marvin Gaye's singing and Jordan's just being Jordan and looking so fine wreaked too much havoc on Mia's well-being. Especially as a vision of their cocoa-brown bodies, naked and sweaty, on the pallet flashed hotly before her very eyes.

She closed her eyes against a wave of desire for him that caused a familiar flood to rise between her legs. "What's going on, Jordan?" she asked, her voice strained.

As he explained how Rajahn admitted to him how he and his siblings had been plotting to get their father and her together, Mia was shocked. Who knew kids could be so manipulative?

She was also very touched. Even though she saw herself as the worst possible candidate for a mother, they wanted her. Blame it on PMS, or stress, or just plain overwhelming emotions, but tears filled Mia's eyes and began to silently stream down her cheeks. Those beautiful children wanted *her* to be their mommy!

The children were all gathered on the staircase in the foyer. Grandpa Clinton was in the kitchen warming up the dinner Ms. McKnight had left for them, the key to the basement in his pocket.

"At least she stopped banging and yelling," Tia said, studying her fingernails.

Everyone nodded in agreement.

The faint strains of music filtered through the door. They had set the CD player on a timer. They all smiled at the sound.

"Grandpa says no couple can deny Marvin," Kimani said brightly, her glasses perched precariously on the tip of her nose. She pushed them back up with a slender finger.

Smiles turned quickly to frowns as the music abruptly ended.

Jordan started toward her when he saw the tears glistening on her cheeks, but then he stopped himself. He started again, and then stopped himself again. He started. Stopped. Anger and compassion battled for victory inside of him.

Compassion won out.

He pulled her into his arms tightly, and it felt as though it was where she belonged. "Why are you crying, Mia?"

She felt like an overly emotional, hysterical female. That was a stereotype that didn't sit well with her. "They did all of this for us?"

Jordan nodded, moving his hand up under the blanket of her soft curly hair to her neck, using light pressure to massage that area. He felt the dampness of her tears against his neck.

Earlier, just a second before Mia had entered the picture, he had seen a twelve-pack of Trojan condoms near the pallet. He knew then for sure that his father had to be in on the bizarre matchmaking scheme tonight. He didn't tell Mia that. No need for her to know that his father was a horny toad.

To think he had believed his daughters when they came screeching into his office saying they had seen a snake go under the door to the basement.

"What lie did they tell to get you over here?" he asked, his breath fanning against the hair on her cheek.

Mia composed herself when she felt herself lightly rocking her body in the comfort and warmth of Jordan's arms. She lifted her face from that addictive spot in the hollow of his neck. Knowing he was angry at her and probably just holding her out of pity for her emotional breakdown, she stepped out of his embrace with bitter regret. "Rajahn told me you had fallen in the basement."

The fact that she moved away bothered Jordan. *So, now she doesn't want my touch. Last night she was damn near begging for it.* "As if you would care," he snapped.

"I don't feel like arguing, Jordan. I have more important things to waste brainpower over."

"Like what, work?"

"Yes, as a matter of fact."

"Big deal."

"It is for me."

"That's the problem."

"No, Jordan, you're the problem."

"Me?"

"Yes. I said I was sorry for missing our date. You need to get over it. I'm only human, not a superwoman."

Jordan laughed mockingly. "Don't start quoting lines from a Karyn White song to me."

"Aw, shut up, Jordan," she snapped, feeling one helluva headache creeping up on her.

"You shut up."

"Whatever." She sighed, glancing at her watch. *I'm going to miss the charity auction. That was a perfect opportunity to network—*

"Fretting over missing your work-related evening?"

"No," she lied.

"Whatever."

Mia walked to one end of the basement and Jordan stalked over to the other.

* * *

Their father's and Mia's angry voices reached them, far clearer than the music had earlier. Clinton walked out of the kitchen. He immediately noticed the gloomy look on his grandchildren's faces. What he wouldn't give to see them smile. He loved them as if his blood actually flowed through them all.

"It's not going so well, Grandpa," Rajahn told him.

Clinton nodded slowly. "We're all going into the kitchen to eat dinner. Everything will work out. They just need time. And when they do work it out, you all won't be around to listen. Let's go."

Their grandfather usually had a way of making them believe anything. But the children weren't so sure about his confidence in their father and Mia.

Ten

Mia stopped pacing circles on the bright primary colors of the carpet. She stopped worrying about being trapped in the basement with Jordan. She stopped fretting over missing the charity auction. She stopped blaming Jordan, because he was as big a victim to this madness as she. She just stopped.

Besides, after he had discovered that the cable box had been removed from the big-screen television he had proceeded to lie down on the pallet. Soon his snores filled the silence they both had clung to. His mouth was slightly ajar as he lay on his side, one hand under his head and the other between his knees.

Mia really thought he was way too calm about the whole thing. His children had locked them in the basement and refused to release them. Maybe the calm before the storm brewed in him. Why wasn't he worried about the children being basically in the house alone?

Sighing she glanced over at him again. He smacked his lips in contentment, and she smiled. He looked like a little boy in his sleep with those long lashes curled against his high-chiseled cheekbones.

"Mmmmmm. Mia."

She jerked her head to look over at him. Was she crazy or did Jordan just say her name in his sleep?

"Mia," he moaned again.

Okay, she wasn't crazy. Mia wondered what was going on in his dreams. When his handsome face broke into a sudden smile, her eyes widened. Whatever it was, it was making him very happy.

She slipped out of her shoes, immediately losing two inches from her height. She tiptoed over to where he lay. *He really is beautiful,* she thought, as she carefully knelt down beside him on the pallet.

Slowly she bent over, holding her hair back with her hand, to lightly brush her lips against his, following an intense impulse. She smiled as he grinned in his sleep and then smacked his lips as if savoring the taste and feel of the kiss.

Sometimes you just gotta enjoy the flow, don't fight it!

No man made her feel alive and sexy like this man. Even in his sleep, as she caressed him with her eyes he aroused her. That's how powerful the attraction between them was. Dynamic. Potent. Lusty. Spirituous. Fierce. Profound. Intense. Electrifying. All of those things and much, much more.

Mia tilted her head and reached out to lightly touch his lips. Just the feel of their bodies together in the most minimal way made Mia shiver. *Oh, the wonders these lips can work.*

Sometimes you just gotta enjoy the flow, don't fight it!

Her friend's words seemed so fitting right now. Mia actually felt a flow of energy between Jordan and herself. An energy that drew her like a moth to a flame. So why fight it?

Clinton descended the steps, having made sure all the children were snug in their beds. He paused by the door to the basement. Quiet was all he heard. Shaking his head, he was just reaching in his jean's pocket to retrieve the key to unlock the door when the faint sounds of Marvin Gaye reached him.

He unlocked the door, but did not open it. With a smile and a hope for reconciliation, Clinton turned out the lights in the foyer and climbed the stairs to retire for the night.

"Jordan. Jordan, baby. Wake up."

"Hmmm?" he mumbled in his sleep.

Mia smiled, reaching out to lightly touch his face. "Come on, baby. Wake up."

Jordan popped one eye open and then closed it quickly, thinking he was still in the midst of a very nice dream. See, it had to be a dream, because what he saw was so unlike the reality he had escaped through sleep.

Surely the soft strains of Marvin Gaye singing "Sexual Healing," the candles lit around the room with the lights off, and a smiling Mia clad only in a lacy white teddy had to be strictly of his imagination.

"Jordan, baby, wake up."

The light touch of Mia's hand on his face was too real. Jordan opened his eyes. "Am I still dreaming?"

Mia laughed huskily. "Oh, no, baby this is real."

She stood, and he was mesmerized by her beauty by candlelight. The lacy affair left little to his imagination. The thin straps graced her softly rounded shoulders. Scalloped edges cupped the full swell of her breasts with her dark chocolate aureoles pressed against the flimsy material. Her small waist and rounded hips were emphasized by the high cut of the teddy before long shapely glorious dancer's legs.

Jordan's nature rose with primal instincts. His groin tightened and blood rushed to harden his shaft until it throbbed with a rhythm patterned by his fast-beating heart.

When she smiled and reached out to him, what could he do but rush to reach out and clasp it? With a slight tug she let him know she wanted him to rise, and he did. As soon as he rose Jordan pulled Mia into his arms, taking the lead.

"I want you, Jordan," she whispered, reaching up to lick the lobe of his ear hotly.

"Oh, you do?"

She wrapped her arms around his waist and moved down to clasp his hard buttocks with her hands. "Yes, I do."

As Marvin sang them into ecstasy, Jordan lowered his head to capture Mia's full luscious lips. The flicker of the lit candles was mirrored in her almond depths, but he knew the desire and passion they shared for each other burned much hotter.

Their tongues danced in the air between their open mouths, as they slowly rocked their bodies to the hypnotic rhythm of the music. Jordan moaned in a rush of pleasure as Mia drew his tongue into her cool mouth, sucking the full length deeply.

"You like that, huh?" she asked.

"Yes, my God, I do."

His hands moved up to massage the back of her neck under her blanket of perfume-scented hair. She moaned in pleasure. Only Jordan's hands could do this for her.

After easing what little tension he felt, his fingertips traced a path down to the small of her back, slipping from her shoulders the thin straps that strained under the heavy weight of her perfect breasts. He didn't dally too long there before massaging her body on his path to grasp both of her full chocolate mounds.

"Yes!" Mia gasped, her eyes closed in rapturous delight.

As he teased the peaks with his nimble fingers, his shaft lengthened and swelled even more in response to the feel of heaven in his hands. "So soft, Mia," he moaned against her mouth.

Half out of her mind Mia moved her hands to the hem of his T-shirt, slowly drawing the barrier to his naked skin up over his head. She hated to halt the feel of his hands on her body even for a few seconds as he raised his arms to thrust the garment from his muscled body. She needed to feel his body unclothed under her wandering hands.

Mia felt fulfilled when he gathered her breasts again, the massaging potent. She dipped her head to lick a trail between his two flat nipples, loving the feel of his soft chest hair against her tongue. When she moved to take a nipple into her mouth she felt a shiver rack his body. Feelings of power filled her as she saw the reactions she wrought from him.

Jordan moved one hand along the smooth expanse of her stomach to her back, to gather a fleshy smooth cheek of her buttock into his hand. The teddy, now around her waist, was a barrier he could definitely do without.

"Take it off," he demanded softly.

As Mia moved back to step out of the skimpy lace, Jordan rushed out of his sweatpants and boxers. Naked, they stood before each other. With feasting eyes they devoured the sight of each other in the candlelight. Perfection personified.

In harmony they stepped back into each other's arms, a hypnotic Sade ballad now their musical interlude. They both gasped at the heated and electrifying feel of their bodies pressed close together. Her softness against his hardness, from their thighs to their chest. A perfect fit.

Jordan felt as if he were floating. Just as if he had jumped off a cliff and then drifted up in the air to soar. She did this to him and for him, as no other woman could. With the candles as his guide he swung her luscious body up into his arms and carried her over to the pallet. Gently Jordan laid her down and kneeled beside her. "You are so very beautiful, Mia," he whispered, almost in awe by the sight of her naked body lying there before him.

"You make me feel beautiful," she returned softly.

Her hands sought and found his lengthy erection as

his own hands massaged her feet and legs. With long strokes she caressed him, impressed by his size. She used the small trickle of his release to lubricate her hand, smoothing the up-and-down motion on his shaft. She knew from the way Jordan licked his lips that she was pleasing him.

He moved up to stroke her full shapely thighs with deep rotating motions. When she opened her legs, exposing her innermost femininity, he inhaled of her womanly scent and wasted no time delving into the pool hidden beneath the soft curly triangular bush. Her hips arched up off the pallet as he stroked her, his thumb simultaneously massaging the bud. "Jordan, don't stop—"

"I won't, baby."

"Please, don't stop," she begged, her hand pleasing him as well.

She began to move against the pressure of his fingers. Jordan watched her face intently as she enjoyed first one and then another climax that left her shivering and near tears. "Jordan," she whispered.

He arched his wrist to delve one and then two fingers inside of her. The feel of heat and wetness caused him to release a primal growl from deep in his chest. "Open your legs, Mia," he said hoarsely, moving to kneel between her thighs.

Her scent hung heavily in the air like an aphrodisiac, and it drove him wild. Grabbing one of the pillows, he slid it under her hips, raising her lower body up off the floor. This gave him much better access to the wonderland in which he yearned to frolic.

Using his fingers to open the moist folds, he exposed her slick, wet bud. Slowly Jordan lowered his head to taste of her nectar. He made love to her core with his tongue, savoring the taste and feel of her. It was like nothing he had ever imagined—a very intimate and pleasing bond between them. He received just as much pleasure from it as she did.

More sweat dripped off Mia's body as Jordan's head remained buried between her thighs, the suckling noises he made echoing in the basement. She felt as if she were losing her mind. "Jordan, Jordan!" she sang, actually hitting a high note just before she began to buck wildly with another release.

He moved quickly to roll on one of the condoms before he plunged his shaft deeply into her throbbing sheath. It was the completion of two halves into a whole. A union of two souls. Spasm after spasm caused her to clutch and release against his tool. He tensed, battling for control, holding her close to him.

Mia clawed wildly at his back, his buttocks, and his head as she thrashed wildly beneath him, yelling his name at the top of her lungs. "Jor-dan! Jor-dan!"

Feeling his own waves of release reside, Jordan began to stroke deeply inside of her, adjusting his body to suck and lick the peaks of her globes. Every stroke was a bolt of lightning, threatening their sanity.

Mia moved her legs up until her knees touched her shoulders, causing Jordan to moan deeply at the tightened feel of her walls. Sweat dripped off his body onto her as they rocked together, finding a little piece of heaven right there on earth.

Mia felt her fourth climax rising, and she worked her hips up against his grinding to achieve it for both of them. "Jordan, I'm coming again, baby."

He sucked her raised chin, lightly dipping his tongue into her dimple. "Me too, baby. Me too."

His strokes deepened and quickened like a piston. "Mia!"

"Yes, baby. Come on, baby. Come for me."

"Mia."

"Come on, baby," she urged, looking up deeply into his eyes.

"Mia!"

"Jordan!"

As the O'Jays begged "Let Me Make Love to You,"

as only they could, Mia and Jordan both yelled out in unison as their release shook them. She grasped his sweat-drenched buttocks, pushing him farther inside of her sweetness, as she worked the muscles of her walls to draw every bit of his release out of him.

Exhausted and spent they slumped against each other, panting, their hearts beating wildly, their bodies slick with sweat and their sweet release. They were speechless.

Mia's eyes caressed Jordan as she watched him walk back from the small bathroom in the corner of the basement, a wet soapy washcloth in his hands. Words could not express what had just happened between them. It had been a connection beyond the physical.

As he cleansed her she intimately leaned up to kiss him. He looked down at her with a deeply intense gaze. Jordan said nothing as he moved under the covers to gather her naked body against his own.

They lay that way, quiet and reflective, in each other's arms long into the night. Mia couldn't help but wonder what Jordan had been thinking when he looked at her with such intensity.

Jordan looked down at Mia as she slept contentedly. He tried to fight the urge but let his finger trace the side of her beautiful face. He knew he could lie like this forever. There was so much still left unspoken between them. So much that he felt that scared him. Surely it was too soon for his feelings for her to be so strong.

But he missed her when she was away from his side. He wanted no other man to possess her. He respected her intelligence and cherished her relationship with his children. His heart pounded wildly whenever she entered his line of vision. Her laughter lifted his spirits.

His stomach clenched at the thought of her. No other woman could compete in his eyes. She was the one.

Mia stretched as Jordan shook her awake lightly. When he told her it might be best to carry this to her house, she readily agreed, thinking of the children. So they dressed, never more than a few inches from each other. Grabbing just the picnic basket and the bottle of champagne, they blew out the candles and turned on the lights before making their way up the stairs.

"What if it's not open?" Mia asked, thinking of how she had pounded and pleaded earlier with no success.

"Just after you woke me up I heard someone unlock the door."

Mia paused in her steps, her face incredulous. "And you didn't say anything?"

Jordan looked down at her. "Aren't you glad I didn't?" he asked, the meaning clear.

Mia dropped her gaze. "Very glad."

The door indeed was open, and they stepped out of their passion-filled prison for the first time in three glorious hours. Funny, neither was all too happy about their freedom now. Hand in hand they headed for the front door in the darkness.

She stopped. "What about the children, Jordan?"

"My father's here with them."

"Your father?"

"I'll tell you about it later."

Arm in arm they walked to Mia's house, entering through the back door she had left open in her haste to check on him. He insisted on going inside first to make sure there were no intruders lurking because of her thoughtlessness. Moments later he waved her in.

Mia was an independent woman, more than capable of taking care of herself, but it did feel good to have someone look out for her. It felt real nice.

Jordan had already turned on most of the lights when

he checked the house. They made their way upstairs to her bedroom. Once inside Mia headed straight for the bathroom and emerged moments later wearing the oversize T-shirt that she usually slept in. Jordan had laid out their picnic on the floor in front of her cold fireplace atop a throw cover from her bed.

She smiled at his thoughtfulness. "I am hungry. What do we have?"

"Remember, please, that neither my father nor the children are good cooks," he joked. "Let's see. There's fried chicken, dinner rolls, sandwiches, chips, and fresh fruit."

"It'll work."

They ate the meal laughing over Jordan's weak threats of punishment for his matchmaking children. He also filled her in on his father, whom Mia was now very anxious to meet. Surely he couldn't be as sexist as Jordan proclaimed. Not with an incredible son like Jordan.

After their feast Mia turned on the thirty-inch television in the corner while Jordan cleaned up. She found an Alfred Hitchcock movie on the late late movie. Together they snuggled on the bed, laying their heads at the foot in comfort.

Mia was sprawled on her stomach, a pillow bunched up under her chest as she watched the black-and-white mystery. Jordan lay next to her on his side, his hand resting on the small of her back.

During the movie Mia would look over at him, just happy to be able to share something so sweet but intimate with Jordan. A huge Hitchcock fan, she turned back to the movie again becoming engrossed in the story. It had been so long since she just chilled out and enjoyed watching a good movie. Tonight was a night for many firsts.

"Mia?"

"Hmm?"

"You don't have any underwear on under your shirt," he said, as if making a joyous discovery.

"No, I don't and hush up, I'm watching my movie."

Jordan moved on the bed to kneel over her prone figure. "Well, just keep watching your movie. Don't mind me."

"I'm not paying you any attention, believe me."

He lifted the oversize T-shirt to massage the back of her thighs with his strong hands. Mia caught a moan that almost spilled over her lips. *Now that feels so gooooood!*

Jordan leaned over and began to suck her buttocks, his hand dipping between the small junction between her thick thighs to feel the wetness he already knew was there. He smiled in satisfaction as he extracted a glistening wet finger.

Mia fought hard to ignore the good vibrations he was causing. She strained to keep her face blank as she looked at the screen with feigned interest.

"You still watching the movie, right? I wouldn't want to interrupt it." He lifted her T-shirt over her head.

Mia counted to three for composure before she spoke. "I sure am."

"Okay."

Jordan removed another of the trusty condoms that had proven to come in handy. He put it on after he stripped, flinging his clothes in a ball across the room. Naked he lay on top of her, the soft swell of her buttocks cupping his arousal like a bun. He bit his lips to keep from yelling out.

Struggling for control he licked her shoulder, grinding his hard length into the soft mounds of her cheeky flesh. Using his knee he opened her legs beneath him. With a shaking hand Jordan probed her moist flesh before finally finding the sweetest place on earth.

His mouth framed an *O* at the feel of her heaven as he used his hips to push deep inside of this incredible woman. It was everything. All at once. Sweetness. Softness. Heat.

Jordan closed his eyes, sliding his hands under her

soft body to grasp her breasts, his fingers massaging the now swollen nipples.

When he opened his eyes, Mia's head was to the side, her pillow in her mouth as she bit down, trying to control her own passion. Laughing huskily he asked, "You still watching that movie, baby?"

Mia began to roll her hips upward under his, now matching his strokes. "To hell with that movie."

Mia didn't know what woke her first, the persistent buzzing of her alarm at 5:00 A.M. or Jordan's loud snoring in her ear. Either way, she was up, and she had to get to work.

Somehow today she just wasn't that anxious to see the steel and granite of Stromer, Wiler. Discussing mergers and acquisitions, asset allocations, dividend reinvestment plans, and portfolios was not the most exciting aspect of her life. The man lying behind her, cuddled in the spoon position, was the reason for that.

But work was work. She had to be there and on time. Mia moved to get out of bed but an arm, surprisingly strong in sleep, grasped her around her waist like a band of steel. When Jordan's hand dipped down to play in the soft curly hairs between her legs, she knew he was awake.

Before Mia could speak Jordan lifted her leg up over his arm. Soon his protected hardened mass filled her slowly and Mia's head rocked back against his shoulder, caught up in his passion. He filled her completely. He nuzzled her neck, licking circles that drove her wild as they both moved their hips to unite his shaft inside of her sheath, again and again.

They spoke no words, their bodies said it all as Jordan stroked Mia's body to a shuddering climax. She tightened and released her walls. She knew his own climax was near as he tensed. His hands wildly teased her aching nipples, his mouth sucked at the back of her neck as he growled with unleashed passion. With strength and passion, he stroked deep into her pulsating core one last time.

They stayed together that way—united, falling back asleep. Mia knew, as her eyes drifted closed and her breathing slowed, that for the first time ever she would be late for work. She didn't care.

Eleven

Mia's view was particularly scenic with skies a perfect shade of azure and clouds that looked as if they were formed from cotton. The water rippled from the surprising morning breeze beneath a sun that was a brilliant shade of gold. It all seemed surreal. The perfect backdrop for relaxation.

It was just too bad that Mia's current telephone conversation was just about to ruin it.

"Mother—" Mia tried unsuccessfully to interject into her mother's tirade.

"I don't understand you, Mia. Can you imagine how foolish I felt when Dr. Blanchard told me you had broken it off with him?" Clara sighed. "First off, why didn't you tell me before I had my appointment with him today? Secondly, why'd you do it?"

Mia rubbed her temple with her free hand. "Mother, my personal business is my concern."

"Oh, I see," Clara said, sounding hurt. "I'm only your mother, Mia Renée Gordon."

Oh no, not my full name! She leaned back in her chair, preparing something to say to appease her mother's hurt.

"First, you won't move out of that jungle of a city and you bought a house there—"

"A home you've only been to once," Mia countered tightly.

Clara continued as if Mia hadn't spoken. "I arrange

for you to meet a good man and what do you do, the same thing you've been doing your whole adult life, mess it up. We got along so much better when you were a child who listened to her mother."

That hurt, but Mia laughed it off huskily to help diminish the stinging pain she felt. "Nothing says I love you like good old-fashioned criticism, huh, Ma?"

"I'm only trying to help you, Mia. Dr. Blanchard is a good man—"

"Then why don't you date him?"

"Child, you are insane!"

Well, it must run in the family. "The limb doesn't fall too far from the tree," she muttered, rubbing her hand over her eyes, which were tight with tension.

"Are you calling me crazy?"

Mia could see her mother with one of her eyes squinted, and her head rotating as she asked that question. *"You* called me crazy. Look, Mama, I'll call you tomorrow, okay?" she lied.

"No, you won't, but I'll let you get off the line anyway. Your father wants to see you. You are going to visit us sometime soon?"

It had been a while since she'd seen her parents and she would love to spend some time with her father. "I'll stop by this weekend sometime. I don't see why you two can't come visit me again."

"You want me to come to Newark! You're lucky I made it out when you first moved in."

Mia rolled her eyes heavenward in exasperation. "Mama, you were born and raised in Newark, so why put on all those airs?" she said, sighing. *Lawd save us from the bourgie!*

"I don't know what's gotten into you. Whatever crawled up your little sassy behind, you need to poop it out and get over it. You hear?"

"I'll see you this weekend, Mother."

"If you know like I do, you better call Dr. Blanchard."

"Bye, Mother."

Mia immediately stood and crossed the carpeted floor to lock her office. Her shoulders and neck were so tense, a headache was steadily creeping up on her. After informing her secretary, via the intercom, that she wanted no interruptions for the next fifteen minutes she kicked off her red leather pumps and slipped out of her tailored red linen jacket. There was only one way to try to erase the tension her mother had brought into her life. Mia pulled one of her armless chairs from in front of her desk to lock into place in front of her view. With long-time experience and ease she folded her legs into position after she took a seat, and turned her palms up. She stared into the waters, breathing slowly, deeply, and calmly.

Deadly Deal, his eighth mystery novel, was complete, and Jordan was definitely in the mood to celebrate. He loved writing a new novel; it was like the creation of a child. But there was nothing like the feeling of accomplishment when it was completely finished. Now he would have plenty of free time to spend with his family.

This would also mean more time for Mia. But only if she would make him feel as though she was willing to share more of herself and her time with him. Last week they shared an explosive night of passion that lasted until she left for work almost two hours behind schedule. But that seemed to be the only aspect of their "relationship" that had changed.

Each night after she got home from work she would call him, and he would slip over to her house to share the most thrilling sex he had ever known. It was like floating over heaven, but then she would send him home with excuses of work she brought from the office that had to be completed. He hated sharing something so profound and intimate with her only to have to go home alone to sleep in his bed with nothing but thoughts of her as his companion. He was starting to feel like a studhorse, only suited for pleasing her physically. Emotionally she kept her distance from him after that first night. If only he could say the same.

He had envisioned them on a whole new level together. He had looked forward to leisurely walks in the park, romantic dinner dates, Sunday afternoons relaxing with the children, and many sultry nights in her arms. Unfortunately, one out of four was bad.

He had even pondered asking her to take time off work to go with him and the children on their annual week long vacation to Disneyworld. Doubts plagued him though. Would Mia be willing to take a week off from her precious job?

Just the other night, when he managed to slip in a conversation with her before she banished him to his house, Mia had admitted to him that she hadn't taken a real vacation since she joined Stromer, Wiler. He had been surprised—no, amazed—no, shocked, definitely shocked. He loved writing, but even he could look forward to a break from it every now and then. Mia was truly a workaholic.

Jordan stood and stretched, his bones cracking lightly as he did. He wondered if anything would ever be as important to Mia as work. She didn't even discuss her parents on a regular basis. Only business acquisitions and new clients seemed to dominate her conversation. He respected the intelligence, drive, and hard work it took for her career to be so successful, and he would never expect her to give it up. Scaling back a bit couldn't hurt, though, could it?

Twice this week she canceled dinner plans they made because of work. "At least she called this time," he muttered, balling up a piece of paper to fling across the room missing the wastepaper basket by a very long shot.

"What's up, Dad?"

Jordan whirled around to see his son leaning against the doorway of his open office door, casually attired in a white tank top and oversize Nautica jean shorts. "How was the movie?"

Rajahn twirled the basketball he had under his arm up onto his finger. "Cool, except when Grandpa almost got us thrown out of the theater."

Jordan groaned. "What happened?"

"Grandpa didn't agree with the end of the movie and started yelling at the screen," Rajahn said, laughing.

"Where is my father?"

Raised voices filtered from the kitchen down the hall. Jordan looked over at his son, who just shook his head with a crooked smile. "Never mind," Jordan said, instantly figuring it out.

He headed straight toward the commotion, nearly tripping over the ball Rajah accidentally let slip from his hands. After kicking it out of the way in frustration he continued, his son directly on his heels. His mouth dropped open in shock when he reached the entrance to the kitchen.

Jordan knew he shouldn't laugh but he did anyway. "Now, I didn't know my daddy was a *white* man."

Clinton's black eyes shot daggers at his son beneath the cloud of flour covering his head. "Jor—dan," he warned in a tone that had worked when his son was young.

Rajahn squeezed past his father to step into the kitchen. His laughter joined his father's. "Looks more like Ghost Dad to me."

Ms. McKnight sucked her teeth, the telltale empty bag once holding the flour still in her hand. "He's a jackass, plain and simple," she snapped.

Jordan stopped laughing, and elbowed his son to do the same. He became more respectful to the anger she obviously felt. "What happened?"

Clinton began to shake the flour off his head and shoulders with his hands, causing the white powder to rise like a cloud around him. "All I did was ask her what she was cooking, and she slugged me with that bag of flour."

"Liar!"

"Old hag!"

"Pervert!"

"Shrew!"

"Retard!"

"Okay, okay. Enough!" Jordan yelled, coming to stand between the two as they squared off. "What happened, Ms. McKnight?" he asked, wanting something closer to the truth than what his father said.

She shot Clinton one last hateful glare over Jordan's shoulder before purposefully focusing on Jordan's face. "That good-for-nothing—"

"Ms. McKnight," Jordan said.

"Okay. He came into the kitchen and grabbed my . . . my . . . behind"—she whispered the last word "—and asked me 'What's cooking in this kitchen besides you? heh heh heh.' "

Jordan had to hide a smile at the sound of her imitating his father's voice, and quite well at that. "I'm sorry, Ms. McKnight. I will speak to my father again about appropriate behavior. I'm sure he's just bursting with apologies."

Clinton ignored the meaningful hard stare his son cast in his direction. "Oh, if I massaged it the right way she'd be purring like a kitten and not spitting like a she-devil."

Rajahn laughed, bringing him a hard look from his father. "Sorry," he mumbled, biting his bottom lip.

Ms. McKnight stomped her foot in frustration, before using the torn flour bag to reach around Jordan quickly and slap Clinton upside his head again. "You need Jesus!"

Rajahn jumped out of the way as she stormed out of the kitchen. "You've really done it this time, Grandpa."

Clinton brushed more flour off his body. "One helluva woman, isn't she?" he asked with a smile, winking at his son and grandson.

"Dad, why do you tease her that way?"

"Son, I haven't lived to be sixty-three to still be as dumb as when I was twelve. That woman loves to see me coming," he answered with confidence.

"Dad, I'm going to have to ask you to keep your hands to yourself. I need her to help with your grandchildren, and I won't have her quit because you're sexually harassing her every time you visit."

"I'll keep my hands off," Clinton acquiesced, making Jordan feel somewhat better. "But she'll sure be missing it."

That last bit caused Jordan to shake his head wearily. He sighed. "Whatever, Dad. Do you remember when you used to tell me 'You'll catch more bees with honey than vinegar'?"

"Point made," Clinton answered after a thoughtful moment.

"Good."

The girls' day camp van's horn blew outside, and Jordan heard Ms. McKnight open the door, assuring the driver that someone was home before he allowed the girls to leave the safety of the van. Moments later they all entered the kitchen with Ms. McKnight bringing up the rear, purposefully avoiding looking at Clinton.

The girls all looked at their grandfather with a wide-eyed expression. The twins laughed behind their hands. Kimani's wise eyes took in the bag now empty on the floor and the splattered flour on Ms. McKnight's hand, instantly putting two and two together. "Grandpa, you've been teasing Ms. M again, haven't you?"

Tia reached up to brush his flour-filled beard. "That would explain him looking like the Ghost of Christmas Past," she smirked.

"Yes, I was teasing Ms. McKnight, and I was just about to tell her how sorry I am." Clinton walked over to stand in front of her. "I apologize. Every man must know when to draw the line of improper behavior instead of crossing it."

Jordan watched as Ms. McKnight smiled like a schoolgirl up at his father. *Funny,* he thought, *I think I can hear the distinct buzz of bees surrounding Dad!*

"On your mark, get set . . . go!"

Kimani, Tia, and Rajahn all jumped into the pool at the lowering of their father's raised arms. He cheered them on as they swam to the other end of the pool. The twins were frolicking in the inflatable baby pool with toys. But they looked on at their older siblings' glee, cheering them on as well.

Tia stretched out her arms to touch the side of the pool first before thrusting her body up through the water, her arm raised in victory. She had always been the best swimmer of the bunch. She was a natural in water. Rajahn and Kimani congratulated her before they all swam leisurely back to where their father stood at the other end.

"Good job, Tia," Jordan told her, reaching to help her out of the water first.

She looked up at him with a mischievous glint in her slanted eyes. "Thanks, Daddy-O."

When she reached up to take his hand, she tugged with all her strength, sending him flying into the azure depths with a surprised yell.

The children all laughed as Jordan came sputtering to the surface. Clinton glanced over at his son from where he was grilling hot dogs and steaks. "Tia got you good that time, son," he hollered, joining in the merriment.

This was the scene Mia walked up on still dressed in her office gear, her briefcase swinging by her side as her Jones New York leather pumps clicked on the asphalt. She had heard the fun as soon as she got out of her car and walked over to see what her favorite family had on the agenda for the evening. She smiled at the sight of Jordan fully dressed and soaking wet as he pulled himself out of the pool. The T-shirt he wore clung to every well-defined muscle of his chest and back. He truly was a fine male specimen, and she immediately felt her body respond hotly at the sight of him. She craved to be in his arms again.

On impulse she sneaked up behind him, holding her finger over her mouth to keep Clinton from alerting his son to her presence. The children saw her and also fell quiet. Mia set her briefcase on a lounge chair before walking up to Jordan. She tapped him lightly on the back. "Boo!"

Jordan whirled and froze in surprise at the sight of Mia, who with a devilish smile and a saucy wink used her index finger to push him right back into the pool. Her laughter was abruptly cut short as Jordan grabbed her arm, pulling her into the cool azure depths with him.

"Aaaahhh," she shrieked.

They sank together but when they rocketed to the top they were in each other's arms locked in a sweet kiss filled with longing. Jordan pushed Mia's wet strands out of her beautiful face. "One good dunk deserves another," he said lightly.

Mia looked deeply into his eyes before laughing. "Truce?"

"Truce."

The children all looked on with bright smiles at their father and Ms. Gordon. They all could see the happiness they shared in their faces. This was a part of what they had plotted and planned for. There was still another hurdle to get over: making Mia an official member of the family.

Mia stretched her long curvaceous frame beneath the thin sheet feeling relaxed and sated. When Jordan pulled her body to his for a tight hug she nearly purred from the good feeling. In fact the feeling was too good. Addictive even.

"I'll be so glad when I'm done with this newest acquisition," she began with another stretch against the length of his body. "I do believe this is the hardest account I've ever worked on."

Jordan stiffened because he knew what was coming next. It was becoming as predictable as rain in April. He remained quiet as he waited for her to drop the "Baby, I'm sorry but I have to work" line. Well, he had a surprise for her. He was not in the mood for it tonight.

Mia rolled away from the warmth and strength of his body to rise from the bed. Jordan was becoming like an addiction to her. Her body craved him. Those feelings were not a part of her plan. "I probably won't get to have some real sleep until well after midnight, just like last night."

Jordan watched her from where he lay naked on her bed, sweaty and spent with his legs tangled with the Egyptian cotton sheets. She walked naked and proud to the adjoining bathroom. Even with his rising hurt and anger he couldn't help but admire the smooth, sleek, and curvaceous lines of her body. She was the epitome of a sexy and alluring woman.

But that didn't stop his irritation at being just a sexual tool to her. He kicked off the covers in frustration. They had just shared the most incredible sex and now her mind was already refocused on working. "Mia," he called out shortly.

She emerged from the bathroom, her glorious body hidden beneath the short blood-red kimono she wore. "Yes, Jordan?"

He looked into her beautiful face, long and hard, the sound of the shower loud and clear in the background. He knew that she would hop right in, without inviting him, wash and change into sweats, and walk him to the door with a brief kiss before heading straight to her office.

Well, not tonight!

"Yes, Jordan?" she asked again.

"What time do we share together outside of hot, passionate sex in this bedroom?"

Mia looked at him with an incredulous expression on her beautiful face. "So what are you implying?"

"That beyond my sending you into ecstasy physically, you have no use for me," he said simply, although his eyes bore into her like nails. "I feel used."

Her gasp of shock mirrored the look on her face. "Get real, Jordan."

He sat up in bed. "I think if you could disconnect this"—he gestured toward his penis—"and not bother with me, you would."

Mia looked away from the truth uncomfortably, before turning to walk back into the bathroom. "I see why you're a best-selling author. Your imagination runs wild."

Jordan jumped up and his limbs tangled with the sheets, causing him to go flying face forward on the floor. Darts of pain shot through almost every part of his body as he moaned. When he opened his eyes it was to look directly at her perfectly manicured feet.

Mia squatted and the erotic scent of her womanhood surrounded him, along with a rather up-close and personal look at her treasure. "You know what, Jordan?" she asked, as she lightly touched the side of his face.

"What?"

"Tia's right. One of these days you're gonna . . ."

"I know, I know. Kill myself, right?"

They both laughed and their anger dissipated like a fine mist. Unfortunately the truth of his words still rang like a hollow bell. She offered her hand to him, pulling him to a standing position.

Jordan captured Mia's upturned face. "Mia, you are a dynamic and vibrant woman. Your intelligence stimulates me, your beauty enthralls me, your caring nature nurtures me, and your wit humors me like no other.

You are too special a woman for me to be satisfied with just exploring your physical attributes—as wonderful and explosive as they may be. I need more . . . I want more, Mia."

The intensity and truth of his words shone brightly in the liquid depths of his mocha eyes. Mia was intrigued by what she saw. She was touched by his words and warmed by his touch. *God, I can get so lost in this man,* she thought as she turned her face into the palm of his hand.

Fear and excitement dwelled within her. This man was like no other. Special. One of a kind. Incomparable. Peerless. Many women would love to be in her place right now. So why wasn't she relishing the moment instead of dwelling in her fears?

Jordan pulled her into his arms, holding her close to him. They fit perfectly together. His hand massaged the back of her neck beneath the curly curtain of her hair. "Let me show you how it can be—no, should be—between us."

Mia inhaled deeply of that erotic scent in the hollow of his neck. At that moment everything seemed so possible, so believable . . . so right.

"Show me, Jordan," she said softly, her breath fanning against his neck, "but please don't let me down."

"I won't, sweetheart. I swear."

Jordan stripped off his clothing, not bothering with his usual bedtime garb of pajama bottoms and T-shirt. The cool crisp sheets felt good against his naked skin although sleep eluded him. Thoughts and visions of Mia were uppermost. Tomorrow held many prospects for his future with the beautiful and vibrant woman from next door.

Tonight he hadn't minded as much when she brought up that she still had work to complete. Not with tomorrow night on the horizon. He had so many plans. He was going to romance her. He was going to sweep her off her pretty feet. He had to.

Even as he dreamed of uniting with Mia in a lasting and bonding way, innocent comments she had made plagued him:

That's why I haven't started a family yet. I worry that I won't be able to give children the time they need.

Okay, he knew that Mia was career-oriented and set in the ways of a single, independent woman. But she loved his kids. Just look at how she kept the girls' hair braided every two weeks, or how she supported Rajahn in his extracurricular activities.

Yes, but . . .

I could never imagine myself being able to cope with five children.

No! He couldn't be discouraged. Fate had seemed to have drawn them together, along with some help from the children. He just had to make her realize that her future held something more substantial than building on an already successful career. Her future was with him and five wonderful children who loved her to death. He had to make her realize that she could have it all: career, family, and love.

This was the opportunity he had been waiting for. He would do whatever was in his power to make her see that this connection between them was unique and not to be ignored or belittled.

Mia rubbed her eyes and leaned back in the chair away from her computer. She couldn't work, even as badly as she wanted and needed to. How could she when she was filled with trepidation about her date with Jordan tomorrow?

Okay, so they had put the carriage before the horse by becoming physically involved before actually dating. Even if it wasn't a real first date, that didn't quell the butterflies fluttering around busily in her abdomen.

Who knew when she bought her dream house in her hometown that all her well-organized plans would go awry? Somehow five beautiful children and one hopelessly clumsy author had woven themselves within her intricate plans.

Instinctively she knew tomorrow night—her very real first date with Jordan—was the start of something new between them. So if she had so many doubts why did she look forward to it like a child on the eve of Christmas?

Twelve

"So tonight's the big night, huh?"

Mia jumped in her seat, surprised by Reese's sudden appearance in her office. "Girl, you scared the crap out of me!" she exclaimed.

Tyresa shrugged her slender shoulders. "Sorry, but you were staring off into space again. Thinking about your big date?"

Mia watched as the other woman took a seat on the edge of her desk. "Jordan just called to remind me. He said he didn't want to get stood up again."

"Can you blame him?"

"Ha, ha, Reese."

"So what does Mr. Banks have planned?"

"I don't know," Mia said, picking up the gold frame holding the computer-generated thank-you card that Kimani had made for her. "He said it's a very special surprise."

Reese looked impressed. "Lucky you. I love surprises."

"I don't."

"Don't I know it," she mumbled under her breath.

Mia looked at her sharply. "What was that, buddy o'mine?"

"Look, Mia, your life does not always have to be planned down to the minute." Reese reached over and tapped her long slender finger against her friend's nose. "Remember, just go with the flow. Okay?"

Mia looked uncertain. "Just go with the flow, huh?"

She nodded. "Let him worry about all the plans and details. Let him spoil you the way he obviously wants to. Just enjoy yourself. Not only do you deserve a night like this one, you *need* it."

"You know what?" Mia asked softly. "You're right."

Reese scoffed. "I usually am."

Jordan replaced the phone. Everything was set. All his plans were under way. Tonight he would woo Mia. He smiled in satisfaction as he thought of the pleasure with which he would bless her. She deserved all of it and so much more.

"What has you smiling like a Cheshire Cat?"

He grinned even more broadly at his father, his hands folded behind his handsome head as he leaned casually back in his chair. "Mia," he answered simply.

"It's good to see you happy, son," Clinton said, a very familiar grin on his handsome face as he took the seat in front of Jordan's cluttered desk. "You are happy?"

Jordan looked into the eyes that were so like his own. He saw concern in the depths. Had his father picked up on the varying levels of emotional involvement Mia and he had invested in their "relationship"? Yes, he felt that his feelings for her ran a lot deeper than hers for him. But he was patient. He had time. She was worth the wait.

Realizing his father was waiting for an answer, Jordan said, "Yeah, I'm happy."

Clinton nodded. "If you're happy, then so am I."

"Believe me, Dad, right now I'm floating on cloud nine.

"Daddy! Dad—dy! Mia just pulled up!"

Jordan winced visibly in his private bathroom as all of his girls yelled in unison to alert him to Mia's arrival.

Some of the tight tension of his abdominal muscles eased a bit. *At least she's home on time this time.*

He would admit only to himself that he had been worried about work claiming all of her attention again tonight. "So far so good," he mumbled as he walked over to his closet. He laid his suit, tie, and shirt on his bed.

Seconds later the phone began to ring. He made a quick reach for it before one of his nosy kids could get to it. "Hello."

"Next time tell the girls to close the windows if they're gonna yell out my arrival."

Jordan laughed, his eyes crinkling at the corner. "They were that loud, huh?"

"Yup," she answered emphatically with humor in her husky tone.

"They're very excited about our date tonight," he told her dryly, as he sank on the edge of the bed, not mindful that he was wrinkling his suit.

"Well, then we all have something in common."

His heart hammered in his chest at her husky tone, and her implied meaning. "Then my vote makes it u-nanimous."

"Good."

"How soon can you be ready?"

"Anxious?"

"I'm very anxious to be in the company of the most beautiful woman I've ever laid these four eyes upon."

Mia laughed huskily. "I'll be ready in an hour."

"Thirty minutes," he insisted. "It's already after seven."

"Forty-five," she bargained.

"Deal."

Mia put the finishing touches on the elaborate up-sweep. The style brought out her eyes and the elegant long lines of her slender neck.

With one last pat she stood from the cushioned bench in front of her glass-and-brass vanity table. Her skin glistened from a long steaming bath and a luxurious pampering with Pleasures scented lotion and perfume. All she needed to do was choose an outfit. She had narrowed her choices down to two.

"Okay, ladies, which should it be? The lavender knit dress by Kevan Hall of Halston or the black knit dress by FUBU?" Mia picked up both from the edge of the bed, turning to face her very own miniature ladies-in-waiting.

Four sets of eyes scrutinized both dresses. Mia was leaning toward the lavender because it was her favorite color, but the black fit her shape nicely and was a bit more daring.

Tia spoke up first, of course. "The black would be nice—for a funeral," she finished dryly.

Kimani rolled her eyes heavenward. "Must you be so overly critical all the time, Tia?" she snapped, pushing her glasses up in irritation.

Mia smelled an argument brewing and moved quickly to calm the waters. "Focus, ladies. Focus. Which dress?"

"The wavender," the twins said in unison around the plump thumbs in their mouths.

Mia nodded and turned to the two older siblings. At their nods of agreement she carelessly flung the costly black ensemble back onto the pile of clothes on the bed. "The lovely lavender Halston it is then."

Jordan checked his appearance one last time before turning to his father and son for their approval. Clinton gave him the thumbs-up from where he lounged on the bed and Rajahn made an okay signal.

He was ready.

Ready for his first date with a beautiful woman. Ready to romance her. Ready to be with her. Ready to love her.

Question was: Was she ready for him?

* * *

"You wook pretty, Ms. Gordon," Amina said, her neon green Teletubbie clutched to her chubby side.

Mia twirled one last time for the girls, and they all smiled in approval. Their watching her and helping her get ready felt so much as if they were really her daughters.

"I just hope your father thinks so."

"Oh, he will," Kimani said with confidence.

"I'm gwad you're gonna be our mommy, Ms. Gordon," Aliya offered.

Mia's eyes widened in surprise. But before she could explain to the little girl that a date with her father didn't mean they would be married, the doorbell chimed. All of the girls went racing out of the bedroom. The sounds of their sneakered feet clamoring down the stairs echoed loudly.

Turning she faced her reflection. "Ready or not, Jordan, here we go," she said softly, before leaving the room as well.

Jordan's breath caught in his throat at the sight of her as she stood at the top of the staircase. She was breathtaking—from her upswept hair of riotous curls to the stunning lavender dress she wore. The color perfectly offset her beautiful bronzed skin.

The form-fitting knit dress had long delicate sleeves with a daring square neckline. The material tastefully but sexily outlined her full breasts, slender waist, and rounded hips before stopping at a hemline just above her knees and never-ending legs. The matching lavender strappy heels she wore accentuated her slender ankles and pedicured feet.

Who knew a dress so seemingly simple could look so devastating? Hell, this woman could bring a potato sack to life with that body!

"Daddy, doesn't Ms. Gordon look good?" Tia prompted, as she nudged him with her shoulder. She didn't understand that her father was quiet because he was awestruck.

He nodded as Mia slowly descended the stairs. Each step brought her closer to him, allowing him to inhale her unique scent, to feast upon her beauty face-to-face, to have her in his arms.

Mia didn't need words to know that Jordan was mesmerized by her. She saw it all in his eyes and was heated by it.

"Ready?" he asked, as she stepped directly in front of him.

He looked so masculine, handsome, and virile that she was dumbstruck herself. All she could do was nod as he brought a beautifully arranged bouquet of two dozen lavender roses from behind his back.

Clinton waved off the happy couple from where he stood on his son's porch. If everything his boy planned worked out, then Mia was in for a very special evening indeed. He was impressed by his son's romantic spirit. It inspired him.

He entered the house, quickly looking in on the children, gathered in their playroom. Clinton entered his son's office, slipping into the leather chair. He looked beneath the clutter of paper and discarded cups for the telephone.

Seven digits later the line began to ring. He smiled at the sound of the voice on the other end. "Hello, Minnie. Clinton here."

"Clinton?" she asked, mildly surprised. "Is everything okay with Jordan and the children?"

He laughed, his fingers lightly dancing across the keyboard. "Everything's fine. In fact Jordan and Mia just left for a romance-filled night."

"Good. I'm glad," she said with pleasure, her love for the couple evident.

Clinton cleared his throat, surprised at the nervousness he now felt. "I didn't call you to talk about my son's love life."

Silence reigned supreme for a few long seconds before she answered. "Why did you call? I'm certainly not in the mood for one of your wisecracks, Clinton Banks."

"No, no, it's nothing like that at all," he rushed to assure her. "I'm calling about . . . well, you and me serious like. How about it?"

Her answer brought a huge cocky grin to his handsome face. With renewed confidence he propped his legs right atop the clutter and leaned back in the chair. A very long and fulfilling conversation ensued. He knew he was definitely not in any rush to get back to Virginia now.

"Just where are we going, Jordan?" Mia asked, her voice revealing just how relaxed she felt as the SUV cruised under his direction.

"We're almost there."

Mia felt cherished, and they hadn't even left the confines of the sports utility vehicle. During the drive Jordan had caressed her hand as the melodic sounds of Marvin Gaye filled the vehicle.

During many of the songs, their voices blended softly as they accompanied the music. They would look over into each other's eyes, holding hands, just enjoying each other's company.

Jordan slowed down. "Almost there."

Mia's eyes widened in surprise when he pulled into the crowded parking lot of Mahogany's. The downtown restaurant and bar was popular for its live jazz music.

The restaurant's decor, food, and atmosphere cleverly showed the music's influence. In just two years it had garnered quite a reputation. Mia couldn't wait to hear the live band, sip a margarita, and enjoy the jambalaya that was the buzz.

Jordan had chosen well for their first date, and he could see the pleasure in her face. But the night had just begun, and the best was yet to come. "Our table awaits," he said with a flourish before tucking her hand under his arm.

Mahogany's was located in a renovated brick building, which once housed a factory. The two-level structure's almost plain exterior gave those who entered quite a surprise. The atmosphere was warm and comfortable, and the contemporary decor inviting with its deep mahogany, rich vibrant blues, and gold accents perfectly bringing the artfully decorated brick walls to life. The hardwood dance floor and stage were on the lower level with a classy wrought-iron spiral staircase leading to the similarly decorated dining area upstairs.

The place was alive with the sound of soft, sultry music, dancing, and people who were having a good time. Mia loved it instantly. "I could stay here all night," she whispered to Jordan as they followed the hostess up the staircase to a great table right on a balcony overlooking the stage.

Jordan reached for her hands across the table. "As long as you are with me, I don't care where I am," he said with sincerity, the candles from the brass centerpiece flickering in the depths of his eyes.

Mia's face infused with heat, and she just squeezed his hands tighter. She didn't have a chance to speak as the waitress appeared at their table. Mia looked surprised by the bottle of champagne she carried with two gold-rimmed crystal flutes.

"Hello, Mia and Jordan. My name is Tanika, and I'll be your waitress for the evening," she said with a warm,

comforting smile on her pretty face. "If you don't re-
quire anything, I'll be right back with your first course."

And she was gone. Mia turned back to Jordan. "How
did she know our names? Well, you're a famous writer
but I know she's never seen or heard of me. And our
orders, how does she know what—"

Jordan quieted her with a finger to her lips that
caused her to shiver. "I called ahead to place our orders.
I hope you don't mind?"

Mia shook her head as she watched him skillfully
pour the vintage champagne. "No, I don't mind. May
I ask what you ordered? No, let me guess, it's a surprise,
right?"

He laughed deep and husky before handing her a
flute. "That's right. All you have to do is sit back and
wait to be served. Trust me."

Mia smiled before she slowly sipped the liquid. "I
do."

And everything turned out to be divine. The music
was soft and alluring. The service was top-notch with
Tanika bringing every course and meeting every wish
while still giving them privacy. And the food was scrump-
tious. Jordan had chosen well and impressed Mia to no
end. She particularly enjoyed the roasted red snapper
with oyster and mushroom stuffing.

During their dinner they spoke of everything, filling
each other in on just about every detail of their lives.
He had even massaged her feet under the table, totally
unaware that the feel of his hands drove her past the
brink of sanity. What was between them was chemistry.
Electricity. Destiny.

They were sipping after-dinner drinks and holding
each other's hands as they looked down on the band.
Suddenly Jordan stood. "Dance with me?"

Mia forced herself not to envision Jordan being a
total klutz on the floor as she took his hand and let him
guide her to the crowded dance area. He positioned
them right near the front, pulling her into his arms

with more skill and ease than she would have guessed he possessed.

She wrapped her arms around his neck and pressed the length of her body close to his. She enjoyed how it felt as if her body fit his like a key to a lock, and she sighed in pleasure as she snuggled her face in that spot in the crook of his neck with which she was becoming obsessed.

Slowly they danced, their bodies moving in unison. It almost felt as if they were making sweet, slow, passionate love. It was as if no one existed in their world but them as they moved, their eyes closed as they imagined just that. Their hearts beating a similar tatoo against each other's chest. Their souls releasing emotions that were too strong to be denied. It all felt so right. So beautiful. So meant to be.

Even after the band slowly ended the song, they remained in each other's arms, unaware of the eyes that looked upon them. The younger couples yearned for the connection they saw between Mia and Jordan. The older couples smiled fondly and reminisced on their days of young passionate unions.

"We'll be taking a fifteen-minute break before the next set," the bandleader said into the microphone.

It broke the spell that Mia and Jordan had cast upon each other. Slowly and reluctantly they broke apart but didn't move too far from each other.

Mia caressed his cheek. "Jordan, this night has been absolutely perfect. Thank you."

He lowered his head to quickly capture a brief but sweet kiss. "I'm not done yet. You ready to go?"

"It's your night. I'm completely in your hands," she said softly, enjoying being spoiled.

"Okay, sit here," he said, guiding her to an empty table. "I'll be right back."

She watched as he climbed the stairs. He gave Tanika money and she passed him a small blue paper bag with

Mahogany's emblazoned on the side in gold. Soon he was back by Mia's side and leading her out the door.

"I'm stuffed. How about a stroll to walk off some of the food?" he asked, his arm draped around her waist.

"That would be nice."

They left the car in Mahogany's private parking lot and made their way down Broad Street. "I should have ordered dessert," Mia said, as she gazed up at the star-filled night of the metropolis. "I would have loved a big slice of—"

"Let me guess, banana-and-toasted-almond cream pie."

Mia looked over at him in surprise. "How'd you know that?"

"I'm right, aren't I?" he asked with confidence.

"Yes."

"I know you, that's all there is to it," he said, coming to a stop on the corner. "Now you have to close your eyes for your next surprise."

Mia looked up into his handsome face, giving in quickly to the urge to taste his lips. "More?"

"Lots more."

Jordan tied a bandanna around her eyes so that she wouldn't cheat. Carefully he guided her to their destination, ignoring her pleas to tell her what the big secret was. He couldn't wait to see the pleasure on her face. So far the night was going even better than he had planned.

Mia tried to figure out where in the world in downtown Newark he could be taking her at nine o'clock. For every possible thought she got she just as quickly dismissed it. She did know that they crossed the street twice and that they had entered a building and then rode up on an elevator.

Jordan's hands were warm and assuring on her arms as she heard a door open and close behind them. "Okay, Jordan, please let me look. Enough of the darkness," she pleaded. "We have to be there. Are we?"

But on they continued. "Step up once," he advised.

She did as he said and was soon engulfed by the scent of something sweet and exotic. Seconds later the blindfold was removed. After her eyes adjusted to the sudden light, she gasped in pure pleasure at what she saw. Immediately she turned into his arms and kissed him with all the passion he evoked from her.

If it were at all possible to re-create the Garden of Eden, then Jordan had successfully done it in a simple hotel room. The lights were dim with plenty of aromatic candles lit for illumination, giving the spacious bathroom a soft, romantic glow. Flowers of every color and variety filled every available space, including a rose petal trail to the sunken tub in the middle of the tiled floor. It was a den of delectation.

The music from the stereo continued Marvin Gaye's serenade softly from the corner as Jordan moved his hands slowly and seductively to unzip her dress. "You have never looked as beautiful as you do tonight in this dress," he said softly, blessing her with a kiss at the base of her slender neck as the garment fell to a lavender pool at her feet among the petals. "But you definitely are bewitching like this."

Carefully he bent over to remove her sandals, before rising to take her hand. He led her like a goddess to the tub. Following his lead she stepped into it, the bottom covered with more petals that tickled her bottom as she sat down.

Jordan turned the bathwater on slowly to an invitingly warm temperature. Soon lavender-scented bubbles began to shield her nude beauty from his eyes.

Mia sighed in pleasure at the feel of the warm water and the soothing scent of lavender, sinking down beneath the slowly rising depths around her body. "Oh, Jordan, this is divine," she purred.

Slowly he undressed, removing each article of clothing in sync to Marvin's sultry serenade. The candles cast a bronze tint to his skin. Disrobed and unashamed he knelt by the tub on a plush towel, planting a kiss on her eagerly awaiting lips as he turned off the water. Mia eyed him heatedly, awestruck by his glorious nude body.

He serenaded her in an off-key but sweet manner as he bathed her from head to toe with long, caressing strokes that drove her over the brink of sanity. Nothing was left untouched.

She felt like a goddess being worshipped by her subject. She felt relaxed by the atmosphere, the warm aromatic bubble bath, the soft music, and the smooth feel of Jordan's hands on her body beneath the water. She felt herself come alive. His seduction was breathtaking.

Mia gasped when he spread her legs with his strong hand, sliding his adept fingers into the delicious folds of flesh. Her head arched back against the rim of the tub as his other hand deeply massaged her breasts. The warm water intensified his caress.

"Jordan," she purred, her eyes closed in rapturous delight.

He laughed huskily at her reaction to his seduction. "You like?"

"I love," she moaned lazily.

Jordan left her side, and Mia instantly felt the loss. He returned seconds later with a long-stemmed crystal flute of champagne, handing it to her with flourish. "Just relax and sip on this."

She accepted it. "More surprises?"

"The night is young."

Mia giggled like a carefree girl, blowing bubbles from her hand into the air. "I don't think I can take anymore pleasure tonight."

"The best is yet to come."

He returned just minutes later carrying a stack of fluffy towels, dressed in a robe that hid his body from her view. "Miss me?" he asked.

Mia stretched lazily in the bath. "Like crazy."

He held out his hand, pulling her easily to a standing

position. His loins tightened in awareness, and his shaft hardened at the sight of her magnificent body gleaming as the water slid down off her. Droplets of water hung from her hardened nipples teasing him, and with a growl of unrestrained hunger he captured the tempting drop and her nipple into his open mouth to suck quickly.

Jordan lifted Mia out of the water, pressing her body to his while pulling the towel around her. His lips met hers with urgency and need until he felt he had quenched but a small bit of the thirst he had for her.

Standing among the petals and the beautiful glow of the candlelight, he dried her from head to toe with a towel as soft as cotton. Intermittently he kissed the tantalizing spots on her body that he couldn't resist. His words of praise were a soft, husky breeze against her damp skin.

Once he draped another dry towel around her he swung his lady up into his strong arms. "Hold on," he advised, alluding to his clumsy nature.

But Mia felt secure and cherished in his arms. "Oh, I'm not letting you go," she said seriously, her arms around his neck.

At her words, Jordan stopped in his path out the door. "You mean that?" he asked softly, his face just inches from hers.

The flickers of the candles burned in the depths of their eyes, but the passion and devotion they felt for each other at that moment burned much hotter. Mia nodded, initiating a soul-searing passionate kiss that shook them both.

He carried her easily into the bedroom where the romance theme continued with more lit candles, more scattered rose petals, more seduction. Marvin's voice carried from the bathroom to continue his soft, sultry serenade. Mia gave in to the joy of being pampered.

Jordan removed the towel and lay her naked on top of the petals strewn across red satin sheets. Quickly he removed his robe and lay beside her. There they lay, naked and aroused among the petals, resembling Adam and Eve in the Garden of Eden.

They fed each other fruit and sipped champagne in between just touching and kissing each other. Their nakedness was intensified by the silky smooth feel of the satin against their skin.

"Lie on your back," he instructed her, the desire he was consumed with evident in his voice.

She did as he asked, her eyes closed in total relaxation. "Do I deserve all of this?"

"You deserve it and more."

Jordan bit deeply into a plump ruby-red strawberry and then squeezed the juice over her breasts. Swallowing the fruit he leaned over and licked the sweet trail with his tongue. He felt her shiver and knew she was pleased. Moving to straddle her hips Jordan rubbed his hands together before using his fingertips to brush over her face, barely touching her. He held his hands just above the surface of her skin, brushing the fine hairs to cause a sensual sensation created by static electricity. He traced the delicate outline of her forehead, her eyes, her nose, her ears, and her neck.

Mia loved the technique. It was like a massage but with just minimal physical contact. Shivers ran up her spine, and she was aroused by the slight tickling sensation.

He glided his hands in a slow hypnotizing motion over her smooth amber body. From her face to her thrusting full breasts, from her flat stomach and long shapely legs to her feet, he massaged her. For nearly five minutes he aroused himself and Mia.

Never had she felt so stimulated and excited. Never had she felt so alive and relaxed. Never had she wanted Jordan so much. "Please, Jordan," she begged, her voice hoarse as she began to squirm with desire.

He just laughed. He moved his hands back to her face and began a fingertip massage. His hands followed the same path, sculpting to the delicious curves of her frame. He loved it when she cried out at the first feel of his hands massaging her hard and taut nipples.

When he massaged the aching bud between her legs, he found her wet and swollen with want. He knelt there, her knees up around his head as he lowered slowly to taste her nectar. He felt himself harden more.

Mia let the tears flow. Jordan had moved her beyond words and now he kissed her core with such sweetness that an unknown feeling exploded in her chest.

Unable to resist, Jordan moved up between her legs and kissed her deeply before sliding a condom onto his shaft and moving into her heat and wetness with one deft stroke.

They both gasped in pleasure, shivering at the feel of each other. Tightly they held each other because they felt as if they were free-falling through space. He kissed her tears and stroked deep within, uniting them in the most primal of ways.

They praised each other with whispered words, caressing touches, and long, revealing stares as they made love to each other. Every fiber of their bodies was in tune to their electricity. This was like nothing either had ever experienced. It went beyond sex. It was another level.

And they made love for a long, pleasure-filled time. Neither giving in to the end that was on the brink of cooking. It was just too good to give up. It was the best for both of them.

Finally as they both began to shiver with release they kissed deeply, tightening their hold on each other, as the first waves of an earth-shattering climax shook them. They cried out, their bodies gyrating on the sweat-soaked sheets as white-hot spasms controlled them.

As the waves finally receded, Jordan pulled her onto his chest. Their hearts pounded furiously. They both breathed deeply, completely speechless by what they had just experienced.

* * *

"I never knew a city sky could be so beautiful."

Mia turned to smile up at Jordan, who had just joined her on the balcony. He, like her, was dressed in a robe. "Did I wake you?" she asked, as he folded his arms around her waist from behind.

"I rolled over, and you were gone. Couldn't sleep?"

She shook her head, leaning back against his strong chest. She clasped her hands over his. They gazed up at the full moon and the star-filled sky in reflective silence.

"You sure you don't want to change your mind about going home tonight?" he asked hopefully, wanting to wake up with her in his arms in the morning.

"Oh, I would love to but it might not be a good example to set for the children, especially the girls," she insisted. "They would wonder why we stayed out all night and what we were doing."

"We're both adults, Mia."

"I know."

"I know I'll regret it when I'm in bed alone but we'll play it your way—this time."

She lifted his hands to kiss them. "Thanks."

He kissed the top of her head. "Hungry?"

"As a matter of fact, I am. Lord knows you should be. You worked up quite an appetite."

They both laughed. "Wait here," Jordan said before moving quickly inside.

Soon the sound of Marvin could be heard, and Jordan reappeared with the bag from Mahogany's in one hand and a chair in the other. Sitting down he patted his lap. She instantly moved to him.

"What's in the bag?" she asked eagerly.

He reached in and Mia gasped in pleasure and surprise when he pulled out a container holding two generous slices of banana-and-toasted-almond cream pie. "Do I know you, lady, or what?"

She smiled and kissed him before taking the container. Mia wiggled in his lap in pleasure. The pie was as good as she thought it would be. "Thanks, Jordan. It's delicious."

They fed each other until every bit of both slices was gone. Jordan took the container from her hand and set it on the balcony floor before motioning for her to rise.

When she did he stood as well and pulled her into his arms. As Marvin sang "What's Going On?" they danced in the moonlight.

Thirteen

That night of their first date everything changed between Mia and Jordan. It was evident that they were much closer. The time they spent together was precious. Dinner and movie dates were frequent. Outings with the children were constant on Sundays.

Mia had to admit that she was happy in terms of her social life, but the more focus she put into her relationship with Jordan the more she felt she was losing her edge at work. Did she want to cut back on building something with Jordan so that she could revert to the work hound she had been just one month ago? But then did she want to lose her career behind sharing good times with her man and his children?

She looked deep at her reflection in the mirror of her vanity table. *What to do, Mia?* she asked herself.

Her phone began to ring, breaking into her reverie. Mia stood from the bench where she was sitting to pick up her cordless phone from the bed. The caller ID showed Terrence's name and number. She dropped the phone back on the bed and let it ring.

The man was persistent but she was not interested in resuming their lukewarm relationship. Jordan was all the man she needed. After seven rings, the call ended abruptly.

She shuddered as she reclaimed her seat when she remembered the look on Jordan's face when her an-

swering machine clicked on and the good doctor's voice
had filled the room pleading with her to return his calls.

Jordan had never mentioned it and would not discuss
it whenever Mia would broach the subject, but she knew
that it bothered him deeply. She understood his feelings
and respected them.

She knew that if another woman, especially that scan-
dalous Amanda, were calling her man regularly, she
would turn green with angry jealousy.

Her phone rang again, and she retrieved it. "Yes,
Jordan?" she said with a smile.

He laughed huskily. "How'd you know it was me, Miss
Know-it-All?"

"Caller ID."

"Oh yeah, I forgot," he admitted. "You almost ready
over there? We should get on the road within the next
twenty minutes or so."

"I'm just finishing my makeup. I'll be ready in
twenty."

"Ten?" he asked hopefully.

"Fifteen," she insisted.

"Deal."

Newark Symphony Hall's Terrace Ballroom was filled
to capacity. Every table was loaded with spirits and a
variety of food. The band was jamming and the dance
floor was packed with gyrating bodies doing everything
from the latest hip-hop dances to the hustle. Overall
the annual charity ball held by a fraternal organization
was a roaring success.

"Did I tell you how beautiful you look?" Jordan asked
Mia, leaning toward her so that she could hear him over
the music.

She tilted her head toward him as well, enjoying the
warmth of his unique scent. Following an impulse, she
pressed a luscious kiss on his smoothly shaven chiseled

jaw. "Yes, you have, but don't stop. In fact, tell me again," she said playfully.

He held her delicate dimpled chin with his hand. "You're beautiful, Mia," he said, looking deeply into her eyes beneath the flashing colored lights.

Instinctively they kissed. It was sweet and short, but fulfilling and steeped with promise of more to come.

Mia licked her lips as if to savor it. She smiled when she saw Jordan do the same. *This man is addictive.*

The band began to play the beginning strains of "You're My Lady" by D'Angelo. The song was from 1995 but it was a classic to Mia. She began to rock her hips in the seat.

Suddenly Jordan stood, causing his chair to push back and hit the one behind him. "Sorry," he told the older woman, who shot him a nasty look.

After making more apologies, he turned back to Mia, his hand outstretched. "Dance with me?"

It reminded her of their first date, and she immediately accepted, taking his hand. With a smile he led her to the crowded dance floor, pulling her toward him with his hands warmly on her hips. Mia wrapped her arms around his neck and leaned her head on his broad shoulders. As always their bodies molded together.

Softly in her ear Jordan began singing along with D'Angelo, and Mia laughed. She closed her eyes, lulled into a comfort zone by the warmth of Jordan's strong hands on her hips and the gentle sway of their bodies as they rocked together.

She wished it could go on like this forever. Being in Jordan's arms seemed so right. At that moment none of her earlier worries mattered. That's how it was for her when it came to Jordan. None of her insecurities about their relationship surfaced until she was out of his overwhelming and powerful presence.

"Are you my lady, Mia?" he asked softly, his voice deep as he leaned her back to look down into her face.

She nodded. "Yes. Yes, I am."

Right there in the middle of the dance floor, surrounded by hundreds of people, they shared one of their most passionate kisses ever. Jordan pulled her body closer, and she moaned deep in her throat at the feel of his lengthy erection pressed into her stomach.

Damn, will I ever get enough of this man?

Fevered and frenzied they feasted upon each other's lips, finally breaking apart with reluctance when someone yelled out, "Damn! Go get a room!"

That's how it was between them. Whenever they were together, they could never seem to get enough of each other!

"Jordan Banks? Funny running into you here!"

He stiffened at the vaguely familiar voice. Turning, his suspicions were confirmed as he came face-to-face with Amanda Langston. The smile on her pretty face was the total opposite of the last time he had seen her after the fruit-punch incident.

Clearing his throat Jordan forced a smile onto his face. His eyes quickly darted through the crowd for Mia. *This could get real messy, real quick.* "Hello, Amanda. How've you been?"

"Just fine. Just fine. Could've been better if things had turned out differently between us," she purred, caressing the lapel of his suit jacket with scarlet fingernails. "If I knew that I would see my favorite author when the paper asked me to do this assignment, then I would've worn something more . . . appropriate."

Against his better judgment his eyes darted down, taking in the strapless red sequin dress she wore. It left very little to the imagination. Clearing his throat he looked into her face, making his expression bland as he attempted to step away from her. "Enjoy the rest of the ball, Amanda. I'm—"

"Don't run off just yet," she said quickly, stepping

over to block his path. "The night is young, and so are we. Say, what brings you here anyway?"

"Me," a voice answered sharply from behind.

Jordan looked over Amanda's bare shoulder directly into Mia's stormy mocha eyes. She brushed quickly past the woman to wrap her arms around him, clearly a possessive move.

With a smile as false as wooden teeth, Mia looked her nemesis directly in the eye. "Hi, Amanda, it's nice to see you again."

Amanda's eyes widened in mild shock and then squinted with understanding. Totally ignoring Mia and her greeting, she turned to him. "Jordan?"

He shifted uncomfortably under Amanda's intense stare and the subtle tightening of Mia's hold on his arm. Amanda wanted him to deny the obvious, while Mia wanted him to confirm it. *Women!* "Amanda, you remember my girlfriend, Mia Gordon?"

Mia's smile was like that of a cat who had just eaten a fat rat. Okay, she knew she was being childish but what the hell, Jordan was her man. She shot the other woman a hard stare with a clear warning. *He's mine, so back off. Got it!*

Amanda's eyes answered. *He's yours now, but for how long?* She smiled falsely. "Yes, I do remember Ms. Gordon. She was leaving for her date with that gorgeous doctor," she said sarcastically. "How is the good doctor, Mia?"

Mia felt Jordan stiffen at the mention of Terrence. She moved her hand down his arm to entwine her fingers with his. "It was nice chatting with you, Alissa—"

"Amanda," she corrected sharply.

"Whatever," Mia countered breezily with a dismissive wave of her hand. "Jordan?"

"Uh, good luck on your story, Amanda," he said, moving past her with a brief wave. Mia was close behind him. "Good-bye."

"Oh, I'll be seeing you, Jordan," she called behind them.

Amanda smiled when she saw that Jordan had to forcibly pull Mia behind him. "Oh, and the sooner the better," she finished with a mocking laugh.

Jordan glanced over at Mia's stoic profile for the hundredth time since they left the dance. She hadn't said a solitary word to him, and any attempts he made at conversation were shot down with a nasty "Don't say one word to me" look.

They would each be home within minutes, and it pained him to know that their evening would end on such a sour note. But he also refused to be insulted by her childish behavior. He decided to make one more attempt; after that, if she still wanted to sulk, then so be it!

Quickly he reached out with his right hand and captured hers in a tight grasp. "Why are you letting her destroy what started out as a wonderful evening, Mia?" he asked, ignoring her daggerlike stares and tugging to be released from his grasp.

"She wants to be where you are," he said, as if reasoning with her. "But I want you by my side, not Amanda."

Mia just sucked her teeth.

"If I wanted Amanda, I would be with her," he said, growing weary of her childish silence.

"You were with her, that's my point," she snapped.

"Huh?"

"You were supposed to be going to the bathroom. When you took so long I came looking for you. What do I find? You huddled up in a corner with that *thing.*"

Jordan sighed, awkwardly using his left hand to turn the sizable vehicle down their brick-paved street. "I would hardly say we were huddled in a corner, Mia. You act as if I knew she was going to be there. You're acting like I wanted her to be there."

Again silence. He pulled into a parking spot in front of his house. When Mia didn't immediately move to jump out, he hoped he was making headway with her. "I have never been interested in Amanda no matter how much she is interested in me."

"You have an odd way of showing it."

At that moment Jordan gave up. *Let her believe what she wants. Hell, I'm not the one with exes calling my house!* "Good night, Mia. Give me a call when you get over it."

He released her hand and climbed out of the SUV. Ever the gentleman, he intended to open Mia's door for her but she was already halfway up her stairs before he got the chance. He just stood on the sidewalk framed by the yellow streetlight as she slammed the front door.

Bbrrrinnggg . . . bbrrrinnggg . . . bbbrrrrinnnggg.

Jordan groaned in his sleep, his head covered by pillows. The persistent ringing of the telephone woke him. Half out of his mind he reached out in the darkness for his cordless. His hand knocked over the glass of warm milk he had carried to bed.

Bbrrrinnnggg . . . bbrrr—

"What?" he said gruffly. *Who in the hell could this be at*—he glanced over at the digital clock—*two in the morning?*

"Jordan? Jordan, it's Mia. Were you sleeping?"

He sat straight up in bed at the sound of her hesitant voice. "No, I'm awake," he lied, afraid she wouldn't finish what she had called to say.

"Liar," she said softly with a husky laugh in the darkness of her bedroom. "Look, I can't sleep. I've just been tossing and turning. I'm sorry for how I acted. I was being childish and stubborn. Do you forgive—"

Mia jerked up in surprise as the line went dead sud-

denly. Confused, she leaned over to turn on the light.
Before she climbed out of her bed the bedroom door
swung open. Jordan stood there, breathing as though
he had run a 5K, still dressed in his pajama bottoms.

Mia's look of shock turned into a broad smile that
made her more beautiful, if that were at all possible.
"Forgiven me, huh?" she asked smugly.

Jordan kicked off his slippers, sending them flying
in the air. He was naked before he reached her bed.
With a wink he began to sing "You're My Lady" as
he lay down next to her. He pulled her into his arms
and showed her quite thoroughly just how forgiven
she was.

The moonlight glistened through the open window
casting their naked bodies in a shimmering silver glow.
Mia lay on her side with her head on Jordan's chest,
her leg strewn across both of his. She couldn't sleep
even though Jordan was resting quite comfortably. So
she counted the stars scattering in the skies instead.

No words were spoken. They moved together as if
joined by their minds. As if by instinct. As if they were
meant to be this way . . . forever.

Jordan rolled Mia over onto her stomach before using his hands to massage every beautiful bit of her
smooth unmarred back. She moaned in pleasure as
he moved on to work the length of each of her arms.
Down he continued to tend to the most delectable
derriere he ever had the pleasure of caressing. His job
would not be complete if her long shapely legs were
ignored.

He aroused himself as he pushed her toward mindless ecstasy. His hardened mass stood erect and awkward. It pleased him just knowing he was pleasing her.

From the way she squirmed beneath his hands and
sighed with pleasure, he knew he was successful in his

task. Especially when he carefully massaged her before taking each tantalizing toe into the heat of his mouth.

At the first feel of it Mia bucked upward, her eyes closed against a sharp wave of intense pleasure. She shivered in response. "Jordan," she moaned.

Not yet finished he moved upward retracing with his mouth and tongue the same path his hands had taken. The taste of her was heady, especially when he placed a pillow under her prone hips and began to kiss her most feminine essence ever so intimately from behind.

Soon Mia began to shiver with the coming of her first climax. She clutched the sweat-soaked sheet as the first tide rolled over her body. Just as she began to moan deep in the back of her throat and shake with release, Jordan opened her legs using one of his hands. He quickly opened a condom and shielded himself before guiding his shaft into her sheath deftly.

Mia yelled out hoarsely, her climax now intensified as they began to move together and then apart in unison. It was their own dance. Their own unique tango, waltz, and hustle blended into one.

To Jordan, being inside his woman was like no other experience. The feel of her soft buttocks touching against his body as he stroked deep within her sent him over the edge. He lost control as sweat beaded on his body before dripping off him to land on her back.

He was near his own release but he could not, and would not, give in until he was sure his lady was satisfied. Using his hips he began a wicked circular motion inside of her, before deftly switching to a counterclockwise move that was vicious in its attacks on her senses.

Jordan didn't need to ask if she liked that. He knew that she did. And the look of rapture on her face as she bit her bottom lip was proof. The whimpers deep in the back of her throat were a testament to his lovemaking skill.

And he knew as the muscles of her walls began to rhythmically clutch and release his shaft that she was nearing yet another climax. It was then that he allowed himself to release. He deepened and quickened each stroke. The sounds of their coupling echoed in chorus with their moans. Hoarsely they both cried out in symphony as they reached the pinnacle of their passion together.

The next day at work Mia shivered as she recounted every detail of last night with Jordan. No man pleased her like he did. No one. He was truly one of a kind. A mix of boyish charm, aged intellect, and virile maleness. The clumsiness and absentminded nature gave him an endearing quality that she now adored.

"I wonder what he's doing?" she pondered aloud, looking out the window at the waters.

Since she had become serious with Jordan she couldn't remember needing one of her once-important meditation sessions. He was the ultimate in relaxing her.

Were his thoughts filled with her as well? Was he reminiscing on the most recent passionate coupling? Mia shook her head. "He's probably out shooting hoops with Raj or playing with his dad or volunteering at the day camp with the girls or starting an outline for a new novel—"

"Mia?"

She turned to find Tyresa standing in her doorway. At least she thought it was her assistant because the person's face was covered by a beautiful and elaborate bouquet of lilac and white roses with lilies. Without asking she knew it was from her man.

As she took them into her own eager hands, Mia vaguely heard Reese mutter, "Now why doesn't Royce send me flowers?"

She buried her face in the fragrant floral depths, intoxicated by the smell and the knowledge of who had sent them. She wanted to be alone to read the card she unpinned from the wrapping paper. "Reese, would you please get me a vase from somewhere around here?"

She didn't know why—because she didn't consider herself overly emotional—but Mia felt tears well into pools in her eyes. Blinking rapidly to stop them from falling, Mia looked down at the note:

My Mia,
We have shared many wonderful nights of loving, but last night will forever remain uppermost in my mind, words cannot explain what we shared. Words cannot say how happy I am that "You're My Lady." (Smile)
Jordan

It was so like Jordan to be so in tune with her needs. His timing was ideal. Just when she was wondering if he was thinking of her, the flowers arrived. Just on time. Just perfect. Just her Jordan.

Fourteen

Mia felt totally powerless as she watched Jordan finish packing. This would be their first time apart in two months. And for four whole days!

"I wish you didn't have to go," she said softly, rising from the head of the bed to wrap her arms around his midsection from behind.

"I wish you would go with me," he returned quickly, as if the comment had been sitting on the tip of his tongue waiting to fall off at any time.

"You know I have to work."

"And you know the speaking engagement at the conference is work for me, too."

Yes, she understood him needing to promote *Deadly Deal.* So, yes, she understood that he had to go even if he didn't want to. But, no, that didn't make it any easier for her to see him get on that plane today.

So they remained at a standstill. He wanted her to take a week off work and attend the conference with him. She didn't want him to go. Neither got their wish.

With a rather dramatic sigh Mia moved away from him to stand by his bedroom window. She made a beautiful sight dressed all in white and framed by the sunlight. Jordan felt his breath taken away. *My own earth angel,* he thought. If only Mia would reconsider. He would love spending his spare time sightseeing in Washington with her. But alas, once again work came first for her.

"I'm all set," he said, snapping his Samsonite suitcase closed. "Ms. M is going to stay here and watch the children. That will be good for her because I know she's missing my dad."

Mia smiled at the surprising love that had blossomed between the older couple. "He is coming back from Virginia after he handles his business?"

"Yeah, but I don't know for how long. He loves Virginia, and Ms. M loves Jersey. But then they love each other."

"What are they going to do?"

"Who knows."

Mia could sympathize with the older woman. Just the thought of being away from Jordan for a week was pure torture for her.

"There is one thing I do know though," he said, coming to stand behind her at the window.

She turned into his embrace, pressing her face into his neck and enjoying his scent. "What's that?"

"I'm going to miss you like crazy, Miss Mia Gordon," he said, his voice ever so deep and resonant.

Mia looked up into his handsome face. "And I miss you already, Mr. Jordan Banks."

The kiss they shared was long and amorous. Already they were trying to make up for the hundreds of kisses they would miss out on during their separation. Both longed for Sunday to arrive.

Only two hours had passed since Jordan departed in the hired limo to catch his plane at Newark's International Airport. Already Mia felt an intense need to meditate because the day was not turning out to be her day.

She was about ten seconds fresh off another one of the "conversations" that she loved with her mother. Mia had barely worked up a lukewarm response to Terrence before she and Jordan got together. Admittedly she was too caught up in the man to even allow another to raise her internal temperature one degree. So why didn't her mother understand that you can beat a dead horse in the head but that still wouldn't make it rise and run? Of course Mia realized that she was being a coward by not telling her parents of her relationship with Jordan, something she knew would absolutely send her mother into horrified shock.

Her mother's call came right on top of her discovering a miscalculation in her proposal for the acquisition of Lucent Textiles by the larger conglomerate Texcom Inc. She was slipping, and she knew it. Not even in the very beginning as a financial analyst had she made any errors this major. Her game had always been tight. Her edge was now softening. What would go next, her ability to add?

Mia released a troubled sigh. She had a little under two days to get her act and her proposal together. "With Jordan in D.C., I won't have any tempting distractions," she said aloud to herself as she bit the tip of her Cross pen. "Hopefully nothing else will go wrong today."

Her phone began to ring, a shrilling break into the quiet of her office. She eyed it with trepidation from the corner of her eyes. Mia picked it up warily, ending the insistent ringing. "Gordon here," she said with more confidence than she actually felt.

Moments later her eyes widened in shock before she ended the call slamming the receiver down on its base. She gathered her purse and car keys before sprinting out of the office like a world-class track star in her slate-gray Via Spaga heels.

Jordan looked down at the telephone in a state of confusion. There was no answer at the house. Mia wasn't in her office, her cell phone kept announcing that she was unavailable or out of her calling area, and neither her assistant nor her secretary knew where to locate her.

Something was definitely up.

Then again maybe his creative imaginings were running wild, ever in search of a mystery.

He tried another round of calls to no avail before forcing himself not to worry. With a long, drawn-out sigh he finished unpacking among the luxurious surroundings of his hotel suite in Washington, D.C. He smiled as he put away a couple of pairs of sweatpants and T-shirts that were just beginning to soften with age, just the way he liked them. He hung his slacks and dress shirts in the armoire.

Not yet ready to be surrounded by the masses attending the conference that was being held in the hotel, Jordan flopped on the bed and grabbed the leather-bound menu from the nightstand. Quickly he surveyed it. *Uhm, decisions . . . decisions.*

Recently Mia had been getting on him about his less-than-healthy eating habits. Okay, he was a junk-food, fast-food addict. With Ms. M enlisted as a cohort it had been nearly three weeks since he had enjoyed a good, fatty, greasy, artery-clogging, but ever so delicious meal.

"Tonight's the night," he said high-handedly to himself as he eyed several dishes he could devour easily.

"No," he said, rather dramatically. "Mia would want me to have this grilled skinless chicken breast, a salad, and a baked potato."

Jordan reached over for the phone and dialed the proper extension. "Oh, no, wait a minute. Mia's not here, and what she don't know won't hurt her," he said smugly with a gleeful laugh. With mouthwatering anticipation he ordered a Reuben sandwich platter with extra Swiss cheese.

By the time he showered and changed into his beloved and comfortable navy blue sweatpants and gray T-shirt his food had arrived. His stomach grumbled at the thought of the steaming corned beef topped by sauerkraut and Swiss cheese on rye bread.

Jordan nearly danced as he removed the contacts that

he detested and slipped on the glasses he had repaired to no one's knowledge. This was his time to please himself and no one else. He planned to enjoy it totally. He moved to the door, opening it so that his utopia could be wheeled in on a cloth-covered cart.

Yes, he missed Mia and the children but this was the life!

Today just ain't my day!

Mia ran both of her hands through her mass of curly hair as she slumped down onto the cocoa leather sofa in Jordan's den. She released a troubled sigh before turning to look into each and every face of the children. First Raj, then Tia, Kimani, Aliya, and lastly Amina.

She was now faced with the responsible task of baby-sitting while Jordan was away. Today Ms. McKnight had slipped on one of the children's toys and broken her leg. Rajahn had called her, and Mia had had to fly there to carry Ms. McKnight and the children to the emergency room.

They had driven Ms. McKnight to her daughter's house in South Jersey once the leg was cast. This left Mia in quite a bind. With Jordan's father back in Virginia, she could either take over watching the kids for him or call him back from his conference.

As much as she would love to have Jordan back in town, she would never be that selfish. Jordan was important to her, and the conference was important to him. What else could she do but take on the task?

Although this was the worst possible time. How in the world would she manage working and monitoring the girls who were finished with their summer day camp? Especially when she needed to focus on fixing those portfolio figures in just two days.

Lord, how do working mothers do it?

To top it off her culinary skills only went as far as

boiling water for Cup O' Noodles, scrambling eggs, and having a wicked speed-dial punch for takeout.

Quickly she decided it would be best for her to stay here with the children instead of her house, especially since she was wary of them breaking any of her valuable African collectibles. Besides, her fridge contained nothing but bottled spring water and fruit, while Jordan kept his stocked for an army.

Tension tightened her lower back muscles, her shoulders stiffened, and she felt a headache coming on strong. After she called Jordan, she was planning one helluva meditation session for herself.

"Looks like I'll be camping out with you until your daddy returns," she said finally, resigned and filled with panic that caused her left eye to jump.

She must have looked like a deer caught in headlights, because Kimani walked over to wrap her slender brown arm around Mia's shoulder. "Don't worry, Ms. Gordon. Everything will work out just fine."

Mia forced a smile as she looked up at her. In the fresh clear depth of Kimani's eyes was trust, assurance, and love. "You're right, sweetheart," she said softly, her smile softening as she smoothed her hand over Kimani's braided hair. "Just fine."

The phone began to ring, and Tia dashed off with thunderous feet to answer it. The next ring ended before it even began. "Mia, it's Daddy."

Mia dropped her keys onto the coffee table before rising. She wanted to race to the phone and rip it from Tia's hand but she maintained her composure.

"Here she is, Daddy, so calm down. We're not gonna throw a party," Tia was saying, her eyes rolling expressively upward in her pretty face. "Count to ten, Daddy, you're getting postal on me."

Mia gently removed the phone from her grasp. "Jordan?"

"Baby? What's going on? I knew when I couldn't

reach anyone that something went down." His voice was frantic. "I just knew it."

"Ms. McKnight broke her leg, and the children called me at work—"

"How is she?" he interrupted.

"She's fine, they cast it, and I took her to stay with her daughter while she—"

"Of course I'll handle all her expenses. Oh, and she can't watch the kids," he broke in again.

"Of course," she countered dryly. "So I'll—"

"I'll be on the first thing smoking. Could you just keep an eye on them until I get there?"

If he cuts me off one more time I'll scream, I swear it! she thought, giving him a chance to speak before she tried to finish a sentence. "Now, Jordan, you don't have to—"

"I better call the airport right—"

"Aaaaahhhhh," Mia screamed, releasing a high-pitched sound. When it came to a drawn-out end the children all looked at her with bug-eyed expressions.

"Mia? Mia! Are you okay? What's happening?" Jordan's voice echoed into the room.

God, that felt great. Mia cleared her throat. "Now that I have your attention, I will watch the children so you don't have to leave the conference."

She rushed out the words so that he couldn't interrupt again. The line was totally quiet when she was done.

"Are you sure, Mia?"

"Yes," she said slowly, drawing it out and sounding anything but sure.

"Thank you, sweetheart" he said, his voice filled with emotion. "I'll have to show you just how appreciative I am when I get home."

Mia smiled at the thought. "The sooner you get here to thank me, the better."

"I was so worried when I couldn't reach anyone. You didn't even answer your cell."

"My cell!" she exclaimed. "It's in my briefcase, at the office with all my papers."

"Mia?"

"Huh?" she asked vaguely, her mind envisioning her Coach briefcase sitting under her desk.

"You okay?"

"Yes, I'm fine. Just enjoy your conference and don't worry about a thing at home. Okay?"

"I really miss you, baby," he said softly and with total honesty.

She sighed. "And I miss you, too."

"Oh, brother," Tia groaned from behind her. "They're about to get goofy. Just look at her face. I'm outta here."

Mia barely noticed the children file out as she listened to Jordan tell her in very explicit detail what he planned to do to her his first night back in her arms. It definitely wasn't a conversation for a child's ears.

Mia steered the sports car more carefully than she normally would as she followed her usual route to work. She had to get her briefcase. Even if it meant taking the children with her. Besides she figured they would get a kick out of seeing where she worked.

They chattered and argued, sang along with the radio, and played car games. Mia felt one hell of an even bigger headache looming. If someone could bottle the energy of one child and market it, somebody would get rich.

Rajahn sat in the front passenger seat and saw Mia grimace when the twins began to play tug of war with one of their stuffed animals. He turned in his seat and shot them a nasty look, which they ignored. So he turned to Tia, who immediately got the picture and made the twins cease.

Mia was grateful when they quieted down. She had a lot of planning on her mind to better utilize her time.

She pulled into her reserved parking spot. "Okay, gang. We all have to be very quiet in the offices, okay? I just need to pick up my briefcase and make some calls."

They sure did look out of place in the brisk, business atmosphere. Women and men, young and old, looked very stern and formal in their Saville Row, Brooks Brothers, and Jones New York tailored suits. Mia was well aware of the odd stares she and the children received. This was hardly the place to find children. Boldly she met each and every stare with one of her own. She dismissed any person who looked down on them. She felt defensive and protective of the children.

Relief was her friend when they finally reached her office. Like little angels they all found seats and were quiet as she worked. Rajahn played games on her computer with Tia, Kimani read a magazine, and the twins played contentedly with each other on the rug.

"Heard you were back in the office. Where on earth did you go flying to?"

Six pairs of eyes swung to look up at Tyresa as she stood frozen in the office doorway. The rest of her words froze on her lips.

"Come in, Reese," Mia said, ignoring the confused look her assistant gave her.

"Hello to you, *Mama Mia,*" Reese said playfully with a wink before strolling over to the sofa where the children sat. "You all must be Mia's next-door neighbors. Now let's see if I get these names right."

Lightly she touched each of the twins' cheeks. "You little angels are Amina and Aliya."

"I'm Amina and that's Awiya," one of them corrected her with a huge toothy grin.

"Okay," Reese acquiesced, moving to stand before Kimani. "You're Kimani, right?"

"Yes, ma'am."

"Rajahn, of course, our lone young man."

"That's me."

"And little Miss Tia, right?"

Tia gave the tall slender beauty the once-over. "Okay, now that you've won the grand prize on Name that Kid, who are you?"

"Tia!" Mia gasped in reproach at the girl's rude behavior. "You're going to get enough of being so grown. Now apologize."

"Sorry," she said halfheartedly.

"That's cool, Mia. She reminds me of me when I was her age. She'll grow to do wonderful things, trust me." Reese smiled. "Everyone, I'm Tyresa, better known as Reese. Mia's best friend and highly efficient assistant."

"And I am very glad that you are so highly efficient, because I'm taking a couple days off, and I need you to man the ship."

Reese pretended to swoon with shock, her bottom lip nearly to the floor. "You're taking time off? You?" she shrieked in amazement. "The world must be about to end."

Mia's hands stopped their rapid flight across the keyboard of her notebook computer. "I'm watching the kids while Jordan's out of town."

"Say what?"

Quickly Mia explained about their caregiver's broken leg and Jordan's conference. "So I'll need you to stay in close contact with me and keep me abreast of everything while I'm out of the office."

"That's no problem," Reese assured her. "And you make sure to call me if you need any advice."

Mia scanned the room to look at her little bunch as they continued to play quietly. "Everything's going to be fine. Right, kids?"

"Right!" they all exclaimed with enthusiasm.

Back at Jordan's the children had separated through the house as soon as they arrived. Mia made them promise not to harm one another or themselves while she rushed to her house and quickly packed an overnight bag.

Alas she was taking a short vacation anyway. Too bad it wasn't at a scenic island resort or even sightseeing in the nation's capitol with Jordan. She longed for him and for his touch, his smile—even his clumsiness would be welcomed right then.

After hanging up her tailored mint Donna Karan suit, Mia changed into one of the T-shirts Jordan had left at her house and some sweatpants. She inhaled deeply of his scent. It was a sad replacement for the real deal.

After tugging on her sneakers, new, thanks to Jordan, she headed back next door. She smiled at her very Jordanesque relaxed look. Mia knew Jordan loved to see her out of her business attire and more comfortable. Oddly, it was a turn-on for him.

Soon though she was glad for her dressed-down attire. As soon as she stepped through the gate all of the girls came running at her at full speed. Mia's eyes widened in shock just before she felt herself fall backward to the ground.

"You're it!" they yelled, laughing.

The afternoon sun was bright. She was missing Jordan like crazy and looking for a diversion. Besides, the girls' smiles were catching. *Looks like I'm about to play tag,* she thought, before she winked up at the girls.

"Well, ladies, I hope you all have your running shoes on!"

They all squealed as she jumped to her feet in fast pursuit.

It felt odd being in this bedroom, *his* bedroom, without him. Mia never imagined that the first night she spent here she would be alone. She swallowed a pang of longing as she looked around.

His presence was everywhere. The faint scent of his Joop! cologne, the discarded clothes on the chair in the corner, the oversize black teddy bear she won for him at the carnival downtown. She missed him terribly.

Sighing, Mia moved from where she stood in the door frame. Slowly she closed the door behind her and set her overnight bag on the edge of his king-size bed. She walked around the room lightly touching Jordan's possessions and wishing they were him.

A light yawn escaped from her. She felt exhausted. Keeping up with five intelligent and energetic children had drained her, and she yearned for rest. Right then she felt envious of the slumber they all enjoyed tucked away in their beds.

If only she could be sure that sleep would claim her just as quickly. But it would be so hard in that bed, in this room, in this house, without Jordan.

As she undressed Mia wondered what Jordan was doing. Did he miss her as much as she missed him? Somehow she knew that he did. Jordan was affectionate and compassionate. He was a mix of strength and tenderness. A rare man indeed.

As she lay between the cool crisp sheets in the darkness of his bedroom and inhaled deeply of his scent, which clung to the pillow, Mia wished like hell that she had joined him in Washington.

She had just reached out in the darkness for the phone when the bedroom door creaked open allowing a sliver of the hallway's light to beam in. It thickened as the door opened. Two small shadowy figures stood in the portal.

"Amina? Aliya?" she said softly as she turned on the bedside brass lamp. "What's the matter?"

"Can we sweep with you?" one asked, tightly clutching a top to her chest.

"We're scared," the other added.

Mia immediately moved over and flipped back the covers. Her reasons were slightly selfish. For the majority of her adult life Mia had lived alone. Alone but never lonely. But tonight she felt so lonesome that she welcomed their presence.

She tucked them in, one on each side of her, before turning off the light to bask them in cooling darkness. "Good night, girls, don't let the bedbugs bite," she teased softly.

"Good night," they answered in sweet, melodic unison, sleep already in their voices.

Mia's head had just hit the pillow when the door creaked open and the shaft of quickly thickening light reappeared. The shadowy figures of Kimani and Tia appeared.

"Can we?" Tia asked into the darkness.

Thank the heavens Jordan has a king-sized bed, Mia thought as the girls climbed onto the bed as well. Once she made sure everyone was comfortable Mia snuggled under the covers. The twins were so close to her sides that she feared if she turned over she would crush one of them. Not that she had much room to turn anyway.

With thoughts of Jordan and the comfort of company, Mia finally felt her body relax as she slipped into slumber and the waiting arms of her lover in her dreams.

Jordan tossed and turned for the hundredth time in the comfortable but unfamiliar bed. Its bed linens were all disarrayed and tangled with his strong limbs. The luxury hotel suite felt as desolate and lonely as him being the man on the moon.

With a frustrated growl he punched his pillow. Sleep eluded him. His thoughts were filled with long, shapely honey-bronzed legs and beautiful, intelligent eyes that twinkled in mischief and glazed with desire.

It was 11:40 P.M.

It was late.

He knew he shouldn't but he did anyway. Quickly Jordan picked up the phone and turned on the light in one swift movement. Squinting against the sudden brightness he slipped on his specs and dialed home.

It rang just once.

"Hello," she answered groggily, her voice a hoarse husky whisper. "Jordan?"

"Yeah, baby, it's me." He smiled at the sound of her voice. His heart raced at the image of her lying in his bed. His loins tightened in a hot rush of desire for his woman.

Fifteen

The summer sun was a crimson red disk in the lavender-blue skies, signaling the start of a new day. A new day of beginnings, a new day ripe with hope and possibilities. Birds chirped as they dug for worms, squirrels rattled the branches in the trees as they searched for their nutty breakfast. Already the sound of the city awakening was alive and fresh.

Mia sat in Jordan's window enjoying the sweet smell of summer and rediscovering the season's wonders. She sighed. Right now she knew she should be lying in Jordan's arms, his chin on the top of her head, his heart beating a sensual tattoo against her bare back as they enjoyed the horizon together.

I miss you, Jordan, she whispered to the skies as if the air could float the words to him.

"Morning, Ms. Gordon."

She rose from the chocolate padding of the window seat as her bedmates began to stretch their small bodies. "Mornin', ladies," she answered as four pairs of eyes peered sleepily at her.

"Up and at 'em." Mia clapped her hands, moving over to the bed to pull the covers back quickly from over their bodies.

They all squealed and giggled. The twins tried to crawl beneath the covers. "Just five more minutes," Tia pleaded, turning her back to everyone to lie on her side in a fetal position.

"Nope," Mia said over her shoulder as she slid on Jordan's robe. With one last warning glance she left the room.

She was determined not to let this week get the best of her. Her confidence felt a little bit stronger this morning. If she could handle double-digit million-dollar deals without breaking a sweat, surely five children would not be the end of her sanity.

Jordan rose early slightly uncomfortable in the unfamiliar bed. After pulling on his glasses, he immediately reached for the phone, dialing his house. As if they had just met, Jordan's heart hammered in anticipation of hearing Mia's sultry voice.

"Banks residence."

He smiled. It wasn't his woman but he was just as pleased to hear Kimani's bright voice. "Guess who?"

"Daddy! Daddy!" she yelled, causing him to pull the phone a few inches from his ear. "We miss you."

Laughing, Jordan sat up in bed. "I miss y'all, too, pumpkin. Where's Mia?"

"Right here making breakfast."

Jordan started in surprise. "Mia's cooking?" he asked.

Seconds later she was on the line, all smiles, warmth, and tenderness in her voice. "Good morning, Mr. Banks."

"Morning to you. Cooking, huh?"

Mia snorted, very unladylike. "If you consider pouring five bowls of Cap'n Crunch cereal and making toast cooking, then yeah, I'm cooking up a storm," she said, laughing, leaning her shoulder against the wall by the phone. Lightly she tangled her fingers in the cord.

"What are you wearing?" he asked suddenly and only somewhat seriously.

"What?" she asked softly in surprise as she turned her back to the children's openly observant faces.

"I said, what are you wearing?"

"Your robe."

Jordan whistled low in his throat at the image. He was instantly aroused by the thought. "And what else?" he asked huskily.

"Nothing," she lied, hearing the desire in his voice and wanting to enflame it further.

"My Lord," he moaned deep in his throat, having to rub his full-fledged erection to ease the throbbing ache. "I wish I could reach through this phone line and touch you."

Mia pressed her thighs together as heat infused her. "Where?"

In low and intimate tones Jordan explained in intricate and very intimate details the delicate parts of her beautiful body that he wanted to touch, to taste, to tantalize.

Mia moaned deep in her throat, closing her eyes in divine rapture as she tried to live out his words. She started to explain to him in return how she yearned to send her tongue for a dip in his navel when she remembered that she wasn't alone. Turning to face the children, Mia felt her face infuse with embarrassed heat at their odd expressions.

Clearing her throat, she made her voice way less husky and definitely more cool and reserved. "That would be nice, Jordan. I look forward to it all."

Jordan laughed, immediately understanding her plight. "Not easy to simulate sex over the phone with kids looking down your throat, right?"

Mia glanced over her shoulder at them quickly. "Right."

Regretfully they both let the conversation turn to a more sexually neutral area. Yet the visions of what they would share that first night back together never strayed far from their thoughts. They both looked forward to it with great anticipation.

"In closing, I believe that being a successful African-American writer in the mainstream market is something to be commended and supported. The diversity of African-American literature today makes fulfilling all the needs of our community possible," Jordan said, ending the ten-minute speech he had just given on African-American fictional writers in the twenty-first century.

Finally his nerves subsided, the worst of it was over. He absolutely hated public speaking. He took a deep breath of relief as he gathered his note cards and moved from the podium to his seat alongside the rest of the panel members.

"I want to thank Jordan Banks again for his speech, and at this time we would like to open the floor for a Q and A session. Please keep your questions and/or comments as short as possible. Also please walk to the microphone at the center of the room so that you can be properly heard."

Jordan took a healthy sip of his ice water as the female moderator spoke at the podium. Even with the AC on, the lights that were focused on the six-member panel of African-American authors caused sweat to bead slightly on his upper lip.

The first few questions from the 200-plus crowd in the hotel's ballroom were not for him, and he began to doodle on the notepad supplied to him. Almost absentmindedly Mia's name flowed from his fingers, as if he were in grammar school with a crush.

"Jordan. Jordan?"

He looked up from his notepad, his hand jerking out accidentally and knocking over his glass of water. As he righted the now empty container he realized that all of the occupants of the room, including his fellow panel members, were looking at him. "Yes?" he asked weakly with a smile on his handsome face.

"There was a question addressed to you. Madam, could you repeat it please?" The moderator smiled, but Jordan could tell that she was annoyed at him.

"Uhm, yes. Hello, Jordan, my name is Amanda Langston from the *Newark Star Gazette*. Being from an urban community like Newark, New Jersey, and it being common knowledge that your best-selling novels are usually set in Newark or in the surrounding cities in Essex County, I wondered what role do you believe you can play in changing the negative images and hurtful stereotypes of the city?"

Jordan's deep-set eyes widened like saucers behind his spectacles as he swung his head to look over at the woman. *What in the hell is she doing here?*

He cleared his throat and reached for his glass. Remembering that the contents now lay on the tablecloth, he cleared his throat again. He was looking for composure because the smug look on her pretty face did not bode well at all.

He could barely remember what answer he gave her or anyone else during the remainder of the conference. His mind was filled with the drama that would enter his happy life with Mia if Mia found out that Amanda was here in Washington. He shook his head, letting it drop in his hand.

Jordan was more than glad when the moderator brought the event to an end. He shook hands with the other panel members before gathering his materials and sliding them into his Coach leather portfolio. He spotted Amanda heading straight in his direction. She wasn't hard to miss in the form-fitting lemon sundress she wore. Every bit of her femininity was accentuated. It was not a dress that spoke of a newspaper journalist, and the look on her face was that of a cat who had just spotted a big bowl of cream.

He had just stepped off the podium when she reached him. "Uh, hi, Ms. Langston—"

Amanda wrapped herself around his strong arm, meaning to press her bosom against him in a clear invitation. "Ms. Langston?" she purred with a scolding air. "That's a little formal for old friends, isn't it, Jordan?"

He pulled his arm from her surprisingly vicelike grip. "It's quite surprising to see you here in D.C."

Amanda smiled and licked her bronze-tinted lips as she looked him directly in his eyes. "I'm not one to be coy. I read about the conference and your speaking engagement on your Web site. It was my idea to approach the editor with the idea of covering the conference with most of the focus on our hometown celebrity. She loved the idea."

Jordan looked around uncomfortably. It was then he noticed that several of his fans waited nearby for him to autograph his latest novel. "Please thank your editor for her support, but I must be going."

"How about dinner?"

"I don't think so," he said, nervously pushing his glasses up on his nose, although they fit perfectly.

Amanda reached up and stroked his cheek before he could move away. "Sure 'bout that?" she purred. "I'll supply dessert."

Jordan's handsome face became incredulous by her forwardness. He didn't find it appealing. "I have to go, Amanda, enjoy the conference."

"I'm in suite 1106 when you change your mind."

Quickly he walked away before she could stop him. The woman was like a bee to honey, a widow spider to her prey. Hardly the subtle allure of his beautiful woman.

And there was no way he could tell Mia that Amanda was in D.C., especially with her staying in the same hotel. He hated to lie, but what choice did he have? Besides he had no intentions of giving in to the woman's obvi-

ous advances. Mia was the only woman who could
quench the thirst she created in his body. She was his
only desire, and the sooner Amanda realized that, the
less disappointed she'd be.

"Are you done yet, Ms. Gordon? Huh, are you?"

Mia looked around the computer monitor at the
twins. They sat together, perched in the chair before
Jordan's cluttered desk. "One minute, okay?"

She had fixed their hair into two ponytails and managed to get them nicely dressed in lavender GAP over-
alls with matching printed tees. They looked adorable
but that didn't stop them from persistently stopping Mia
from concentrating on her botched proposal that
needed to be repaired by tomorrow. She understood
that they were bored now that day camp was over but
she really needed to get this done.

Of course Rajahn was old enough to baby-sit but she
had already given him permission to go the community
pool with his friends. She would hate to ruin his summer vacation by making him stay in the house to watch
his little sisters. That didn't seem fair.

Kimani was on the porch reading, and Tia was in the
playroom. She had to separate the little deviants after
a vicious hair-pulling fight over who would help Mia
wash the breakfast dishes and who should dry. Now
there was a stack of nasty encrusted dishes in the totally
wrecked kitchen. Before she could even contemplate
dinner she knew she had to tackle those dishes.

That left the twins waiting impatiently for her to finish working so that she could supervise them in the
pool as she had promised.

Mia felt like screaming. No, she felt like crawling into
a bed and pulling the covers over her head to avoid all
the drama. How in the hell did working mothers do it?
No, the better question was: Why would they?

She felt like a rag doll whose limbs were being

stretched as she was pulled in all directions. Finish your work . . . entertain the children . . . finish your work . . . supervise the children . . . finish your work . . . cook for the children.

Her head was spinning. As much as she loved the little darlings, she couldn't wait for Jordan to come home and take over his parental duties. It was just too much for her.

On top of a messy kitchen, being more than an hour late in fixing lunch, and supervising bickering and whining children, Mia was having a hard time accessing her files on Jordan's archaic computer. *Can we say upgrade, sweetheart?*

"Ms. Gordon, we're hungry," Aliya said, coming around the desk to stand by her.

Mia turned around in frustration. She couldn't be angry at a child for being hungry. She saved the program quickly. "McDonald's?" she asked softly, deciding that she'd better take a break.

"Yeah!" the girls yelled, both running out of the office calling their sisters' names.

Mia sighed as she grabbed her purse and keys. Her focus toward her career was fading. It had everything to do with her growing relationship with Jordan. She loved being in his presence and enjoyed time with him and the kids, but every extra moment she pulled from her life to give to her happiness seemed to negatively influence her work.

She loved the nights she came straight from work and watched a movie with him in the den. She treasured his surprising her with visits to her office, as did many of her female coworkers. And she looked forward to her weekends devoted to sightseeing, or going to museums with the children. But it was beginning to show in her work performance.

For so many years she had been an overachiever, and now that she sought happiness outside of her career her performance was still above par but that didn't satisfy her employers. It seemed 110 percent was not good enough when they were used to her giving 210 percent. She loved her career but she loved the taste of freedom from work that she was beginning to experience. Could she find a balance for both?

Mia stepped out onto the porch and instantly felt the smooth caress of the wind against her face. The rays of the sun kissed her bronzed skin. After being cooped up in the office all morning it did feel refreshing to be in the outdoors.

But she still had a desk filled with paperwork to sort through that just couldn't be ignored.

It took thirty minutes to zip the girls through the drive-thru window at McDonald's on Elizabeth Avenue. Soon she had them settled in the playroom watching television. After putting Rajahn's lunch on the stove, Mia hurried from the kitchen, trying to ignore the total chaos.

She carried her own cheeseburger and soda into Jordan's office, reclaiming her seat behind his desk. Soon she was focused, intent on finishing up today and putting herself one day ahead of her schedule.

And with Jordan returning Sunday evening, Mia wanted to look cool and relaxed for her man, and not harassed by working on the proposal all tomorrow. She even planned to attempt cooking dinner. That was if she ever got rid of the disaster area in the kitchen.

With total concentration, and with the girls out of her hair, Mia gained access to her files and had the proposal prepared by the time Tyresa rang the front doorbell. One of the girls screamed that they would answer it.

Tyresa strolled into the office. "Hey, boss lady," she sang cheerfully.

"I'm just printing it out. Have a seat," Mia mumbled around the pencil she clutched between her teeth.

"Well, well, look at Ms. Corporate Black America. She's turned in Donna Karan suits and Via Spaga pumps for T-shirts and sweats. No perfectly applied neutral makeup. A fuzzy ponytail instead of a bun," Tyresa teased. "Looking like a female Jordan over there, girl."

"Ha, ha."

"It suits you," Tyresa said, almost reflective. "I was worried you would start getting those nasty frown lines in your forehead."

Mia snorted.

"Adventures in baby-sitting wearing you out?"

Mia looked directly into her friend's laughing eyes. "Definitely," she said with total seriousness. "I love 'em but it's a lot different when Jordan is the one doing all the yelling and chastising. I'll be glad to see him tomorrow for more than one reason."

"Craving the loving already?" her friend asked, tongue in cheek.

Mia leaned back in the chair and stretched her shapely frame, her eyes closed. "Hey, when it's good, it's good."

"Hey," they both sang in that sister-friend fashion before bursting into soft, melodic laughter.

"Girl, don't talk about it 'fore I take off the rest of the day and surprise Royce in his office with nothing on but a thong and a smile."

Mia raised a brow. "Oh, you a little closet freak, huh?"

Tyresa raised one finger. "Hold up. Only for my husband."

Their laughter winded down into silence.

"Seriously, girl, you look happy."

"I am happy," Mia admitted, as she removed the pages from the printer and placed them in a binder with the company's logo on the front.

"There's nothing like love to make you see the world through rose-colored glasses."

"Love!" Mia shrieked. "Now who said anything about love?"

"You don't have to say it. It's all in your face and in

your actions. Girl, you know you love Jordan, and he loves you," Tyresa said with an omniscient air as she took the proposal from Mia's hands.

"I care for Jordan, there's a difference."

"Whatever."

"Besides, Jordan hasn't told me he loves me," Mia said, hating to admit the way her heart raced at the prospect of Jordan's feelings running that deep for her.

Tyresa sucked her teeth and rolled her eyes heavenward. "That's what's wrong with sistas. Always banking on those three words, which ain't diddly but just that—three words. Actions do speak so much louder."

Mia fell silent. She was not ready for this discussion with her friend or herself. "Everything cool at the office?" she asked, purposely changing the subject.

Tyresa nodded her head slightly, acknowledging her friend's wish to change the subject. "That reminds me. I am the bearer of bad news. The appointment date has been moved up. You'll need to fly out tonight to make the meeting in Houston tomorrow."

"When the hell did this happen?" Mia roared, shooting up to sit on the edge of the chair, her ponytail swinging wildly behind her.

"About ten minutes before I came here." She reached into her purse, extracting a notepad. "Your secretary already made the plans. Your flight leaves at seven tonight and you're booked at the Radmont Hotel in Houston—"

"Reese!" Mia exclaimed, her pretty face shocked. "I cannot go to Houston tonight!"

"Why not?" she asked flippantly.

"The children," Mia answered, her tone disappointed.

Tyresa had the good grace to flush. "Oh yeah, Mia, I forgot. Sorry."

Mia dropped her head in her hands. "What am I going to do now?"

"This is a huge deal, Mia."

"You'll have to go in my place," she said suddenly, looking up.

"Me! I've never done a presentation alone."

"I know you can handle it."

Tyresa's pretty face was one of total shock. She had actually thought Mia would pay whatever fee necessary for a baby-sitter to make this meeting. Instead she was delegating work, passing on a top-notch meeting. Was the world about to end?

"Don't look so shocked. I'll call ahead with an excuse and make my apologies. Tell Fran to send flowers ASAP. You and I will go over all the details. So what's up? You down?"

As Tyresa nodded, still shocked by it all, Mia felt only a slight bit of remorse. She would have loved to fly out to Houston tonight for the deal but then she would have missed Jordan's return tomorrow. For that she would have been sorry. All she could do was prep her able assistant and pray that everything turned out well.

Jordan yawned as he entered his suite, enjoying its quiet coolness. After a long day of signing books, meeting fans, and doing interviews, he was ready for sleep. But not until he called Mia and the kids first. That was his top priority.

Besides, he needed an early night. Tomorrow he was renting a car to drive into Virginia to his father's. The two men were going to drive back to Jersey together. And the sooner he got back to Mia and his kids, the better.

Jordan didn't bother turning on the lights as he made his way to the bedroom. Of course he wasn't surprised when he nearly fell over the end table. He just took the fumble in stride, correcting his posture before continuing. The hairs on the back of his neck stood on end as soon as he entered the bedroom. Suddenly he felt as though another presence was in there with him.

But as he hit the switch to bask the room with bright light, he looked around quickly and saw nothing out of place.

"Let's not get paranoid," he said to himself.

With all haste he moved to the phone, quickly dialing his house. A smile broadened his handsome face and illuminated his brandy eyes as one of the twins answered. Patiently and lovingly he spoke to each of his children before finally he was blessed with the sound of Mia huskily saying his name in that voice of hers.

"How's my girl?"

"Missing you like crazy."

"Same here," he said, moving to lie down on the bed. "So how's everything going? Kimani said she and Tia fought."

"Yeah, neither one wanted to help me with the dishes. It would've been a battle to the death if I didn't stop it."

"I'm sure you handled it fine," he said, although he knew he would've sent them straight to their bedrooms, but he didn't want to make her feel guilty.

"So who washed them?" Jordan asked, loosening his tie as he did.

"I did about a half-hour ago."

"You did what?"

"Did I do something wrong?"

"No, not you," he said, lowering his tone. "It's a part of their chores to wash the dishes when Ms. M is away, and they know that."

"I didn't mind, and I wasn't in the mood for another wrestling match between Killer Kimani and Tia the Terror," Mia joked.

That made Jordan smile. "Next time my little rugrats do the dishes, and not you. Deal?"

"Are they old enough?" Mia asked with doubt.

"Not the twins but, my God, Mia, the rest are eight,

eleven, and thirteen," he said, his handsome face incredulous. "Trust me, they know how."

"Whatever you say, old man."

"I'll show you how strong my back is for an *old man* when I see you tomorrow night," he said, his voice low and cocky.

"Don't make promises you can't keep."

"Only time will tell."

As Mia filled him in on the rest of their evening, Jordan's eyes widened as the closet door opened and a long shapely brown leg appeared. "What the hell?" he roared, his eyes like saucers as his hand with the phone dropped to the bed.

"Jordan? Jordan, what's wrong?"

The leg was followed by a curved hip and then a slender arm before a plump breast appeared. Seconds later Amanda was walking toward him as naked as the day she was born.

"Jordan!" Mia's voice shrieked through the phone line.

Wisely sensing a terrible situation about to get worse, Jordan jerked the phone back to his ear. "Mia, baby, let me call you back."

"Is everything okay?" Mia asked, obviously concerned.

"Yeah, I saw a mouse in my room," he lied with uneasiness, his eyes on Amanda as she massaged her full heavy breasts. "Let me call you back."

Jordan hung up just as Amanda opened her mouth to speak. "What in the hell are you doing in here?" he roared, as he stood to rip the coverlet from his bed and fling it at her.

She just as quickly flung it from her body with flair into a corner. She knew that she was desirable, and she always got what she wanted. She was going to have Jordan—right here, right now.

"You have five minutes to get dressed and leave. Have some respect for yourself."

"What are you, gay?"

She pushed him down on the bed with both of her hands. Jordan barely rolled away before she fell down on the spot where he lay. He threw his hands up in exasperation. "Wouldn't you like for me to prove I'm not?" he said mockingly, losing his glasses in the frenzy.

"A faithful man, now, isn't that rare?" she mocked as she moved to sit in the middle of his now jumbled bed.

"I'm with Mia and very happy," he asserted. "Now please get dressed and leave."

He left the room, slamming the door on her laughter as he did. Five minutes later she emerged dressed in a black mini that was hardly more than her being actually naked. He immediately stood from where he sat on the couch, not quite sure she wouldn't pounce on him and pin him down. "Have a good evening, Amanda" he told her, his voice firm.

The temptress caressed his face as she walked past him. "I've never seen a man turn down filet mignon for cubed steak," she said softly. "When you change your mind, call me. It's worth it, believe me."

With one last wink and a blown kiss over her shoulder, she was gone, leaving him with quite a memory. She certainly did a lot for his ego.

After Jordan hung up, Mia sat looking at the phone waiting for his return call and pondering the odd manner in which he had disconnected the line. Finally she realized that no matter how long she sat there with her gaze fixated on the instrument, she couldn't will it to ring. He said he was going to call her right back, and he hadn't. That was unlike Jordan.

What was he doing?

She gave in to the temptation and called his room. Uneasiness settled around her as his phone continued to ring. When prompted to leave a message by the hotel's answering service, she hung up. *Where in the hell is Jordan?*

Sixteen

Jealousy was not an emotion that Mia succumbed to, but as she lay in Jordan's bed, she felt herself sinking in it. She hadn't been able to eat the takeout she ordered for their dinner. She hadn't been able to focus on the game of Monopoly that the kids cajoled her into playing. She hadn't been able to do anything but wonder what was going on with Jordan.

He hadn't called her back at all. That disturbed Mia. All kinds of fears and then accusations swirled around her as if she were in the eye of a turbulent tornado.

Was he hurt?

Why did he rush off the phone in the first place?

He couldn't be with another woman, could he?

Why hadn't he called back?

What was he doing?

And who was he doing it with?

Those questions and many more claimed her consciousness as the alarm clock mockingly blinked 12:13 A.M. at her. Frustrated, angry, hurt, and filled with fear, she tossed onto her side beneath the covers, punching the pillow with force before lying upon it.

"Something wrong, Ms. Gordon?"

Dismayed that she had awakened one of the girls, Mia sat up. She had forgotten that they slept in Jordan's big bed with her again. She saw that it was Tia looking over at her with sleep-filled eyes. "Everything's fine, sweetheart. Go back to sleep," she whispered, reaching over to smooth her braided head.

"Okay," she answered sleepily, before her head dropped back down on the pillow. Soon she was back in slumber.

I wish I could get to sleep so easily, Mia thought, as she settled back in bed.

Her head had just hit the pillow when the phone rang extremely loudly. Quickly her hand shot out to grab the cordless from the nightstand. Mindful of the sleeping children, she left the bed. "Jordan?" she whispered urgently, as she left the room to enter the dark hallway.

"Yeah, baby, it's me."

Relief flooded her in waves. "Jordan, where in the hell are you?" she asked, her voice concerned.

"I drove down to my father's house in Virginia."

Mia's face became a mask of confusion. "I thought you weren't going to Virginia until early in the morning?"

"I decided to just jet down tonight."

"Any particular reason?"

Jordan cleared his throat several times before answering. "This way I can get to sleep earlier and leave in the morning sooner."

Something did not sit well with Mia about Jordan's reason for going to his father's. And the fact that he cleared his throat really filled her with unease. She realized over their months together that he usually cleared his throat before he told a lie. Nothing big, usually just something to tease her or fool her. But now in this context the thought of him lying did not sit well with her at all.

"Why didn't you call me back and just tell me you were driving into Virginia tonight?" she asked, hating that she sounded like a detective.

Again he cleared his throat, and Mia's grip on the

phone tightened considerably. "Mia, I just left spur of the moment. I'm sorry."

She nodded her head as if he could see her. "You should've gotten to your dad's three hours ago. Whatcha been up to—"

"Just talking to my dad. I should have called you sooner. I'm sorry. Look, baby, I miss the hell out of you."

His voice sounded as though he was desperate for her to believe him. Yet, she couldn't get over the uneasiness she felt. Was Jordan lying to her and if so, why?

"I'm really tired, Jordan, why don't you call me tomorrow, okay?" she said quickly, suddenly feeling an urgency to get off the phone with him. "Good-bye Jor—"

"Mia," he cut her off. "I said I miss you, baby."

"I miss you, too, Jordan," she said, softening. "Good night."

Mia disconnected the line. She sat there in the coolness of the dark staring off into space for a long time, her mind racing and not liking one bit where it was speeding.

Jordan hung up the phone in the guest bedroom of his father's house. He hated the way he felt. He didn't like lying to Mia, which was why he had stalled on calling her back. But he couldn't tell her the truth, especially not now.

He had just hightailed it from the hotel worried that he would wake up from sleep and find Amanda naked in bed with him. He would never cheat on Mia but he could tell from the way she had acted on the phone that she probably thought just that.

"Damn!" he swore, before plopping down on the bed.

* * *

It's funny how the weather sometimes perfectly matches a person's mood. It was pouring rain that summer day in Newark. The skies were cloudy and turbulent. Thunder rumbled like a bear. The sound of the rain against the windows was unrelenting.

Mia found great irony in that, especially with the way her soul felt barren with all the doubts that plagued her about Jordan. Would he cheat? Had he?

She sighed from where she stood in the den looking out the window at the storm. A vision of Jordan making love to a faceless woman flashed in the cloudy mirror, and Mia shut her eyes tightly to block the image. He wouldn't. He couldn't.

A huge part of any relationship was trust. Isn't that what Iyanla Vanzant had said on her new talk show? And Mia wanted to trust Jordan and believe him. She didn't want her accusations to be based on the fact that he cleared his throat. That was asinine.

"I have to trust him," she said softly to her blurred reflection in the window. "I have to."

"What's the matter, Ms. Gordon?"

Startled by the new arrival into the den, Mia whirled to see Kimani standing behind her in a floral sundress, a book in her hand. "Nothing's wrong," she assured her, letting a smile replace her frown. "And what are you up to on this rainy day?"

"Thinking about my future," Kimani said, with the utmost seriousness. "I look up to you, Ms. Gordon."

She rubbed her hand across the little girl's cheek, touched by her words. "You do?"

"Especially after we went to your office yesterday. I didn't see a lot of women or black people, so it's like you're good at doing something that people wouldn't expect a black girl to be good at," she said with amazing insight.

"That's true, there aren't many African-American women in my field. I'm very proud of my success in this career."

Kimani leaned her head against Mia's side. "If I tell you something, you won't laugh?"

"Of course not."

"I want to be a pilot. Silly, huh?" she asked, her voice doubtful.

"Of course not. If you study and work hard you can be successful at whatever you choose to do. Never let your gender or your race hold you back. Instead let it inspire you.

"Are there a lot of black girls who grow up to be pilots?" she asked, looking up at Mia.

"There sure are. Like M'Lis Ward and Patrice Clark-Washington."

"Really!" Kimani said with excitement. "Ever since we first went to Florida I've loved airplanes. I never told Daddy. I thought he wouldn't like it because I'm a girl."

"I know what, let's hop on the Internet and check out some info on aviation, okay?" Mia hugged her to her side. "And I'm sure your father would support all of you in whatever you choose as long as it's positive. So talk to him."

"Cool."

The rain continued at a relentless pace. It was such a gloomy day that all the children were upstairs in their beds enjoying a late afternoon nap. Mia was curled up in the middle of Jordan's bed reading a book on money management that he had bought for her during his weekly trip to the ABC Bookstore downtown on Halsey Street. Today was the first real opportunity she had to enjoy it.

Reese had called to fill Mia in on the details of the meeting. All had gone well, and they were to forge ahead on the project. Jordan had called, and he and his father were on the road and headed north up I-95, due to arrive this evening. For the first time in a long time she had some free time to herself.

Later, deciding to take a break from reading, she headed downstairs in her socks. In the kitchen she found a couple of Ms. M's recipe books. After flipping through the pages Mia found what she thought would be the easiest dish to prepare. Twice she read through it, finding the steps relatively easy.

"I'm just going to take my time and do this," she assured herself, as she began to pull ingredients from the pantry.

The rain had softened to a mist as evening reigned. The city streets were slick beneath the yellow glow of the streetlights. The many porches and street corners were nearly empty because of the weather, about the only time you could find urban streets without inhabitants.

Jordan was glad to be home. Home to his children, his house, and his woman. Everything he cared for most in the world was waiting for him, and he felt anxious to be surrounded by the familiar.

He peered out at the streets as his father drove the minivan they rented. With every passing intersection and streetlight he was closer to his family.

His father slowed the car down in front of the house. Lights were ablaze, the yard was free of its usual clutter, it looked very inviting. It was home.

Just as he stepped out of the car the front door opened and there she stood, waiting for him. *She's never looked more beautiful,* he thought, as he swung his garment bag over his shoulder.

He didn't take his eyes off her even after his father pulled off on his way to surprise Ms. M. Jordan opened the gate and entered his yard, his eyes never straying from her.

Mia dashed from the porch and ran into his open arms halfway up the walkway. They pressed their bodies together as if trying to physically blend into one. Fevered and rushed kisses were bestowed. Whispered words of missing each other caressed their cheeks. As they held each other, a steady rain began to fall, but neither even thought of moving apart.

Jordan grasped Mia's beautiful face and with a ravenous growl he plunged his tongue into the warm depths of her open and inviting mouth. Their kisses tasted of the heat they created and the cool rain falling upon them couldn't diminish their fire.

Thunder roared in the sky and lightning crackled. Finally the sounds of nature's fury broke through. Jordan grabbed his garment bag in one hand and Mia's hand in the other. They dashed up the stairs and into the house laughing.

"We're soaking wet," Mia gasped, as a chill racked her to the bones "We need to get out of these clothes."

Greedily Jordan pulled Mia to him again. "You're absolutely right," he moaned against the addictive softness of her slender neck as he carelessly dropped the luggage to the hardwood floor. "Where are the kids?"

Mia immediately knew where his thoughts lay and hers weren't very far off. "They're asleep, but, Jordan, we can't."

He leaned away from her to give an "Are you crazy?" look, before swinging her quickly up into his strong arms with more adeptness than she had ever seen him claim. "We'll just get a quickie before they awake, baby, that's all."

Mia laughed and wrapped her arms around his neck. Silently she prayed that he didn't lose his agility and fall on the stairs. Showing off, he took them two at a time. Thank God they made it safely to the top in one piece and quickly entered his bedroom. He kissed her before setting her on her feet in the darkness of the room. They peeled the damp clothes from their skin, letting them fall heavily to the floor.

Mia moved to pick them up. Jordan's hand on her wrist stopped her. "Leave them."

"But the floor," she protested.

"I don't care right now, baby," he insisted while quickly putting on a condom to protect them. He then lay on the bed and pulled her naked body down beside him.

Only the flash of lightning outside offered any light as they tasted and touched each other with urgency. The pitter-patter of the rain against the roof mingled with their moans of pleasure and delight. The skies filled with a thunderous roar as they climaxed together with tangled limbs and shuddering sweat-soaked bodies.

Jordan rolled off Mia onto his back, his breathing ragged as he pulled her soft, pliant body to his side. He stroked the soft damp tendrils of her wet hair. "Mia? I lo—"

Just then the doorknob was rattled from outside. They both immediately jumped out of bed. "Hurry and get dressed," Mia said in a rushed whisper, walking over to her overnight bag to pull out dry clothes.

"Ms. Gordon? Why's the door locked?" Tia asked from the other side, again rattling the knob.

Mia jerked on a crewneck shirt and snatched up linen drawstring pants. "Hurry up, Jordan!" she whispered to him when she saw him still looking through his drawers for something to wear.

"Ms. Gordon, are you talking to yourself?"

"I'm coming, sweetie. Is something wrong?" Mia yelled out as she straightened the damp covers on the bed.

"We're all waking up, and we're hungry. What will it be tonight, Dominoes or Pizza Hut?"

"I cooked something."

"You what!" both Tia and Jordan exclaimed in shock.

"I know I ain't crazy. I heard my daddy!" Tia said excitedly. "Daddy's home! Daddy's home!"

Jordan and Mia opened the door, standing together to find five pairs of eyes looking at them. As the girls all rushed their father, sending him backward to the

floor with an umf, Mia sniffed the air hoping the scent
of their sex did not linger.

Rajahn stepped into the room as well, flipping the
switch to bask the room with a dozen sources of light.
"Welcome back, Dad."

Jordan reached his hand through the girls' tangled
limbs to share a pound with his son. "Girls, please let
Daddy up. You're killing his back."

One by one they stood, but never moving too far
from their father. Mia watched as Rajahn helped him
off the floor with a tug.

"Hey," Tia said suddenly. "What took you so long to
open the door?"

Mia and Jordan shared an amused glance. "We
were . . . uhm," Mia struggled for an explanation. "We
were—"

"Reading," Jordan finished with finality in his voice.

"In the dark?" Kimani asked, obviously confused.

Rajahn gave them a knowing look before smiling
broadly. Jordan eyed him, deciding then it was time for
a refresher course of safe and responsible sex with his
son. "Did I hear right? Mia, you cooked dinner?" he
asked, intentionally changing the subject.

"I sure did. So how about you little rugrats washing
your faces and hands. We'll all meet in the dining room
in five minutes."

The kids all filed out and as soon as they were alone
Jordan grabbed her from behind. He bit her shoulder
lightly. "One more round?" he asked, pressing his erection against her soft backside.

Mia turned to face him, molding her body against
the length of his. She kissed him deeply and passionately. "Later," she spoke into his mouth, before turning
out of his embrace and quickly leaving the room.

"Dad, I don't know if you know it or not but Mia
can't cook."

Jordan shot Tia a stare, his eyes darting back to the entrance leading into the kitchen where Mia was warming up the supper. "I'm sure everything is delicious," he lied from his usual seat at the head of the dining room table.

Uneasiness was on everyone's face as Mia began to carry in covered dishes one by one.

"You want some help, baby?"

"No, just sit and relax," she said over her shoulder on the way back into the kitchen.

"God help us," Tia prayed, her hands actually together under her chin.

"Tia!" Jordan warned.

Mia returned with a basket of rolls, setting them next to the casserole dish. She took the empty seat at the other end of the table. "Pass your plates."

They all did so reluctantly and she piled each plate with a piece of fried chicken, a scoop of red rice and sausage, a helping of string beans, and a roll.

"It looks good, baby," Jordan assured her. He picked up his piece of chicken and bit into the crispy thigh. He didn't know why but something just didn't taste quite right.

Mia looked at everyone. "Eat up," she encouraged them as she used her fork and knife to cut into her chicken thigh. Dismayed, she frowned as blood sizzled out of the meat. It wasn't done to the bone as she had thought.

"My rice is hard," Aliya complained, her face frowning as she used her fork to play with it.

Jordan's mouth was filled with the rubbery, funny-tasting meat but he found enough space around it to say, "Aliya, don't complain. It's rude."

Mia looked down at her own plate with disgust. "No, she's right. The chicken's bloody, the rice is undercooked, the string beans bland."

"Don't forget the rolls," Tia added, picking up the

one from her plate to hit against the wood table. It made the same dense sound that a small rock would.

Mia dropped her head in her hands. Soon her shoulders began to shake. Immediately they all moved to surround her.

"It's okay, Ms. Gordon. We're still alive," Kimani told her.

"It's pretty good for your first meal," Rajahn tried to assure her, his hand on her shoulder.

"Just stick to investing, that's all," Tia piped in.

Mia's shoulders shook even harder.

"See what you did, Tia," Rajahn snapped at his younger sibling, his eyes flashing over Mia's head.

"We wuv you, Ms. Gordon, even if you can't bake us cookies," one of the twins said quietly, placing her Teletubbie doll in Mia's lap as if it would console her.

They moved back as Jordan stepped closer to her. He wrapped his arm around her shoulders. "Mia, please don't cry, baby."

Mia's head jerked up. "Cry! Who's crying?" she shrieked, her eyes free of any tears but filled with laughter. "Dominoes, everyone?"

One by one they all joined in with her until the dining room was filled with laughter.

After the day's rain, the night sky was all the more beautiful. A dark shade of purple scattered with stars that looked like diamonds in the celestial regions. The white disk was full and fluorescent. It was all the perfect physical backdrop for a revelation.

And that's exactly what Mia had as she lay naked on her side and gazed down into Jordan's sleeping face illuminated by moonlight. How could she deny the feelings fluttering in her chest?

This wonderful man with his loving, dependable nature, his intensity, his brilliance, his compassion, his raw sex appeal, his beauty, even his endearing clumsiness occupied every inch of her heart.

Completely. Uniquely. Satisfyingly. Undeniably. Unashamedly. Unabashedly. Definitely and eternally, she loved Jordan Banks.

Tears filled her eyes as she traced the long curled lash against her cheek. "I love you," she mouthed, afraid to expose herself.

Seventeen

Physically it was a typical Monday for Mia. She woke up at five and completed her morning ritual of a twenty-minute shower, ten minutes on her hair, ten minutes doing her makeup, five minutes rubbing her body down in lotion, and finally the selection of her tailored wardrobe for the workday.

Downstairs by six she ate her usual breakfast of a toasted bagel, piece of fruit, and juice before collecting her briefcase and papers from her office. By six-thirty she was in her car and headed to work by her usual route.

At work she parked in her reserved spot and by 7:00 A.M. she was at her desk in her elite corner office. By 10:00 A.M. she was called into a meeting with the senior partners of Stromer, Wiley.

During the meeting her recent decline in work had been discussed and reprimanded. Although angry at their censure she had promised to step up her game to her previous above-par level. Afterward she felt she should have stood up more for herself. She should've told them that they were foolish to believe that her entire life had to be dedicated to her career. But as an African-American female who had risen in the ranks she knew they thought she should be grateful. And they thought she should do whatever she could to maintain that status with the firm.

Sighing she kicked off her shoes, locked her office

door, and told Fran, her secretary, to hold all her calls.
She took her place before her view searching for her
comfort zone.

Mia had just settled into her sitting position with her
palms up, breathing deeply, when the shrill ring of the
phone jarred her roughly. Frustrated she sighed,
quickly unfolding her long shapely legs to stand. She
stalked over to her desk to snatch up the phone angrily.
"I thought I said to hold all my calls, Fran," she
snapped, irritated.

"Yes, Ms. Gordon, but it was your mother and she
said it was an urgent emergency. She sounds upset."

Mia released a long breath. "Put her through."

"Mia?"

"Hello, Mama. What's wrong?" she asked, concerned.

"Nothing," she answered simply.

"Then why did you tell my secretary that it was an
emergency?" She talked slow and deliberate, searching
for control.

"I knew she would put me through, that's why," Clara
said with confidence. "Anyway, how about coming to
lunch today. I'm making a mini-seafood feast."

Seafood, especially fried butterfly shrimp, was Mia's
weakness. If no one else knew that, her mother did. "I
can't, Ma."

"Mia, all I'm asking for is one hour. Your daddy
would love to see you."

Another weakness, her love and closeness with her
daddy. "Okay, I'll be there by noon, but I can only stay
for half an hour, okay, Ma? I'll see you later."

Mia hung up her cordless and slumped in her bungi
chair. After glancing at the crystal clock on her desk
she picked up her phone again. Pressing two on her
speed dial sent her straight through to Jordan.

"Talk to me."

Mia smiled at his odd greeting. "Hey, lover."

"How's my baby?" he asked, his voice filled with pleasure.

"Feeling indecisive, troubled, frustrated, beaten down, and unappreciated."

"Whoa. What's wrong, Mia? What's going on?" His concern was evident in his tone.

"Nothing I can get deeply into right now. I just needed to hear your voice. Right now you're just about the only thing in my life that I know is right," she said softly, her eyes looking over to her view.

"You're just as important to my life," he assured her with emotion in his deep, husky voice.

"Think you'll have some spare time for me tonight?" Mia asked, leaning back in her chair, her eyes closed as she thought of him. "I really need to talk over some things with you and get your advice."

"Can we talk now?"

She smiled at how he was always there for her. "I wish but I'll probably be reprimanded for even making a personal call. I also have some calls to make and a staff meeting in a few minutes. Then I'm going to lunch at my parents'."

Jordan became quiet. "When will I get the chance to meet the people who created such a wonderful daughter?" he said finally, his voice pensive.

"Soon," Mia said. "I'm just jetting over there for lunch and coming right back to work."

"Okay, some other time then," Jordan said, although his voice was obviously doubtful. "I'm taking the kids to get their shots for school this afternoon."

"Okay," she said softly, knowing he was bothered that he had yet to meet her parents. *Baby, you just don't understand.* "I can't wait to see you, hold you, touch you, and kiss you."

Jordan laughed low in his throat. "Same here, baby. Same here."

Mia leaned forward to hang up the phone. Knowing that at the end of her hectic workday that she would be in his company, his arms, and his bed made her feel a helluva lot better.

* * *

Her parents' block did not look any different than
the street where Mia lived in Newark. She knew for a
fact that her house, which was recently renovated and
twice the square footage of theirs, was a lot less expensive. All because of the differences in the cities in which
they resided.

Mia turned her car into her parent's paved driveway.
Her mother had worked very hard to make the land-
scape as beautiful as her neighbors', and she had suc-
ceeded.

Before she could knock the wood door opened and
she was engulfed in arms holding her tightly to a chest
as hard, solid, and wide as a brick wall. She inhaled the
familiar scent of Aqua Velva and cigar smoke. How she
loved her father.

"Hey, old man," she teased, blessing his cheek with
a brief kiss as he led her inside the house.

"How's my baby girl?" he asked, his voice gruff.

"Getting older every day," she said as she dropped
her purse onto the mahogany table by the door in the
foyer. "Where's the queen?"

"Real funny," a familiar voice said from behind them.

Mia turned as her mother entered the foyer from the
hall leading from the kitchen "Hey, Ma," Mia said before stepping forward to kiss the smooth cheek of a face
so like her own.

"I'm doing fine. I'm just bored a lot with all this time
on my hands. Plenty of time to baby-sit some grands."

Mia ignored that last dig. "I'm starving. Where's—"

The chime of the doorbell interrupted her. Clara
wiped her manicured hands on the dish towel she carried from the kitchen. "I'll get it. I invited one more
guest for lunch. I hope you two don't mind."

For a hot second Mia thought her mother had invited
Terrence, but she immediately eradicated the idea. Her
mother wouldn't dare.

Niobia Bryant

"Welcome, welcome, Terrence. I'm, I mean we're so glad you could make it."

Mia felt two thousand tiny little red devils run up and down her now rigid spine. She turned and was face-to-face with him. Unable to do anything but be polite, she smiled. "Hi, Terrence, how have you been?"

"I'm doing much better now since I'm seeing you."

Clara looked on with a beaming smile. "Warren, don't they make a beautiful couple? Terrence, this is Mia's father Warren Gordon."

"Nice to meet you, sir," Terrence greeted the older man, extending his hand.

"Mama, may I speak to you in the kitchen please?" Mia asked through a forced smile.

She walked stiffly down the hall into the bright airy kitchen before her mother could put up a protest. Mia stalked around the island in the center of the tile floor as she heard her mother make excuses to her guest. Seconds later she strolled into the kitchen.

"Mia, that was very rude of you—"

"I am so angry with you that I could scream," Mia spat, her eyes blazing. "How could you invite him here without my permission?"

"First off, this is my house. Secondly, you won't seem to get your love life straight, and I'm only trying to help you," Clara said, one hand on her hip, the other wagging at her daughter.

Mia threw her hand up in the air in exasperation. "Are you my mother or my pimp?"

Clara gasped in horror and shock. "How dare you say that to me, Mia Renée Gordon!"

"How dare you try to run my love life!"

"What love life?"

They squared off, both with their arms crossed over their heaving chests in anger.

Very deliberately, Mia said in a clear and concise voice, "I have a man, thank you very much."

Clara's face filled with disbelief. "Yeah, right. Where

is he?" she asked, looming around the kitchen comically. "Why haven't you invited this invisible man to meet your parents?"

"If you weren't such an overbearing, undermining, complaining, spirit-breaking person, then I would have told you months ago about Jordan."

Clara's face became filled with horror.

Warren dropped his head to his chest. He was filled with embarrassment for his wife, his daughter, and himself, but also for the young man who stood beside him. Although he had to give the fellow credit. From his stoic profile you would never guess that he had been witness to the heated family argument.

"If you'll excuse me, Terrence. I better go play referee," he said, already heading down the hall.

The words "You mean that wrinkled mess with the kids next door to you?" preceded him, followed by the sound of something falling.

So that's why Mia hasn't been returning my calls, Terrence thought as he studied his immaculate reflection in the mirror. *She's actually involved with that clown with the brood of children. A mismatch if I ever saw one.*

A cell phone began to ring. He checked his own Startac in the breast pocket of his blazer. "Not mine," he said in a bored air.

Then he noticed the antennae sticking out of Mia's purse on the table beneath the mirror. Looking quickly down the hall to make sure he was alone, he slipped the phone from her purse. Stepping outside he flipped it open. "Yes?"

The line was silent. "Is this Mia's cell?"

"Yes, it is. Who's this?" he asked arrogantly.

"Jordan, who's this?"

Terrence smiled as opportunity knocked. "Look, we're enjoying lunch with her parents. Call back, or better yet forget the number."

"Who is this?"

He closed the phone, ending the call. He pushed the power button off before stepping back into the house and the foyer. With a decidedly satisfied air he slipped the phone back in her purse just as he had found it.

Terrence wanted Mia. She was brilliant, wealthy, beautiful, and connected. She had all the attributes he wanted in a wife. Together they could make a powerful couple. Of course he'd have to break this connection she had to that city of hell she called home.

Casually leaning against the wall, he listened to the rest of the argument.

"Why would you want a man with five children?"

"Clara."

"Oh, be quiet, Warren, you don't care who she chooses to be with."

"As long as she's happy, you're right I don't and neither should you."

"Daddy, don't argue. I can fight my own battles," Mia said. "Mama, I love Jordan. I'm with Jordan, and nothing you can say will change that."

Seconds later Mia strode down the hall and into the foyer. She grabbed her purse, flinging it over her shoulder. Sighing, she turned to Terrence. "Terrence, I'm really sorry you had to hear all that." She smiled weakly before leaving the house.

Terrence watched her go from the window. The mother was on his side, the father was indifferent, and Mia just had to be made to see what she really wanted—him.

Jordan tried to reach Mia by her cell phone for the hundredth time in the past two hours. The same message played: "The wireless customer you are calling is not available at this time. Please try your call again later."

Right now as he sat on his porch, his cordless phone in his hand, Jordan knew several things for sure: Dr.

Suave had been the man to answer Mia's phone today, Dr. Suave had been to Mia's parents with her, Mia had not wanted him to meet her parents, and lastly, Mia was not able to be reached.

Nothing made sense, especially after her call this morning about how important he was in her life. Why call him with those lies and then meet another man at her parents'?

Were they still together? Is that why she wasn't answering her phone? Why wasn't she back in her office?

Jealousy burned in him like fire. Never would he have guessed that Mia would cheat. He thought they had been in a committed relationship. He'd been wrong, and that hurt like hell. He loved her, and she had betrayed him.

Right now he didn't know if he could stand the sight of her. After two hours he didn't want any explanations. He just wanted her out of his life for good.

Knowing that he wanted to avoid her, he quickly strode into the house to recruit his father for baby-sitting duties. After showering and changing, he jumped in his SUV as soon as his father arrived. Desperately needing a diversion he headed to Mahogany's.

Bad choice.

He was reminded and mocked by his memories of the night they had shared there. He sat alone at a single table in a darkened corner. Foolishly he thought alcohol would erase her from his memory.

Jordan wanted to forget the smell of her perfume, the soft husky quality of her laugh, the pure pleasure of her dimpled smile, and the searing of her unique brand of loving to his soul. Hour after hour, drink after drink, he sat there listening to music that mirrored his injured soul and berated himself for his stupidity.

Soon he was quite drunk and even more irate and saddened than before. Constant images of caramel-bronzed limbs entangled with another man haunted and angered him. The alcohol had served no purpose except to make it impossible for him to drive himself home.

Mahogany Woods, the owner of the establishment and a stunning beauty in her own right, came over to greet the well-known author who was a frequent visitor. Immediately noticing his inebriated state, she offered the service of calling a taxi to drive him home. She assured him that his vehicle would be safe and secure in the parking area until he retrieved it.

As Jordan looked up into her friendly smiling face a vision of Mia replaced it instead. "I'm going crazy," he muttered to himself.

He knew that it was time to take Mahogany up on that offer. He pulled his billfold from the back pocket of his baggy jeans. He handed her a fifty-dollar bill to cover the tab. "Thanks, Mahogany. And I'll be needing that cab ASAP."

He felt nauseated, and he just wanted to go home. He was glad when she moved away. The woman reminded him too much of someone he wanted very much to forget.

Tonight was her turn to sit, wait, and worry. Mia glanced down at her watch, using the light on her porch to illuminate the dials. It was after eleven. *Where is he?*

After leaving her parents' Mia had driven to Westside Park, near where she grew up. For hours she had sat there, hurt and angry over the vicious argument with her mother. Her time at the park had been a chance to reflect on a better time when she and her mother had been inseparable. Her family had spent many an afternoon in the park, cooking out, watching local softball games, attending neighborhood events. Where had her loving, understanding mother gone?

Deciding to take the rest of the day off, and needing to talk to Jordan, Mia had headed home. She had been more than a little surprised when Clinton told her that his son wasn't home. She had tried his car phone to no avail. As late afternoon became early evening Mia became more worried. Now as late night reigned she was near distraught imagining the worst.

Twin headlights flashed in the troubled depths of her eyes as a car turned the corner. She felt intense disappointment at the yellow cab she saw coming down the street. It wasn't Jordan's SUV.

Mia rose from the top step on which she sat, deciding to go inside. It was then she noticed that the cab slowed down and then came to a stop in front of Jordan's house. Seconds later Jordan stepped out of the back and paid the cabbie before the car pulled away into the night.

"Jordan," Mia called out to him as she slowly descended the steps. *Where's his car?*

He turned, surprised by her sudden presence. He just glanced over his shoulder before quickly continuing up the path to his porch. An obvious dismissal that left her feeling confused.

Mia raced behind him still dressed in her gray pinstriped suit and matching heels. She reached out for his arm just as he stepped up onto the porch. "Jordan, what the hell is wrong with you?" she asked, holding on to an arm that felt like a band of steel.

He stiffened visibly at her touch before jerking from her grasp. With eyes that froze her soul Jordan looked down into her upturned face. He said nothing, but that spoke volumes.

Mia actually flinched and moved back from the fury she saw in his mocha eyes. "Jordan?" she asked warily.

His square jaw clenched. "Do me and my family a favor and stay away from us."

"Why? What happened?" she asked frantically, her eyes filled with panic as she felt a barrier quickly building between them.

"I know about Terrence, that's what happened," he barked over his shoulder as he continued up the steps.

Mia's look of confusion was not feigned. "Terrence?"

Jordan whirled on the top step of the porch to face her completely. He looked directly down into her anxious eyes and had to steel himself against the twin pools that could allure him. "Was he at your parents' or not today?"

Mia hesitated, surprised by his knowledge of that fact. "Jordan—" she began, climbing the steps quickly to stand beside him.

His hand slashed the air, cutting her off. The eyes that once were warm and comforting like cognac, now glittered dangerously like diamonds. "Yes or no?"

Mia licked her full luscious mouth, biting slightly on her lower lips. She felt his eyes flicker down to watch the move, an obviously nervous gesture on her part. Her eyes met his briefly before looking away.

Jordan raised his hand slowly, lifting her chin so that he saw full into her face. "Yes or no?" he asked again, his voice low but unrelenting and cold.

"Yes," she answered reluctantly. "But—"

Jordan instantly released his slight grasp. "There's nothing more to be said," he said, cutting off any words from her. "I won't put up with a woman who thinks I'm not man enough for her."

"You won't put up with?" Mia asked, each word punctuated with increasing ire at his assumptions and his arrogance. "You know what, Jordan. To hell with your foolish accusations, your foolish ways, and your foolish arrogance."

He watched as she turned and walked away. "No, Mia, to hell with you."

Eighteen

Mia was looking out her living room window when Jordan returned with his SUV the next day, late in the morning. Her heart had flipped at the sight of him, so masculine and sexy in the tan outfit that he wore. She bit back a smile as he hit his head on the door of the vehicle as he exited.

She felt hunger as he stepped out of her line of vision. Admitting to her love for him was fresh and new. Now, like a flash, it had been tarnished.

Mia wrapped her arms around herself, wishing they were Jordan's. She didn't know how Jordan found out that Terrence had been to her parents', nor did she know why she had allowed him to believe the worst last night. There was only one thing she did know for sure: she loved him too much to let him go so easily.

"Now is as good a time as any," she told herself, as she stepped from the window to check her appearance in the mirror.

It was a dress that shouted "Notice me," "Want me," "Listen to me," and "Ravish me." The fuschia knit halter frock by Gigi Hunter was definitely more daring than her usual attire. It had been a gift from Tyresa for her birthday last year. The material clung to every bit of her shapely body and accentuated the bronze tint of her amber skin. The hem stopped just below the knee to show off her shapely calves and delicate ankles in the strappy sandals she wore.

It was lethal! How could Jordan resist?

Yesterday had been a big misunderstanding that she was going to clear up right now! Mia headed out of the bedroom with determination etched in her beautiful face. She was just descending the stairs when the doorbell rang.

"Jordan!" she gasped, just knowing it was him coming to apologize.

Jordan stared over at Mia's house from where he sat on his large wraparound porch. He still couldn't believe that she had cheated on him. Another man had been blessed with her smile, her sweet scent, her touch, her glorious body. Sleep had eluded him last night until he felt as if sandbags now weighed down his eyes. Every time he closed them he saw a vision of her riding another man.

Angry, he slammed his fist down upon the railing with force. "How could she?" he asked, closing his eyes against a sharp wave of pain.

The sound of a car door closing caused him to jerk his eyes open. The pain he already felt spread through his chest at the sight of Dr. Suave stepping up onto the sidewalk in front of Mia's house.

Red-hot rage filled his vision until he thought it would melt his contacts. Jordan wanted to slam his fist into the man's smirking face. He wanted him to regret having ever touched his woman.

And Mia. To think she would plan a date with her other lover so blatantly in his face. *So she couldn't wait for the chance to flaunt the pompous bastard!*

It took the control of a thousand men not to walk over there and beat the hell out of Dr. Suave. A show of violence and jealousy would only serve to make him look like a fool who couldn't handle losing his woman. No, he would not stoop to that level.

Besides, she wasn't worth the effort.

* * *

"Terrence?"

The look of disappointment on her face was clearly evident. She forced a smile as his eyes took in her sensual garb. "What are you doing here?" she asked, stepping out onto the porch to keep him from expecting an invitation inside.

"There's a jazz festival at NJPAC, and I would love for you to accompany me," he said, a smile on his handsome face.

"No, thanks. But I hope you enjoy yourself," she said politely, about to step back into her house.

Her eyes widened in surprise when Jordan's SUV squealed out of his parking spot and down the street. *Oh Lord, he probably thinks I invited Terrence over here!*

Mia's face saddened at the entire situation.

Terrence grinned in satisfaction.

Halfway down the block Jordan convinced himself that he had left so suddenly because he had to join his father and the kids at Ms. M's for an impromptu cookout her family was throwing. He actually made himself believe that seeing Mia in such a dress for another man hadn't spurred his actions. What a big fat lie.

How in the hell was he going to survive living next door to her and not being with her? How would he take seeing her and not speaking to her? How could he take her having another man claim her in the bed he had thought he alone possessed?

As he drove, Jordan envisioned them in the doctor's flashy sports car laughing as they sped off for a Saturday afternoon date. His hand hit the steering wheel as he slowed to stop at a red light. He noticed the woman in the SUV beside him casting curious and interested glances in his direction.

She was pretty in a classic sense, like Amanda.

"Amanda," he said slowly with satisfaction.

As the light turned green, the woman sped off with a honk of her horn. He picked up his cell phone, quickly dialing the seven digits. "Amanda? This is Jordan. You feel up to joining me at a cookout?"

"Y'all kids come and get something to eat," Clinton called over to his grandchildren where they played in the large backyard at Minnie's.

They immediately followed his order, coming to line up by the buffet table. Clinton fixed the twins a plate each, leading them to one of the patio tables.

"Clint, bring the twins over here with me," Minnie called over from where she sat under a large shaded tree. "I haven't seen the children since I hurt this leg."

He immediately did as she bid. "I don't know where that son of mine is," he said upon reaching her.

"I'm sure he's on his way." Minnie assured him, looking up at him adoringly.

Clinton winked at her roguishly before leaning over to plant a firm kiss on her lips. "Love ya."

"Love ya too," she said, sighing with happiness.

The kids all began to fill Ms. M in on their activities since they last saw her. She agreed to let them all sign her cast. Their chatter was nonstop in between bites of food, until they saw their father's SUV pull into the already crowded yard.

The silence around the table was deafening as the seven pairs of eyes—eight if you counted Kimani's glasses—all watched as he helped Amanda out of the vehicle.

Rajahn's young face was a mask of confusion. "What's *she* doing here?"

Kimani removed her glasses, cleaned them methodically with her shirt's hem before replacing them on her slender amber face, only to be disappointed. It was Ms.

Langston that she saw wrapped around her father's arm, and not their Mia.

The twin's lip pouted. "We don't wike her," Aliya piped up.

Tia waited until the couple neared the table. "Where's Ms. Gordon?" she asked, dismissing the woman who stood before them in a white sundress.

Jordan actually fidgeted under his children's piercing stares. He realized now that bringing Amanda like this had not been appropriate, especially with them being unaware of his breakup with Mia. But what could he do now? "You all remember Amanda?"

Clinton stared long and hard into his son's eyes as the children greeted a woman they obviously disliked. Last he knew, Jordan had been deeply involved with Mia. Now here he was with another woman. What the hell was going on?

"How do you do, Amanda?" he finally greeted her with a charming smile, before turning back to his son. "Have a seat, young lady, while my son helps me with this grill."

Amanda sat at the table by Rajahn, her eyes warily on Tia and Kimani. She smiled at everyone as Clinton and Jordan walked away together. When Jordan had asked her to accompany him to a cookout she had envisioned a few older couples under a netted tent, dancing and listening to music, their menu made up of grilled salmon and vegetables with iced alcoholic beverages. Certainly she didn't expect this loud family gathering with hot dogs and hamburgers. *The things women do for a man,* she thought, as she swatted an aggravating fly away.

Clinton opened the lid on the grill and slowly began to turn the barbecued chicken. "What's going on, son?" he asked, briefly looking into Jordan's troubled eyes. "Where's Mia?"

His son's face hardened immediately at the mention of her name. "We're finished," he snapped, using his hand to redirect the acrid smoke from his direction. "And no, I don't want to talk about it."

With that he walked away from the man whose eyes were all too knowing.

Mia decided to have a "Pamper Me" day. She meditated for a long time to release the inner turmoil she felt about her love life—or lack of it. With total quiet and the soothing scent of her incense and Tranquility potpourri called Tropical Sunset, Mia attempted to soothe her soul through peace. She inhaled deeply of the unique blend of geranium rose and coconut by the African-American-owned company. Their products of teas, bathtub teas, potpourri, essential oils, and herbal teas were a godsend to those seeking relaxation.

As she drew a bath with chamomile, Mia made a steaming pot of relaxing Instant Herbal Flash. The tea was an intriguing blend of roasted chicory and guarana seed.

The blend of fragrant scents swirled in the air around the house. Mia actually felt as if she were floating as she set her cup of tea on the small table by the tub and undressed by the candlelight. With a sigh she eased her naked body beneath the steaming fragrant waters, settling against the bath pillow with her eyes closed.

She didn't want him to but Jordan entered her mind so easily. She missed him. She loved him. But no! She was resolved not to focus on her bullheaded, jealous love. This day was all about her, not him!

Mia reveled in the bath until the water cooled nearly twenty minutes later. After stepping out of the tub she wrapped her wet, curvaceous body in a plush bath towel, moving around the spacious area to blow out each scented candle.

In her bedroom Mia put on a jazz CD, humming to the soulful music as she smoothed her damp body over with Pumpkin Pie Cocoa Butter Body Jam. It was a handmade product by Carol's Daughter, an African-American-owned boutique in the Fort Greene section of Brooklyn, and it worked wonders for maintaining her skin. She loved the feel of it on her body and the smell of it was a treat in itself.

Satisfied, Mia wrapped her naked body in a plush toweling robe and slipped her feet into equally fluffy slippers. She felt damn good. How long had it been since she had taken time out for herself?

And she had to give credit where credit was due. Jordan had taught her how to kick back and enjoy life. A few months back she would've been holed up in her office working herself into an early grave for a company that she now knew didn't give a damn about her.

For the gift of learning to enjoy to relax, Mia knew she would love her stubborn man forever.

As the partygoers moved to clear the tables from the portion of the yard that was covered by asphalt, the sun was just beginning to lower in the sky. The adults began to line up, because a party with black folks wasn't a party without the Electric Slide.

It was then that the children cornered their father. Jordan looked down at them as he felt the fence bordering the backyard press against his back. They had caught him off guard. The questions they asked were rapid like automatic gunfire. "Hold it!" he yelled, drawing anxious looks from nearby guests.

"Where's Ms. Gordon, Dad?" Rajahn asked.

"Yeah, where's Ms. Gordon?" the rest of the children chorused.

His gut clenched at the mere mention of her name. He had to tell them the truth, especially with Amanda being his date. This wasn't going to be easy, they loved her just as he did. "Mia and I are not going to see each other," he said finally. "I know you guys love her, but this is for the best."

He couldn't take the disappointed looks on their faces. They were children, and they didn't understand. They couldn't possibly understand the pain Mia had caused him. Seeking solace from their aggrieved expressions, Jordan walked away, pretending to fix himself something from the buffet table.

"Whatcha think happened, Raj?" Tia asked her brother.

"I don't know."

Grown-ups are dumb," Tia snapped, her thin amber arms crossed over her chest. "All our work gone to waste. They messed up everything."

Rajahn looked over at his father, before turning back to his siblings. "Maybe not yet."

Kimani rolled her eyes heavenward. "Why should we keep trying to put them together if they keep breaking apart?"

"Do you want *her* to be our mother?"

They all followed Rajahn's finger, which he pointed at Amanda. She sat uncomfortably on the edge of her seat looking very much as though she'd rather be somewhere else, anywhere else as a matter of fact. She had the warmth of a freezer toward them, no matter how much she melted on their dad.

"Once again, it's on," Tia said.

Clinton wiped his palms on his jeans before he lowered the volume on the portable radio/CD player. All eyes were turned on him.

"Excuse me, everyone, but Minnie and I have an announcement to make," he said, his voice loud, authoritative, and masculine.

Minnie looked at him from where she sat with her leg propped on a pillow in a chair. She held out her hand to him, amazed by the love she had for this man who turned out to be everything and yet nothing like she expected. This Clinton Banks was a teddy bear, and she realized his brusque, chauvinistic manner was a front to the loving man he truly was.

Clinton walked to her, clasping her hand in his warm grasp. "Minnie has agreed to be my wife."

Everyone gasped in mild surprise before breaking off in applause. Her family gathered around the couple with congratulations. Jordan shook his father's hand and clapped him soundly on the back.

He could admit to no one the envy he felt for his father. If Mia hadn't tarnished his loving image of her he could see himself jumping the broom with her. Pain clasped his heart like a fist because it would never be.

Mia was relaxing in her backyard on one of her plush lounge chairs, now dressed in a gauze slip dress that did wonders for letting cool air flow through to her skin. She took another sip of lemonade and turned the page of the book Jordan had bought her. What an absolutely lazy day she had had, and she enjoyed every minute of it, even if she had been lonesome without him and the kids.

"Well, well, speak of the devils," she said with warm pleasure, as she caught sight of the SUV through the break in the hedges.

"Ms. Gordon!" the girls all exclaimed when they, too, caught sight of her.

At least they still like me, she thought, as she closed the nonfiction work. She stood just as they came running through the break in the hedges. "How are the little princesses—" her words froze in her throat as she looked directly into the faces of Jordan and Amanda.

The other woman's look was smug as she placed her arm around Jordan's waist. Together they walked up the stairs and into the house. Jordan had ignored her completely.

Pain clawed at Mia's throat like a rabid dog. Tears filled her luminous eyes and threatened to fall. "Girls,

I . . . I have to go," she stammered, as she gathered her personal items.

Mia raced up the stairs and into the kitchen, closing the door just as the tears fell like rain down her cheeks. She slid to the floor, desolate, as she felt her heart shatter into a million little pieces.

Saddened by seeing Mia so obviously upset the girls went home. They wished Rajahn were there but their grandfather had wanted him to help clean up after the barbecue. He would have known what to do.

They didn't understand grown-up love. They didn't understand why adults hurt each other. All they knew was that they loved their father and they loved Mia like their mother. They wanted a family, and they were determined to have it.

Amanda accepted the glass of wine Jordan gave her. "Thanks," she purred softly, her eyes looking up at him with temptation.

Jordan looked down into her pretty face. "I'm just going to shower and change. Have you decided where you want to go?"

Amanda nodded, allowing the liquid to pool in her mouth to savor the taste. "Mahogany's."

His handsome, lean face closed immediately. "No," he said shortly.

She looked up in surprise. "Why not? Good music, good fun, it's the hottest spot going. Our paper gave it a four-star review."

"Look, anywhere but there," Jordan said, his voice hard, brooking no argument as he stared off at a spot above her head.

Amanda set her wine goblet down, moving from her seat—like a tigress—to massage his shoulders. She was undeterred when he stepped away from her touch.

"You shower, and I'll think of a new locale for our first date."

"Good."

She watched him walk out of the den, aroused by the sight of his hard buttocks and broad shoulders in the casual clothes he wore. She pressed her thighs together to stop the ache.

As soon as Amanda knew he was in his room she rose. Quietly and quickly she left the house and made her way next door. With cruel intentions she rang Mia's bell.

Mia looked up from where she sat huddled in the corner of her leather tuxedo chair when her doorbell rang. "Reese," she spoke into her cordless phone. "Hold on, someone's at my door."

She set the phone on the table, wiping her damp eyes as she moved stiffly to the door. "Who is it?"

"Amanda."

After a moment's hesitation, Mia flung the door open in anger. "What the hell do you want?" she snapped, her eyes blazing like twin fires as she looked at her nemesis with open hostility.

Amanda breezed past her with no invitation, turning in the middle of the foyer to face this woman she couldn't stand with a false smile and a deceptive look in her eyes. "I wanted to make sure there were no hard feelings about . . . well, Jordan and I being together."

Mia stepped back holding the door open wide. "I could care less if Jordan isn't mindful of the company he keeps. Now get out before I throw your ass out," she said, her voice speaking of promise and not just threat.

"We had a wonderful time in Washington." Amanda threw that over her shoulder as she stepped out onto the porch.

Red-hot anger shot from Mia's toes to her head like the mercury in a thermometer in boiling water. She felt ready to explode. "You what!" she exclaimed, disbelief on her face as she frowned.

Amanda turned slowly on her heels, a look of pure satisfaction on her face. "Washington was wonderful. The hotel was worth every star."

In a flash Mia thought of the night Jordan had ended their phone call abruptly and then was unreachable until late that night when he called from his father's. She had been suspicious of his actions then and her thoughts of betrayal were confirmed now.

"That bastard!" Mia spat, slamming her front door closed behind her as she pushed past Amanda to stalk over to Jordan's.

"Where do you think you're going?" Amanda yelled, racing on her stilettos to catch up with a fast-retreating Mia.

But Mia ignored her and was up the stairs, in the house, slamming the front door closed before her nemesis could even reach her. As she marched up the stairs she heard the woman rattling the knob in an effort to open the locked portal.

How dare he accuse me when it was him that was cheating! she thought angrily. In his bedroom she heard the shower running and immediately headed for his bathroom.

Not caring, she flung the shower curtain back. "You have some nerve, you stupid bastard."

Jordan yelled out in surprise. He turned off the shower and turned to face her with cold, uncaring eyes. "What the hell are you doing in my house?"

Mia slapped him, hard, but felt little pleasure or relief of her anger from it. His mocha eyes glittered in anger as he cockily rubbed his jaw, but she was not deterred. "You were with that tramp in Washington?"

Jordan checked his surprise of her knowledge of that fact. "I don't have to explain myself to you."

Mia bit her lip as sharp pain radiated through her body. She had wanted him to deny it, and he hadn't.

This time she wanted to slap him out of sheer need to inflict some kind of pain on him. Swallowing back the tears, she swung.

His hand caught her wrist, stopping her. "You don't want to do that," he warned, his tone ominous.

They looked a sight. Once lovers, now glaring angrily at each other, she in her nightclothes, he wet and naked as he stood in the shower stall. He released her, and Mia left the room without another word spoken between them.

Nineteen

"Your turnaround the past couple weeks has been commendable. Your handling of the Morgan and Capital merger was reminiscent of your starting days as VP of mergers and acquisitions."

Mia looked directly into the eyes of the partners who owned the firm where she worked. The three gentlemen were definitely representative of the old boy network: rich, white males. She focused on Raymond Stromer's baritone voice as he finally got to the reason they had called this meeting with her.

"A partnership certainly looks to be in your future here at Stromer, Wiley . . ."

The rest of his words blurred. This was what she had worked hard for her whole career. And the benefits that would accompany the offer were astounding. A partnership!

Without Jordan in her life she had refocused on her work and the bigwigs had taken note. It was now time to reap the rewards for her years of struggling up the corporate ladder. She deserved this, and she *wanted* it.

"Congratulations."

Mia smiled at the employees assembled in her office when she stepped through the door. They all applauded and raised their flutes of champagne to her in praise.

"Thank you," she said softly, as Tyresa handed her a flute.

"Congratulations," she said softly, touching hers to Mia's briefly, the crystal ringing clear in the air. "You're too much for me."

Her smile was forced. "Thanks to you all again."

Sensing that her friend needed one of their sista chats, Tyresa soon corralled everyone out of her office. "It's still a workday," she explained weakly.

"Thank you again," Mia called out from behind her desk as Tyresa closed the door on the last suited straggler. She set her flute on her desk before removing the Liz Clairborne jacket she wore.

"They implied that a partnership was in my future. Half of me is excited and validated . . . and . . . and . . ." Mia released a breath, unable to find the words. "But the other half of me remembers how stressful this career can be for me working here. I had to return to a seventeen-hour workday for them to make me an offer. How long can I hold up like that without getting burned out?"

Tyresa set her own flute on the desk. "As long as I've known you this has been a goal for you. I'm surprised that you're even hesitant about accepting the offer when it comes."

"I'm not the same person I used to be," she answered softly, her eyes filling with tears because she knew whom she had to thank for that.

They hadn't spoken since that night in his bathroom. They didn't even bother to speak when they passed each other in the street. The hostility and pained feelings of betrayal were ever-present.

Attempts at matchmaking by the children failed miserably until even they had given up. It was over, and although Mia had thought Jordan to be her one true love, slowly but surely she had come to deal with the fact that he did not love her and probably never had.

Amanda was his companion and in retaliation and

need to uphold her pride, Mia had finally accepted Terrence's constant offers for dates. No, she wasn't happy with him as she had been with Jordan, but somebody beat nobody when the man you loved was loving someone else.

Jordan and Mia were finished. Yes, she still cried for what they had thrown away. She still ached for the man she had fallen in love with. All she could do was pull the good memories together and put the bitter memories in her past so that her soul could survive.

At least she still had her relationship with the children. They were still constant visitors to her house. She loved them, and she *knew* they cherished her as well.

Mia sighed, wrapping her arms around herself. Just then the phone rang. Tyresa answered it for her when she saw the troubled light in her friend's eyes.

"Mia, it's Terrence."

Her heart didn't jump as it had at the mention of Jordan's name. The way it still flip-flopped whenever she saw his handsome and sexy, cheating face. Taking a deep breath she accepted the phone. "Hi, Terrence," she said, forcing happiness into her tone.

Jordan's book was still on the best-seller's list as it had been the past four weeks, but his mind was focused on beginning the next in his Slim Willie series, after he took the children to the Catskills before they began school the following week. With them in school his time would free up.

He was sitting on his porch reading *Forced into Glory: Abraham Lincoln and the White Dream,* a book that questioned the myth of Abraham Lincoln as "The Great Emancipator." He wasn't able to put the proper concentration into it though, especially when he looked up just in time to see Mia's car pull up into her driveway.

He heard the car door open and close. Was he crazy

or could he smell her Tresor perfume actually waft over to him? He shook his head to remove the sensation.

Above the hedges he saw her head with the full profile appearing slowly as she climbed the steps onto the back porch. She turned suddenly and their eyes met and held.

God, I miss her, he admitted to himself, although he kept his face unreadable. *Why can't I get her out of my mind?* Anytime he saw her with Dr. Suave, it cut him to the core like a knife. He couldn't get her out of his system.

A car door slammed, and his head swung away from Mia to see Amanda make her way up the walk. Jordan's head swung back to Mia's porch, but Mia was gone.

Mia was just settling into her office when her phone rang. She reached out to answer it. "Hello."

"Hi there, Mia. This is Minnie."

Mia smiled with pleasure. "Hi, Ms. M, how are you? It's good to know you're up and at 'em again. Excited about your big day?"

The older woman laughed. "I sure am. In fact I was calling to see if you changed your mind about attending. Clinton and I really want you there."

Mia fell quiet. "I don't think so. Jordan wouldn't—"

"So you still haven't told him the truth about your mother inviting Terrence for lunch that day?" she asked with obvious disapproval in her tone.

Mia had confided in the older woman during one of their many phone conversations. Times like these she regretted her candor. "No, I haven't."

"I've always found the truth to be the best way. Take my advice. Tell him. You might be surprised."

"I doubt it."

"I'm not going to beat a dead horse but we've gotten to be close. I really wish you'd change your mind."

"I'll think about it," Mia said softly, her eyes misting with tears as her throat constricted with pain.

"You do that. You think about *everything.*"

Mia hung up the phone, using both of her hands to wipe her eyes. The tension she felt behind them was increasing.

"I've always found the truth to be the best way. Take my advice. Tell him. You might be surprised," Ms. M had said.

Surprised by what? Mia couldn't help but wonder what Ms. M meant by that. Did she know something she wasn't telling? Besides, the older woman didn't understand, clearing up the truth about Terrence with Jordan would not erase the fact that *he* had cheated with Amanda. No, Ms. M had no idea of the black hole of pain that Mia constantly felt herself dwell in.

Purposefully pushing the hurting thoughts away Mia stood and stretched her long shapely frame. She had to get ready for a date with Terrence. Sitting here thinking of Jordan wasn't going to do it, for sure. Glancing at her watch she saw that it was a little after 7:00 P.M.

She thought of Terrence as she climbed the stairs. He certainly had the patience of Job. They'd been out on about five dates, and so far he had been content with the sisterly pecks she gave him on his cheek. Not that he had a choice because that was all that he was getting.

But as she entered her bedroom she felt that familiar guilt. She was not interested in Terrence in the least. In fact, if she were honest with herself, she was just using him to fill the enormous void Jordan left in her life. He was a boost to her ego, a buffer against some of the pain.

Mia knew that sooner or later she was going to have to end it because she had no intention of taking their placid relationship to the next level. Besides, cheater or not, it would take a special man to top Jordan's skills in pleasing her, particularly in bed.

As she stood under the spray of the shower Mia gave

in to her memories of Jordan's unique brand of loving. She closed her eyes, and recalled their last intimate moments while letting the water pulsate against her skin. The way he tasted of her core. The feel of his hands on her body. The strength and intensity of his deep strokes within her.

She shivered just thinking about it! The bud between her legs swelled. "Oh, Jordan," she moaned, leaning back against the wall, wiping the tears and the water from her face with both hands. "Why do I still miss him?" she cried out in anguish, her voice echoing against the tiled walls.

Quickly, she reached to switch the steaming water to cold, hoping it would freeze the desire for him that ran through her veins like fire.

It didn't work.

Mia rushed through her shower and left the bathroom wrapped in a plush peach towel. With her eye on the clock, she dressed. She had just slipped into her shoes when the doorbell rang.

"I'm ready, Terr—" the words froze on her lips as she looked up. "Jordan?"

Her eyes devoured every bit of him as she held her breath. He stood there tall, athletic, strongly built, and so damn beautiful in black casual wear. She wanted to kiss away their past and start anew with the future. Her heart swelled in her chest. She had to bite her lip to keep from telling this man that she loved him completely.

This was the closest she had been to him in weeks, and she was overwhelmed by him. "Hello, Jordan. Is something wrong?" she asked, her voice soft as she watched him slide his hands deep into his pants pockets.

"On your way out?"

Mia used a finger to push her curly hair back behind her ear. "Yes, yes, I was."

He lowered his head briefly before clearing his

throat. "I just wanted to assure you that you shouldn't miss the wedding on my account."

Hope died in her chest like a doused fire. "The wedding?"

He nodded, his deep-set eyes uncaring as they flickered over her dismissively. "Ms. M just called and said that you wouldn't attend, and I want you to go for her sake. I know that you want to and the only reason I can think you wouldn't go is our breakup. I can handle it if you can."

Mia said nothing, she just looked at him, nervously licking her lips.

"I wonder, little Mia," he said suddenly, his tone mocking and insulting, his eyes cold and distant. "Does he make your toes curl the way I used to?"

Mia gasped. "Go to hell, Jordan," she said softly, dropping her eyes from his to hide the pain his words inflicted.

He lightly trailed her bottom lip with his finger. "I'll see you there."

And he was gone, leaving Mia shivering with an odd mix of desire and anger swirling around her in an explosive blend until she didn't know if she were coming or going.

Jordan watched from the shadow of his porch when she left with her new lover. He could just as well have called her but he had wanted to see her, be near her. The wedding had just been an excuse. The little vix was in his blood.

And she looked so damn beautiful in her soft pastel dress that he had to put his hands in his pockets to keep from touching her. How many times had he dreamed of loving her: slow and sensual, fast and feverish, deep and delightful? *When will she mean nothing to me?* he wondered, before moving to enter the house.

He went down to the playroom where his children were assembled. They all looked over their shoulders at him, briefly, returning their attention to the movie playing on the big-screen television. Jordan sat down among them on the floor as they made room. The twins immediately climbed in his lap.

"Dad, you forgot the popcorn," Tia scolded him.

"I sure did."

"I'll get it," Raj volunteered, rolling to rise.

As he made his way up the stairs the phone began to ring. "Unless it's Grandpa, I'm not home," Jordan yelled up behind him.

He was avoiding Amanda for the moment. He needed a break. The woman was persistent and outspoken on her desire to have him in her bed. He made sure to limit the time they spent together. Jordan was in no way interested in becoming seriously involved with her. He just knew it irked Mia to think he was involved with her.

Truly he was getting tired of the whole game. He was a man with five children and not a child himself. He looked forward to leaving for the Hudson Valley in the morning. It would give him a break from it all.

Rajahn returned carrying a large bowl of buttery popcorn, the scent preceding him down the stairs. "That was Amanda on the phone," he said, as he set the bowl and the napkins he had carried down to his family.

"Thanks, Raj." Jordan felt the children's eyes on him but he ignored them, feigning interest in the comedy they were watching.

"I'm gonna miss Ms. Gordon while we're gone," Kimani said.

"Me too," her siblings agreed.

He released an anxious breath until the children turned back to the movie. He just couldn't take another session of "Why aren't you with Ms. Gordon?" He just thanked God they had ceased their matchmaking antics. They had even tried to trick him and Mia into the basement again.

He felt sad as he thought of that first night of passion he and Mia had shared together. He glanced over at that corner, with a clear vision of their naked entwined bodies by candlelight.

Shaking his head to clear it, Jordan was determined to put Mia in his past and move on. The love he had for her and the trust he put in her had been a mistake. A mistake that he would not make again.

The next morning Mia rose early as the September sun was just beginning to rise over the city. She dressed and performed her usual daily routine in the bathroom.

Once in her sneakers she jogged down the steps and left the still-dark house. She smiled when she saw that they hadn't left yet. Mia wanted to wish the children well on their weeklong summer vacation.

As Mia approached, Rajahn and Jordan were loading the last few items into the back. She bit back a smile when Jordan's end of the cooler slipped from his hand and landed soundly on his foot.

His expletive of pain echoed throughout the early-morning empty streets. The look of discomfort was evident on his handsome face but it quickly turned to surprise and then dismissal when he saw her slowly walking over to them.

"Ms. Gordon!" Kimani exclaimed happily, running over to hug her around the waist tightly. "Are you going with us?"

The hope in her voice tugged at Mia's heart. "No, I'm still not going. I just wanted to see you off safely."

She hugged each to her and kissed the top of their heads, even Raj, who fidgeted as young teen males do when given affection by a family member. As she did, Jordan said nothing to her before going to sit in the

SUV, ignoring her completely. That hurt Mia, but she swallowed it down with a false smile for the kids.

Reluctantly, as the sun rose steadily in the fast-appearing clouds above her, the children climbed in, each buckling in safely. She turned and watched them as they waved at her until the SUV disappeared around the corner. With one final wave she silently wished them a safe trip.

Jordan watched her in his rearview mirror until he turned the corner and her image was gone. His heart hadn't stopped pounding yet from the mere sight of her. This week would be both a blessing and torture. The part of him that still ached from the pain of her betrayal looked forward to the reprieve from seeing her. But the other part of him that seemed to be ruled by his unloyal heart would miss the rare glimpses of her every day from next door.

"Dad?"

Jordan looked briefly over at his son as he headed for the New Jersey Turnpike. "Yeah?"

"Can you explain to me, why the Catskills over Disney-land?" Rajahn's skepticism rang out loudly in his tone.

Jordan laughed. "It's closer to home. It's something different for a change. You'll see something besides an urban environment."

"Disneyland isn't exactly urban, Dad."

"True," Jordan said as he switched lanes effortlessly. "We're staying in a renovated Victorian castle sitting on the edge of a lake."

"For real?" he asked, some interest now evident.

"No, for fake," Jordan joked. "Trust me, son. We're gonna have fun."

"We'll see."

During the two-hour drive the children played travel games and quizzed their father endlessly on any and every topic that popped into their heads. With patience he answered each one as best he could. Jordan was encouraged. So far the trip was starting off well.

Soon he pulled the SUV into New Paltz, which was located in the Catskills region of the Hudson Valley. The children were more than relieved when he stopped in the parking area of the Mohonk Mountain House. He and Rajahn had to carry each of the sleeping twins, with Tia and Kimani closely at their sides.

Jordan looked upon the thousands of acres of unspoiled scenery. The land was rich and fertile, the air clean and unpolluted, the skies the perfect blanket of azure, the trees tall green testaments of nature.

He smiled, his chin on Amina's head as he surveyed the lush habitation. Rajahn didn't look pleased by what he saw at all, that was obvious from his frown. "Trust me," Jordan advised before his son could complain.

That night Mia took a long, hot shower and washed her hair, before settling on the couch in her living room to watch television as she worked on a speech she was giving on increasing minorities' participation in investing. She was just reading over her first draft when the phone rang.

Picking it up, she didn't recognize the number on the caller ID. "Hello."

"Ms. Gordon."

She sat up, pressing the phone closer to her face as she recognized Kimani's voice. "Hello there, little lady. Does your daddy know you're calling me?"

"Yeah, he's right here. You want to talk to him?"

Yes! "No, that's okay."

Mia's heart hammered in her chest just knowing he was within listening distance of their conversation. "How's the trip going?" she asked, eager to change the subject.

"We're having fun," Kimani exclaimed. "We're staying in a castle and today we went horseback riding."

"So the little princesses finally get to stay in a castle," Mia said with feigned seriousness.

Kimani giggled.

One by one she spoke to the children. Mia missed them, and they had only been gone one day. She relished the happiness in their voices, especially the twins, who were excited about the ponies they rode. She was reluctant to hang up but she knew it was close to their bedtime. "Okay then, good night," she said softly to Kimani, who had reclaimed the phone.

"Bye."

The line disconnected.

After replacing the cordless on the base, Mia picked up the remote, continuing on her wandering through the cable channels. She had just settled on a rerun of *The Jeffersons* when the phone rang again.

Laughing as Sherman Hemsley did his character's unique dance, Mia reached for the phone again. "Hello," she said, humor still in her voice.

"Is Jordan there?" a female voice asked with open hostility.

Mia frowned with surprise and disapproval. "Excuse me?" she asked, as she picked up the remote, placing the television on mute. "You have the wrong number."

"No, I don't. Now put my man on the phone!"

Mia rolled her eyes heavenward. "If he's your man then why are you calling my house?" she snapped sarcastically.

With that she ended the call. When she checked the caller ID she saw that the number had been blocked. She turned on her phone and pushed the code to activate the feature on her caller ID that did not accept blocked numbers.

Next she scrolled back and retrieved the number where Jordan and the kids were staying. Her adrenaline was running high with indignation as she dialed the number quickly.

"Jordan Banks' suite please," she said politely when the clerk answered the phone.

It rang just once.

"Hello."

Mia took a deep breath and then it rip. "I would appreciate it if you would advise your women not to call my house looking for you."

"Mia?" he asked, surprise obvious in his deep, husky voice.

"Yes, and I meant what I said. Tricks are for kids and I ain't in the mood."

She hung up before he could speak. She waited with the phone in her hand, expecting him to call back, but he didn't. Neither did the woman.

The nerve!

Twenty

The day of Clinton and Minnie's wedding dawned bright that September morning two weeks later. The brilliance of the neon disk in the azure sky was the ideal backdrop for the legal and spiritual union of two souls who loved each other dearly.

Against her better wishes Mia was attending the nuptials. That meant she had to have a date, so she invited Terrence. Besides she wanted to join in their celebration, even if the kids told her that Jordan had invited Amanda as well.

And the fact that the beautiful woman would be there had absolutely nothing to do with Mia spending nearly all day in Sweet Things, the full-service day spa/salon she had visited the day before. Nor was it the reason why she spent the rest of the day at Short Hills Mall shopping for just the right dress. Topping Amanda was not her motivation.

Well, okay, maybe it was.

With a pleasant sigh Mia turned gracefully in the full-length mirror, more than satisfied with her appearance. A little vainly she blew a playful kiss at her reflection. "Now let me see Miss Amanda outshine this," she said with confidence.

Her shoulder-length tresses, which she usually wore loose and curly from a biweekly rod set, had been highlighted with auburn and then wrapped to now flow in an ultrastraight blunt bob that framed her face and caressed her delicate collarbone. Following the advice of her stylist she wore a lightweight supersheer foundation that added just a hint of shimmer to her caramel complexion for a sun-kissed glow. The rest of the makeup was very minimal.

Now the dress was lethal. The yellow one-shoulder number was as bright and as inviting as the sun that blazed in the sky. But it was the design of the Emanuel Ungaro Parallele summer dress that had drawn Mia to it. Flowing ruffles lined the top as the soft material clung lovingly to her full breasts, falling to fit her flat stomach and curvaceous hips before the hem fell in a flowing asymmetrical cut from just below her hip on the left down to below her knee on the right. It had been worth every delicious cent she spent on it. Glass stilettos complimented the outfit and showed off her pedicured toes. The dress was totally sexy, totally feminine, and totally destined to be the showstopper she wanted it to be.

Mia had just slipped on her two-karat diamond stud earrings and three-karat tennis bracelet when her doorbell rang. With one last glance at herself she left the room and descended the stairs. The look on Terrence's handsome face when she opened the front door said enough about her success in creating the optimal feminine presentation.

Gone was his usual reserved manner as his eyes widened in approval. Leisurely he looked at her in awe from head to toe. "Mia, you look beautiful."

"Thank you," she said uneasily, as he looked at her wolfishly. She closed her door. "Now close your mouth," she teased as she passed him to descend the front porch.

When she didn't hear him following behind her, Mia turned, well aware of the dangerous hemline that swirled up around her well-toned thighs and curved hip. Terrence stood transfixed in the same spot with his eyes hotly upon her, his mouth slightly ajar.

That was exactly the response she hoped for but not

from him. *Jordan, eat your heart out*, she thought with a mischievous smile, deepening the dimple in her chin.

"You nervous, old man?" Jordan teased his father as he clapped him soundly on the shoulder where they waited in an anteroom of the church.

Clinton ran a finger around the inside of his collar, looking very distinguished and handsome in his morning suit. "Just ready to get out of this getup."

Jordan laughed before pulling his father into a tight bear hug. "I'm happy for you, Dad."

"I thought I would never love anyone after your mama died. But Minnie is special, and I had my eye on her for a long time," he told his son with a roguish wink. "I hope she can keep up."

"Let's go before she changes her mind."

The two men left the room and climbed the stairs that led them to the front of the church by the altar. Jordan froze in his steps just as he crossed the threshold. He didn't even move when his father bumped into the back of him. He wasn't able. He was awestruck.

The double doors of the small church opened and in walked Mia, framed by the beaming sunlight in one hell of a dress that rivaled the brightness of the sun against her supple bronzed skin. Jordan's eyes devoured her from her newly styled hair, her beautiful face, the body-molding dress with a hemline that wrecked his senses.

She glided down the aisle drawing attention from everyone before slipping onto the seat to which the usher showed her. Slowly, as if meaning to torture him, she crossed one shapely leg over the other exposing a smooth expanse of thigh.

Clinton stepped to the side of his son, his own face knowing as he followed Jordan's transfixed gaze.

Clinton bit back a smile. It sure was a good thing they were partially hidden by the floral arrangements, because the look on his son's face definitely wasn't appropriate for the church.

But besides the lust, Clinton saw love. "Son, we need to talk," he said with humor, as he slapped him loudly on the back to jar him.

"Huh?" Jordan asked, confused and turning to face his father.

Without another word Clinton led his son back through the doorway they had just entered. "Let's go, boy."

The twins went running past them, both dressed in their floral flower girl attire. Clinton stopped them and gave each a message to deliver. They left to do as they were told.

"What's this about?" Jordan asked, obviously recovered. "We're supposed to be upstairs."

"There's something you need to know first."

Mia sighed as Terrence slid closer to her and placed his arm possessively around her where they sat on the walnut pew.

The wedding guests were dressed in pretty pastel colors with large impressive matching hats. The men were finely dressed in their suits. The small church was decorated perfectly with candles, ribbons, and lush floral arrangements.

"The church is so beautiful," she said softly as she looked around.

"Not as beautiful as my lady," he whispered, his breath tickling her ear.

Who said I was your lady? she thought as she forced a smile and tilted her head away from him.

Mia's entire body stiffened when she felt something moist and warm pressed to her shoulder. *I know he didn't just kiss my body,* her mind shrieked.

"Ms. Gordon."

She was stopped from reprimanding him by a soft

voice. Mia turned to see Amina standing beside her. "Don't you look beautiful, sweetheart," Mia said, raising her hand to touch the neat ringlets in her hair. "And your hair!"

"Daddy took us to the beauty parwor," she answered. "Ms. M wants you."

Mia accepted her small hand. "Excuse me, Terrence," she said as Amina pulled her through the people standing and mingling in the church.

Minnie smiled at her daughter in the mirror as she helped settle the wide-brimmed ivory hat with satin trim that matched her beautiful embroidered satin two-piece suit. "Thank you, baby."

"You make a beautiful bride, Mama," Alyssa said with a soft smile.

A knock at the door of the room interrupted them. They both turned to see Aliya enter. Minnie smiled at how adorable she looked. "Yes, sweetheart?"

"Grandpa said to go ahead and tell Ms. Gordon."

Minnie immediately understood, and as if on cue Mia and Amina entered the room hand in hand. "Hello, ladies," Minnie said warmly.

Mia smiled a greeting at Alyssa before immediately walking over to kiss the soon-to-be-bride's cheek "Aren't you beaming, Miss Thang," she teased.

"I'm happy, that's all," she told her. "Alyssa, will you take the twins? I need to talk to Mia."

"Sure, Mama."

"Is something wrong, Minnie?" she asked after they left.

"Yes. You and Jordan not being together."

"Marriage is a lifelong bond signifying the union of a man and a woman who are in love."

Mia listened to the minister's words with only half of

her attention. She was too lost in the revelation Minnie had made.

Was it true?

Could it be that she had falsely accused Jordan?

She cut her eyes over to where he stood by his father, serving as the best man. She could only see the back of him, but even that was impressive. Just his stance as he listened to the minister's words was tempting. It was all a lesson in subtle arousal.

She bit back a smile when he suddenly cast a chastising, hard look at Kimani and Tia, who giggled together where they stood with the rest of the bridal party.

He truly was magnificent.

Now there was a chance that this anger and mistrust between them was all for nothing. Could it really be possible? She couldn't deny the hope that sprang alive in her chest.

"Love is a wonderful thing, and it comes when you least expect it," the minister's voice rang out.

Mia's eyes went right to Jordan's tall figure again, and she gasped in surprise when she saw that he was already looking over his shoulder directly at her. Her heart pounded in her chest as she nervously licked her lips slowly.

Terrence leaned over and kissed her bared shoulder again. "That will be us one day," he whispered.

Mia stiffened, and Jordan's face hardened before he turned back to face forward. She attempted to scoot away from Terrence's persistence, but he only moved closer.

"By the powers vested in me, by our Lord and the State of New Jersey, I now pronounce you husband and wife for all eternity." Minister Franks closed his Bible and smiled broadly. "You may now kiss your beautiful bride."

Mia was one of the first to applaud as Clinton pressed his mouth down upon Minnie's with obvious love and devotion. She and the rest of the guests stood as the minister instructed.

"I now present to you Clinton and Minnicent Banks."

The beaming couple exited with the wedding party following behind them. Mia blew kisses to the girls and winked at Rajahn as they passed her. Before she even turned, she felt Jordan's eyes on her. She felt the energy between them magnify. She wanted to pull him into her arms and kiss him, but she didn't. He still had lied about that night in Washington.

Jordan couldn't take his eyes off her. She was beautiful, especially in that dress. He couldn't believe that she had allowed him to think the worst about her concerning Terrence, but then hadn't he done the same about Amanda and himself? As he looked at her standing there like sunshine he wanted so desperately to believe that she hadn't betrayed him. He wanted to wrap his body into her body and just enjoy the feel of her. He wanted to kiss her so deeply that he tasted her soul. He wanted this incredible woman back in his life.

But there were too many questions still to be asked and answered. Like why in the hell was Terrence's hand on her as if he possessed her? And how far had their relationship gone in the past weeks?

Even as he walked past her, Jordan turned to look back over his broad shoulder. As he did, it seemed as if time ticked slowly. The look of disappointment on her face tugged hard at his heart.

Mia and Terrence were walking side by side into the hall where the reception was being held, just as Jordan and Amanda were walking side by side out of the building. The two couples nearly collided.

"Hello, Mia." *Damn, I love this woman.*

"Jordan." *Why do I love him so much?*

The two stared deep into each other's eyes as Amanda wrapped herself around his arm. Terrence slid his hand across Mia's back to settle low on her waist. Both of the lovers shook them away.

"We need to talk," they both said in unison.

Jordan grabbed Mia's hand and quickly pulled her behind him back into the hall. Amanda and Terrence stood speechless as their dates entered a room and soundly closed the door.

Amanda smoothed her hand over her perfectly coifed upsweep. "How rude," she said with false calmness to the silent man left standing beside her.

Terrence folded his tie back into his single-button suit jacket. "Exactly."

"I don't have to put up with this foolishness, she snapped, her anger rising as she turned to needlessly fix her immaculate makeup in the oval mirror on the wall.

Terrence's eyes skimmed over her, now quite tired of Mia's games. "You certainly do not."

Amanda turned, hearing the approval in his voice. Funny, she hadn't really noticed just how handsome the doctor was before. Definitely more her upscale style than Jordan with his brood of children. She flashed him her brilliant smile and extended her slender hand. "Dr. Blanchard, right?" she asked with a seductive lick of her lips.

Mia looked around the small room that obviously served as a storage area. Jordan leaned against the door, his arms folded across his heart as he watched her intently.

"Nice dress," he said huskily after another lengthy perusal.

Mia whirled in the middle of the floor sending the asymmetrical hem up around her hips in yellow billows. "It is nice, isn't it?"

Jordan took one large step to pull her to him from behind, his arm like a band of steel around her waist. He inhaled deeply of her scent, was aroused by the feel of her plush buttocks against his swelling manhood. "Did you spin like that for Dr. Suave?" he asked, his face close to the hollow of her neck.

Mia shivered at the feel of being in his arms. She closed her eyes in pleasure. "I don't want Terrence," she said softly with conviction, as she moved her hands to rest lightly on his arm.

Jordan laughed lightly, mockingly. "I can't tell."

"I only started seeing him because I was mad about you and Amanda," she admitted, tired of the games, her voice barely a whisper.

"And I only started seeing her because of the time I saw him pick you up." Jordan's heart pounded, echoing in his ears like drums. "Baby, I'm sorry for lying about that night in D.C. I swear she sneaked in my room—"

Mia stiffened before using all her strength to push out of Jordan's grasp. "She was in your room?" she asked in disbelief as she turned to face him.

Jordan pulled her back into his embrace, this time using all his strength not to let her go. "I didn't want her there. I threw her out."

"Did you sleep with her?" Mia asked, anger still in her voice as Jordan attempted to massage the back of her head.

"Hell no," he swore. "And I still haven't. I swear."

"She told me you invited her."

Jordan's body stiffened. "Why would I when I practically begged you to go with me?"

Mia didn't know what she believed, but she knew it was so good being close to him again. With the fast beating of her heart, the race of her pulse, the tightening of her nipples, and the rising throb of the bud between her legs, her body had already responded.

"Did you sleep with him?" he asked hoarsely as he bent his head to nuzzle her neck.

"Hell no," Mia answered, looking up into his brilliant mocha eyes just as she raised her face to his for the kiss they both longed and trembled for.

Their eyes remained open as Jordan licked the sweet contours of her luscious mouth. Mia did the same before seeking entrance into the cool hollow with her eager, wandering tongue. They both moaned as their tongues danced hotly in the air between them.

Feverishly the kiss intensified as they allowed their hands to explore the contours of each other's body. "Oh, Jordan, I—I love you so," Mia admitted into his mouth, unable to hold back her feelings for him any longer.

"I love you, too, baby," he answered hoarsely, as he captured her tongue.

The door swung open. They broke apart slowly turning to see the surprised waiter who stood in the doorway. "You're not supposed to be in here," the nervous man stammered at the sight of them.

Jordan and Mia laughed as he grabbed her hand and led her out of the room to the hall's foyer. He immediately pulled her back into his embrace. "Your body feels so damn good," he moaned.

She smiled as she kissed his strong neck. "You feel good, too, baby, but I don't think this is the place to make up for lost time."

"Right," he agreed reluctantly. With one last tender kiss Jordan placed Mia's hand on his arm.

"Tell me you love me again," she said softly, looking up into his handsome face.

"I love you," he said fiercely, as his hand softly caressed her full bottom lip.

And Mia saw the love in his eyes and felt it in his caress. Together they entered the ballroom, hand in hand.

The children all smiled their approval at the sight of the couple. Clinton and Minnie waved from the center of the dance floor where they rocked in each other's arms.

"Well, I'll be damned," Jordan said in amazement.

"What?"

He pointed across the room, and Mia, too, was amazed to see Amanda and Terrence dancing quite closely together. "Good," she laughed, feeling no jealousy. "Now they'll leave us the hell alone."

She looked into his handsome, strong face and saw that he, too, lacked any jealousy over the loss of Amanda. "Shall we?" she invited with a curtsy.

With a grin he pulled her into his arms. Together they began a slow grind. They held each other tightly as they danced the night away.

Clinton pressed his wife closer as they swayed. "We did good," he said, as he nodded toward Jordan and Mia, who seemed to be in their own world.

"Yes, we did."

"I sure hope you're ready for the honeymoon. Can you handle it?" he asked, his voice low and husky, as he lowered his hand to clasp her buttocks.

In the past Minnie would've become shocked and angry by his boldness. Now she lowered her hand to his backside and did the same, amused by his shocked expression. "I've been handling it so far," she said saucily, before throwing back her head with a laugh.

"How about a nightcap at my place?" Amanda said softly into Terrence's ear before she sucked the lobe lightly. "There's nothing here for either of us anymore."

He leaned back to look down into a beautiful pair of honey-colored eyes. "I don't regret that now. Do you?"

She shook her head just before he lowered his head to hers for a kiss that shook her to her toes. "Let's go."

Hand in hand they strolled past an entwined Mia and Jordan and out of the building into a night of new beginnings.

"I can't wait to grow up and fall in love," Kimani said as her father planted a kiss on Mia's brow.

"Love ain't easy," Rajahn advised.

Tia sighed heavily. "We ought to know. Look how hard we had to work to get those two together."

Twenty-one

Fall in the city was alive but at a much more sedate pace with the return of children to school and the coming of night's darkness an hour earlier. Gone were the giggles and screams of school-age children delighting in outside games. But always the sounds of activities remained: the blaring of horns, the muted whir of distant ambulances and police sirens.

Mia turned in her seat to look at Jordan as he drove. "Shopping is high on my list of accomplished skills. This will be a breeze," she told him, speaking of the trip they were taking to the mall to buy more clothes for the kids' winter wardrobe.

He reached over to capture her soft hand in his, cherishing the bright smile she gave him.

To think just a couple of weeks ago they had passed each other in the street without speaking, had complicated their lives with Terrence and Amanda, and had almost thrown it all away. Now the kids were happy, Jordan's father and Minnie were smug, and he and Mia were more in love than ever. Mia hah invited him and the children to a big party at her parents' later that afternoon.

"I want to go to the GAP for my clothes," Tia said as Jordan turned the SUV into the entrance of Woodbridge Mall.

"How about I take Tia and Kimani, you take the

twins, and Raj shops alone," Mia suggested, as they all climbed out.

Rajahn's eyes lit up at the prospect of being able to choose whatever he wanted for however much he wanted. Jordan frowned in immediate disapproval. "How about Rajahn picks out his clothes and puts them on hold until I approve them and then pay."

His son's face became crestfallen. "Dad, I can shop for myself."

"You also believe it's okay to pay eighty dollars for a top just a little better than a T-shirt," Jordan said wryly, as the ladies all looked on impatiently by the SUV. "Polo, FUBU, and Tommy will not be the end of me."

"Dad, we're rich. We can afford it," Raj countered, basically placing the final nail in his coffin.

"I'm rich, you're not, Jordan told him, only half joking.

Mia bit back a smile. "Looks like we have a plan then. Shall we?" she asked, as she accepted the crisp bills Jordan gave her.

Jordan nudged his son before offering the sullen teen a pound. Grudgingly Rajahn returned it.

They had agreed to meet at Friendly's at 2:00 P.M. Mia and the girls appeared at the restaurant first, each burdened with several shopping bags. Ten minutes later Jordan and the twins strolled up, with Rajahn walking a short distance behind as he read the latest issue of *Vibe* magazine.

The adults looked flustered while the girls filled one another in on the latest additions to their wardrobes. Jordan took all the packages. "Get a seat while Raj and I take these to the SUV."

Mia's feet hurt but she wasn't sure it was quite as bad as the throbbing in her head. She immediately kicked off her mules as soon as they were seated. The children shared the booth directly behind her. Basically she was ready to go home.

"Wasn't such a breeze, was it?" Jordan asked, as he slid into the booth across from her.

"Hell no," Mia moaned. "Who knew kids were so picky? And the clothes were as high as mine almost."

Jordan reached under the table and pulled her bare feet into his lap. "Welcome to my world," he said, as he began to massage them.

Mia sighed in pleasure at his ministration. "You deserve an award."

The waitress walked up and Mia lowered her feet to turn in the booth and supervise the children's ordering in the booth behind them. He stared at her beautiful profile as she pushed her ultrastraight hair behind her ear. He truly adored her. He liked having someone to share responsibility with. He liked having Mia's influence in his life and his children's lives. He couldn't lose her again. Jordan just didn't think his heart could stand it.

"Nervous?" Jordan asked, as he watched Mia bite off her lipstick.

Mia smiled at him, far too brightly and falsely. "Why would I be nervous, Jordan? Don't be silly."

"Maybe because you're taking me to meet your parents for the first time?"

Mia just laughed lightly. She didn't trust her mother's mouth or her actions. In fact, they had hardly spoken since Clara had found out her precious Dr. Terrence was now steadily dating Amanda. In fact it was her father who had extended the invitation for the surprise party they were throwing for some friends. He had assured Mia that her mother would behave.

She firmly believed her father was swimming in denial, and she didn't mean the river in Egypt!

Jordan caressed the inside of her palm with his

thumb. "I'm sure you're worrying for nothing, baby. Okay?"

Baby, you just don't know, she thought, but said, "Okay" as if she really believed his words.

"Make this right at the light. It's the second house on the left," Mia advised him as they neared their destination.

Jordan did as she told him and soon they were parked in front of the brick house. They were all climbing out of the SUV as the front door swung open.

Her father's face beamed as soon as his eyes lighted upon her. He immediately strode over to them. "Mia, how's my baby girl?" he asked with love, before enfolding her into a tight hug.

"Hey, Daddy."

"And this must be Jordan," he said with warmth as he extended his hand. "So you're the fellow who's got my girl smiling, huh?"

Jordan shook the hand offered to him. "I try my best, sir. It's nice to meet you."

"Daddy, this is Rajahn, Tia, Kimani, and the twins, Amina and Aliya." Mia introduced them with pride, lightly touching each as she did.

Warren slid his hand into his pockets. "Looks like I might have some candy somewhere in here," he teased them, his gray eyes bright. With a laugh he pulled out five lollipops, handing them each one.

"What are you supposed to say?" Jordan prompted.

"Thank you," they chorused.

Mia's heart swelled with love for her father. Impulsively she kissed his weathered cheek and hugged him tightly around his neck.

"Aren't you going to introduce me to your friend, Mia?"

She stiffened at the sound of her mother's voice. Slowly she turned to face her. "Hi, Mama, this is Jordan . . . Jordan Banks and his beautiful children," she finished, listing their names again.

Clara extended her manicured hand to him with a soft smile. He warmly enveloped her hand in his own. "So you're Jordan?"

"Yes, ma'am." He warmly enveloped her hand in his own.

"He's quite handsome, Mia," she said, causing Jordan to drop his head bashfully. "And the children are all adorable. Let's get them inside."

Mia's face was frozen with shock. Was this her mother? Jordan gave her an "I told you so" expression as he and the children followed Clara farther into the house.

"Mia, would you help me in the kitchen?" her mother said over her shoulder as she walked toward the hallway.

"Sure," Mia said reluctantly, following her. *This is odd!*

"Those really are beautiful children. His son's going to be quite handsome," Clara began.

Here we go. "I love them like my own," she said defensively, surprising herself as she finished making the fresh-squeezed lemonade by the sink.

"Oh, that's wonderful," Clara said with a smile.

Here comes the but—

"But they're not your own. Is it good to form such an attachment? What if the relationship doesn't last?" she asked kindly, as if concerned for the children. "That wouldn't be fair to them."

Mia wasn't buying it. "The relationship will last."

"Like the one with Terrence?"

Mia slammed the spoon she was stirring the lemonade with onto the countertop. "Don't start."

"I just don't understand the decisions you make. Why would you take on a man with five children? I don't—"

"Because I love him," Mia yelled out in frustration. "I love him, and I love those children."

Clara turned her back on her daughter. "Don't come running to me when it doesn't work. I'll only say I told you so."

Mia laughed bitterly as tears filled her amber eyes.

"Do you actually think I would call you for compassion? For what, to hear more criticism, more put-downs. I doubt that seriously. You're not exactly the mothering type. In fact it would be a cold day in hell before I nominate you for mother of the year."

She ignored her mother's gasp of shock, continuing. "This was a bad idea. Anytime we talk or see each other we argue. Why don't we quit trying so hard at something that obviously isn't working?"

Mia turned, grabbing her purse from the stool by the entrance, and left the kitchen. She ran right into a solid chest and knew it was her Jordan.

"Baby, don't cry," he soothed, as he wrapped his arms around her tightly, trying to will her some of his strength.

From behind them Warren left the living room to step into the foyer. He closely watched the obvious affection the man had for his daughter. The love between them was obvious.

"Daddy, I'm sorry," Mia said, when she saw him standing there. "Kids, we're leaving," she yelled out before breezing out of the house.

Jordan followed behind. "It was nice meeting you," he said with a final handshake, before he, too, followed the children out of the house.

Warren entered the kitchen, his steps heavy. He found his wife arranging deviled eggs on a platter. "I'm tired of you making my daughter feel unwanted and unhappy in my home." His voice was hard with anger.

Clara turned sharply to face him. "Your daughter. I'm her mother—"

"Then why don't you act like it?" he snapped. "You and I are going to have a long and much needed talk."

With that he left the kitchen and eventually the house with a final slam of the front door that caused Clara to jump.

* * *

Jordan watched Mia closely as she worked on her computer in her office. They hadn't spoken of the incident at her parents' since they got back. When Mia had told him that she had some work to complete, Jordan had immediately sent the kids home with Rajahn in charge, and then invited himself along to her house, not wanting her to be alone.

Jordan began to work out the rough outline for his newest novel. But his eyes were constantly drawn to her sullen figure. When she rubbed her eyes with her hands he immediately moved to stand behind her.

Mia smiled lazily as his hands massaged the tension from her shoulders. "That feels good," she moaned languidly.

"You want to talk about today?"

She shook her head. "No."

"But—" he began.

"Please, baby. Not now," she pleaded, her emotions raw and exposed as she replayed the argument in her mind. It hurt her to sever ties with her mother. But if all they did was argue and bring pain to each other, then what was the purpose?

"I've been thinking about heading up an investment club," she said, purposefully changing the subject. She whirled in her swivel chair to look up into his handsome face. "It would be a good opportunity to encourage African-Americans to plan ahead for their future fiscally. Maybe with a joint venture they would feel more secure about it."

Jordan accepted her initial deflection with a nod. "You ever thought of starting your own business?"

"Me?" she asked in amazement as she kissed the palms of his hands.

"Yes, you."

"I hadn't really thought about it." Mia watched him as he reclaimed his seat, moving with strength. "Lord knows I'm not reaching many blacks at Stromer, particularly those who are working class."

"Well, you've been complaining about not feeling appreciated at your firm. You could still work, set your own hours—"

"Do more for African-Americans and investments," she said softly, considering the idea.

"Do it."

"No," she said, shaking he head. "I can't just turn my back on everything I've built up there. They are on the verge of offering me a partnership."

"Put the same dedication into your own business and build it up."

"But who says it'll be successful? Then I'll be giving up a secure position for what?" she asked, unsure. "Right now only half of middle-class blacks invest while nearly eighty percent of whites do. Who says I have what it takes to make blacks understand the importance of relying on more than just saving accounts."

"This self-doubt from a lady who plans multimillion-dollar acquisitions. You can do it, if you want to," he said, moving his hands to caress her nipples beneath the silk material.

Mia stood and walked from behind her desk. Slowly she slipped the straps of her sundress from her softly rounded shoulders. "Do you know what I really want?" she asked huskily as the fuschia silk fell around her feet.

She held out her hand and he took it, and reseated himself on the couch. She stood before him, naked and proud as his malehood lengthened and swelled in response.

"What do you want, Mia?" he asked, his voice tight with desire.

With a teasing, husky laugh Mia straddled him. "What do you think?" she asked, before capturing his lips in a soul-searing kiss.

As the week began and then progressed, Mia found herself working long hours. She and Tyresa, along with a small but skilled staff, had never seen so much of one another. Each night as she dragged herself home at eight o'clock she began to see less of Jordan against both of their wants. But whenever she thought of the possibility of a partnership, she was spurred forward. She wanted it, and she was determined to get it. Jordan complained but he would just have to understand her ambitions.

That night, after a week of hardly any time together, Mia and Jordan made love with much intensity and whispered words of love. Spent and sated the couple rolled away from each other, breathing deeply, only to move back closely together.

"Marry me, Mia," Jordan moaned so suddenly against her throat. The intensity and passion in his words could not be denied as he rolled onto his side to look down into her beautiful face.

His heart swelled with love for her. He knew she was destined to be his wife.

"Are you serious?" she asked weakly, stalling.

"I've never been more serious about anything in my life. I didn't plan ahead, so I don't have a ring, but my words and feelings are just as binding as jewelry." Jordan caressed the side of her face with his strong able hands. "I love the hell out of you," he told her fiercely, before possessing her lips.

Mia felt panic swallow her like quicksand. Afraid that she would reveal her reluctance on her face Mia quickly turned on her side, scooting backward so that they lay in a spoon position instead.

"Mia?"

"We haven't known each other long, Jordan," she said softly in answer to his prompt.

She felt him stiffen behind her. Moments later the warmth and comfort of his body was gone. She turned onto her back to see him out of bed, already dressed in his baggy pajama bottoms.

Nervously Mia bit her full bottom lip as she watched him pace in the darkness.

"Are you saying no?" he asked, his voice soft but decisive as he came to stand by the bed to look down at her, his hands on his narrow masculine hips.

Mia exhaled a deep breath and pulled her body to a sitting position in the middle of the bed, the sheet wrapped tightly across her breasts. "What I said was that we haven't known each other long," she insisted, looking up into his handsome face that was as remote and hard as a stone statue.

Jordan bent to turn on the bedside lamp. His movements were deliberate as he sat on the bed facing her.

His eyes locked with hers in a gaze she couldn't break. "Mia, will you marry me?" he asked again, finality obvious in the ominous depth of his throaty tone.

Her lip quivered as she bit down on it. "I'm sorry, Jordan. I love you, but I'm not ready—"

The rest of the words died in her throat as Jordan thrust his tall muscular build from the bed. Her eyes widened as he strode angrily around the room, presumably looking for his discarded clothing. She couldn't lose Jordan forever, not like this!

Uncaring of her nakedness Mia flew from beneath the tangled sheets to him. "Jordan, don't leave like this. I love you," she said quite loud and desperate as she clung to his muscular arm.

"Maybe you agree with your mother. Is that it? You don't want to marry a man with five children?" he said, only meaning to be sarcastic. His handsome face was astonished when he saw the truth in her eyes.

Jordan laughed bitterly as he looked down into her face. The face of the woman he loved and wanted to share the rest of his life with. The face of the woman he wanted to be a mother to his children. The face of the woman who turned down his proposal from the heart. "No, Mia, I love you," he said, his voice cold, hard, and unforgiving. "My children love you."

"And I love them," she screamed, tightening her hold on him.

He shook his arm, easily removing her clinging naked frame. Even in anger he felt arousal at the sight of her gloriously nude body.

Mia felt cold beneath his stare and wrapped her arms around herself, covering her breasts. "Let's talk, Jordan. Let me explain why," she said softly, just as he moved to the door.

He stopped, his hand on the knob with his muscled back to her. "Right now I don't want to hear a damn thing you have to say." His voice was pained.

And he was gone with the quiet closing of the door.

Mia sank onto the bed, curling herself into a knot as tears racked her frame. Maybe it was best that he left. Mia just didn't feel ready for the responsibility of being a stepmother to five children even if she loved them like her own. And now Jordan was lost to her forever.

Jordan was glad that his father and Minnie had taken the kids to Virginia with them for the weekend. Right now the quiet solace was welcome as he entered the house. Furious and pained he entered the den and strode over to his locked bar. Using the key on his ring he opened it and extracted a bottle of Crown Royal and a glass.

"To hell with her," he muttered, as he sat down on the sofa before the twenty-seven-inch television.

Uncaring that the drink splashed onto him, Jordan poured himself a generous portion, taking a swig. It went down his throat like liquid fire.

But he knew that even a drunken stupor wouldn't stop the pain he felt at Mia's rejection. With a growl he viciously swung the crystal glass against the far wall. It shattered into a million pieces.

Just like his heart.

***

"You did what?" Tyresa shrieked into the phone.

Mia sniffed and then held the phone away from her ear until her friend quieted down some. "Reese—"

"Don't Reese me," she interrupted her friend. "You are the biggest fool going."

"Marriage is a big step, Reese. You should know that."

Tyresa sucked her teeth. "What I do know is that I'm not letting my man go for nothing," she finished vehemently.

Mia exhaled deeply, tucking her bare feet beneath her in the bed. "My career—"

"What about it?"

"I love it, and I don't want to lose it. To stay on top I need my edge and when I'm with Jordan I'd rather make love than work all night. I'd rather go to the museum than be stuck in my office on the weekends."

"And you hated that the firm was upset with you because you wanted a personal life. What are you going to do, stay single forever? And after you burn out, then what?" she snapped, obviously frustrated with her friend. "I'm your assistant, and I want success. I look up to your accomplishments but I have balance. It is not impossible."

"It's not just that. I'm not ready to be some child's mother, far less five children."

"Bullshit."

"What?" Mia said shocked by her friend's candor.

"You love those kids. You're always talking about them and buying them things, and you see them just as much as any working mother would see her kids anyway. You're already their mother and you know it."

Mia was silent a long time.

"Girl, I have never seen somebody fight off happiness," Reese told her, her voice now soft.

"You're so busy rooting for Jordan," Mia said, looking down at her pedicured toes. "I thought you were my friend."

"I am, but you have what a lot of women are looking for and are throwing it away. Excuse me for not throwing a party."

"Reese, you don't understand."

"You're right. I don't," Tyresa said. "Look here. You might like being alone and successful in your career, but I have my husband waiting for me with a certain look in his eyes. I'll see you tomorrow at the office, 'kay?"

"Okay."

They disconnected.

How she wished she had a mother in whom she could confide. But knowing Clara Gordon, she would throw a party if she found out that Mia had turned down Jordan's proposal.

With a groan Mia fell back in the bed, pulling the covers over her head.

Jordan enjoyed a long hot shower before pulling on his favorite pajama bottoms and sitting in his cushioned windowsill. Reflective, he looked up at the full moon, his spectacles in place.

He refused to believe that Mia resented his children. He knew that she loved them as much as she loved him. She was afraid, that was all.

This all came to him after his initial reaction of anger had subsided.

He wasn't going to lose her but he was going to give her space. Maybe with a little time alone she'd realize just what she was giving up.

Twenty-two

Mia was so glad to see Friday come that her step was filled with pep as she dressed for work. She promised herself that she was not taking any work home tonight, and she was leaving the office before 5:00 P.M. Hell, tomorrow was her birthday.

"Happy early birthday to me . . . happy early birthday to me. Happy early birthday to me. Happy early birthday to me," she sang sadly. Without Jordan in her life, she sure as hell didn't feel like celebrating.

All her attempts at reconciling with Jordan had failed. She hadn't seen him or the children in two weeks. They weren't staying in the house, and she didn't know how to reach them.

When she called Minnie, the older woman had advised her that Jordan and the children were safe but she wouldn't tell Mia their whereabouts. That had at least been some assurance.

She assumed he was so hurt over her turning down his proposal that he didn't want to chance running into her. That hurt, but what could she say? Turning him down had caused him pain.

And for what?

Her career.

She loved the investments arena, but she loved having a personal life as well. At this firm there seemed to be no balance for her. Yes, she wanted that partnership but not if it meant losing nearly everything else in her life that was important.

Jordan was important. And so were his children. Mia loved them all. These two weeks she craved their company, their hugs, their smiles, their love. How could she even imagine her life without them?

She wanted her family back!

During the ride to work she listened to the D'Angelo CD that Jordan had given her, reminiscing. Her thoughts were filled with him. Her body craved him. Her heart ached for him. *Come home, Jordan!*

As she was reviewing her e-mail there was a soft knock at her door. "Come in," she called, her fingers frozen above the keyboard.

The door opened slowly. Mia was quite surprised when her mother stepped into the office. "I hope I'm not interrupting you," she said softly, hesitant.

"No, no. Of course not. Come in and sit." She waved her hand toward the chair in front of her desk, hating how reserved she felt. "Is everything okay?"

Clara smiled nervously before taking a seat. "Does something have to be wrong for me to visit you at work?"

"Considering that you never have before, I just assumed so." She couldn't hide the censure in her tone.

Clara shifted uncomfortably, licking her lips as she glanced down at her folded hands. "I thought I would take my daughter out for a birthday lunch as a surprise. If you're not too busy here at work."

Mia looked at her as if she had two heads. "My birthday is not until tomorrow."

"I thought Jordan and you might have something planned to celebrate, so I wanted dibs on today," she said pleasantly. "Did your young man plan something nice?"

Mia's eyes widened. Who was this woman, one of the Stepford wives? She certainly wasn't her mother, Clara Gordon. She even said Jordan's name without a look of distaste. Was this her way of showing her approval of him? Still, there was no way she was telling her mother that she and Jordan were apart.

Clara sat on the edge of her seat and reached across Mia's cluttered desk to grasp her hand. "Work with me, Mia. I'm trying to bury the hatchet. I didn't realize that doing whatever I thought I should so that you would have the best made you feel I didn't love and appreciate you. I'm sorry."

Tears misted Mia's eyes but she blinked them away rapidly. "Why the sudden enlightenment?"

She squeezed her daughter's hand, wanting her to squeeze it back. "A long talk with your daddy and an even longer talk with myself."

Clara took a deep breath before she continued. "I just wanted you to have it all. The older you got, the more you focused on your career, which I'm very proud of you for, but you didn't seem to give a damn about all the other things you deserve, like love and a family. Always it was just work, work, work.

"You were my baby girl, and I had dreams for you since you were small. I went about it the wrong way, but I only want you to have it all. Career, love, and beautiful babies to raise. I was afraid that you wouldn't realize that you could have it all. You don't have to sacrifice one for the other."

"Mama," Mia said softly, her voice filled with emotion as she wrapped her fingers tightly around the hand that held hers.

"And now my baby's in love," she said. "I was so mad that you didn't fall for the man I picked that I wanted no dealings with Jordan. Didn't give him much of a chance, did I?"

Mia laughed. "No, you certainly did not."

"Still think he has too many children—"

"Mama," Mia shrieked, disturbed because she had thought the same thing.

She held up a well-manicured hand. "But I respect your choice."

"Thanks."

"Your father's waiting in the reception area. If we are finished being mushy, let's go eat." She squeezed her daughter's hand one last time before releasing it.

Mia logged off her computer and grabbed her purse. "How about Ms. J's?" she asked eagerly.

Clara froze and turned. "You mean in downtown Newark?"

Mia sighed as she came around the desk. "It's my birthday. My choice."

Clara rolled her eyes heavenward. "Oh, okay. Your daddy will be glad to hear that," she said as she left the office.

Mia shrugged. "She's still bourgeois, but she's promised to stay out of my love life. It's a start," she mused aloud, as she left her office, closing the door.

Tyresa knocked once on Mia's door before entering. "Before you hightail it out of here, I wanted to give you this." With a smile, she brought a small wrapped package from behind her back. "Happy B-day."

Mia slid the last of the folders into her Coach briefcase, a goofy grin on her face. "My big day is not until tomorrow," she said, as she accepted the lightweight gift.

"Just in case I didn't get to see you tomorrow."

"I'll be home maxing and relaxing," Mia said.

"Well, you never know," Reese said vaguely.

"What is it?"

"No," Reese yelled out, her hand raised as Mia started to tear into it. "You must promise not to open it until later."

"Why?"

"Just promise," she insisted.

"Fine," Mia agreed, placing it under her arm as she grabbed her purse and briefcase. "I'm outta here."

They left the office together. "You heard from Jordan?" Reese asked.

Mia's face clouded. "No, he really hates me, I guess," she said, her voice husky as her spirits plummeted.

Reese hugged her shoulders as they walked. "He'll come around. Enjoy your weekend," she told her before heading down the hall.

Mia hummed a sad song as she rode the elevator downstairs alone. She felt gloomy. She and Jordan were completely off. He was in hiding with the kids. She had never felt so alone. She was rushing home, and for what?

"Surprise, Mia."

She gasped in sheer surprise when her eyes lighted upon Jordan as the elevator doors opened. "Jordan, what are you doing here?"

He kissed her briefly, as if they had seen each other just that very morning, before reaching to take her briefcase and Reese's gift from her hands. "Come on, baby, let's go."

Mia followed him, curious when he walked past her car in the underground parking garage. She stopped in her tracks, getting angry at his assumptions after disappearing from her life for two weeks. "Jordan," she shouted.

He stopped, turning to face her, now outside. "Come on baby, the limo's waiting."

She glanced back at her Benz before following him slowly. "Limo?"

There parked on the street was a stretch silver limousine with a uniformed chauffeur awaiting them by the opened passenger door. The man immediately took the briefcase from Jordan and placed it in the trunk, while placing Reese's gift on the seat inside.

Jordan pulled her into his arms when she finally reached him. With a laugh, he kissed her, her face a mixture of confusion and surprise. "Close your mouth, baby."

"Jordan, what are you up to?"

With a bow he waved toward the vehicle. "Your chariot awaits."

Mia climbed in with Jordan behind her. Soon the luxury vehicle pulled off into traffic. Jordan removed her pumps before pouring two glasses of champagne. She accepted hers warily with a nod. "Nice."

"Here you go," he said, handing her a thick manila envelope.

Eyes flashing like lightning, she threw it onto the other seat, where it slid onto the floor. "Screw that," she said, nodding her head briefly at the envelope. "Where in the hell have you been?"

He calmly sipped from his flute, noticing that her eyes dipped to watch his full sensuous mouth press to the crystal rim as he did. "My father and Minnie's house," he answered simply.

"So they've been lying to me?" she said softly, hurt by that.

"At my request."

Mia punched him. "Why?"

"For the greater good of you seeing just what you threw away," he said, his mocha eyes on her intently, effectively reminding her that she had said no to his proposal.

Well, it worked, she thought, her anger subsiding.

Carefully holding his flute he leaned down to retrieve the envelope. "Now will you open it?" he asked with a charming smile that gleamed against his bronzed mocha skin.

Mia's heart swelled with love for him but she didn't show it, instead snatching the envelope out of his outstretched hand with a sullen air. "What is it?" she mumbled, looking over at him briefly.

"Open it."

She handed him her flute. Just as she slid the flap he snatched it back. Mia looked up in surprise. "What?"

Jordan handed her Reese's gift. "Open this first."

"My, aren't you nosy," she snapped.

Jordan looked heavenward in irritation. "Open it," he said, his deep tone insistent.

Sighing, more than agitated, Mia cast him a resentful look as she removed the wrapping. "You're not going to snatch it, are you?" she asked.

"Mia!" he said, his jaw clenching.

"All right . . . all right."

Inside the white box she found a rather expensive Norma Kamali metallic gold swimsuit. "Now why in the hell would Reese give me this? It's almost October?" she asked, confused.

Jordan handed her the envelope again. "Now open this."

"Are you sure?" she asked.

He said nothing.

Mia opened the flap. Inside were two tickets. "We're going to Puerto Rico?" she exclaimed, her mouth open.

Jordan nodded, taking a sip of the Moët. "For the weekend. Your bags are all packed in the trunk, thanks to your mom. Nothing to worry about. Happy B-day, Mia."

"Since when did you and my mama become thick as thieves?"

"Since I called her and expressed to her just how much I love you and that I would never hurt you."

"You called my mama?"

"Sure did."

"And she didn't tell me?"

"Sure didn't."

That explains a lot. Mia set the flutes in the holder before leaning toward the mouth she craved to taste. Just before landing her lips on his, she asked, "What about the kids?"

"With my dad and Minnie."

Satisfied, she pressed her mouth to his and kissed him with all the passion she could muster.

* * *

"Happy birthday, Mia."

Mia slowly opened her eyes just as Jordan pressed a kiss to her forehead.

Using her hand to cover her mouth she said, "Thank you."

He smiled as she threw back the brilliant white covers to dash naked across the red-tiled floor to the bathroom. He knew she was going to brush her teeth, a vehement enemy of morning breath.

When she emerged, her face was scrubbed clean, her mouth minty fresh, and her glorious nude body covered by a thin cotton wrap. He could have done without the latter, especially since he was still naked as the day he was born. Mia sat back down on the bed, leaning down to kiss him. "Now, good morning," she said softly.

Jordan turned in the bed to remove a slender wrapped gift. "Your present or breakfast?" he teased.

Mia reached across him to snatch the gift. "Don't play," she warned with hard eyes as she removed the wrapping and opened the jewelry box. "Oh, Jordan," she gasped, the glitter of the diamonds reflected in her eyes.

He pulled the fourteen-karat gold charm bracelet from the case and secured it around her slender wrist. Wanting her to be happy he looked into her eyes with a question. "You like it?"

"I love it," she said huskily, as she fingered it. "I thought the trip was my gift. Thank you."

"You're welcome."

He made to rise, flinging back the covers. "I can't wait to explore San Juan with you."

Mia untied her wrap, letting it gape open to show the seductive curve of her breasts and the smooth expanse of her thigh. "I thought we would . . . uh, you know."

Jordan turned where he sat on the edge of the bed.

His eyes clouded with desire at the sexy image she portrayed. "San Juan can wait," he growled, as he lay down and pulled her into his strong arms.

"It certainly can."

They didn't leave their room at the El Convento Hall until early afternoon. Having missed breakfast they dined on tea and delicate desserts, or *postres,* before leaving the historic converted convent to explore their surroundings.

Mia and Jordan walked hand in hand up the cobblestone streets wearing shades to shield their eyes from the rays of the ultrabright sun. Leisurely they strolled, trying to absorb as much of the history and the culture as they could.

The town's square was four hundred years old and surrounded by narrow streets lined with cars. There was a fortress built in the early sixteenth century by Spanish colonizers. The old city that served as the heart of San Juan was beyond words. Sightseeing around the city was a lesson in contradictions: a blend of the old and the new. Hotels and condominiums that kissed the azure sky lined the streets as well as grand decaying churches dating back to the sixteenth century. The Spanish colonial houses were a rainbow of pastel colors with wrought-iron fences and balconies.

Mia and Jordan spent the entire day taking pictures and envisioning themselves in the old world as it must have been centuries ago. They absorbed everything and enjoyed all of it. They rested at the *Plaza de Darsenas* located in front of the port in the heart of Old San Juan. They sat upon a bench overlooking the plaza.

"It's so beautiful here," Mia said, as she took a picture of the native people who mingled with the visitors.

An elderly *piragÜeros* with weathered tanned skin approached them pushing his brightly painted cart. Jordan immediately rose to buy two tamarind *piragÜa* from him. *"Gracias,"* he told him as the man moved away to solicit more customers.

Mia slipped her shades up on her head, her hair pulled back in a ponytail. "Puerto Ricans used to sell these in my neighborhood during the summers," she said, before taking a bite into the shaved ice cone covered with the colorful sweet syrup. "Do they still?"

"I don't think so."

"Me neither," she said around another satisfying bite.

Mia looked over at children throwing pebbles into the circular brick fountain surrounded by beautiful statues upon pedestals, reminiscent of the fifteenth-century architecture surrounding the plaza. "I wonder what the kids are doing?"

Jordan raised her chin with his hand. "I love my children but this weekend is about you and me. Agreed?"

Mia nodded, wondering if he would propose again or just accept her earlier refusal. "Agreed."

Sweetly he kissed her forehead, her cheeks, and finally, blessfully, her mouth.

They finished up the afternoon shopping and browsing the art galleries that showcased local work among the international pieces. San Juan's music, art, and food were influenced by the unique blend of Taíno, African, Spanish, and American cultures. Mia and Jordan purchased a beautifully carved mask and walking stick for her parents from The African Shop on Calle San Justo, along with little carved statues for the children, and a traditional African drum for Clinton and Minnie.

Laden with their purchases and tired from their walking, they stopped at an outdoor café. The sunset was a ruby red as it caressed the fading blue as night approached.

Mia stretched in her wrought-iron chair "I would've never imagined a McDonald's and such here."

"You want a Big Mac?" he teased.

"I can have that at home. I'm here in Puerto Rico and I'm going to have some traditional *arroz con pollo.* How 'bout you?"

Jordan studied the menu just as the pretty olive-skinned waitress arrived at their table. "The seafood stew," he decided.

A short while later, she returned with two steaming plates followed by another smiling girl holding their pitcher of tart passion-fruit juice. They fed each other, their hands interlocked on top of the glass table.

"Jordan, don't you think we need to talk about the proposal?" Mia said, asking a question that had been burning in her chest all day. How could they just ignore that night and all the pain?

He shook his head, his eyes intense as they looked at her. "Yes, but let's enjoy your birthday weekend. We can discuss that once we're home."

"But—" she began.

"You really are a beautiful woman," he said, his voice deep and husky, sending shivers through Mia's body.

"And you are one sexy man," she returned, allowing him to change the subject.

As if in harmony they leaned forward to kiss, straining their bodies forward to feast upon each other's lips. Wanting more, but knowing this wasn't the place for it, Jordan paid for their meals. They strolled away arm in arm down the cobblestone street, the sun fading behind them in the distance.

Mia moaned in pleasure as she pressed her dampened nude body closer to her love. A thin cotton sheet lay haphazardly across their tangled limbs. Would the heights of their passion ever stop climbing? She just didn't think so.

Jordan kissed the top of her mussed hair as they lay sedate and sated in the cool darkness of their room. A light breeze blew in from the open balconies as the moon beamed in to highlight their bodies. "You enjoy your birthday?"

She nodded, kissing his chest. "I'm going to hate to leave tomorrow. It's all so beautiful," she said, her voice husky with exhaustion.

"I don't want to leave either. Mia, I love you so much."

But she was already asleep. "Tomorrow," he promised her and himself, before straightening the covers over their bodies. With a final kiss on her forehead he joined his one true love in slumber.

The lovers spent the next day, their last in the capital of Puerto Rico, in a very similar way to the first. They ordered *majorce* and *cafe con leche* for breakfast at an outdoor café beneath a green umbrella table. After being filled by the sweet thick bread and coffee with milk, they strolled off for another day of exploring the city.

They lounged on the sandy beach, frolicking like carefree children. After browsing through all the historic sites they could, like the San Juan Cathedral and the museum *Museo de Arte e Historia,* Mia and Jordan walked hand in hand up the cobblestone streets, stopping in front of a tangerine Spanish colonial house with beautiful ornate wrought-iron work on the porch. An elderly couple looked down upon them as they kissed, smiling at their young love.

Mia wiped the lipstick from his mouth with her thumb before they continued their stroll. The street suddenly opened up to reveal a sweeping panoramic view of the San Juan bay. It was quite a sight, and Jordan instantly snapped more photos.

Together they approached the twenty-foot-thick ancient city wall. Mia leaned against it, and Jordan stood close behind her. They were awed by the history and the beauty as the ships slowly pulled into port. Mia felt relaxed and transfixed by the jewel-like beauty of the greenish blue waters. This was the perfect setting for romance and love.

"Can you believe how incredible this is?" Mia asked, her voice filled with awe. "I'm glad we stopped here before leaving."

The view of the sun setting on the horizon against the backdrop of El Morro Fort was truly magnificent. El Castillo San Felipe del Morro, or El Morro, was the fort constructed along the peninsula of San Juan to ward off enemy attacks. The formidable structure still remained after almost five hundred years.

As evening descended, the clouds were shades of white and a hazy orange tinge as the sun deepened in color. Those in the distance were a deep navy blue against the powder blue of the sky, blending with the frothy waves of the teal-tinted waters surrounding the stone fort. It was truly a magnificent and tranquil sight.

Taking a deep steadying breath, Jordan turned Mia to face him. "You are a remarkable woman with strength that I admire. You are brilliant and beautiful. I think of my life ten—no, thirty—years down the line, and you are right there beside me."

Mia's heart hammered in her chest as they looked deeply into each other's eyes. His words were hypnotic as he continued, his voice deep with raw emotion.

"I have found my soul mate. And I don't want to live my life without you in it. I can't live my life without you in it," he finished fiercely as he held her hands in a tight grasp.

With a press of his lips down upon hers, Jordan kneeled before her surrounded by the beauty and tranquility of Old San Juan. He reached into his pocket to retrieve the ring he had searched hours for: a two-karat marquis-cut solitaire with one karat of baguettes flanking it in a unique design.

"Mia, bless me with the honor of being my wife?"

She thought of her life, of the two short weeks without him and the children. She knew she could be a good mother. She wanted to be their mother. She wanted a family and now as she looked deep into the eyes of the man she loved, she finally realized that a ready-made family wasn't bad at all. She thought of Tyresa's words of advice. She even thought of her mother's approval, but mostly she thought about his unique brand of love and not having it in her life to comfort her any longer. How in the world could she let that go? She loved this man like no other. "Yes," she said softly, and then with more strength and conviction. "Yes!"

Jordan slipped the ring on her trembling finger. "I can't wait to lie with you in my arms every night and wake up to that beautiful face every morning. Next week too soon?"

"Jordan, it takes at least a year to plan a wedding."

"Uh-uh. One month," he mumbled against the hollow in her neck where he planted dozens of passionate kisses.

Shivering, Mia whispered, "Six months."

"Three."

"Deal."

As the waves beat against the strength of the fort's wall he swung her up in his arms, their lips locked in unison. Right then they knew their love would stand as strong and last as long as the five-hundred-year-old fort where they stood.

Twenty-three

Friends and family lined the oak pews, quietly talking as the musician softly played ballads on the piano. At precisely eleven, the minister, Clinton, and finally Jordan took their spots in front of the candlelit altar. The groom was quite handsome in his Maurice Malone light gray wool suit with a silver silk tie, as he faced the rear of the church where his bride would enter.

The romantic sounds of a classic ballad floated from the piano as two ushers opened the double doors. One by one the small wedding party marched down the aisle. Rajahn, an usher, was quite handsome in his gray suit as he escorted Clara and then Minnie to their seats at the front of the church. Both were pretty in soft lavender suits and wide-brimmed hats. Clara smiled softly at her handsome soon-to-be son-in-law before taking her seat in the oak pew. Minnie winked mischievously at her loving husband before she did the same in the opposite pew.

Amina and Aliya, the flower girls, were angelic in their mauve silk-tafetta ruffled dresses. Carefully they dropped ivory, pink, and lilac rose petals. Their father looked on with pride.

Kimani and Tia were stunning bridesmaids in their gray silk organzas with mauve sashes carrying their bouquets as first one and then the other joined their family by the altar. Clara instructed the children she had come to love to stand tall and smile.

Tyresa, resplendent in a lilac bias-cut slip gown with a cowl back and a beaded tulle inset, entered next as she performed her matron-of-honor duties. She blew her husband a kiss as she clutched her sweeping floral bouquet.

The pianist began to play the wedding march, signaling the arrival of the bride. Everyone rose from their padded seats and turned to greet her, just as another usher unrolled a brilliant white runner down the aisle. A collective gasp raced through the wedding-goers.

Mia stood posed in the doorway alone, framed by the light piercing through the stained-glass windows behind her. The bride wore a Manalé Dagnew dress in light champagne. The Ethiopian designer had truly created a gown fit for a queen. The A-line strapless satin-faced organza with intricate floral beading delicately enhanced Mia's voluptuous shape and captured her pure beauty. She wore no veil, with just diamond studs in the elegant upsweep of her hair.

Her eyes instantly sought and found Jordan. He looked at her with such fierce intensity that Mia knew that she was loved. She knew that he was pleased with her choice of gown for their day.

As her father took his place at her side she never broke their gaze. With every step down the aisle she was brought closer to her one true love. One step closer to her destiny. One step closer to eternal happiness.

Their eyes spoke of promise, devotion, and fidelity.

Even after her father placed her hand in Jordan's and they turned to face each other before the minister, Mia looked deeply into the eyes in which she drowned with love. Tightly they squeezed each other's hand. Their hearts pounded in unison. They were lost in their own world, anxious for the ceremony that was but a symbol of the commitment they promised each other.

During the entire ceremony they both were emotional and caught up in just each other. It took the min-

ister two tries to garner their attention to say their vows.
Everyone laughed happily at the two enamored lovers.

Their words were deep and heartfelt as they vowed
to cherish, love, and honor each other until only death
did they part. Jordan wiped away a single tear that raced
down her cheek, earning him a smile more brilliant
than a thousand rays of sunshine.

After fiercely spoken "I do's" Mia Renée Gordon became Jordan Jahman Banks' wife, legally and spiritually.
With all the love he felt for her, all the devotion he kept
for her, and all the desire he had for this remarkable
woman, Jordan kissed her thoroughly and quite length-
ily. This was a union meant to be—thank goodness the
children had known it.

As Mia and Jordan turned to face the well-wishers
they picked up the hands of the children now surrounding them. They all left the church together, their hands
serving as a physical bond among them. It was not a
man and wife that walked down the aisle, but a family.

Epilogue

Brrrinnnggg . . . brrrinnnggg . . . brrrinnnggg.

The ringing of the telephone broke into the quiet as Mia typed furiously away at her computer. One hand still on the keyboard, she picked up the receiver. "Yes, Jordan?" she said, already knowing that it was her husband calling.

"Your mother's having a fit," he mused, his voice filled with humor. "She says it's Saturday, for goodness' sake."

"I'm leaving now. Love you."

"Love you too."

Mia saved her program and then turned off the computer. She was just as anxious to get to her parents' annual barbecue as her family was for her to get there. But when you owned and operated your own business, working half a day on Saturday may be needed to be a success. And Banks Investment Services was just that.

In the five years since she had turned down the partnership offer at Stromer, Wiley, Mia had worked hard to start a successful business. Now she served customers from the hard-working blue collar, to the mayor of the city and other professionals. Her past successes at Stromer, Wiley had given her a good foot in the door for acquiring clients.

This was her dream accomplished, she thought, as she surveyed her surroundings. She had converted her house into the offices for her business since she had moved into Jordan's house when they married six years ago. They were planning to convert the unused upstairs into an apartment for Rajahn, nineteen and a sophomore at Seton Hall University. It would be quite a surprise for their handsome son.

To think she had had doubts about motherhood, and now she was having it all. A good stable, loving, and still wildly passionate marriage. Her business was a thriving success. She had six beautiful children who loved her. Oh yes, Mia had a son whom they all spoiled and adored. Little Malik at three was the star of the family.

She was blessed. She had it all.

Mia grabbed her keys and left the office, securing it with the alarm system. She looked with pride at the gold embossed sign on the lawn: BANKS INVESTMENT SERVICES. With love she looked over at her home next door. Now painted bright white and adorned with flagrant floral arrangements, it was a house filled with love.

She deactivated her alarm and climbed into her car. She sped away for a day of fun, food, and family. As the silver Benz faded over the hill her license plate read: 3XLADY.

A NOTE FROM THE AUTHOR

More than 60,000 African-American children are waiting for adoptive homes in the United States. I truly believe that adoption, foster care, and mentorship are important aspects needed to rebuild the black family.

For more information on adoption, please contact:
    State of New Jersey's
    Department of Human Services
    Adoption Resource Center
    800-392-2843

    or

National Adoption Center
1500 Walnut Street, Suite 701
Philadelphia, PA 19102
1-800-TO-ADOPT
www.adopt.org

For information on being a foster parent please contact:
    National Foster Parent Association
    1-800-557-5238

Please look into mentorship programs in your local areas. They are invaluable and immeasurable services to our communities.

Thanks,

Ni

ABOUT THE AUTHOR

A native of Newark, New Jersey, Niobia Simone Bryant currently resides in South Carolina. She is a graduate of Seton Hall University with both a Bachelor of Science in Nursing and a Bachelor of Arts in Social and Behavioral Science, with an accompanying psychology minor.

After having ten short stories published by a popular romance magazine, she dived into her very first novel, *Admission of Love*. With a four-star rating from *Romantic Times* magazine, she knew she had found her calling for telling stories of love that would last a lifetime. An avid fan of many genres of African-American literature, she enjoys reading a good novel as much as she enjoys writing one. Currently she is busy at work on her third novel, tentatively entitled *Heavenly Match*, where the town of Holtsville from her first novel will be revisited. She can be reached at one of the following:

E-mail : niobia_bryant@yahoo.com
or
Write: Niobia Simone Bryant
      PO Box 2181
      Walterboro, South Carolina 29488

More Sizzling Romance from
DONNA HILL